Somnalia
The Metamorphoses of Flynn Keahi

Praise for
Happiness & Other Diseases: The Metamorphoses of Flynn Keahi

"A twisted descent into arousal, madness and mad arousal, *Happiness and Other Diseases* pulls no punches as it peels back the layers of the human experience to reveal our soft, creamy centers. Take that how you want, but if you are looking for a disturbing, sexually charged read with solid writing, Sumiko Saulson delivers."
> — Angela Yuriko Smith, Bram Stoker Awards® Nominated author of *In Favor of Pain*

"If you enjoy unsettling dark paranormal romances that place power dynamics in sexual relationships under the microscope, look no further. Sumiko Saulson gives us body horror, what feels like an insiders look at mental illness and the mental health system, dysfunctional families, semi-obscure mythological characters, and an excellent depiction of how many of us teeter on the fence between sex and death. *Happiness and Other Diseases* is a sexy, funny, disturbing, and unflinching tale of the insane lengths people will go to in search of love and acceptance."
> — Michelle Renee Lane, Bram Stoker Award Nominated author of *Invisible Chains*

"In this entertaining novel, Saulson incorporates mythology into what might appear to be normal, everyday life. However, characters, Flynn and Charlotte, are far from normal. I enjoyed how Saulson keeps their relationship lively but honest – even sweet, but not in a saccharine way. Buy this book! For sheer enjoyment, it's a keeper!"
> — Marge Simon, multiple Bram Stoker winner, HWA Lifetime Achievement Award winner

"It is a very unconventional book that offers a supernatural dimension to the mysterious, sometimes mind-bending world of psychological pathological conditions, psychosis, and disorders."
> — Justin Boyer, bibliophilesreverie.com

"*Happiness and Other Diseases* by Sumiko Saulson is a tragic love story that includes dark humor, Greek mythology... moments of pure horror."
> — David Watson, HorrorAddicts.net

Somnalia
The Metamorphoses of Flynn Keahi

Sumiko Saulson

Rock Hill, SC

Copyright Notice

Paperback ISBN: 978-1-962353-13-7
Copyright ©2024 Sumiko Saulson
Second Edition

Cover Art Photograph by Garrett Sohnly
Cover Art Model: Wednesday T. Friday
Additional Cover Art by Maya Preisler
Editor: S. H. Roddey
Proofreader: Nicole Givens Kurtz
Publisher: Mocha Memoirs Press

First edition editor: Michael Minch
Proofreaders and Beta Readers: Amy Bellino, David Watson, Buffie Peterson, and Turner Morgan.

Acknowledgements

First Edition Editor:
Michael Minch

First Edition Proofreaders and Beta Readers:
Amy Bellino
David Watson
Buffie Peterson
Shane Chase
Paul Prince
Sabrina Johnson
Turner Morgan.

Other Works by Sumiko Saulson

The Metamophoses of Flynn Keahi (Series)

Happiness and Other Diseases
Somnalia
Insatiable- Coming Soon!
Akmani-Coming Soon!

The Moon Cried Blood (Series)

Legend of the Luna
Bloodlines
Dreams of the Departed
Death Omen
Shadows and Substance
Ghosts of Time
Moon Shadow
Dark Luna

Other Novels

Solitude
Warmth

Collections

Things That Go Bump In My Head
The Void Between Emotions
Spit and Pathos
Within Me Without Me

Poetry Collections

The Rat King: A Book of Dark Poetry
Melancholia: A Book of Dark Poetry
Anthologies Edited By
Black Magic Women
Black Celebration
Scry of Lust 1
Scry of Lust 2
Wickedly Abled

Graphic Novels

Agrippa
Dreamworlds: Beyond Somnalia
The Complete Mauskaveli
Ghost Cat is Best Cat, Drain Monster, and Other Tales of Terror

Introduction

Sumiko Saulson interviewed me for *Women in Horror Recognition Month* (WiHM) and I was immediately impressed with the research ze did to come up with specific questions for me. I never asked how much time ze spent digging up background information but I would bet it was significant. Later ze authored a non-fiction book, *60 Black Women in Horror Fiction*, creating a source that had never been gathered before of black women writers. Clearly Sumiko cares deeply about writing and supporting other writers.

I became curious about this author who wrote non-fiction, fiction, and poetry. Ultimately, I bought Book One: *Happiness & Other Disease* of the Somnalia Series and read it. Sumiko's first book in this series (not hir first book published) was a unique dark fantasy of mythological creatures' desires and power struggles and the humans that become the subjects of their diversions.

Every author does research to create their particular world. Sumiko's clear love of digging into existing material and then using hir imagination to create hir mythology shined brightly in Book One. Hir work is character driven in a well-defined universe. The elaborate level of interactions between the supernatural creatures and humans can be sensual but is by no means sentimental. Sumiko knows how to write dark fantasy with a bleeding edge.

Book Two: Somnalia unfolds in this same universe introducing new levels of powers and feuds. Some of the characters from the first book are in the second book which is a comfort for readers of Book One in the series. However, Sumiko does a great job of telling the reader what they need to know from the first book so they aren't lost if they haven't read it. I won't say anything about elements common between the two books because it's a wonderful surprise when they reappear.

The poet in me loved finding music in Sumiko's prose. For example,

"The blackness of night, born of Chaos, was pouring forth into the skies before the Earth and its creatures crawled out of their primordial ooze…"

The Gods and Goddesses in the series are written with a mix of callousness and heart that makes the human reader care. When horror is visited on humans in the book we can't turn away. It is clear in the writing that Sumiko cares about hir characters, powerful or human, and that caring comes through in the depths of their reactions and decisions.

Sumiko is a writer that puts heart and mind and music into hir work and takes the reader on a roller coaster ride of edgy fantasy. You will not be able to predict the twists and turns as this story unfolds. In the end you'll be fulfilled and ready for more to come in the next book.

Linda D. Addison, award-winning author of four collections of poetry and prose and the first African American recipient of the HWA Bram Stoker Award®. See her site: www.lindaaddisonpoet.com, for more information.

our love has ever been
pedestrian
an unimpressive thing
built of safety
and trust
imperfect, and small
no ships
by its beauty launched
not a single city
burned in its name

Prelude

The twins were quite alarmed when it happened. They had no idea what was going on. None of the somnali did. Nine hundred ninety-nine Oneiroi overpowered Brash and his children and tossed them into the Lethe. The Lethe wasn't a mere conduit to reincarnation. It was the mechanism that ensured the reincarnated forgot who they once were.

Mercy and Sympathy would have forgotten, as well, if Thanatos hadn't gone to fetch them.

"Did you know that all of the Oneiroi are male?" Thanatos asked the girls.

He had cornered them in a remote area of Brash's kingdom in the dark realms. It was a private niche where the two were fond of engaging in their carnage. It was a brazen crack in the center of darkened volcanic rock that seemed to have been smashed into the side of the mountain with a giant axe. The inside of their cavern was lined with the screaming visages of corpses, their death throes frozen into stone. The décor was inspired by the unsuspecting dead of Pompeii. This was Sympathy's home, a place only Mercy knew of. On this day, the girls hid there, cowering away from their many uncles.

"I have always been amazed Brash had so many daughters," Thanatos continued. "At first, there were only men in the Demos Oneiroi, except for when Mother visited. Then, some of the Oneiroi took female consorts, and others had daughters. The underworld desperately needed a feminine touch before you, the granddaughters of Somnus, were born."

"What is happening to our brothers and sisters, Grand Uncle?" Sympathy cried out in alarm. She was by far the most simple-minded of Brash's children. Mercy and Sympathy were twins, born seconds apart.

Mercy was the oldest. She was very attached to her idiot little sister.

"Charlotte's consort died," Thanatos enlightened them. "I was surprised that it was such a beautiful death, relatively peaceful and painless. You know, I preside over those kinds of deaths, so naturally, I was there. I can thank Maribelle Metaxas for that, she poisoned his coffee. I should imagine you'll curse her, though. Upon the moment of Flynn's death, Nyx enjoined you and all of Brash's immortal children to enter the cursed human cycle of birth, death, and reincarnation until such a time as she decides you all have paid your penance."

"Penance for what?" Mercy said scornfully. "I wonder why she feels such affection for these inferior beings Prometheus made. Why do they exist, if not to feed us and fulfill other needs?"

Sympathy did not share Mercy's cockiness, and was slowly backing into a tiny, slanted corner of the chamber in a futile effort to hide. She was in one of her cephalopod-like forms and was attempting to squish her boneless body into the slit like a fleeing octopus.

"She thought there would be a certain poetic justice in your punishments," Thanatos explained. "Since you were so eager to live in their realm, she's arranged to send you there. She calls yours a crime of envy."

"Envy?" Sympathy said incredulously, ceasing her squirming escape attempt due to her need to defend herself. "Why would we envy them?"

"Nyx thinks you did," he explained, "and particularly you two, so jealous of your little demi-somnali sister. But yours was hardly the greatest crime of this little melodrama. The greatest crime was committed before you were born. Your father angered Zeus with his ardent pursuit of young human maidens. He had the poor taste to impregnate at least one girl who had caught the eye of Zeus himself, perhaps more than one."

"What has that to do with us?" Mercy demanded.

"Well, if your little plan to rend asunder the veil between your world and theirs had worked, your father could wander over to Earth any time he wanted," Thanatos proclaimed. "The curse would be broken, but that does not mean Zeus could not, once again, be provoked to anger. Your father has little self-control with the ladies… or the men, for that matter. It's just that he can't inseminate the men. Nyx could not afford another war with Zeus over your father's philandering, so she had to put the lot of you in check."

Sympathy shrugged. "Our father has already been reincarnated. Our sisters and brothers are being dragged down to the Lethe by force as we speak, having their memories wiped away. Have you come here to drown us in the Lethe, Uncle? Will you force us to forget who we are?"

"No," he said. "I know my mother won't rest until you've been reincarnated, but I thought perhaps I could arrange a little something special for you two. You would still be born human, but you would be born with all of your memories. You would know who you are. I could also arrange to keep the two of you together."

"Twins?" Sympathy asked.

"Twins," Thanatos reassured them.

"Thank you, dear uncle," Mercy answered quickly, making the choice for both of them. She knew that time was running out. "Please do so."

Thanatos snapped his fingers, and Mercy and Sympathy found themselves in a dark place, blind and unable to hear, surrounded by fluid. Mercy immediately regretted her choice, to be self-aware in such a wretched condition.

How could the human beings stand it? Being trapped in this little bit of temporary, eventually-decaying flesh was dismal. At least she wasn't alone.

Somewhere, in this vast wasteland called a womb, her sister was with her.

Act I: The Consort

The Conversation

Somnus visited his mother often, now. The events surrounding his son's passing and the inheritance his granddaughter would receive necessitated it. Even now, they watched over her from afar.

"See how she continues to write her illustrated epics?" Nyx said admiringly, looking down upon young Charlotte in her studio. "In this day and age, there are no Homers or Ovids, but perhaps, through one such as her, our stories can once again become legend."

"I agree, Mother," Somnus said. "As I recall, that Neil Gaiman comic *Sandman* put the name of Morpheus on the lips of many a mortal, Maribelle Metaxas included."

"Yes," Nyx said, nodding her head. "I believe Brash capitalized on that fact during their courtship. Wasn't Thanatos a woman in that series?"

Somnus laughed. "When I see him, I'll be sure to ask."

Charlotte and Faelyn stayed in the downstairs guest bedroom in Hannah and Shelby's home. The women created an art studio for Charlotte out in the garage. Her comic, *Somnalia*, was becoming quite successful. She was making enough money from it that she was now able to afford to move out on her own, but she didn't want to be alone. She was still mourning Flynn.

She was out back painting, coming up with cover art for the next issue of *Somnalia*.

"She has so many paintings of her young man," Somnus observed. "They are very beautiful. I suppose it must be very difficult for her, being separated from him."

"She is so like you," Nyx said with a sigh. "You both feel you can protect that young man from everything. You sedate him to prevent him from suffering. She is allowed to experience her grief. By contrast, he is once again imprisoned in the name of protection. Again, he has voluntarily relinquished his liberty, but do you think this is best for him?

"Don't you realize you are taking away his ability to experience anything? His grief over his death and separation from Charlotte is natural. It is part of what it means to be mortal. How can you take that from him?"

"I will consider it," Somnus said. "However, consider carefully. I am protecting more than just the boy, himself. He holds all her power within him, power that Phobetor resents. Brash and his children more than slightly overstepped their bounds and trampled on Phobetor's toes, as he, not Brash, is the god of nightmares."

"Phobetor is not in charge here," Nyx complained. "I have enough trouble with the likes of Zeus. The last thing I need is discord among my grandchildren. The Demos Oneiroi is big enough for all of your thousand sons. You tell him I said so."

Somnus nodded.

The Joining

She didn't mean to awaken him. In fact, she had no idea that Flynn existed in a form that might allow her to do such a thing to him. She thought he had moved on, but he had not. He was still in suspension, still attached to her. She couldn't see him, or hear him, or feel him.

But he felt her.

She had been inexperienced in the use of her native powers when she originally cast the spell on him. If she had known better, she would have realized what she'd done. Once, some time ago, she had decided she wanted him to know what it felt like for her, when he pleased her physically. She performed that trick a little clumsily. There were still remnants, bits and pieces of the magic she used to put him underneath her surface, into her body so he could experience the sensations the same way she did.

Once again, he was feeling with her skin. It started with his flesh tingling, prickling sensations running across its surface as their senses became one. He broke out in gooseflesh as though his skin was being bathed in cool air. It was beginning.

It was an accident. She didn't intend to awaken him from the protective sleep Somnus had placed him in. Indeed, she had not known that Flynn existed in the Demos Oneiroi, let alone that he slept there.

At first, she went looking for him in her dreams. For Charlotte, the clarity of her dream world was fading. With her somnali blood stripped from her system, and her powers fading, her nocturnal activities became increasingly human. Her dreams were flighty things now, easily forgotten in the mornings.

When she woke up this morning, she couldn't remember roaming the visceral landscape of her dreams, searching for him everywhere. She couldn't recall being unable to find the secret places they once dwelled in together as lovers in the dream realms. She didn't know that they were locked away from her.

All she knew was that she woke up in tears, desperately missing his touch. She clutched at his old shirt – the one she slept with, the one that for the longest time, smelled like him. Years had gone by and it didn't smell like him anymore. Deprived of his scent, she sorted through her stack of memories, recalling a time when they were together.

Finally, she remembered a night when she instructed him to go down on his hands and knees and to give her pleasure. When he had brought her to climax, she had put her hands on him and used her powers to make him feel exactly what she felt. She daydreamed that she could still make him feel. She imagined that somehow, somewhere, he was experiencing what she did when she pleasured herself.

When she thought of touching him, she touched herself.

In the cave where he waited, he lay fast asleep in the warmth of his blankets, under cover of darkness, he felt it somewhere deep inside. He felt every gentle touch as she began tenderly stroking her arms with her fingers. He felt the sensation of caresses on his belly and thighs when she touched herself in those places. They were her fingers on her skin. He was in her skin and could feel everything.

That was when he woke up, his back arched, his face contorted with pleasure as he anticipated sweet release every time she stroked and touched herself while thinking of him. His breath became labored, sweat poured from his body, and he found himself brought to the edge of orgasm several times but not allowed to climax.

"Oh Charlotte," he moaned. "Please don't tease me."

His body exploded and trembled with powerful sensations. She had no idea how much pleasure she gave him as he slept, somewhere deep inside of her. She didn't know how closely they were bound together. She didn't have the power to work this trick alone, but since her power was imbued in his form, they could work it together.

Awakened

When he woke up, Charlotte was gone. Flynn was alone.

Remembering the dream, he put his fingers in his mouth and sucked them. Was it a dream? He could still remember what it tasted like when she was putting her fingers in her mouth after touching herself last night. He could still remember exactly what she tasted like, but he was no longer able to taste her.

He undressed himself under his blanket and tossed the clothes out from beneath onto the floor. He loved the feeling of the furs against his naked skin. His hands roamed over familiar surfaces of his frame, recollecting differences between the shape of her body and his own. He caressed his chest, thighs, and his genitals, remembering. He remembered her touching herself, warm abbreviated touches giving way to the hot and hungry need. He remembered being with her every step of the way as she nestled her hand between her legs, her long fingers searching out the source of her pleasured release.

When he put his hand between his own legs, he found an old friend, and smiled.

It came back to him suddenly: he was no longer among the living. He was surprised that his body was so substantial. He half expected his fingers to pass through his ribcage into his chest, or his hand to merge into his thigh. He didn't pinch himself to see if he was awake, he pinched himself to see if he was alive.

The form he was in didn't occupy space in the same way his old one did. All of him was so recently encased, somehow, inside of Charlotte. How very strange it was.

He pushed the blanket off his body and stood naked in front of the fireplace. There was no one here to see him, what did it matter if he wore clothes? The warmth on his skin was pleasing. He extended his hand over the flames to see if the fire could hurt him. The sensitive flesh of his palm grew unpleasantly warm, and increasingly uncomfortable.

He was tempted to shove it into the fire to see if it would burn, to let the scent of his searing flesh reassure him that he was real. Instead, he pulled it back. Sometimes he felt like the weight of knowledge would send him tumbling into a psychotic fit, ranting and raving and foaming at the mouth. He wondered if that was where all the stories of raving earthbound spirits came from. Maybe other dead people were just as totally freaked out as he was right now.

He wished he wasn't alone with his disquieting thoughts.

There was a cauldron of water hanging from a metal hook that sat in the center of a wooden beam over the eternal fire. He took the dirty clothes he had stripped from his body earlier and tossed them in the water. Although he knew he had no physical form, performing these functions bought him a sense of comfort and stability. Without them, he felt that the strangeness, the newness of things was overwhelming.

There was a stick beside the fireplace, and a bar of rough oatmeal soap on top of it. He broke a piece of the soap off with his fingers and tossed it into the pot. Taking the stick, he stirred the soap into the clothes, but no matter how hard he stirred, there weren't any bubbles. The muscles in his upper arms began to ache with the exertion. He took the stick out of the pot and sat it against the wall.

Flynn held his fingers under his nose and smelled the soap, rich and earthy. He tasted his fingers, wrinkled his nose at the bitter taste of the soap under his fingernails, and lulled himself into the pleasant illusion that he was still a living man.

He had to. He was terrified of himself, the ghost in this house.

Walking further into the cave, he found a pool of fresh, clear water that was fed by a narrow rivulet flowing down from a ledge up above. He cupped his hands in the narrow stream and drank the refreshing liquid that poured forth. Next, he dipped his feet into the pool. He expected it to be cold, but as he slipped in he realized it sprang from some natural hot spring below. He let himself sink into the temperate waters.

The oatmeal soap was slightly rough and contained some sort of sandy grit designed for scrapping away dead skin. Charlotte used that kind of soap to try to clear up her acne. It had tiny bits of apricot pits and the like within. It was beautiful here. The air smelled of honeysuckles and tangerines. There were so many little details he hadn't noticed when he'd been here with her. He missed her very much.

He was too consumed by his grief to understand that he was also nursing barely pent-up hostility about his losses. He'd been plucked out of life, everything he knew and loved had been left behind, and now he was nowhere. Without consciously thinking about it, he began to rub his skin raw with the stuff. The flesh on his arms rose up, red and angry. It felt good to feel something. He closed his eyes and let his head fall back against the stones.

Flynn thought to himself how much he could use someone to talk to right now. Any listening ear would do. He suddenly missed his therapy sessions with Dr. Lester. He certainly could use a good psychiatrist right now, or even group therapy. At least in the psych ward, he wasn't so incredibly alone with the voice in his head.

When he opened his eyes and looked down at himself, his chest was raw and wounded with dozens of self-inflicted scratches. He shook his head. Old habits die hard. He remembered when he first met Charlotte, she told him he didn't have to hurt himself. She could do that for him. He shrugged. She wasn't here now. Bleeding made him feel alive.

But he wasn't alive. He was dead. He decided to examine the damage he'd done.

Inspecting his skin, Flynn noticed the scrapes and cuts were not the only thing unusual on its surface. There was a black marking of some kind on his chest that resembled a tattoo. It was a small circular emblem, about two inches in circumference. Upon closer inspection, he could see it was a serpent eating itself. It was Ouroboros, the Greco-Roman snake god that fed on its own tail. It was one of the symbols of life, death, and rebirth. He had no recollection of getting it. The marking was simple and primitive, but beautifully done.

He considered masturbation, thinking it might make him feel better. After a few fumbling attempts at fondling himself, he realized he wasn't in the mood. He was distracted by disturbing thoughts which reminded him that he didn't really have a body, or a penis, or hands. Too depressed to beat off, how sad was that? He soaked a while, and then got up and returned to the furs before the fire.

He used the stick to fish his clothes out of the pot and then hung them from the same pole that held the cauldron. Having something to do, he felt more ordinary, almost normal. Looking around the cave, he found a piece of thick linen cloth that could serve as a towel. He dried himself with the cloth in the warmth of the fire. He enjoyed the rough texture against his battered skin.

He reconsidered the possibility of masturbation. Maybe if he did, he could tire himself out enough to fall back asleep. He didn't want to stay awake. This was all too overwhelming.

When he pulled down the blanket, for the first time, he got a good look at the furs he'd been sleeping on. One of animal hides was the spotted fur of a leopard. He recognized it as the skin from the leopard form Charlotte had assumed when she'd consumed his flesh during the Feast of Tears ritual. He laughed. She must have left it here for him at some point as a joke, thinking they would return here together.

He lay down and stroked the soft fur with his hands. He rubbed against it. He enjoyed the feeling of what had been her fur against his naked skin. He decided if the skin was there, then Charlotte, as the leopard, must have died here. He had died here. Maybe life and death didn't mean what he thought they did. He was here nestled away in a safe place Charlotte had built for him. It was a home, one of many homes that were to be part of a life they would have had together.

For the first time, he let wash over him the idea that life was not truly over. It was just on hold.

Flynn rolled over and fell back to sleep again.

Cat

Charlotte missed Flynn, but she had her hands full with Faelyn and *Somnali*. Her daughter was twenty-six months old and in the middle of potty training. Her enrollment in the same Suisun preschool as Hannah and Shelby's son, Kyle, was dependent upon her potty-training success. The preschool didn't take kids in diapers. Until she graduated to the potty, Faelyn was stuck in the daycare center that provided the afterschool program for Kyle's nursery school.

Kyle was a year older than Faelyn and was already potty trained when the couple fostered him six months ago. Just two weeks ago, they were finally able to adopt him. His name was Kyle Cohen-Baptista. Hannah's name was Hannah Cohen-Baptista. Shelby's name was at the end of their compound name, primarily, because she was the most reticent when it came to the whole topic of marriage. That, and Hannah couldn't handle the idea of a blended name like Cohista or Baphen at all, although they still jokingly called their coupled selves Hanby.

Hannah got off work earlier than Shelby and she picked both kids up from daycare. Charlotte had a nervous breakdown after Flynn died and was no longer able to steady her hands or her nerves well enough to drive. The preschool opened up earlier than the daycare, so Hannah was not able to drop Faelyn off in the morning on her way to work. Charlotte took her two-year old to daycare every morning on the bus. She was eligible for free childcare because she was still in college. She stayed in classes until one every afternoon, then caught the bus home where she worked on *Somnalia* in her art studio. She would work uninterrupted until Hannah came home with the kids around five. Shelby got home around seven-thirty.

She was walking home from the bus stop when she first saw the cat.

It was a big, black cat with long matted fur. She didn't notice it at first, but after a couple of blocks of continually seeing it, she decided it was following her. She didn't recognize it as belonging to any of her neighbors.

"What's up, boy?" she asked it. "Don't you have a home?"

The cat rubbed its filthy face against her calves and began to purr. It was so big she had to steady herself to keep it from accidentally knocking her down. She bent down and rubbed the scrubby fur between its ears. This cat did not seem feral. It seemed like a domesticated stray.

He followed her all the way home. Charlotte wasn't sure she was ready to have a pet. She wasn't sure if Shelby and Hannah would even allow her to have one, but she felt sorry for the big old gnarly tom cat. She opened a can of tuna and left it out on the front porch for the cat.

While he was eating, she carefully combed out a few of his matted locks. She was surprised when the alley cat put up little to no protest against her fur-maintenance routine.

Separation

When Brash died and was cast into the Lethe by Nyx, along with all of his somnali children, Charlotte's somnali half was stripped from her.

She was the sole heir to his kingdom, yet she was powerless. She was human now. There were many things Charlotte was no longer aware of now that she was human. She could only enter the dream world in the limited way that humans do.

Her human body was unable to contain the power of Brash, so it was taken from her to protect what remained of her mortal existence. When she died, she would return to the Demos Oneiroi to claim her inheritance and take the throne. Until then, she was trapped on planet Earth with the rest of the mortals; left there to endure and to muddle through it all just like them.

The price of her inheritance, and her daughter's safety from otherworldly influence, was the loss of her future husband. Flynn had been prematurely torn from this mortal coil. Charlotte was a bit of a doubter. She suspected, even hoped, that they would be reunited in the afterlife, but she didn't entirely believe.

Before Flynn died, she'd been demisomnali, the half human and half somnali child of Maribelle and Brash. Now she was entirely human, allowing her to carry an entirely human child who was no longer under the sway of Brash or any of his inhuman offspring.

She missed Flynn terribly. She daydreamed about holding him and touching him. Sometimes she had a vague sense that in some way, he was still there. It was a kind of unspecified emotional warmth humans often experienced with regards to lost loved ones. It was nothing she could prove to be real. She couldn't actually feel his touch in a literal, physical way.

She couldn't feel him, but unbeknownst to her, he felt her. He perceived every delicious stroke of her fingers against his tingling flesh, and he remembered. This was how it would be until they were reunited.

Nyx and Somnus shielded Flynn and the power he contained to keep him safe from the many challengers Charlotte would face when she came into power. How much easier would it be for any of them to unseat her by proxy, taking what was owed to her from Flynn?

They both had been busy, and neither of them had picked up on the fact that Flynn had revealed himself and was sleeping naked and exposed on a leopard skin rug, out in the open where anyone could see him.

Boring

Thanatos couldn't send Mercy and Sympathy anywhere too close to the San Francisco Bay Area without attracting the immediate, negative attention of Nyx. The closest he could place them without raising alarm was six hundred miles away, in Boring, Oregon. Boring was a small city of about eight thousand people a little over twenty miles southeast of Portland. It was a nice little town with parks and trails and wildlife. There were a number of nurseries that provided wholesale trees and plants to customers in and out of town. Boring had enough nature to be able to share it with others, one might say.

The town's slogan was, "Boring, An Exciting Place to Live."

The twins were Geminis born on June 9th, "Boring and Dull Day," the day that the people of Boring met with a representative from their sister city, Dull, Scotland.

Their human mother, Alice Carter, worked at one of the local nurseries, and was going to go out on maternity leave on June 15th, since the twins weren't due until June 30th. No one knew they were going to show up three weeks sooner than expected.

Their human father, Timothy Carter, was an auto mechanic. He took off from work early when his wife called him, asking for a ride to the hospital. They only owned one car between the two of them. He took Alice to Salem Hospital, where she had been receiving prenatal care.

The first year and a half of the children's lives were uneventful. It wasn't until they were nineteen months old that the local rumors about the black-eyed children began.

The twins were having difficulty controlling their little human bodies. Having to operate through flesh made it hard to impinge on the consciousness of even the weak-minded humans with delusions or waking dreams. The genius of the black-eyed children was that only a tiny bit of the human perception had to be changed. The girls only had to convince their victim that the child they were looking at had solid, black eyes.

The first time it happened, an ordinary human teen was knocking on the door trying to get Alice Carter to let her in to make a phone call after a car accident. The girl claimed her cell phone had been tossed out of the car through the window during the accident. The Carters lived in a fairly isolated area. When Alice asked where the car was, the girl claimed it crashed into a tree half a mile out on the highway.

Alice was about to let her in, when the twins used their combined powers to convince her that the girl she was looking at had vacuous, pure-black eyes, with no whites to them. Their mother screamed and ran out of the living room, terrified by the monster that lay in wait at the other side of the door.

Both girls laughed and laughed at their little trick. Later, they would pull the same prank on a man at their mother's job, only making their own eyes look like beckoning pits of despair. It was wonderful!

It wasn't until about a year later that the girls would start to grow dissatisfied with these spooky little games. Mercy was especially dissatisfied. It would be much more fun if she could actually hurt someone.

Nightmare

Flynn was crying in his sleep when the animal arrived in his cave. It was a large black housecat, an unaltered male Maine Coon. It was not just a fat cat, although it was indeed overweight. It was also long, with a stocky build, consistent with its breed. It had a ruffed neck, like a bobcat.

He was still sobbing into the leopard skin when it snuggled up against the space at the back of his neck. It was hot against his neck and shoulders, and its long and voluminous fur tickled the back of his neck.

It was not the body heat the cat generated, but its very audible purr. The buzzing sound and vibration against the back of his head reminded him of an old-fashioned manual coffee bean grinder his mother used to have.

Flynn sat up and scooped the fluffy creature up into his arms to take a closer look at it. What a heavy thing it was! The cat seemed to weigh at least twenty pounds. It wore a silver collar around its neck with a little round yellow name tag dangling from it. Reading the tag, he learned the cat's name was Nightmare.

"Hey, what are you doing here?" Flynn asked Nightmare. He sat the cat down and began to pet it. It purred and rubbed its heavy body against the side of his thigh. Soon, the cat began kneading the skin with its claws.

"Hold on a minute," Flynn said, getting up. He pulled his pants and underwear down from the pole. They were dry now. They were the same pants he was wearing the day he died: tight black jeans that Charlotte liked to see him in. She said he had a nice ass, but he never really checked it in the mirror, so he took her word for it. The material was thick enough to offer him some protection from the vigorous, sharp-clawed affections of a twenty-pound housecat.

Flynn was happy to have the cat's company. He had been so lonely.

Nightmare knew he couldn't keep this visit a secret forever, but he would try to shield them for as long as he could. The dome-like structure he set over the cave wasn't as powerful as the cloaking blanket of Nyx, but it was better than nothing.

Phobetor

Flynn was pretty hip to his Greek Mythology, and whatever he didn't know when he'd first met Charlie, he studied up on, or gleaned from reading her comic *Somnali*. He was especially familiar with the Oneiroi, Charlotte's thousand uncles. He might have recognized the cat as Phobetor, but he was too desperately lonely to marvel over the presence of the animal.

Phobetor, the god of nightmares, frequently appeared to humans in both the waking world, and in dreams, in the form of an animal. Each of the thousand dream deities was responsible for a different type of dream. Some of them were in charge of types of dreams humans were happy to have. Prodromia, for example, was the god of prodromic or healing dreams. Numinor was the god of numinous or cosmic dreams.

Others, such as Phobetor and Brash were in charge of less than welcome dreams. Most mortals were familiar with Phobetor, if not by name, then by the many words constructed from his name, notably phobia. His dreams struck fear into the hearts of men.

There were many deities on the "Dream Team" whose duties involved various kinds of erotic dreams. Some of these erotic dreams bordered other kind of dreams. Paraphilia, for example, was a type of sexual arousal by objects. Phantasos commanded dreams about objects, but Paraphos handled the dreams in which objects were eroticized.

Brash and Phobetor's spheres of influence similarly overlapped. Brash supervised nightmarishly erotic dreams. All of the "Dream Team" had been born with personalities well-suited to their job titles. The children of Brash had inherited these proclivities, although some of his children, such as Mercy and Sympathy, were particularly enthusiastic and forceful in these tendencies.

Even Charlotte had these types of urges. Flynn's fear of being exposed in public heightened her pleasure when she undressed in public or convinced him to wear revealing clothing. If she had not been partially human, she might have been a lot more ruthless.

That was Phobetor's concern.

Mercy and Sympathy were greedy, and so was their father. Phobetor was one of the few dream deities who could easily traverse the veil and travel between Earth and the Demos Oneiroi. Brash and his kin envied that power and sought to gain it for themselves at every turn.

If this Happiness was going to be equally, well, brash, he had no desire for the competition. He had a certain amount of gratitude and sympathy where the girl's consort was concerned. Phobetor could not deny the fact that without the young man's sacrifice, Brash and his brats would still be polluting the dream world and doing their best to spread their infernal contamination to the mortal realm.

Phobetor decided to observe Flynn for a while. Unfortunately, the longer he was around the dead human, the more an atmosphere of irrational fear would settle upon Charlotte's consort. Phobetor had to be careful not to stay too long.

He hoped he might discover how or where Somnus and Nyx, his father and grandmother, had hidden the girl's powers. If he did, he would have the power to usurp her. He wasn't sure, but perhaps the dead boy would give him some sort of clue as to where the key to her power might be found.

He had no desire to harm Flynn, but he would if it was the only way to obtain the power he sought. For now, he kept the dead human company while it slept. He found it a little morbid the way the creature cuddled up on its mate's furry pelt. He wondered if the human knew that Mercy had skinned the leopard, peeling this fur from its slaughtered carcass shortly after the big cat devoured his tender flesh?

Artist

One of the few powers Charlotte hadn't lost when Flynn died was her ability to draw the activities that concerned the somnali. It was a gift of otherworldly insight that she'd inherited from her mother's side of the family. Her relation to Brash only influenced the selection of material. She still would have seen things she shouldn't have seen otherwise, but those visions would have been attributed to madness. Now that the somnali were gone, there was an element of the prophetic in her drawings. They no longer took place exclusively in the present.

Her visions continued to influence her comic book series which, as Brash's oracle had predicted, became wildly popular. The latest issues featured the slaughtered somnali reincarnating at various disparate global locations. Fans of the comic praised the new cultural diversity. Although in diapers, the character of Mercy was already showing signs of becoming a young Jeffrey Dahmer. Some fans found she had a Dexter-like appeal.

She wasn't drawing the somnali now, though. She was drawing Flynn.

In the new pictures, Flynn somehow gained a tattoo. The tattoo was of a small black serpent. It was currently curled up on his breast, swallowing its own tail like Ouroboros. It wasn't always in the same place, though. Sometimes when she drew it, it seemed to be in the process of moving to some new location on his body. The first time she saw it, it was curled around his belly button. The snake was about two inches in circumference when it was in its Ouroboros form.

Painting or drawing Flynn was bittersweet. She loved the way the drawings helped her remember what he looked like. Even the tiniest details, those that would have faded over time, were held in place in her memory by the drawings that renewed her vision of them. Yet recreating him on paper made her miss him all the more.

Hannah came in while she was painting. She often visited the studio, usually talking shop about the comic, or whatever new merchandising line she intended to spin off the series. She was eating a frozen yogurt dessert with a spoon and had an obnoxious habit of talking with her mouth full.

"Who is that standing behind Flynn?" Hannah asked, pointing with her spoon at a drawing on the table.

"What?" Charlotte asked. Hannah was mumbling. Her face was full of yogurt. She swallowed and tried again.

"In the drawing, tall black dude with big Oneiroi wings standing behind Flynn, kind of looks like Tony Todd?" Hannah expanded upon her original question.

Charlotte came over and took a look at the drawing. "You're kidding, right?" she told Hannah. "He's maybe twenty-two, much younger than

Tony Todd. His face is longer and narrower. See how pointy his chin is? Both of them are tall, dark and handsome, though."

"You left out 'pensive'," Hannah said. "See? He has those brooding eyes, like in Candyman. He has that kind of sullen, wounded look. Totally has the Byronic thing going on. Did you know that Heathcliff in *Wuthering Heights* was a brother? Guys aren't really my thing but, damn he's hot."

"I see," Charlotte said with a chuckle. "Well, that's Phobetor. He's the god of nightmares. See? He's the cat in the other sketch, the one I'm painting now." She pointed at the canvas.

In the painting, a large black cat was wrapping itself around Flynn's ankle. Flynn was shirtless and barefoot, wearing only a pair of tight black pants. The cat's tail encircled the cuff of the pant leg. The painting was very stylized, and the smoky fur of the cat's tail seemed to almost extend from the page.

"He's been popping up a lot lately. Here is another picture of Phobetor," Charlotte said. She walked across the room, a garage with high ceilings and unfinished rafters. On one of the high horizontal boards was a long metal slider with indentations to receive and hold hooks. There were long metal wires hanging down from the hooks, which were intended for mounting paintings at different heights.

She gestured towards a painting of a blue roan stallion whose lips were curled back as if he were in a terrible rage. The beast's eyes were blood red. Its mane and tail were composed of writhing black serpents, like an equine Medusa.

"I understand Phobetor is your uncle," Hannah said amiably. "I think you have his eyes."

Charlotte laughed. She went back and checked the other painting, and sure enough, the cat had the same copper-colored eyes as Charlotte. She imagined that in the sketch of the winged man, they would be more amber. Faelyn had the same type of eyes, although from the distance, they appeared brown.

"Do you think Flynn is really with Phobetor?" Hannah asked her.

"I don't really know," Charlotte said. "I think these are probably just artwork, things that come from my imagination. I guess I would like to believe he still exists somehow, somewhere. The thing is there isn't any evidence to support it. It's just something I want, and I can't trust my feelings."

"But you won't see anyone else," Hannah pointed out. "You must, on some level, think there is a possibility of reunion."

"I don't know," Charlotte repeated. "I feel like he's with me somehow. I guess people always say that kind of thing about loved ones, don't they?"

"Maybe they're right," Hannah suggested.

"But I don't feel like he's here as a conscious, communicating entity. I feel like he's here like a dormant part of me, the way your leg is when it falls asleep," Charlotte said, gesturing blindly in the air. "It sounds so stupid, doesn't it? To say he's a part of me."

"But he is a part of you," Hannah said. "Look at your art, and how much of him is in it. Look at your beautiful daughter. He'll always be with you, Charlotte."

Charlotte's poignant expression was heartrending, but she nodded in agreement. Hannah gave her old friend a hug.

"It's time for me to pick the kids up, Charlie," she said at last. "Maybe you should come with me, get out of here for a bit."

"Alright Hannah Banana," Charlotte said, putting her paintbrushes in a mason jar filled with water. "Just give me a minute to put my art supplies up. It would be good for me to get out of the house."

It was only natural for Hannah to be concerned about Charlotte and want her to move on. Her friend lost more than her fiancé that day almost three years ago when Flynn's bloated, half-eaten corpse was fished out of the Sacramento River. Early reports of an accidental drowning soon gave way to the coroner's report, giving poison as the cause of death.

The deaths of Michael, Tess, Flynn, and even Cory surrounded the group of friends like a low-hanging swampy mist for a long time. In many ways, they were all still recovering. For Charlotte, it was worse. Hannah knew that Charlie suspected her mother, and maybe even Maribelle's witchy friends of Flynn's poisoning. His death was still unsolved, relegated to the cold case files.

Most people believed Flynn had committed suicide. Even his mother was of that opinion, although the two weren't very close. Only his friend, Danny, and Charlotte stalwartly insisted that could not be the case. They both said that he was happy about the baby and looking forward to the future. But when the police interviewed her, Charlotte had to admit that Flynn was devastated by what had happened to Mike and was thinking of going back into the hospital.

"It's sunny out today," Hannah said, watching Charlotte set out the last of her brushes to dry. "Don't forget your hat and your sunglasses."

Charlotte grabbed her things, and they headed out the door.

The Watchers

"Do you see this, Mother?" Somnus asked. He pointed down at the tableau visible in his mother's little scrying pool. He was pointing at Charlotte Metaxas in her studio with her series of paintings of Phobetor, often accompanied by Flynn.

"Does this shock you?" Nyx asked. They were in her palace on Venus, far away from the crowded corner of the underworld where Somnus lived with his small city of progeny. There was no need to worry about the possibility of spying by the likes of Thanatos, Phobetor, Morpheus, or Phantasos, each of whom would have had some stake in seeking out the source of Brash's powers before Charlotte could inherit them.

Of course, Phobetor was much closer than he realized.

"Does which part shock me?" Somnus asked. "That my granddaughter is a weak bit of an oracle, or that you allow Phobetor to encroach upon her territory right under my nose, and say nothing?" The usually calm Somnus was absolutely livid about this last bit.

"Either," Nyx said casually. "Brash was well-aware of Maribelle Metaxas' lineage when he sought her out to bear his child. Did you think of all the women on Earth, he only accidentally fell upon a woman of

Greek ancestry whose forebears were well-noted oracles? This was no accident; it was by design. When Brash lived, she was his oracle.

"Do you not realize what has happened? Now that Brash is human, she is your oracle. As an oracle of Somnus, she is able to see all of the activities involving your children, the Oneiroi. Additionally, she continues to see the activities of your grandchildren, the somnali. She is focused on her own siblings, but she could see her cousins as well, if there ever was a need. Her comic, *Somnalia*, is no longer about Brash. It is now about you, Somnus. Phobetor is your son, so naturally, she can see him. Because he is with Flynn, she sees him as well."

Somnus stroked his chin thoughtfully. "It is a good thing to have an oracle on Earth," he said. "I hadn't considered it, but as you explain it, this certainly makes sense. What a wonderful development this is. Still, I want to understand how you can allow Phobetor to invade Charlotte's home and spy upon her consort."

Nyx waved her hand over the scrying pool. It was a wide, shallow marble basin filled with clear water which sat upon a single, low, ionic column. In the waters was an image of Flynn asleep on his belly with the cat Phobetor curled up on his back.

"Does he look like he's trying to hurt the boy?" Nyx asked Somnus.

"No, but he's looking for the source, and if he stays there, he will find it," Somnus warned.

"And what does it matter? The source is nothing that can be taken or stolen. It is something that can only be given. It will remain dormant with the young specter until he chooses to release it to someone who can actively use it."

"But Phobetor will see it," Somnus complained.

"You are overprotective," Nyx said. "The young dead man can't even control his own spectral form. All he does is putter around his little hovel pretending to be one of the living. So what if Phobetor sees? Then the poor soul can have an adventure, defending himself against the rampaging god of nightmares.

"It would be better for him to spend the next forty years mastering the use of his new form as he runs through the Demos Oneiroi hiding from Thanatos and Phobetor. That would be better than to leave him there, languishing in that dark corner, sedated and asleep, a passive vessel. How will he learn to protect Charlotte? What kind of consort can he ever be if you keep him so overprotected?"

"But he…" Somnus began.

"But nothing," Nyx said. "He is stronger than you think he is. If he gets into too much trouble, we can intervene. Until then, let him learn what he is capable of."

The Serpent

Two days went by before the tincture of nightmarish despair began to permeate the air of the cavern in which Flynn resided. Phobetor didn't intend to alarm the dead boy, but fear kind of oozed out of his pores when there were humans around. If Flynn had accepted his own death, he might have been impervious to the stench of terror emanating from Phobetor. It was his desperate clinging to the illusion of mortal life that made him vulnerable. Unfortunately, his waking nightmares eventually revealed the source of Charlotte's power to Phobetor.

Flynn was asleep on his belly when the writhing beneath his skin awakened him. He quickly rolled over and sat up in bed. The serpent tattoo sat on his left pectoral muscle a few inches above his heart. It had been flat up until now, but suddenly the skin was raised. He brushed it with his fingers. The snake was moving.

Flynn was disturbed by the wiggling sensation underneath his skin. The creature slid up and over, to the position of his right atrium, and then plunged itself deep inside of him. Its forceful penetration felt like a stake through his heart. He clutched his hand to his chest and began to wail.

Serpents were one of the common forms Phobetor assumed when he appeared to humans, so he was quite familiar with their types and breeds.

He recognized the serpent as miniature black mamba. The mamba could reach as much as fifteen feet in length. Even at birth, it would have been three to four times larger than the little four-inch serpent that made itself at home in Flynn's breast.

The feline Phobetor barreled forward after the snake, landing all twenty-two pounds of his furry form squarely in the center of Flynn's chest. The weight and velocity of the cat missile dropped Flynn's upper body back down onto the floor. The serpent's tail was still twisting back and forth on his chest as the creature's upper body slid further into him. The cat sunk its claws deep into his skin and muscle to gain purchase. It quickly sunk its teeth into the serpent's tail and attempted to extract it from Flynn's body.

"Fuck! Fuck fuck, that hurts, shit shit," Flynn screamed, skittering backwards on his knees and the palm of his hands, hoping to get away from the battling animals.

The poisonous snake was Charlotte's power emblem, and Phobetor was having a great deal of difficulty extracting it. Pulling against him, the snake increased in size, until its bulk was too great for the mouth of a housecat. A good four feet of tail as thick as Flynn's wrist thrashed about and repeatedly hit the head of the wildling feline.

Hoping to increase his physical strength, the god of nightmares transformed into a fine gryphon, as black as night and with the same beautiful wings as the Oneiroi. Flynn felt the increased weight of the creature upon his sternum and recalled being torn apart by Charlotte. This creature could tear him apart, but that did not seem to be its goal. It was after the snake. However, it didn't seem to be terribly concerned about the terrified Flynn becoming collateral damage.

Already dead, Flynn couldn't escape his body the way he did when Charlotte dismembered him. He had no choice but to stay there and suffer. When the gryphon used its sharp beak to pry a hole in his chest, he looked down in horror at his own beating heart. The snake reduced in size and slithered inside of it. It seemed to have an endless series of evasive maneuvers to outwit the determined hunter.

The gryphon seemed to have a similar arsenal of hunting maneuvers.

This went on for several hours before Nyx arrived to put a stop to it.

"You aren't going to be able to pull it out of him, Phobetor," she chided, shaking her finger at the great beast. "It can't be taken, only given. It can only be given with Charlotte's consent, so you waste your time."

Flynn, who resembled a frog on a dissection table, meekly greeted her with a whispered "Hello."

She pointed her finger at the dead human. "Get up off the floor, spirit. Pull yourself together." Flynn stood up, and a mess of broken bones and disemboweled organs fell from his abdomen. Unaware of how to repair himself, he simply stood there with his hand on his hip while his elders spoke.

Phobetor resumed his human form and stood next to his grandmother. He was a tall black man with impressive wings, and the same ink-dark hair as his grandmother. "How can you allow such a great power to reside in such a fragile vessel?" he asked disgustedly.

"Is the titan Prometheus a weakling because he suffers at the hands of Zeus?" Nyx asked.

Phobetor shrugged. "No, I suppose not. He is indeed weaker than the mighty Zeus, so he can be made to suffer. This doesn't necessarily mean he is weak. It only demonstrates that Zeus is formidable. I suppose to suffer for mankind, his creation, shows some sort of moral fortitude on his part."

"Exactly so," Nyx agreed. "And neither is Flynn a weakling if he takes his wife's side and suffers at your hands for it. You are more powerful than he is, and you can make him suffer. Yet, he is strong enough to protect and defend his wife and her inheritance, as well he should."

Both Phobetor and Flynn noted that Nyx twice used the word *wife*. She put a great deal of weight on the word, and it was significant. If there would be a marriage, then Flynn's home was here. He would be a permanent fixture in the Demos Oneiroi.

Phobetor began to see the wisdom in allying himself with someone who clearly had gained both his father's and his grandmother's approval. He frankly couldn't see what the fuss was about, but the dead man was good enough company. If he couldn't have Charlotte's power, perhaps he could exert his influence over her partner by befriending him.

"He is very inexperienced," Phobetor said carefully. "See how he stands there even now, unable to repair his spectral form? Perhaps it would better serve us all if he were to have an education."

"Very well," Nyx said with a wave of her hand. "Feel free to take him under your wing if you like. He is your niece's husband, and her father is dead. There is no reason why you can't stand in Brash's place as his mentor if you wish it. Just be aware that I will be watching you."

"Yes, Grandmother," he said with a smile.

Flynn, petrified, still stood in the corner with a hole in his chest cradling his detached entrails in his arms. Phobetor turned and gave him a mordant grin, which Flynn did not find the least bit comforting.

"Take care of *that*," Nyx said derisively, pointing at Flynn's grisly disembowelment. She waved at them both. "I must be going now. Good day."

"It won't heal because you're thinking about yourself all wrong," Phobetor said with a shrug. "You aren't alive, and your body is not bound by the laws of the living. You should be able to fix that with yourself, but your mind is telling you that this is real. If you went to bed, you would begin to heal immediately, because no conscious part of your mind would be creating those wounds."

"If you say so," Flynn grimaced. "Can I sit down? My guts are starting to get kind of heavy."

Phobetor sighed. "Fine, then. Have a seat" He gestured into the open air, and an easy chair appeared. It was the same one Flynn slept in when he was fighting with Charlotte right after they moved in together. Flynn waddled over to the chair and had a seat. Phobetor picked up a wooden tub and tossed it into his lap.

"There," he said with a contemptuous look. "Pour your guts out into it, and your heart, too, if it has become detached. Perhaps when you tire of soaking in your misery, you can restore them to your abdomen. I have to go now, humans to terrify. It's my job, you understand."

Flynn shook his head. Was this guy kidding? Could he get the fuck out already? "Don't let the door hit you in the ass on the way out, buddy."

Phobetor laughed. He waved as he left.

Pasithea

When Somnus and his wife, Pasithea, came to visit Flynn, Somnus wore his younger form. He was a young man, wings on either side of his head, and completely naked. He no longer wore a beard, nor did he have wings on his back. His wife, Pasithea, was equally young and nude. The troubled Flynn averted his eyes when the naked couple entered the room.

Young Somnus was very dark, almost as black as his mother, the night. Although he was young, his hair was as stark white as that of an ancient man. Pasithea was very pale, with dark hair which piled upon her head in an elaborate Roman fashion. In coloration, they were like a photo negative.

"Does it hurt much?" Pasithea asked Flynn, who was unable to heal himself and holding himself as still as possible to avoid exasperating the excruciating pain.

"Terribly," he said. His anger gave him enough energy to yell after Phobetor on his way out the door, but now that it was spent, Flynn was exhausted and a pitiable sight. His lungs could be seen through the gaping wound in his chest as he labored to breathe.

Somnus looked at his wife. She was, in his eyes, the perfect vision of beauty. He once risked incurring the wrath of Zeus in order to claim her hand in marriage. It was because of Pasithea that he felt such a deep sympathy towards the plight of his granddaughter and her lover. His heart was softened further because Brash had been a child borne of love amongst his many sons born of parthenogenesis. Brash had been the only child of Pasithea, the goddess of mediation and relaxation. Charlotte had inherited her grandmother's talent for soothing touch.

"May we help you?" Somnus gently asked his granddaughter's consort.

"Please," Flynn replied. "I cannot seem to help myself."

Somnus placed his hands under Flynn's head and touched the back of his neck. Immediately, the pain began to fade, and he grew drowsy. Pasithea took him by the feet, and Flynn felt his entire body relax. They both put their arms around him and lifted him from the chair. He found himself back in the bed he'd shared with Charlotte.

He could feel them piling his organs back into his body, but it wasn't unpleasant. It didn't feel like surgery, it was more like they were kneading his body back together as if he were made of clay. After they finished returning what should be inside his frame, they stroked the skin from hip bone to clavicle until it was healed.

Flynn was aware of their relationship to his Charlotte and felt embarrassed by his arousal at the sensual and sedating touches. He tried to roll over on one side, but they gently restrained him while they finished their work.

When they were done, Somnus and Pasithea sat on either side of him, cross-legged, and were magically drinking wine. Flynn had no idea where the wine came from, but they made a toast over his belly, the glasses chiming musically as their rims touched. He felt a drop of wine land on his bellybutton. He felt very drowsy and still.

"To the wedding," Pasithea toasted happily.

"To the wedding," Somnus concurred.

"When we touch you, it relaxes you," Pasithea explained. "It is just a side effect of what we each personify: sleep, and mediation. I used to watch you spending time with our granddaughter. You are familiar with this kind of touch, yes?"

"I am," he said softly. "It reminds me of her."

"My mother says I'm too gentle with you," Somnus told him. "She says I would like to coddle you and lull you into a false sense of security and let you sleep through life."

"He only tries to comfort you," Pasithea told Flynn. "Much as Charlotte did. She loves you so."

"I know," Flynn said drowsily. "I love her, too. But I want to be able to do things for her, not just be taken care of."

"I know," Somnus told him. "That's what mother says. Charlotte left you in my care. I am sorry if I have been overprotective."

"No need to be sorry," Flynn assured him. "You have always been kind to me."

"Good," Pasithea said. "So, Nyx tells us there is to be a wedding? Show us the ring, will you? I've got a gift for you."

Flynn sat up in bed and took Charlotte's ring into his hand. He moved to lift the chain up over his head, but Pasithea just took it in the palm of her hand and rolled it over.

"It's very charming," she said. "Look at it, Somnus."

Somnus took the ring from Pasithea and rolled it over in his hand. He noticed that it was bound with a braid of his mother's luxurious onyx hair. He let go of it and allowed it to drop against Flynn's chest.

"Does our nudity bother you?" Pasithea asked him.

"I uh…" Flynn didn't want to answer. He himself was wearing the remnants of black jeans that had been torn to shreds by Phobetor's claws when the god of nightmares wore the lion-pawed form of a gryphon.

"I know it bothers you to be naked," Somnus said definitively. "I had no idea our nudity would bother you. How odd."

"That's fine," Flynn said nervously. "I live here now; I need to get used to your customs."

"I made you this bouquet," Pasithea said. It was a collection of exotic wildflowers from the glen where he'd spent so much time with Charlotte in the dream world. Many of them were poppies, the opium flower, which was emblem of both Pasithea and Somnus' personified power for sleep. Pasithea was sometimes also associated with hallucination.

Flynn was used to being drugged, drugged by therapists, by Charlotte, by Somnus, and now by Pasithea. He believed they were all a bit too concerned about his supposedly fragile nature. He was glad to know that Nyx, at least, did not think of him as weak. He recalled her little speech to Phobetor about the resilience of Prometheus. He took the flowers in his hands and examined them more closely.

They were bound in white lace, the same lace Charlotte used to bind his hands before she sent him floating down some tributary of the Napa River. He had no idea what magic had whisked him away on the Lethe. The power that caused him to reemerge two weeks later on the Sacramento River near the place where both the river and Carquinez Strait dumped out into the San Pablo Bay belonged to the man sitting beside him.

The lace, which had been soiled and gray when he arrived here, was now fresh and perfect and new. Flynn fingered it gently, then looked up at Pasithea and smiled.

"It is very beautiful," he said softly. "Thank you,"

"It will never wilt," Pasithea said. "The flowers will never lose their luster. Their beauty will never fade."

"Just like you," Somnus said. "You'll always be twenty-six years old. Of course, if you want to, you can make yourself look older." Somnus passed his hand before his own face and his features underwent a subtle, but steady aging in appearance until his youthful visage gave way to the crow's feet, laugh lines, and graying temples of a middle-aged man. This was exactly how Somnus appeared on the day Flynn met him. Somnus waved his hand back over his face and he was young again.

"You will always be this beautiful," Pasithea said playfully. "Your youth will never wilt or fade, not any more than these flowers."

"He is a beautiful youth," Somnus said, and winked at his wife.

"As are you," Pasithea remarked. "Charlotte finds him exquisitely beautiful, but I think we're embarrassing him."

"You are more beautiful still," Somnus told Pasithea. "You are the most beautiful being I've ever seen."

"Except for Aphrodite," Pasithea cautioned. "You wouldn't want to bruise her vanity. We all remember what she did to Psyche."

Somnus handed Flynn a pile of clothes that, like the wine, had appeared from nowhere. "Here, since you are so fond of covering yourself. You should be able to make them yourself, but I guess it takes time."

"He's only a human spirit," Pasithea shrugged. "I think your mother is expecting rather a lot from an ordinary human soul."

Somnus gave his wife a warning look. "He will learn."

"Well, we must be going now," Somnus added quickly. "We just wanted to congratulate you on the upcoming nuptials."

"Yes," Pasithea. "It's all very romantic. Hera will be pleased, you know. She is the patron of marital love."

The couple got up and left Flynn alone in his cavernous apartment to attend to his affairs. Unable to figure out how to navigate outside of the context of the laws of physics, he proceeded to strip out of his torn pants and threw them into the fire. Noticing that his underpants were tattered and stained, he removed them and threw them into the fire as well.

He was rather disturbed and disgusted to learn that he'd urinated and defecated all over his legs while the snake and the gryphon were doing battle all over his flesh. It was the first time he'd actually relieved himself since he'd been here… apparently close to three years. He hadn't had any food, either. It occurred to him that while he didn't need to eat, drink, piss, or shit, he was still able to do all of those things.

He walked over to the little hot pool and bathed himself. Settling into the delicious caress of the warm water, he realized how sensual he found the experience of bathing. What would it be like to be without a body, and unable to bathe?

He just couldn't fathom it.

As he settled down into the water, he noticed the serpent emblem had reappeared on his skin, only in a slightly different location. It was encircling his left nipple now. He ran his finger over it.

How cute. He stroked it a few times to see if it would move again, and it reared its head back and bit his finger. Fascinated, he poked and prodded at it some more. It became agitated and bit his nipple. He sighed. That felt good.

He relaxed into the steamy water and began to fondle himself. Even if this wasn't his original body, it was his. It belonged to him. He could touch it and use it anyway he wanted to. He planned to take possession of it by stroking himself off in the water.

He just hoped that none of Charlotte's relatives would pop in for a surprise visit while he was trying to masturbate in the bathtub like a normal fucking human being.

The Offer

Phobetor had the good sense and discretion to wait outside while Flynn took care of his business. There wasn't much privacy in the Demos Oneiroi. However, in much the same way that Flynn himself had averted his eyes with Somnus and Pasithea, one could simply choose to look away. The god of nightmares opted to give Flynn the privacy that the young human seemed to crave.

When the boy was done, Phobetor walked up to the bath and cuffed him on the back of the head. He dropped a towel and some clothes in a pile on the floor.

"Dress yourself and then come in the other room," he said curtly. "We need to speak."

Flynn dried himself with the towel, which was a good deal softer than the linen in the cave. He put on the pants, black baggy bondage pants made from parachute material, like the ones Mike had been wearing that night they all went to the club. He looked at the t-shirt before he put it on – it was a black *Somnalia* shirt, just like the one Hannah had given to Mike.

Mike, Hannah, and Shelby had been his friends. He lost them along with his girlfriend, and any chance he had of ever seeing his child. Looking at the shirt, his eyes clouded with tears, and he began to cry in silence. He missed them, and the life they could have had together.

Finally, he dried his tears with the towel, and put on the t-shirt. Phobetor had provided him with socks and shoes, two things he'd been without most of the time he'd been in the underworld. His wet sneakers never seemed to dry properly over the fire. These shoes were platform boots, the kind Charlotte would have adored. Putting them on, he thought how much she would have loved seeing him in it. He hugged himself.

When he came into the room with the furs, which served as his living room, bedroom, and kitchen, there was some new furniture. Phobetor sat at a primitive stone table on one of the four smooth stones surrounding it like a mini-Stonehenge. He was a big man, and he dwarfed the table. Flynn was six feet tall and Phobetor was a good eight inches taller.

There were two simple ceramic mugs on the table without handles. Phobetor held one in his oversized mitt. Flynn sat across from him and put his hands around the second mug. It was steamy, hot, and inviting. It smelled like chamomile tea. He lifted it to his mouth and blew at it to cool off the liquid. He took little careful sips. It was very homey, very relaxing.

"How are you?" Phobetor asked unemotionally. Flynn smiled a little. It was the same uncommitted tone Dr. Lester used to use when they were in therapy.

"I have been better," Flynn said. "I've been having a difficult time adjusting to all this."

"I can see that you are homesick," Phobetor observed. "I gave you some clothes that might remind you of home. How do you feel about that?"

"I cried when I saw them," Flynn admitted, "but I do feel better. I feel more myself. I guess that the pain of loss is better than the numbness I've been feeling. I guess I have to accept what's happening here, even though I don't want to."

"I think that people don't do things without any motivation," Phobetor said finally. "I realized that I wasn't motivating you correctly when I left you here to piece your body back together. You don't care that much about yourself."

"I wouldn't say that," Flynn defended.

"I would," Phobetor said. "I can see that you care for your woman, your friends. You don't really seem motivated to take care of yourself at all. You will allow others to care for you, though. You let Somnus and Pasithea swaddle you like an infant child. I won't coddle you like that."

"Weren't you a cat that slept on my back?" Flynn asked.

"Does a cat care for a man?" Phobetor asked. "Or does a man care for a cat? I appeared as a cat because I knew you were lonely and would seek my company. You humans keep felines as pets, do you not?"

"We do," Flynn answered.

"I have the power to appear in animal form, not only here, but on Earth," Phobetor said. "What if you could appear to your fellow men and women as an animal? Wouldn't you want to see your wife again?"

"Of course I would," Flynn said. "I would love nothing more than to see Charlotte again."

"You wouldn't be able to speak to her," Phobetor warned. "You would be a dumb animal. But you would be able to be close to her. You'd like that, wouldn't you?"

"I would," Flynn said. He wasn't aware of the fact that he was holding his cup in midair now, frozen in the act of bringing it to his lips, not moving a muscle. He was hanging on Phobetor's every word, afraid that he would find out that it was some kind of a trick or a lie.

"She could touch you," Phobetor said. He spoke carefully now. He was trying to seduce Flynn with his words, to obtain his agreement. "Humans often do that, don't they? They stroke their pets. She could pick you up and run her hands over your soft fur. Wouldn't you like that?"

Flynn's mouth dropped open. He swallowed. "Um… yeah. I would definitely like that."

"Fine," Phobetor said. He dropped his cup on the table. "Then you will need to learn to control your spectral form. That is what Nyx asked me to teach you. You will need to learn to control this body you possess now if you wish to learn to shape-shift. Does that seem worthwhile to you?"

Flynn nodded. "Yes, it does. I want to do it. Please, tell me what I need to do."

"First you must learn to control your surroundings," Phobetor said. "You should be able to change your clothes at will, blink furniture in and out of existence here. You should be able to control the environment within this cave as if it were part of a dream you were having. Most of the places in the underworld, in the dream realm, and in what was Brash's kingdom, are not so. But this is a special place that Charlotte made for you. You should be able to control everything within this place.

The pool in the other room is a scrying mirror, not just a bathing pond. You can learn to use it so that you can see your wife and your daughter in its waters and other earthly goings on. You can't do these things because you insist on treating everything as physical space, not as dream space. You will need to learn to control the space you are in, and your body within it, first. We can go on to more complicated lessons later."

"Okay," Flynn said amiably. "Thank you. Thanks for giving me a chance."

"Don't be sentimental," Phobetor said harshly. "I am not doing this out of the kindness of my heart. I need you. I need an ally in my dealings with your wife. Some day when Charlotte comes into power you will act as my ambassador with her. You both have enemies who are more powerful than I. She will surely need my support. You can mediate between us as a trusted adviser. Do you agree?"

"I agree," Flynn swore.

Phobetor nodded. "I know you to be a man of your word, so that will suffice. I have to be going now. Good day."

He stood and vanished without any ceremony or preamble.

Flynn stripped naked and burrowed into his furs, relishing the way they felt when they brushed against his bare skin, and daydreaming about what it would be like to be a cat, and have Charlotte rub him and stroke his fur. For the first time since he died, he felt hopeful, optimistic. At last, there was something to look forward to.

He had pulled the blankets over himself but was too excited to fall asleep. He stayed up, staring at the ceiling. He was trying to make something move or change in the room. After many hours of concentrating, he was finally able to put out the fire in the fireplace.

Satisfied, he rolled over onto his belly and fell fast asleep.

Preschool

Today was the big day. Faelyn was a big girl. She didn't wear pull-ups anymore; she wore big girl underwear. She went to the big girl potty, and she was going to get to go to the big kid school with Kyle. She was riding down to the school in the back of Auntie Hannah's Prius, the one she'd be driving to work in ever since Kyle came to live with them.

Hannah's motorcycle was sitting in the garage Charlotte used for an art studio most days now. Every once in a while, she would bust out the helmets and take Shelby for a ride. Charlotte would babysit the kids. It would be like the old days, before all three of them settled down into alternative rock child-rearing suburbanites.

Kyle kept trying to poke her in the arm and shouting "Fae-fae! Play me."

Faelyn looked at him and said, "Gaaaah!"

Charlotte turned around and looked at Faelyn over the back of the front passenger seat and said, "Use your words, sweetie."

"Stop it!" Faelyn yelled at Kyle. She was a big girl, and she could use big girl words now.

Charlie was grateful for the kids, both of them. She was the only one in the house who didn't have a regular day job, being a part-time student who worked from home. Friday was Hannah and Shelby's date night, so Charlotte watched the kids that night and the following morning. She spent Saturday mornings with her sketch pad on her knee, drawing while the toddlers watched cartoons.

Somnalia was actually doing well, so well in fact that she could say she did have a job that paid her bills. Still, she worked from home. She was still in school… Faelyn's birth and Flynn's death had both delayed her studies some, but she already had an Associates of Arts degree in the multimedia design program, and she would be graduating with a Bachelor of Fine Arts at the end of the current semester.

She was twenty-six years old. It often occurred to her that she was now the same age as Faelyn's father had been when he had died. It was tragic. Twenty-six years had been very little time, and Flynn had barely had a chance to live before dying so young.

She wore a pendant, with his photo in it, on a chain around her neck. She often remembered their brief and tumultuous relationship and all the difficulties they faced. Thinking of Flynn made her feel sad, and more than a little guilty. She should have known that she could lose him. She could have protected him better. She should have recognized how fragile he really was, ignored his bravado and refused to allow certain things to happen.

She shouldn't have trusted her mother.

But the past was over, and today was just one more day, yet another milestone in her life that she and Flynn would not be experiencing together. She steeled herself. She would just have to live thoroughly enough for both of them. Her gentle man was not coming back.

Hannah pulled up to the preschool and parked the Prius. Charlotte was still kind of amazed to be rolling in something so shiny and new that did not belong to her mother. Hannah was at the helm of her company's moderately successful three-and-a-half-year-old print division. She was the genius who came up with the idea of colorful wine-country travelogue saturated with brilliant photographs of the local landscape and lots and lots of advertising. The advertising revenue was impressive. Hannah got yet another raise. Hannah and Shelby were living the middle-class dream, suburban homeowners with a cute kid and a silver Prius.

Somnalia was not the biggest money maker for the Napa Valley Dream Press, but it did well and kept the owner happy. Unlike the touristy magazine, *Somnalia* had an international audience. The comic was becoming more popular, and Charlotte had been getting invitations to speak on panels, or make featured guest appearances, at various conferences for some time now. While she made a token showing from time to time, the vast majority of these invitations were declined. Almost three years had passed since Flynn's death, and people were growing weary of her excuse that she was still grieving. Charlie reluctantly agreed with Hannah that when she had her B.A at the end of the Spring Semester, she would go on her full-fledged first tour.

But that was six months from now. Today, there was nothing going on except Faelyn's first day at preschool. The school was a squat, rectangular building with a huge mural of multicultural preschool kids painted over the front wall.

Hannah, Shelby, and Kyle were perfect poster children for the multicultural family. Hannah was Russian Jewish. Shelby was of African and Portuguese heritage, her parentage resulting from the influx of

African peoples into Portugal from the former colonies. Shelby's African ancestors came from Mozambique. Kyle Puerto Rican and African American heritage so they managed to criticism that many adopters of minority children receive adopting cross-culturally. Shelby was black and the kid was black, so what was the problem?

Of course, some people did have a problem with it. Hannah and Shelby were lesbians. But they lived in the Bay Area and such criticism was minimal.

The Metaxas family was from Greece, and Maribelle Metaxas was a second generation American, but like the Portuguese, the Greek citizenry represented a Diaspora. Maribelle was of Greek and Persian heritage. She and Charlotte were both olive-skinned, brown-haired women. Maribelle had sultry brown eyes and lashes so thick and dark she always seemed to have on mascara.

Coming from two brown-skinned, dark-haired parents, Faelyn was also brown. Her Chinese features were not as pronounced as her father's, but her skin color, the shape of her eyes and her button nose gave her a distinctly Polynesian appearance. She had her mother's dark-fringed red-brown eyes, and her father's jet-black hair. She was a pretty, little child who looked like she stepped out of a Gauguin painting.

They were halfway up the stairs to the preschool steps when Charlotte first spotted the cats.

She recognized the older black cat. She'd actually managed to coax it onto her lap one morning and get it to sit still for a little while as she made some sort of futile attempt to comb out its kitty dreadlocks. That didn't last for long. The cat gave her a dirty stare after a bit and huffily meandered away into the bushes.

It looked a bit like the cat in her paintings, only uglier. The cat in the paintings was sleek and beautiful. This tom was older, hoary, and perpetually covered in filth.

Today, it had younger cat with it, a smoky-gray adolescent domestic short hair. The gray cat must belong to someone. It had a black, braided collar around its neck and a gold and silver tag with shiny little flecks of rhinestone in it.

When Faelyn saw the cat, she dropped her mother's hand and ran over to it. Charlotte's jaw dropped. How could the little one move so fast, when she could barely climb up steps?

Faelyn was excitedly slapping her little hands against the cat's back and screaming "Dada! Dada!"

Charlotte rolled her eyes and scooped up her child. "I'm pretty sure that cat is not your father." She wasn't sure why Faelyn and Kyle both said dada, since neither one of them had a father. She imagined they must have picked it up from the other kids at the school.

She had barely gotten the toddler under control when the little gray cat started rubbing against her pant leg.

"Great," she said. "I can't pet you now, Dada. Go away." She gently shoved the cat away with her foot. She managed her journey up the remaining four steps to the door with minimal interference from the young tom. It was still following her when she went in the building and closed the door in its face.

"That cat probably is someone's dada," Hannah said, noticing it was unaltered. "People need to fix their pets."

The ladies continued into the administrative office, where Charlotte finished up her paperwork and left a few "just in case" pull-ups with the front desk. That was it, the start of Faelyn's first day at preschool.

Hannah dropped Charlotte off at school and continued on to work.

Tea

Flynn shook his head. "I can't believe Hannah drives a Prius."

Phobetor winked at him. "It's a good thing Charlotte didn't take a liking to you," he said. "She probably would have taken you home. Soon, she and Hannah would have been cooking up plans to have you surgically castrated."

Flynn grabbed his crotch and imitated the face of the tragedy mask used in theater productions. "No, don't take away the twins… leave them be, woman. I can't live without them."

"So even you wouldn't find that pleasurable?" Phobetor asked. His tone was nonchalant, but he really wanted to know. "Many of the activities you two engaged in, they would be the stuff of nightmares for another person, you do realize that. Don't you?"

"I know," Flynn said. "Trust me, I know."

"But you enjoyed it?" Phobetor asked. "I mean, being eaten by her."

"Oh, that. Well, afterwards… when she was done, the idea that she could have that much power over me," Flynn said slowly. "It excited me, every much. That she could take me, destroy me, and consume me. All I wanted was to fuck her when I woke up, I can't even explain it. But when she actually killed me…"

"Tell me, were you afraid?" Phobetor asked. He already knew the answer.

"I was terrified," Flynn said. "It was a horrible way to die. She dislocated my shoulder and tore one of my arms off. If I didn't know that I was going to live, well, I wouldn't have done it, frankly. But even so, it was far more painful than I had imagined it would be."

"Humans watch scary movies," Phobetor observed. "They read horror stories. Some part of you enjoys being frightened."

"That's true," Flynn said. "It reminds us of our mortality, I think. It makes us feel our adrenaline pumping, and then, when it's over, we feel so much more alive. It's indescribable."

"Fascinating," Phobetor said. "And she did castrate you, am I right?"

Flynn nervously laughed. "She did eat my junk, but technically, I was already dead by then. I mean she tore my throat out first. I was watching her. Gosh, it was like a horror movie, but with me in it. I think she killed me first on purpose."

"Why?" Phobetor asked.

"Because what you imagine something could be like and what it really is like are often two different things," Flynn explained. "I think she was afraid if I had to experience feeling something like that, I'd be so traumatized I'd never get an erection again. I mean, I already had a history of erectile dysfunction."

"I had no idea," Phobetor responded. He shrugged and sipped his tea. He found nothing this young dead man had to say particularly shocking. The youth clearly needed someone to speak to, and there weren't any therapists here.

"Thank you for not judging me," Flynn said gratefully.

Phobetor laughed. "Why would I judge you? I am the god of nightmares. I've done much worse things to humans in their dreams than whatever little games you and Charlotte played. You aren't the only human who enjoys fear. I'm the god of fear. Phobias are named after me. You won't shock me, don't worry about it. You're fine."

"Oh, okay," Flynn said. "Thanks,"

"I am curious about your human psychology, though," Phobetor said. "Once humans worshiped and made sacrifices to me. Humans still enjoy their scary movies and horror stories, but they don't call me by name anymore. As Charlotte probably told you, we need humans. We gather strength from your attentions."

"Why would you care about me?" Flynn asked flatly.

Phobetor shrugged. "When I first appeared to you, it was to steal away what you hold for Charlotte, that which is her inheritance. Let me see if I can put this in language you humans can understand."

He gestured in the air as if grasping for absent words. Flynn nodded his agreement.

"Okay," Phobetor asked, "Do you know what an heir apparent is, or a regent?"

"Yes," Flynn said. "An heir apparent is the person presumed to be next in line to the throne, one whose claim cannot be dismissed, at least not without a change of law. A regent is someone who can rule on behalf of a monarch who is too young to rule or otherwise unable to do so, such as due to sickness, or disability, or absence."

"And of course you know what a consort is?" Phobetor asked.

"Of course," Flynn answered. "I am Charlotte's consort. A consort in this context is the partner of a monarch, but has no power to rule on his own. This could happen in cases where the consort is not of a high enough standing to rule, such as a lover or even spouse who is a commoner. It depends upon the rules of the land."

"Right," Phobetor said. "So, you are Charlotte's consort. You can't rule in her place, yet she is absent from her throne due to her disabling condition which is known as humanity. Nyx was prepared to leave her throne empty until her return, or even set you as her regent, but you don't qualify. After I… attacked you, she lectured me about it. She says I can't rule your wife's kingdom, but she did invite me to be her regent until she returns. Do you understand now?"

"How does Brash's kingdom… I mean Charlotte's, differ from your own?" Flynn asked.

"Brash was supposed to be in charge of erotic nightmares, you know the kind of thing Mercy was giving you before she got out of control," Phobetor said sourly. "What he and his offspring were not supposed to do was leave the world of dreams and insinuate themselves into the mortal world.

"Charlotte may or may not have told you, but Brash was under a bit of fire from old Zeus over his attempted takeover of the human gene pool. Zeus couldn't have some other god knocking up all of the hot chicks. He had enough trouble with Poseidon and Hades in that department. Zeus wasn't about to tolerate to tolerate such behavior from a little upstart like Brash, and so cursed your father-in-law. The only way Brash could have mortal children was by inflicting nightmarish pain and suffering on humans and conducting sacrifices.

"That curse applied to his entire bloodline, including the demisomnali. Fortunately, for Charlotte at least, there was a kind of a loophole. If she could find someone like you, someone who enjoyed erotic nightmares, well…"

"So, Charlotte," Flynn paused. "So, Charlotte… so she, she is supposed to do what Mercy did to me, to other people?"

"Well, yes," Phobetor said. "But as for the wounds manifesting in the physical world part, that was never supposed to happen. The rest though, that's in the job description."

Flynn grew pale.

"Are you upset?" Phobetor asked him.

"Yes!" Flynn sputtered. "I… no, she can't do that."

Phobetor laughed. "But it's her job. Do you feel less special when you think about her sexually torturing those other people? Are you jealous?"

"Yes and yes," Flynn said, furrowing his brow.

"Well, a lot can happen in forty or fifty years," Phobetor shrugged. "I mean, Mercy and Sympathy have both been reincarnated. So has Brash. They will be adult humans well before Charlotte dies. Maybe one of them will complete the penance Nyx has set before him or her and take the throne so your precious Charlie doesn't have to. You never know."

Flynn shook his head. "I don't want to think about it," he said. "I want to go back to sleep."

"Fine," Phobetor said, "but I will need you later. I'm doing Charlotte's job while she's on Earth, and I need you to advise me, to make sure I am doing it right."

"How am I supposed to do that?" Flynn asked.

Phobetor waved a single, long finger and beckoned for him to come forward. "Come, let me show you," he said.

Flynn stood up and walked over to the larger man. Phobetor didn't rise. He gently placed his hand on Flynn's chest and sent a series of nightmarish images pulsing through his body that set the boy's hair on edge.

"There," Phobetor asked. "How were those nightmares? Were they frightening?"

"Yes," Flynn said. "Whoa. That was something else."

"But were they sexually arousing?" he asked. "

"A little," Flynn nodded. "All scary things are a little sexually exciting to me."

"Okay," Phobetor asked, putting his hand on the same spot. "What do you think about these ones?"

Flynn collapsed to his knees and began to tremble. He gasped, "Yes. Both."

"Thanks," Phobetor said, getting up to go. "That was very informative. You're quite useful."

Change

Flynn buckled and fell to the ground, where he immediately shapeshifted. First, he assumed the form of the woman whose nightmares Phobetor had just fed him. She was an elderly woman who had been in the middle of a particularly juicy nightmare about being swarmed by a pack of starving vampires. When he touched his neck with his fingers, they were covered in blood.

He held his hand in front of his face, observing the wrinkled flesh, the peppering of liver spots. The skin was an unidentifiable faded gray color and very thin and fragile. He held the seasoned hands against his wrinkled cheeks and wondered what it would have been like to grow that old in his own mortal body.

As he curled up on the floor, the withered form of the woman whose dream he recently occupied was replaced by an equally aged version of his own. His bones were thinning, and his arthritic joints ached. The room's edges were blunt and muted through his bleary, cataract laden eyes. Flynn began to weep.

He was on the floor in tears when Nyx came in.

Without thinking, he transformed into a young gray cat. She scooped him up and dropped him in the crook of one of her arms.

"What a clever boy," she said, stroking his soft, hazy fur. "What a pretty boy you are. I see you are wearing that exquisite coat you had on when you saw your wife earlier today. It's a shame she didn't recognize you in it."

Flynn tried to answer her, but nothing came out but mewing noises.

"I know, I know," Nyx said, speaking to him just the way humans will speak to a house cat. "But at least you saw your beautiful little daughter. I'd noticed she'd recognized you."

Flynn still couldn't speak, but he began to purr.

She patted the cat and stroked his fur. He began to arch his back. Soon, he began butting against her hand with the back of his head, demanding to be petted. She laughed and scratched the furry spot between his ears. When he had enough, he tried to nip her hand, but she quickly yanked it away.

"Bad kitty," she said. She set him down on the table, threw one of his blankets over him and restored him to his human form. He was sitting on the edge of the table, feet resting on a chair, with the blanket she gave him when they first met, stretched across his lap.

"You need to be careful," Nyx told Flynn. "You are a shade, the disembodied spirit of a dead man. You will lose your senses if you remain in animal form too long. You will become as Charlotte was as the leopard, eventually becoming completely animal. But it's a comforting form, isn't it? Being a cat, for just a little while? "

"It is," Flynn admitted, sliding down into the chair and wrapping the blanket around his waist.

Nyx picked up one of the empty cups on the table, ran her hand over it, and set it back down. It was filled with hot cocoa, topped with real whipped cream. She slid it across the table to Flynn.

"This is a drink I am told you humans find soothing," she said. "So, the in-laws are a little hard to take, I gather?"

He laughed. "I'm sure everyone means well."

"Don't be so sure," she cautioned. "Phobetor has a vested interest in getting Charlotte to relinquish her claim. Her role as ruler would be a lot less hands-on than he suggests to you. She'd have minions to do her dirty work."

"But still…" Flynn shrugged. "It's just a lot to deal with."

"I know," Nyx said. "It will be a lot for her to deal with, too. She will need you at her side. She'll need you informed; do you understand?"

He mulled it over a bit. "I suppose so. You want me to know what's going on so that I will be able to help her."

"Correct," Nyx confirmed. "Otherwise, we would just pat you and comfort you and keep you sedated, but you would be nothing greater than a pet. I think you should be more."

She stood up straight and unfurled her hidden wings. The wings of Nyx were magnificent… larger and more translucent than the wings of her children and grandchildren. Like her hair, they wound through the air and curled endlessly into the air, tendrils disappearing into the ether. She walked behind Flynn and put her hand on his back, between his shoulder blades.

She tapped twice, and he could feel what was happening to him before he saw it. Great black feathered wings burst forth from his flesh, extending out of muscle and bone. The pain was intense, and he gripped the edges of the table with his fingers, but he didn't cry out.

"I think you should be somnali," she said. She held his face between both hands and looked him in the eye. "I think you should go to your wife and guard her."

She kissed him on the forehead and a series of images burst forth in his mind. They were pictures of Charlotte and Faelyn, under attack by supernatural creatures. He didn't know when and where these scenes would take place, he just knew he had to protect her.

"A danger is coming," Nyx said. "You should be prepared."

"Stand up," she ordered. Flynn stood before her, waiting for the end of his transformation. The tiny serpent on his skin began to unwind itself, extend and expand over the left side of his body. He felt its scales tearing against the underside of his epidermis, his skin was on fire. The beast wrapped its tail around his leg and extended its length over his hip and up the side of his torso. It placed its head on his chest, just below his clavicle. It stopped moving and settled into his skin.

He now had a tattoo that extended from his ankle to the bottom of his neck. He also had wings. The process of growing wings had left him totally exhausted. Suddenly realizing that he was naked, he picked up the blanket and wrapped it around his waist again. Nyx, like her son, had very different attitudes about nudity than Flynn did. She didn't seem to care about it one way or another.

"You'll need to rest now," Nyx told him. "As somnali, you will have the ability to visit Charlotte in her dreams. It is what you want, isn't it?"

"It is," he said. "More than anything, it is what I want. I am very grateful. Thank you."

"She needs a protector," Nyx explained. "Bad things are coming her way. I know you will do your best to guard her."

"I will," he said.

"Then sleep," Nyx told him. "Sleep while you can and have pleasant dreams."

Comfort

For the first time in three years, he slept with Charlotte in his arms. It was strange to be asleep and dreaming of sleep, but it seemed that both of them were doing so. He was on his side, leaning slightly backward with her body partially covering his. She was leaning on one side with her face buried in his chest. One of his arms was wrapped around her hip, with his hand over the small of her back. His other arm was over her back, with his fingers buried in her hair.

He could feel her breath against his skin, soft and steady. He loved the weight of her pressing against him. He pulled her closer against him and covered her face in kisses until she awakened.

"Charlotte, I…" he began to speak, but his voice choked with tears.

"Shhhhh," she said, kissing his lips. "At last, you're here. I've waited for so long."

She was the same old Charlotte, loving but never too gentle. Her tender kisses gave way to rough, hungry nibbles. She shoved him over onto his back, holding him down so she could taste him. He gasped when she bit his lip. He returned her kisses with the heat of desperation, fearing they would be the last kisses. His body responded to her as if his world was one that might never include kisses again. Their hands and fingers found all of the secret places that had been lost to them. Their bodies told the story of need, loss, and separation.

She threw her arms around him, and her fingers stroked his feathers. She stopped kissing him and said his name, her face against his neck, "Flynn."

She broke free from his embrace and looked at him. "Your tattoo is stunning. You are so beautiful. I want to remember everything, so when I wake up, I can draw you. Show me all of you."

Her touch was delicious. She ran her finger up his calf, tracing the line of the snake tattoo. She put her hands on his leg, touching and caressing the sensitive skin of his inner thigh. He rolled forward a little, so she could see the part of the tattoo that ran up the back of his leg. He felt her finger running along the curve at the bottom of his buttock. She followed the tattoo back over his hip and up the side of his waist. Her fingers poked and prodded at the slightly raised flesh over his chest. She stroked his skin until she reached the opposite end of the tattoo. Where it ended, the snake's head curled down, just under his collarbone.

Charlotte kissed him in the crook of his neck. Her lips and tongue retraced the spots where her fingers had been. He shuddered, and his wings began to flutter in response. He pulled her closer. He was afraid he would awaken and she would be gone.

"I didn't think I was going to see you again," he said. "Your family had told me I wouldn't see you for a very long time. I've been staying with them, you know."

"In the Demos Oneiroi," she said. Then she bit him on the soft spot where his waist met his hip, and he moaned. "I need to have you," she said. "Let's talk later."

They were in her bed. Flynn sat up and let his legs hang over the edge so that she could straddle him. She sat on him, facing him, with her legs bent at the knees. For the first time since he gained them, his wings were unfettered. He felt them stretch out to either side, caressed by the air. They didn't hurt any longer. Charlotte tossed her arms around his neck and rocked her body against him.

He wrapped one arm around her back, settling his hand on her sweetly rounded behind. His other hand explored her body, taking note of the changes caused by three years of time and nine months of pregnancy. Her breasts were heavier now, more womanly. He leaned back so he could kiss them and take them in his mouth. For the first time, he instinctively bit down on her nipple. She balled her fist up and hit him on his upper back, but she didn't stop him. She threw her body into him.

She wrapped her legs around his waist and whispered in his ear. "Pick me up, love."

He didn't think he would be strong enough to do it, but he obeyed her command. He was surprised to find that this was something he could now do quite easily. He wasn't human anymore. He put both of his arms around her, pulling her against him so she wouldn't slide down. One of his hands was still under her bottom, cradling her as he pressed deep inside of her.

To be stronger than her, to hold her like this was so strange, so very different for him. It was exciting to think about having so much more power, and willingly relinquishing it to her. He wanted to give all of himself to her. He was thrilled when she began to bite his ears and his neck. Her long fingernails cut into his skin as she clung to his shoulders. It felt so good he wanted to cum, but he wouldn't allow himself to lose control until he knew she was satisfied.

At last, she tensed against him and let out a wail. Flynn collapsed against the bed with her on top of him. When she came, he knew he finally had her permission to climax, and so, he let go.

Charlotte lay on his chest, bathed in sweat and post-coital bliss. For the first time, she noticed the ring he wore on a braided thong around his neck. It was the engagement ring he used when he proposed to her. She sent it with him into the afterlife, but she didn't expect to learn that any of those rituals had worked. She picked up the ring in her hand and looked at it. She remembered using it to bind him to her after death.

"Did Somnus come to get you?" she asked.

"Not at first. Nyx came," Flynn told her. "This braid, it's her hair. She tells me you're my wife and I'm bound to protect you. She is the one who sent me here, at last. But it took years for that to happen. For years, I was grieving. When Somnus came to visit me, not long after I arrived in the underworld, he saw my grief, and he put me to sleep so I wouldn't suffer. I regret being so weak that I slept when I could have tried to return to you. I hope you can forgive me for that. I've missed you so much."

"You're only human. Well, you were only human. Apparently, you're somnali now." she said. "I forgive you. Indeed, I think there is nothing to be forgiven. You look exhausted right now. I don't need any special somnali powers to see that."

"Nyx put her hand on my back and these wings began to erupt from my flesh where she touched me. It was a grueling process. I could feel the muscle tearing away from bone, and my skeletal structure itself, reforming under my skin before the wings burst out of my shoulders. The pain was excruciating, but the hurting wasn't the worst part of the process. It was demanding. It left me physically exhausted and emotionally spent. The wings were very tender when they emerged. They don't hurt now. Would you like to touch them?"

She rolled off of him and propped herself up on one elbow on the bed beside him. He rolled over onto his belly to accommodate her curiosity. Charlotte ran her hands over his back and touched the puckered skin where the wings rose up from either side of his spine. The skin there was still red and raw looking, although she knew that in time it would cool, and blend with the rest of his flesh. It tickled when she stroked and petted his feathers with her fingers. Finally, she ran her finger down his spine and over the curve of his ass. She flattened her palm and smacked him playfully across the rump.

"I know it's tempting to stay up all night," she said at last. "We have been apart so long, and it is frightening for me as well. We are both worried that we might fall asleep and awaken to never see each other again. But if Nyx sent you here, we shouldn't worry. She is a very powerful goddess. Even Zeus himself has had cause to fear her. I have always known her to be trustworthy, but she's never taken such an interest in my life before. It seems you have a very influential patron.

"She's always been kind to me," Flynn said. "I don't know why."

Charlotte took his hand in hers. "Then let's trust that it will remain so. You must sleep."

He nodded. He rolled over on his side and pulled her up against him in the spoon position. It was wonderful to be this close again, naked, skin against skin. He used his wing to cover her, like a blanket. He tossed his arm over her and touched her belly, soft and covered with striations. He fondled her belly and caressed the stretch marks with his fingertips.

"Those are left over from when your sperm fertilized my egg and a tiny human started growing inside of me," Charlotte said drowsily, with a chuckle. "I'm sorry you missed it."

"I saw her once," Flynn said. "I was a cat at the time."

"Dada," she whispered. "Faelyn saw you, and Hannah and I both saw you also."

"I noticed. I heard you two talking about me, you know. Thank you for not having me neutered," he said, kissing the back of her neck.

"Oh no," she said. "We couldn't have that."

Then they snuggled up together and they both fell asleep.

Act II: Children

Mercy and Sympathy

Mercy's name was Candice now, and her sister was Cynthia. They weren't identical, but they did bear a striking resemblance to one another. They had the same mousy ash-brown hair, round brown eyes, and puckishly innocent faces, but Candice's nose was a little more upturned. Their parents weren't enlightened with the latest parental wisdom that instructed them not to treat their twin daughters as color-coordinated little clones. As a result, Mercy and Sympathy were stuck wearing identical outfits. They had the rhyming nickname scheme Candy and Cyndi.

Fast approaching their second birthday, the twins also had a string of these things called words. Mercy called Sympathy "Cyn," because it had a nice ring to it. It sounded a lot like Symp. It also sounded like sin. The Carters thought it was because she was a baby and couldn't pronounce Cyndi. In truth, the two little girls were busy imposing their reality on their working-class parents.

Soon, everyone would be calling them Candy and Cyn, just like they wanted.

Candy was frustrated with the difficulty she had in controlling her human body. She was more advanced than her twin. She had spent the past three months crapping in the nasty little plastic bowl her parents called a potty chair. Cyn was still forced to wear these awful contraptions called pull-ups and sit around with feces smeared all over her buttocks until one of their parents removed it.

With increased control over her own form, Candy found she began to manifest some control over the minds of other humans. She couldn't take over their bodies or anything as sophisticated as all that, but she could make them see things. They were waking dreams known as hallucinations. So far, it had only been little things. Once, at day care, she'd made the other toddlers see and chase after a butterfly that wasn't there. Amused with herself, she followed up the next day by sending them running in terror from a phantom canine.

Little things, but she wouldn't have been able to do anything of that sort at all if not for the timely intervention of Thanatos. Trapped in this human form, she should have lost all of her somnali powers. Somnali, like their Oneiroi progenitors, were able to control various aspects of the human dreamscape. To interact with humans in the waking world and give them a fright was power worthy of Phobetor.

Remembering it made the toddler burst into a toothy grin.

One of the other kids, a girl named Anna, was so frightened that if there hadn't been a fence surrounding the playground, she would have hurled headlong into traffic. Candy was strangely delighted by the idea of herding small humans into the traffic like a sheepdog chasing cattle. She could influence small humans now, and someday soon, she would be able to provoke large ones.

Until then… the playgrounds wouldn't always have fences.

Uninvited

When he woke up, the first thing Flynn did was slip into his clothes, or as many as he could fit on his altered body. He put on his socks and underwear first, and then went through the pile of pants Phobetor left for him. Leather pants, wow, he thought those were pretty cool. He put them on and slipped on the cool platform boots.

He didn't put on a shirt because he couldn't figure out how to get one over his wings.

He spent the next twenty minutes trying to get a stereo system, or at least an MP3 player, to appear before he finally figured out he was doing it all wrong. He didn't need any equipment to play the music. He just needed to concentrate on what music he wanted to hear, and it would simply manifest in the atmosphere around him.

He was sitting on his ass listening to Slipknot and playing video games that were projected on the cave wall with an invisible hand controller when Phobetor showed up. The elder deity smacked him on the back of the head. Stunned, Flynn looked up at him with his mouth hanging open. He resented such treatment but was too afraid of Phobetor to protest.

"Nice wings," he said. "Do you really think Nyx gave you the power of a somnali so you could sit around the house playing with yourself all day? Why are you still wearing the ring?"

"The ring?" Flynn asked stupidly.

Phobetor reached out with a single finger and bounced Charlotte's ring up and down a couple of times. "Yes, the ring. The girl's wedding ring. You just saw her, didn't you?"

"Charlotte? Yes, I saw her," he said, confused.

"And is she still willing to have you?" Phobetor asked. "Or has she found another?"

"I don't think there's anyone else," Flynn said with a shrug. He remembered seeing her last night and began to smile.

"I see," Phobetor said. "So, you saw her, and you bedded her, but it didn't occur to you that she, not you, should be wearing that ring around your neck?"

"Oh," Flynn said, suddenly understanding. "I should have given it to her last night."

Phobetor gave him an irritated look. "Yes. The power that was dormant in you is now active. That means that Nyx, at least, acknowledges you as the spouse of Charlotte. You need to give the girl the ring. Have you thought about what I said?"

"About what?" Flynn said defensively.

"Well, about Charlotte's job," Phobetor said seductively. "Maybe you wouldn't mind it so much if you could be there with her. If you could feel everything her victims feel I believe you might enjoy it. It might drive you insane, though."

Flynn sighed. He remembered that Nyx warned him not to trust Phobetor.

"I don't see how it's any of your business what Charlotte and I do with each other," he said finally.

"But I can show you again," Phobetor purred. "Just like last time, with the blood sucking. You enjoyed that, didn't you?"

Flynn shook his head. "You should go," he said flatly.

Phobetor stood up and took his leave. Flynn was pleasantly surprised. For the most part, the dream world deities seemed to have a poor sense of boundaries and almost no respect for his privacy. He had a lot on his mind, and playing games was relaxing. Being forced to feel whatever Phobetor was forcing onto his victims as Charlotte's proxy wasn't, not at all.

As it turned out, Phobetor was having problems of his own. Some strange reports were coming out of the Pacific Northwest. Something or someone possessed powers that only Phobetor himself should be able to bestow. He needed to find out who this person was, and how he obtained these powers. The last thing he needed right now was any kind of competition.

These disturbances appeared as spikes on his proverbial radar. The god of nightmares was tuned into human fear, and any time there was an outbreak of urban legends, hallucinating nightmares, or other fear-based activity, he was alerted. He remembered how busy bad acid trips used to keep him back in the sixties. Something on that level was going on in Oregon. He had to check it out.

Dada

Flynn was also traveling to the mortal realm, but with a far different earthly mission. He wanted to see his daughter again, and not just in a dream. She was a little over two years old, and her dream life was very surreal. He visited her there once, and she had been dreaming about being back in the womb. They were floating in a sea of warm liquid, and everything he saw was extremely fuzzy and had a reddish tinge. He could hear Charlotte and Maribelle bickering outside, but he couldn't understand a word they were saying. Faelyn's eyes were closed, but she kicked when he tickled her foot.

He didn't want to see her in her dreams. He wanted to see her in the world, with her mother. He borrowed a trick from Phobetor's playbook and appeared as a cat on the steps of Charlotte's studio. This time, he decided to camouflage his unneutered condition, so Hannah wouldn't be staring at his nuts with environmentally sound but nefarious intentions.

He showed up just before Hannah brought the kids back from school. Charlotte was working out back. She'd installed a chaise lounge for those days when she found herself in the need of a mid-day nap. The studio door was slightly ajar, so he walked right in and plopped his furry butt on it. Being a cat, he immediately started licking his crotch.

Charlotte walked over and looked at the cat.

"How did you get in here?" she said. She picked him up with one hand and looked at his name tag with the other. It was a round token interlaced with silver and gold. Although there was no hole in it, it was in the shape of an engagement ring, and the edges were covered in tiny rhinestones. In the middle of the tag was the word "Dada."

She flipped it over on her palm and read the back, "Property of Charlotte Keahi."

Charlie grinned. "Keahi? Are you proposing, Mr. Fuzzybutt?" She sat the cat back down on the lounge chair and walked back over to the workbench where kept her painting supplies. She fished in a little metal drawer and came back out with a ring.

"I got this for you," she told the cat. "Or rather, I got it for Flynn. You are Flynn, aren't you?"

The cat purred contentedly and said nothing.

"Well, it's just a silver band, but it was in the shop getting engraved when he… when you died. I didn't get it back until after we found you a couple of weeks later. I could have buried it with you, I guess, but I kept it. Just in case, I suppose superstitiously."

The simple band had masculine block writing on the inside that read "For Flynn, beloved of Charlotte." She unclasped Dada's collar and put the ring on it, then clasped it back.

"I want you to have it," she said. Then she sat down with him, ruffled his ears, and stroked his back. He walked back and forth, rubbing against her leg and making a happy trilling noise. After a while, he climbed up and sat on her lap. She sat with him about ten minutes before she unseated him so she could go back to work. He gave her a dirty look as she walked off to resume her painting.

Half an hour later, Hannah came in with the kids. The minute she set Faelyn down, the little girl ran to her mother and hugged her legs. Charlotte bent down and picked her baby up. Then, she spotted the cat.

"Dada!" Faelyn screamed, pointing at the cat and squealing. Charlie carried her over to the lounge and sat her down so she could see it. "Dada! Dada!" the little girl screamed, grabbing the poor animal around the neck and picking it up.

"No, sweetie," Hannah said, rescuing the cat from the toddler's strangling affections.

"Put your arm underneath the kitty, like this." She moved both of girl's chubby little arms down around the lower part of the cat's body. "Remember what auntie told you before? Cats don't like it when you hug their neck."

She turned around, looked at Charlotte over her shoulder and pointed down at the cat, mouthing the words "What is this?" without making a sound.

"Oh, uhm… can we keep the cat?" Charlotte asked.

"We will talk about the c-a-t later," Hannah said. By then, Kyle had already toddled over to the source of the excitement and was petting the gray cat. Dada was happily purring, much to Hannah's surprise. She decided the cat must come from a home with children.

"That's a good idea," Charlotte said. "We should talk about him later."

Flynn had been in the cat form too long to understand the English language anymore by then. His emotions were no longer human anymore, either. He was very happy, though.

He wouldn't understand anything that was happening in human terms until after he, the cat, Dada, fell asleep, and he, Flynn, reawakened in the realm of dreams. For now, he was content to be lugged around like a stuffed animal by an enthusiastic toddler.

"That is the mellowest cat I've ever seen in my life," Hannah remarked.

Charlotte laughed. "Yea, he has a really laid-back personality."

Push

Candy and Cyn weren't aware that their activities were registering on Phobetor's nightmare-induced supernatural phenomenon detection system. If they did, they might have considered dialing it back a bit, but then again… knowing those two, probably not. They were vicious, impulsive little creatures.

Together, they could provoke small breaks in reality for humans large and small. Once, they were able to conjure up a fairly large vision, a medium sized pit bull, long enough to spook a toddler and send her running out towards traffic. They couldn't hold up those bigger visions, though.

It was much easier to invoke a smaller, yet equally effective, terrifying image like they were trying to do now. Candy and Cyn could communicate with one another telepathically, and when they were of one mind on a subject, they could work together to make things happen.

Right now, they were both pissed off at Mrs. Jefferson, the kindly, plump fifty-something woman who ran the daycare. Her offense was a small one. She'd refused the twins a second serving of banana after lunch. Cyn loved bananas, but no matter how loud she screamed, "Nyana Nyana! Nan Nan Nan!" Mrs. Jefferson wouldn't give her anymore.

There had to be repercussions for such behavior.

The hallucination imposed upon the unfortunate Mrs. Jefferson was a spider. She had a very bad case of arachnophobia, and any spider would have terrified her, but this particular one was burrowing its way out of her calf just below the knee and crawling up onto her gingham dress.

The alarmed look on her face was priceless. The twins were even more pleased when fear caused her to leap from her comfortable lawn chair and go flying across the yard. In her panic, she failed to look around for objects the toddlers had strewn across the yard. The twins weren't responsible for the opportune placement of little Suzy Finkelstein's tricycle. Mrs. Jefferson tripped over it and broke her hip.

Candy and Cyndi exchanged a gleeful look. This was progress.

No one would suspect that they had anything to do with it. Certainly, little girls didn't control spiders. They weren't the ones who left the tricycle out there. That was the Finkelstein kid.

Positively delightful, the girls thought. Candy clapped her hands and Cyn started to squeal.

Betrothal

They were just playing around when it happened.

Flynn was visiting Charlotte in her dreams. This time, he took her to his apartment, as he'd come to think of it. She was amused to find out that he was living in the grotto. He still used the cavern wall to watch movies or play games sometimes, but not tonight. Tonight, he was on the floor in the animal skins with her, talking and laughing.

"You have some sense of humor," she said, pointing at the leopard skin. "Where did you get this from?"

"It was here when I arrived," he said, surprised. "I thought you left it here for me. It reminded me of you, I know that's weird. Maybe it's kind of morbid, but I've slept in it so many times."

"You remember how Mercy was spying on us that night?" Charlotte asked.

"I do," he admitted. "She was a little bird or something, I guess... I think. When I died, she came and sat next to me. She taunted me while you ate the rest of my body. I was surprised that she wasn't entirely mean-spirited about it. She was just kind of sarcastic. I guess she thought it made for great theater."

"Well, what I didn't tell you is that afterwards, she rammed me through with a spear," Charlotte said. "She killed me in my leopard form, and then she skinned my carcass. I never knew what she did to the hide. Apparently, she tanned it, and left it here at some point. Maybe she tanned it, and someone else left it. I can't say."

"It always reminded me that death wasn't the end," Flynn said. "You are alive, yet your skin is here. It proves to me, that we aren't our bodies. My bones are still out there in the field where you left them, as a reminder. I never go there, though."

"You sound very philosophical about it," she observed.

"I'm not," he said flatly. He came down here to propose to her again, but this talk of death and corpses was quickly putting him out of the mood. He was sitting on Charlotte's corpse. He quickly stood.

"I wanted to show you the water back here," he said, gesturing for her to stand. "It's like a natural spring or some kind of spa. It's really beautiful."

"I know," she said saucily. "I made it. I am the architect of this place. I'm sure my grandfather brought you here because it is my home in the dream world. Now, I suppose all of my father's land is ours, but before, it was just this place and the bit outside I like to call 'the yard.'"

"Well, can we go there?" he said. "Together, I mean."

Charlotte stood up. "Oh... yes, that sounds like fun."

He held his hand out to her. She took it and stood up beside him. She put her arms around him and hugged him. It was a spontaneous display of affection. They were frequent and mutual since they had been reunited. The simple reassurance of shared touch had been denied to them for so long.

"There's an even bigger body of water you probably don't know about," Charlotte said, cradling his hand in her own. "Let me show you." She tugged on his hand and dragged him behind her. He followed her to the same place where he'd bathed so often.

"This is the place I meant," he said.

"I mean under there," Charlotte said enthusiastically, stripping out of her Death Note t-shirt and her boy short pajama pants. "If you hold your breath and swim under the water, you will come to a tunnel that leads to another, larger body of water. Follow me, I'll show you."

Flynn took off his boots and slipped out of his pants. They were the same leather pants he'd been wearing for three days. Charlotte was about to dive in the water when he grabbed her shoulder to stop her.

"Wait," he said. "How will I get through, with these?" He pointed his thumb over his shoulder at his wings.

"Don't you know how to tuck them back under?" she asked.

"No," he said with a shrug.

"Well then just shape-shift," she said. "You do it exactly the same way you turned into a cat, only shift back into your old human form."

"Oooohhh," he said. "Well, wow. Duh."

He did as she asked, and soon he was standing there, naked and human. She climbed up the rocks to the pool. Then she took a dive headfirst into the water. He watched as she slid below. He waited until her foot disappeared, counted to ten. Next, he dove in after to follow her. He could see her pretty, little feet moving back and forth under the water, propelling her forward.

When he followed her up to the surface, they were near a tiny island in the middle of a lake. He climbed onto the land and sat with her on a grassy knoll under a single tree. They were completely underground, but an ethereal light rose out of the water to light the darkness. It was truly beautiful here.

Flynn grabbed her and kissed her. He pulled the necklace up over his head and began to untie the knot that held it together. Charlotte saw what he was doing, and she waited patiently without saying a word. When he was done, he took off her ring and handed it back to her.

"Charlotte Metaxas, will you marry me? Will you have me as your husband? I know I asked you before, but I died, and I…" he paused, fumbling for the words.

"Of course I will," she said, taking the ring out of her palm and putting it on her finger. "And will you still have me as your wife?" She took the ring she'd put on his cat collar earlier and pulled it off the thread that had held it and her ring.

"Of course I will," he said, echoing her words. "I'm yours. I'll always be yours, Charlotte." He put the ring on his finger. He handed her the braid that held the rings around his neck not long ago.

"It's made of Nyx's hair," he told Charlotte. "She took it and braided it in front of me the night I came here. She did that right after she unbound my hands and found your ring there. Did you know she blessed our engagement?"

"No, I didn't know that," Charlotte said. "When?"

"At your birthday party," he said. "She possessed that guy who used to be my roommate, the one who came with Sunshine Green."

"Oh, I remember what he said," Charlotte said. "I don't remember his name, though."

"Howard Lowe was his name. Nyx said he and she were of one mind about it," Flynn said.

"Howard broke up with Sunshine after that," Charlie said. "Or so she claimed."

"They were on a date, they weren't a couple," Flynn said with a shrug. "Anyway… will we marry soon?"

"Soon," Charlotte said. "I mean we have to do it here, in the dream world now, so I guess you'll arrange it."

Bereavement

Out of the blue, Flynn became very upset, and his body began to shake. He began to weep hysterically. It was very alarming.

"Charlotte… the last time, we didn't get married because I died! I mean I am dead, now," he ranted." I'm not even human anymore! I don't know what I am! I can't be with you in the real world, and that's not good enough for you! I hate being dead! I hated dying! I hate being trapped here! I don't have job! I don't have anything to offer you, or our daughter. I can't give you anything!"

She moved close to him and tried to put her arm around him, but he backed away. Charlotte folded her fingers together on her knees and just spoke to him instead.

"That's bullshit, Flynn. You already gave us everything you had to give. You gave me every dime in your pocket. You gave us every drop of blood in your body. Faelyn would have been at the mercy of my father and my family all of her life if not for you."

"I hated dying," he said again, trembling with anger and frustration. "I didn't want to die, and I woke up here all alone. I've been stuck here just waiting for you. It's been so long."

Charlotte raised her eyebrow. "You shape-shifted to get here, didn't you? I mean your wings. You don't know how to just tuck them away, so you changed forms entirely. So, you're not somnali right now, you're actually human."

He nodded and wiped his face with the inside of his arm.

"That's why you are feeling so emotional right now," she said. "Nyx probably changed you to prevent you from going mad down here. It's not a normal place for a human to spend an afterlife. My father said demisomnali came here. I guess I didn't think about it before I sent you here."

Charlotte reached out for him again, and this time he was ready to receive her embrace. Her arms around his waist made him feel like a real person. He pressed his cheek against her shoulder and buried his face in her hair. It still smelled of coconut shampoo.

"You should shift back," she said, gently stroking his bare skin with her still damp fingers. "You're too emotionally vulnerable in this form."

"You always liked me vulnerable," he said. "Doesn't excite you? Didn't you love my being defenseless and exposed? Don't you want to have me now, naked and human? Don't you want to take me here, on the ground?"

Charlotte blushed. "Flynn!"

He handed her the braid and held his wrists out. "You can do anything you want to me, Charlotte. When you touch me, you make me feel alive. Don't hold back."

"We spent six months together," Charlotte said patiently. "Six months when I probably should have spent more time talking to you, and less time groping you. I was supposed to be your protector. All of that time I spent tying you to my bed and fucking your brains out just ended with you being dead. I've been spending the last three years trying to figure out what I could have done differently. Not thinking with my twat has ranked pretty high on my list."

"But I'm not dead now, am I?" he pleaded. "I have died, and I have mourned everything I lost. I lost my life, my hopes, my dreams, and my future. I lost you. I lost the ability to be a part of my own daughter's life. Even now, I can't be her dad. I'm stuck being her cat. Let that percolate for a while."

"I'm so sorry," she said, squeezing his shoulders. Flynn pulled away from her again.

"I don't think you understand," he said moodily. "I slept for eighteen months just waiting for you to come and wake me. When you did wake me, I don't think you even knew about it. Do you remember when you cast a spell on me so I would feel your orgasm?"

Charlotte nodded. "I do."

"Well, it hasn't worn off," he said heatedly. "Every time you think about me when you're touching yourself, I know all about it. I feel everything. It's like I'm in your skin."

She blinked a few times as what he said sunk in. When it finally registered her cheeks flushed beet red. "I'm sorry," she said, "I didn't know."

"I want you to touch my skin," he said. "I want you to caress my body. I don't want to feel like a ghost anymore. I always do, though. Phobetor never calls me by my name. He either calls me The Dead Human, or if he's feeling generous, Charlotte's Consort. Except for Nyx, who considers me a dead hero because of the fall of Brash and his corrupted somnali children, I'm no one here other than who I am in relationship to you.

"You cast me in that role. You sent me here, hands bound, with your ring. I am yours, and I am no longer complete without you. I think it's a little too late to develop moral qualms about what we do in the bedroom. All I've ever wanted was to make you happy. I just want you to touch me so I can pretend I'm alive. Is that too much to ask? Please don't make me sit here and beg you to satisfy me."

Charlotte smiled. He was pouting, something she never remembered him doing before.

"No, of course it's not," she said. "Stand up and show yourself to me."

Flynn stood up and bashfully modeled for her. Now that she was giving him what he wanted, he felt much less bold and demanding. "Do you like my tattoo?" he asked nervously. "It's not a tattoo, really. It's the embodiment of all of the power you will wield as the goddess of erotic nightmares – the power that once was your father's - your inheritance... I'm holding it in my body and it..."

Charlotte clambered up into the tree above him. She reached down, took his hands in hers and pulled them up over his head into the tree, on either side of a low-hanging limb. He stopped babbling and moaned when she bound them together at the wrists.

"... it moves sometimes," he continued. "It bit me once. Phobetor tried to take it from my body, but no one can other than yourself, unless you permit it." Charlotte reached down and touched the head of the snake, where it lay on his breast. She stroked it until it began to move, following her finger. She took her hand away, and the snake lifted its head, seeking her.

Charlotte dropped down from the tree and played with the creature that lived under his skin. He felt it slithering below the epidermis, leaving the skin hot and tender in its wake. Flynn began to whimper. The snake wound around his calf and thigh, coming up below his buttock and tracing the side of his hip and waist until it reemerged, snaking past his left pectoral, dipping down and resting its head above his heart.

She pinched his nipple and tugged on the ring. Flynn tossed his head back, trembled, and said one word, "harder." She pulled the ring harder, and when she let go, she bit his nipples until they were very sore and his dick was very hard.

"Fuck me, Charlotte," he begged.

"Do you think that when I take back this snake," Charlotte taunted, "it will hurt? Do you think it will rip itself from your flesh to return to me?"

"I don't care," he cried out. "You can have me torn and broken on the ground. I don't care what you do to me. I just need you to fuck me right now. Please."

She answered his urgency, breaking the tree branch in her rush to slide his body down on the grass. She pressed his hands down into the grass over his head and climbed on top of him. She felt him sliding inside of her, warm and familiar. She realized he was right. The thought of him pinned down underneath her turned her on. She used to be demisomnali, he used to be human. She used to be strong enough to pin him down. Flynn was always physically bigger than she was, and now, he was also much stronger. He was letting her have her way with him. It was a gesture of submission.

She looked at him, and watched his face contort in pure pleasure. Whatever they were doing really excited him. She could see he was about to have an orgasm.

"Are you sure you're not just feeling lazy?" she teased. "You've got me up here doing all the work."

He couldn't answer her because he was already beginning to shake. He bucked up against her, moaning and trembling, and she could feel him cum inside her. She shook her head and rolled off of him.

"I'm so sorry," he said sheepishly.

"Do you feel better now?" she asked. "Do you?" She leaned in close and bit his earlobe. "Do you?" She rolled him over onto his belly and smacked him hard across the ass. He laughed.

"You love me, don't you?" he asked her.

"I do," she agreed. "I love you very much."

He looked at her over his elbow, which was in front of his face as his arms were still bound over his head. "You didn't have anything to do with your mother killing me, did you?"

"What?" Charlotte protested. "How can you even think that? I had no idea you were dying. When I found out, I was devastated. I've been beating myself up for the last three years, telling myself that I should have known."

"I kind of knew," Flynn admitted. "She kept giving me speeches about how no one should have to bear my burden. It was obvious she was up to something. I wasn't sure how or when she would do it, though. I almost refused the coffee because I thought it might be poisoned, but then, I had another thought, that it might be better if she did kill me. I immediately regretted that."

"It's not your fault," Charlotte said, beginning to untie him. She loosened the knot and took the braid off his wrists. There was something perverse about using her immortal ancestor's hair as a bondage rope. The braid was not very thick, but it was stronger than human hair. It was like tying him up with a plastic zip tie. She took the braid and wrapped it around his right wrist several times then tied the ends together, like a friendship bracelet. Nyx had given him the braid, and a blanket. Charlotte decided they were probably important.

"Nyx thinks I'm some kind of hero for basically allowing myself to die," Flynn said bitterly. "All I did was fail at refusing a poisoned cup of coffee. I don't see how that's heroic."

"If a goddess says you knew what you were doing," Charlotte pointed out, "she's probably right."

"If so, then forgive me for leaving you," he pled.

"I'm sure you can make it up to me," she answered, kissing him. She was running her hand over his back when he started to shift back into his somnali form. Charlotte breathed a sigh of relief. He was much safer this way. Subconsciously, she was a little afraid of his vulnerability now. He already died once. She already lost him. She didn't want to lose him again.

She moved her hand further down to the small of his back and watched as his wings reemerged. They were a part of him now. Letting them freely emerge no longer caused him any physical distress.

He was still on his belly, and so she started playfully fondling his ass. Occasionally, one of her fingers would slip somewhere it usually wouldn't be. He was tantalized by these mischievous, teasing attempts at penetration. She was testing him to see if he was willing to allow her to finger him. He was smiling, waiting to see how far she would go. Maybe someday she would let her do what she was trying to do, but not just yet. They would have an eternity to explore one another's bodies completely.

He smiled at the thought of it.

"I have a surprise for you," he said, rolling over to let her see the physical manifestation of his pleasure.

They both knew that they needed to sit and talk things over, but it was hard to keep things in neutral after being apart for so long. In a lot of ways, they were still like newlyweds, wrapped up in the glow of new love.

Soon, they would be newlyweds.

Charlotte grinned, and they went at it some more.

Coffee

"How is he?" Hannah said, dropping the mug of coffee on the table in front of Charlotte. Charlie looked very relaxed and wore a thousand-yard stare.

"Who?" Charlie said.

"Flynn," Hannah said decisively, taking a seat at the table.

Faelyn looked up as if someone were saying her name. She'd never heard her father's name said aloud. She and Kyle were already at the table in their booster seats. Shelby was feeding Kyle, and both mother and child wore some sort of bib. Shelby had a big apron she wore over her work clothes in the morning to keep the kids from ruining them.

Shelby nodded. "Hannah is the copy editor for *Somnalia*, and we both read it, girl. Fess up."

"Yeah," Hannah said. "We've already read all about Faelyn's Dada. You know the fuzzy gray one you got sleeping in a cardboard box in your studio?"

"And Harpy got a familiar in the comic book," Shelby said. "Some kind of shape-shifting cat man, you know the guy with the pretty wings and awesome ink? What's his name again? Dead Boy?"

"Yeah, so what is up with that Dead Boy?" Hannah said. "I mean, he seems kind of depressed about being dead."

"Totally," Shelby teased. "It's a good thing he has Harpy to cheer him up with all of that freaky S-E-X."

"Shelby," Hannah warned. "Don't spell that in front of the kids. Kyle's already learning the alphabet in preschool."

She looked at the kid. "Say C-A-T, sweetie."

"C-A-T," Kyle said excitedly. "C-A-T, C-A-T. Cat. Cat."

"See a tree, see a tree," Faelyn answered back. Only her tree sounded like "twee." She was just starting to learn short sentences.

"What does S-E-X mean?" Shelby asked him. Kyle smiled back at her adorably but had no answer.

"See? We've nothing to worry about," Shelby told Hannah.

"What is it?" Kyle asked.

"It is candy," Hannah lied. "S-E-E-S, See's candy. It's really good."

"Right," Shelby said. "So, Harpy looks kind of tired lately, like she's been giving Dead Boy candy all night long. That could be exhausting. You look worn out. Would you like more coffee?"

Shelby picked up a silver serving pot from the table and poured Charlotte another cup of coffee without waiting for an answer. Charlie smiled amiably. She was feeling content, and a little drained.

"Shelby looks like that when I've been giving her candy all night long," Hannah said with a wink, passing the creamer. "She loves to eat candy."

"Ah you hush up about that," Shelby said self-consciously. She was eating a bowl of Cream of Wheat and two pieces of toast.

The kids were eating cold breakfast cereal, but that did not stop them from both demanding candy as a result of the conversation. Hannah obligingly handed each of them a Lifesaver from the roll in her pocket. Any more sugar than that, and they'd be bouncing off the walls at school all day today.

"He's fine," Charlotte said, shrugging. "He wants me to call my mom."

Hannah and Shelby exchanged a look.

"But you barely speak with her, hon." Hannah said.

"I know," Charlotte said. "Can we talk about it later, when the kids are asleep?"

Shelby and Hannah both nodded. They both knew that she was angry with Maribelle because she suspected her in Flynn's death. They guessed he must have told her something about it, but whatever it was, it wasn't appropriate to discuss it in front of the kids.

Not that anything they just discussed was appropriate for family breakfast conversation. If these children were going to insist on growing older and increasing their vocabularies, the ladies were going to be forced to come up with more sophisticated code words for S-E-X.

Portland

Phobetor might have pinpointed the twin's paranormal activity right away if it had all taken place within the tiny town of Boring. It didn't, though. Alice Carter had relatives in nearby Portland. Her brother, Bob Henderson, his wife, Daisy, and their preteen son Daniel rented a house in the city of mismatched bridges. So did Alice's parents, Stuart and Georgette.

Enough psychically weird shit was already happening in Portland on a daily basis that when Candy and Cyn pulled a few stunts while off visiting the relatives, it kind of blended in with the general "Keep It Weird" atmosphere. Big cities attracted the kinds of people Candy loved to prey on in her previous incarnation as Mercy. The homeless, the mentally ill, and runaways lead stressful lives and were easily upset by the twin's little parlor tricks. They also hunted the very old and the very young.

Their first Portland victim was an elderly homeless man who was suffering from dementia. His name was Wilson. Wilson was allergic to bees. No one else could see the one he was running from when he skittered out in front of the 75 Cesar Chavez/Lombard TriMet bus. He was lucky to end up in the hospital with two broken legs, instead of on a slab in the county morgue.

Larry was the name of the budding serial killers' first confirmed murder victim. Candy was the one who had the bright idea that, if they could perform a Wilson-type trick near the train tracks, the victim would not be able to come to his senses in time to avert oncoming death.

The setback the twins had when trying to kill Wilson was, he realized, at the last possible second, he was about to go under a bus. He completely forgot about the bee and tried to scramble out of its path. That was why the bus ran over his legs instead of creaming him in the face as planned. For Larry, who had the bad fortune to stop at the train tracks just before Stuart and Georgette Henderson pulled up, there was no time to change his mind and get off the tracks.

He was busy eating his sandwich from Subway, waiting for the train to pass, when the elderly couple with the twin babies in the back seat pulled up on his left. The adorable kids were smiling and waving and shaking their toy rattles at him. He turned around to wave back at them.

That's when the girl sitting closest to him slowly turned around to face the window, grinning. She had a row of tiny, perfectly white, little baby teeth. They were soon overshadowed by her jet-black eyes. There were no whites to them, no irises, only a pair of malevolent oil slicks. Her lip curled with evil intent.

The terrified man impulsively stomped on his gas pedal in an attempt to escape the demon baby and drove right through the red-and-white warning bar. The wood snapped, and his car rolled forward onto the tracks just in time to greet the oncoming train.

If it weren't for Wilson and Larry, Phobetor might have traced the twin's activities to Boring, a city twenty-two miles away, and things would have quickly come to a head.

As it was, though… he spent most of his time looking in the wrong place. Like any big city, Portland had its fair share of the homicidally minded: committers of domestic violence run of the mill thugs, and people who barely kept their fouler natures in check. As the Zodiac Killer proved during his stint in the small town of Vallejo, psychos weren't solely within the realm of big city experience. In bigger cities, there were more anonymous people, so it was easier to blend in. That was probably why the Zodiac moved to San Francisco.

There were 600,000 people in Portland, while Boring had a population of just 8,000. With so many more people in varying levels of fucked-uppitude in Portland, the monstrous twins were able to fly under his radar, for a little while longer. They just had to remember not to shit where they ate.

Frustration

When Phobetor left Portland, he was in a foul mood. He wasn't a bad guy. He was a hard worker. Some might even say he was a workaholic. As the god of fear, nightmares, monsters, and animal dreams, he had his hands full. Some people thought he was evil, due to that whole "striking fear and anxiety into the hearts of men" thing, but not all of the dreams he caused were terrifying. Some of them were just about animals, spirit creatures or familiars. He felt very misunderstood.

By the time he showed up at Flynn and Charlotte's place—and it definitely was Charlotte's, he could smell her stench all over everything—

Phobetor was brooding. He'd spent the past twenty-four hours slinking through Portland's dark alleys in various animal guises, sniffing out the source of earthly evil.

Whoever was doing this shit was pissing him off! They were using phobias to motivate humans to engage in self-destructive, life endangering activities. He was the god of phobias, so he felt kind of like someone was stomping on his toes. This definitely seemed like the kind of thing Mercy was into, but she was dead, off being recycled in the circle of life somewhere.

While Phobetor was busy trying – and failing – to track down his mysterious usurper, Flynn was off surrendering himself to Charlotte again. That boy was so predictable. Unlike Thanatos, Phobetor didn't mock Flynn for his masochism and sexual submissiveness. Quite the opposite, in fact he often thought to himself how delightful it must be for Charlotte to have a lover who found fear such a powerful aphrodisiac. Phobetor was the god of fear. He rather enjoyed their little amusements and the role the emotion played in their games.

Phobetor knocked and asked for permission to enter the premises, although he really didn't have to. "It's me, Flynn. Can I come in?" He didn't bother explaining who "me" was. He doubted he would be confused with Somnus, the only other male who ever visited Flynn's hovel.

Even though Flynn was somnali now, Phobetor could still easily overpower him. The Oneiroi were more potent than their somnali children, and Phobetor was no ordinary Oneiroi. Like Phantasos and Morpheus, he was a god. Somnus and Nyx were more powerful than he was, and Flynn was under their protection, so overwhelming him seemed a bit unwise.

He did like to push him around a little, though. He never went too far with it. He knew that the boy wouldn't take it in the same spirit as he took Charlotte's rough play and vicious teasing. Having been privy to their little conversation about Flynn's body being ripped apart by the snake from the inside gave Phobetor delight. Serpents and all matter of night creatures and monsters were his forté. He would be gifting Flynn and Charlotte with a series of grisly, yet strangely titillating nightmares on the subject. They wouldn't know where they came from.

No creature would recognize Phobetor as the source of a nightmare if it he did it right. He wasn't into grandstanding and forcing attention onto his role in things, like that awful Brash and his horde of undisciplined brats used to do. For Phobetor, a job well done was its own reward. And he absolutely loved doing Charlotte's job. In fact, he loved it so much he had zero intention of ever giving it back to her. He was already plotting up ways to get Flynn and Charlotte to allow him to continue on as regent after she returned. He was so clever. He was convinced he could get them to believe it was their idea all along.

Having this little secret made him smirk. He plopped his oversized frame down on Flynn's undersized stone furniture. He was in his amorphous form now, which resembled an angry cloud of gloom and despair. He congealed his free-floating angst into a humanoid form, for Flynn's comfort. Like his grandmother, Nyx, his true form was composed of darkness. As the mist congealed into the form of a man, he greeted Flynn with a sardonic smile.

Nyx and her sibling consort Erebus, the embodiment of Darkness, were shadowy figures. Somnus was the son of Nyx and Erebus, and although not all of his children (or siblings, for that matter) shared this midnight complexion. Somnus was dark, like his parents. His sisters were Aether, the embodiment of the Air, and Hemera, embodiment of Day. Both were light in color. Phobetor was black. When he transformed into a human form, he enjoyed being in a darker skinned body.

He was also incredibly tall. This day he was even taller than the last. Measuring close to seven feet in height, he dwarfed the round, stone picnic style table. He leaned to its dead center and rested his head on his elbows before he spoke.

"I have a problem," he said in his deep, ground-shaking baritone. "I was hoping that you could help me with it. More accurately, I was hoping you could help me out by getting your wife to assist me."

"She's human now," Flynn countered. "What could she do to help you?"

"She is also a living oracle of Somnus," Phobetor informed him. "She is a seer who has knowledge of my father's activities and those of his sons, and their children. There is an interloper, one who tries to steal my powers. I haven't had any success in locating him. I was hoping that perhaps, Charlotte has seen something."

Flynn shrugged. "You know, she's not like the Oracle at Delphi. You don't need a special appointment or anything. You can just read her comic books. Hannah has her hooked up with a pretty good distribution contract now. Also, some of them are on the internet."

"I do read her comic book," Phobetor snapped. "That's where I read about these."

His hand flew up in an irritated gesture, and Flynn jumped back as a small crowd of creepy black-eyed children appeared in the middle of the room.

"Holy fuck!" Flynn yelped, backing away. "What the hell are those?"

"Black-eyed children," Phobetor said. "I suspect they aren't, though. I think they are perfectly ordinary children who have been made to appear creepy with a very slight mental modification. The black eyes are an hallucination. Someone has been causing nightmare hotspots to pop up all over northern Oregon, around Portland. Some are tiny insects that the victims are afraid of. Others are these creepy psychic contact lenses."

"Why do you think Charlotte knows anything about this?" Flynn asked.

"Because of this," Phobetor growled, waving his arm to bring up another projection. Flynn immediately recognized the artwork as Charlotte's. It was a pair of otherwise ordinary looking toddlers with jet-black eyes, pointing and laughing at a gnarled black cat.

The little girls in the cartoon were almost amazingly nondescript. It wasn't just that they were innocent looking. All children appeared innocent. It was that they were innocuous, unrecognizable. These kids were the most common-looking children imaginable. No one would be able to remember what they looked like. They were far too ordinary. Only their matching gingham dresses indicated that they were female children. The matching clothes, indicating that they were twins, were their most distinguishing feature.

"That cat is you," Flynn said immediately. "Who are the black-eyed brats?"

"I don't know," Phobetor admitted. "I'm hoping Charlotte does or can find out."

"I'll ask her," Flynn said.

"Thank you," Phobetor said with sincere gratitude. His thankfulness was real, but it wasn't sufficient motivation for him to stop plotting against Charlotte and trying to steal her job.

"So, would you like me to show you my latest work?" Phobetor asked Flynn. "The work I'm doing on behalf of your wife, my niece, of course. You want to see that I am doing a good job for Charlotte, don't you?"

"The last time you did that it was, eh, an experience," Flynn admitted. "Unfortunately, it's the type of experience I don't feel comfortable having with my wife's uncle, so I'm going to have to pass on that."

Phobetor shrugged. "As the young humans say, that's your loss, man." He turned his back and smiled to himself when Flynn couldn't see him. He waved his hand and vanished, leaving the boy standing there alone.

He wanted to make the job he was doing for Charlotte as her regent seem as unsavory as possible to Flynn. One way of doing this was to continually, subtly suggest that it might threaten the couple's sexual exclusivity. Monogamy wasn't big among the Greco-Roman gods. Most thought it rather provincial, but it wasn't unheard of. Charlotte and Flynn's sexual fidelity somehow managed to last over their three years of separation. It clearly meant a lot to both of them. They were possessive with each other. Flynn had previously displayed more than a little jealousy at the thought of Charlotte sexually experiencing others.

It was a gap in Flynn's mental and emotional armor. Phobetor recognized it and knew he could take his time in slowly convincing Flynn that Charlotte's duties as the goddess of erotic nightmares were far too depraved for her to sully her precious little hands by personally doing. He would have both of them convinced it was their idea when they turned over the reins to him, allowing him to act as his niece's proxy in the day-to-day running of this business on a longer-term basis.

Possessive spouses and lovers were not unheard of among the gods. Hera was notoriously resentful of Zeus' many earthy dalliances. She had forced her husband to dispose of his pretty little boy toy Ganymede by making him into a distant constellation of stars. Although jealousy was a problem, many of the gods, like Zeus himself, took on an obscene number of lovers.

Phobetor was not any less promiscuous than other male gods such Poseidon, Ares, Brash, and Zeus himself but his sexual tastes were different from Zeus', so unlike the careless Brash, he managed to stay below his ruler's radar. He prowled the Earth in bestial form, spawning a variety of man-animal hybrid creatures with his dalliances. On many occasions, he impregnated human women with crossbreed spawn. He didn't restrict his lovers to humans. Sometimes he pulled a page from Loki's playbook and bred as an animal with an animal. The offspring of such unions were also parahuman. His numerous offspring included centaurs, minotaurs, gorgons, chimeras, werewolves, werecats, and more.

He enjoyed teasing and provoking Flynn. It was the anxiety this created in Flynn that intrigued him more than any sexual underpinnings. He was, after all, the god of fear and anxiety. He flirted with Flynn to get him to squirm in his seat. This was not because he found him particularly attractive. Although he did not appreciate a well-formed young man nearly as much as Zeus and Brash did, Phobetor was not entirely indifferent to the human male physique. He just found Flynn too sticky, sweet, and common.

Flynn, while attractive, was certainly no Ganymede. For that matter, he was no Phobetor.

Fatherhood

Flynn decided he would go talk to Charlotte later. He had other priorities right now. He had given it a lot of thought. He decided that some of his anger over his current situation was misplaced. He had often felt cut off from his loved ones since his death. Now that he was somnali, and no longer a mere wandering shade in Charlotte's kingdom, he had new freedom. He hadn't mastered the art of visiting dreams, but the possibility existed. He could visit people other than Charlotte.

Visiting Charlotte was easiest because she was experienced with navigating the Demos Oneiroi. Consciously or subconsciously, she helped him create sensible dream worlds with linear structure and a sense of time.

The only other person he'd tried to visit so far was his daughter, Faelyn. She did not seem to be dreaming in any way he could understand or relate to. He wasn't sure if she dreamed at all. He found the experience disjointed and confusing. There were brief flashes of light and sound. He had the impression these were memories of the womb, but he couldn't be sure. He didn't know if Faelyn was aware of his presence.

She recognized him when he was a cat. Why didn't she recognize him in the dream if it was a dream? It seemed less like a dream, and more like a visceral reaction her nervous system was having to the foreign intruder.

If the dreams were strange, or surreal, what did it matter? The important thing was for him to try to be there for her as her father. He never knew his own father. Somewhere, there was a guy who probably didn't even know he had a son to mourn. He didn't want Faelyn to go through what he went through. If there was any way for her to know that he was thinking about her and that he loved her, he wanted to make that happen.

He didn't really have enough experience to work this out on his own, so he asked one his in-laws if he could offer some advice.

"She can't dream the way you think she should," Somnus explained. "Babies don't dream, at least not in any way you could understand. They don't yet have the experiences and memories of an older child or adult with which to build coherent dreams. Their brains and bodies are still developing. As a result, their minds are busy learning how to control their limbs and other aspects of their physicality while they are asleep. Their sleep time is all very practical."

"What I saw," Flynn said, "it was like being back in the womb."

"She doesn't even really understand what her memories are," Somnus said. "She wasn't the one accessing that memory, you were. Her mind just did its best to try to accommodate you and what you were requesting of it."

"I just want her to know who I am," Flynn said. "Isn't there anything that can be done?"

"You can spend time with her, if you like," Somnus suggested. "It wouldn't be the same as spending time with a waking toddler. In a lot of ways, she would relate to you the same way she related to her mother when she was in the womb. She would hear you and get used to your presence and the sound of your voice. She wouldn't really be able to communicate with you, though. Not for another year or two."

"I still want to see her," Flynn said.

Somnus nodded, and without saying a word, held his arms out to Flynn. As he extended his arms, a blanket-wrapped bundle appeared in his hands. He handed Faelyn to her father. He took the child in his arms and held her against his chest. She was heavier than he expected.

"Just hold her and talk to her," Somnus said. "You can sing to her if you like. She can hear you."

Flynn stood there in a daze, his precious little bundle passed out and slobbering on his shoulder. He was the oldest grandkid in his family, and she wasn't the first baby he'd ever held. He had a bunch of younger cousins, kids he hadn't seen for years who were probably in college by now. For the first time in a long time, it crossed his mind that if he was still alive, he would be twenty-nine years old. He'd be thirty in about three months. Only, he would never be thirty. He would always be twenty-six. He thought about how young Somnus looked - nineteen or twenty. He was Charlotte's grandfather, but he looked younger than her. He realized that one day his daughter would look older than he did as well. But that wouldn't happen for a long time, and he could make himself look older if he wanted to. Anyway, it didn't matter. All that mattered was now.

He held Faelyn in front of him and bounced her up and down. She was asleep, but grinning. He wiped the drool off her chin. She was the most beautiful human being he'd ever seen, but he was sure that every father felt that way.

"She's so pretty. Just like her mother," he said.

"Flynn, your daughter looks like *you*," Somnus said. He was amused. He didn't share Phobetor's assessment of Flynn's appearance at all. He had beautiful black eyes, and rich brown skin. He wasn't an athlete. His physique wasn't as chiseled and well-defined as Hercules or Achilles. It was softer, like Michelangelo's David, already exhibiting a tendency towards the love handles that would have plagued him if he'd lived past forty. There was something about the slight softness that was attractive. Charlotte certainly thought so. She liked his tenderness.

Flynn didn't think he was good-looking, though. He kind of shrugged.

"She does sort of look like my mom," Flynn said. "Mom is pretty. She used to be in teen beauty pageants before *someone* ruined her figure by daring to be conceived."

Flynn wanted to be alone with his daughter, if only because he didn't want to sing in front of Somnus or anyone else over the age of five.

"Let's go out and get some air," he told the sleeping child. He went out into the forest for a walk. It was the first time he'd gone outside since the first day he came to live here, the day Somnus put him to sleep. Small brush and poppies grew immediately outside of the entrance to the cave.

He always thought that if he had children, he would expose them to all of the really cool bands he liked in high school. He was into Slipknot, Disturbed, Blink 182, System of a Down, Mushroomhead and Celtic Frost. He was, therefore, surprised when he started singing to his daughter and what came out was the old N'Sync hit *The Girl Who Has Everything*.

He would have never admitted he knew all the words in front of Danny, or even Charlotte. The baby seemed to like the song. She smiled and kicked her feet a little. Flynn touched her tiny, balled fist and she opened her hand and clutched his thumb. Her little fingers were so tiny, so perfect. The knuckles were just little dimples.

"This is the river Lethe," he told the sleeping babe, taking a break from his serenade. "If you follow it all the way up to that hill, it goes to your great grandpa's house. That was him, you just met him. He has a lot of kids. Did you know your mom has nine hundred and ninety-nine uncles? That's a lot of uncles, right?"

He didn't know what to say to her, but he was so happy she was there.

"Did you know your daddy could fly?" he bragged. Flynn had only ever floated about three feet off the ground, so it was a bit of an exaggeration, but he floated up a bit anyway. The baby was still sleeping. He thought about how nice it would be a few years from now, when she would be able to see him and talk to him in the dreams.

With his child in his arms, he walked to the place where he'd died so she could be born. It was the first time he'd visited the spot since before she was born. Someone had come through and buried his remains. He thought it was likely either Somnus or Nyx, but an odd thought occurred to him. If Mercy had skinned and tanned the hide from Charlotte's leopard form, she might have also buried his half-eaten body. It sent a chill over his spine flying over his own grave, but holding Faelyn made him feel like somehow it was all worth it.

He wiped a tear from his eye thinking about it.

He checked to make sure no one else was watching before he started singing more schmaltzy songs to his baby girl.

Finally, he found he was exhausted. He landed on his feet and walked down to end of the grove, found a patch of warm grass nearby and settled down onto it. He relaxed and lay on his back, looking up at the sunshine. The baby was still asleep on his chest, head on his shoulder.

She was so cute. She was the meaning of everything.

Motherhood

Nyx looked down at Flynn and Faelyn and smiled. "Do you remember the time I saved you from Zeus?" she asked Somnus. They were sitting in her home at the edge of the Underworld, where she stayed with her consort Erebus. This was the place from which she would be drawn up into the sky when day became night. It was dark and cozy, much homier and less palatial than her other residences.

Somnus leaned back and sipped his hot cocoa. Food was unnecessary in the Demos Oneiroi, but hot cocoa was absolutely delightful. "Of course I remember, Mother. Technically, you did it twice: once through intervention, and another time through deception."

She laughed. "Yes! You are right!"

"He was always a bit intimidated by you, because you were one of the first," Somnus said.

"The blackness of night, born of Chaos, pouring forth into the skies before the Earth and its creatures crawled out of their primordial ooze," she said slyly.

"I was born fortunate to have such a powerful mother," he said, bowing his head in deference.

"And I tell you," Nyx said patiently, "powerful though I may be, nothing motivates like the love of a child. I stood toe to toe with Zeus for the protection of you, my son. Prometheus did the same for the human beings he created; his children. I ask again; is it weak to create, and to nurture and protect that which is created? I asked this of Phobetor when he mocked my champion as weak."

Somnus lowered his head further. "Your champion succeeded where mine could not."

Nyx lifted her head and gave Somnus a serious look. "But you are mistaken. He did everything for the promise of love and family. He did nothing for me. They are two halves of a whole, and now they will be married."

"Pasithea speaks of nothing else," Somnus said with a laugh. "She buried his bones in the grove the other day. She said the place needed to be cleansed so it would be ready for a wedding, although I think Charlotte might prefer their place in the water."

Nyx laughed. "Let them think their secret places are private. Respect their strange human customs, as Phobetor does."

Somnus wrinkled his brow. "Phobetor has come to me with a concern, Mother, one that troubles me greatly."

"What is it?" she asked.

"He believes that somehow, the somnali are active on Earth. Specifically, he suspects the involvement of Mercy in certain earthly activities. How would that be possible?"

Nyx narrowed her eye. "Before reincarnation can occur, there must be death. If there has been any break in the cycle, I think I should have a word with Thanatos."

"He always was fond of Mercy," Somnus said.

"Indeed," Nyx concurred.

Felines

Faelyn was pounding her cereal spoon on the breakfast table squealing, "Ella! Ella! Ella!"

"Who the heck is Ella?" Shelby asked, grabbing an espresso from the fancy new hot beverage machine Maribelle Metaxas had sent over. Charlotte called her on the phone, and she responded to the possibility of a renewed relationship by throwing money around. Still, it was a thoughtful gift, one all three women enjoyed. Even the kids got steamed milk or hot cocoa.

"You don't want to know," Hannah said with an eye roll. "Charlie says the kid's been spending time with her dad in the dream world."

"He's been singing that Rihanna song to her," Charlotte said.

"Aw how cute!" Shelby cheered.

"Is he still a guy?" Hannah asked.

"Yes, he's still a guy," Charlotte said.

"Are you sure?" Hannah asked.

"Oh, I'm definitely sure about that," Charlie said with a wink.

"Um... yea, but anyway. I think it might have been more useful, and less annoying for him to sing her that ABC song, the one they have Kyle learning so he can recite the alphabet?"

"That song always made me think that LMNOP was a single letter," Shelby said.

"I think we were all convinced that the twelfth letter of the alphabet was elemenopee," Hannah confirmed.

Kyle looked up expectantly. "Ay bee see dee elemenopee," he sang, grinning.

"Ellamenapee," Faelyn chortled. "Ella men a pee! Ella men a pee!"

"Okay," Charlotte said. "This is getting really educational, or something."

Shelby laughed. Hannah was a little distracted by the large, black cat hanging outside the kitchen window. She'd seen the same cat every morning for the past week. It was a huge long-haired cat, a Maine Coon or a particularly large Persian of the non pug-nosed variety. It looked homeless, but someone had tried to comb out a few of its catty dreadlocks.

"Isn't that the cat from your picture?" she asked Charlotte, finally. "Nightmare?"

"Yea," Charlotte said, perplexed. "I think so. He's been here for days. Not sure what he wants."

"Let him in," Shelby suggested.

"Can't hurt," Hannah said. "I mean, it's not like he's a vampire, or something. He could get in without an invite, right?"

Charlotte shrugged. She walked over to the kitchen window and slid it open. "Come in, Nightmare."

The cat stepped in through the kitchen window and carefully stepped around the dishes in the sink before plopping on the floor. For a cat with gnarled fur and a semi-feral look, he had a lot of attitude. He strolled right up to the rear door of the house and stood there, waiting to be let out.

"I think he wants to go out back to the studio and talk to Faelyn's Dada," Hannah said.

"Oooh, somebody's in trouble," Shelby said, opening the door and letting Nightmare strut on out.

"Why didn't he just hop the fence?" Charlotte asked.

"He probably needs someone with opposable thumbs to open the door to the studio," Shelby said. "Come on, boy. I'll let you in." Shelby walked out to the back and opened the door for Nightmare. They'd been thinking about installing a cat door but hadn't gotten around to it yet. Charlotte was building a little loft in the top of the garage, because sometimes she slept there. Kyle had moderate allergies, so cats were not allowed to live in the house.

Nightmare went in the studio and leapt onto the chaise lounge where Dada was sitting. Dada stepped down, walked around the studio as if giving the black cat, Nightmare a quick tour, then returned to the lounge. The two cats sat there looking bored until Shelby closed the door and left.

"I'm pretty sure they both came here to talk to you," Shelby told Charlotte when she came back in. "Dada gave the other one a studio tour, and now they are just sitting there." She shrugged.

"They can keep sitting there," Hannah said amiably. "They're cats. That's what they do."

The ladies continued getting themselves ready for work and the kids ready for school. Charlotte would get back to her guest later.

The Oracle

Nightmare was sitting on Charlotte's lap, patiently enduring the last strokes of her pet brush. A small office wastebasket on the floor near her knee was filled with knots and tangles of cat hair. A pair of scissors lay flat on the paint-splattered end table where she kept her brushes and pallet. They had been used to remove some of the more stubborn masses of cat hair.

She finished off and set him down.

"There you go! Much better," she told the cat.

Dada immediately took his place on her lap, happily kneading her thighs and butting the palm of her hand with the back of his head.

"Am I a cat lady?" she purred at the feline. "Are you my cat lady boyfriend, are you Dada? Are you? Yes, you are! Yes, you are?"

Nightmare flopped across the end table between a glass jar filled with paintbrushes and a plastic paint palette. He looked at Charlotte expectantly, as if to say "get on with it." After a moment, he began to yawn.

"Fine, I get it," she said. "I need to take a nap so we can have a talk, right?"

She was rather taken aback when the big, black cat actually nodded.

Charlotte picked up Dada in her arms and walked over to the loft bed. She lifted him up, and then climbed up after him. Napping in the day bed was a common occurrence these days. Hannah and Shelby called the cat her familiar.

She lay on her face, and the cat curled up in the small of her back. About fifteen minutes later, they were both snoring.

They emerged in Phobetor's home in the Demos Oneiroi. Flynn had never been there, but he was surprised to learn Charlotte had. Phobetor swept her off her feet with a big bear hug.

"How is my favorite niece?" he asked.

"I thought you didn't like any of your nieces and nephews," she said.

"I do now," he said with a laugh. Charlotte really was his favorite, but that wasn't saying much. He liked her, but not so much that he was beyond plotting to steal her powers.

"I hear you're out to take my place," Charlotte teased. "The rumors, oh my, they are absolutely everywhere."

"Now, now," Phobetor said easily, "they are just rumors. I am only trying to help you and your lovely companion navigate things. Nyx even asked me to take a paternal interest in the boy. Surely, you do not mistrust my motives."

"I know you, my dear uncle," Charlotte said with no malice and mild affection. "Of course I don't trust you."

Flynn gave Charlotte an expectant look. She paused in her debate to put her arms around him. He was shirtless, warm, and tempting,

His wings brushed gently against her arms, which were tossed over his shoulders. She kissed him on the cheek first, and then on the mouth, before letting go.

"I see you, Flynn," she said, kissing him a third time.

"Your uncle thinks that maybe there are somnali on Earth," Flynn said. "Not me, I mean… you know, your sisters and brothers. Weird things that happened near Portland that reminded him of Mercy."

"Is this so, uncle?" Charlotte asked.

Phobetor narrowed his eyes. He resented Charlotte's asking about his attempts to usurp her. He disliked the way she spoke to him disrespectfully. She fawned all over her dead consort, the same way Somnus did with his beautiful wife. Pasithea had a great deal of power over Somnus due to his infatuation with her. This dead man clearly had Charlotte wrapped around his finger. It was nauseating.

"Are you sure you have time to talk?" Phobetor asked tersely. "Perhaps you'd prefer to take your consort out back to engage in your usual deviant sexual acts? The rumors, as you say, are absolutely everywhere."

"Oh, fuck you!" Flynn scowled. "You're an asshole."

Phobetor quickly grabbed him by the shoulder and whispered in his ear, "Once, I tasted your fear. It was delicious." Flynn dropped to his knees and began to scream. The snake that lived under his skin seemed to be writhing, moving up his neck and into his face. Flynn felt searing pain that was less devastating than the terrible anxiety he experienced. The snake felt like it was threatening to explode out of his face, pressing its head though his eyeball, when Phobetor ended his little torment. Phobetor's illusions were both powerful and absolutely terrifying.

Phobetor gave a wicked laugh.

"Didn't you come here to ask for my help?" Charlotte snapped. "I didn't come here to be accused of sexual deviance by the god of bestiality, or watch you torture my lover."

Flynn snickered but didn't dare to get up off the floor. He knew Phobetor's little display was a show of dominance. Part of him wanted to get up in his face and go to battle over it, but he knew that he would only wind up getting his ass kicked. There was a hierarchy in the underworld, and even under Nyx's protection, he was at the bottom of it. Charlotte's rank was just below Phobetor's, but she currently lacked the power to enforce it. What power she did have was held by Phobetor as her regent or in dormancy within Flynn. The assault was as much to put Charlotte in her place as to punish Flynn for his insolence.

"Fine," Phobetor said sourly. "There have been strange disturbances in the mesh of the human experience. That part of their group consciousness which should belong to nightmares is being overcome by daytime, conscious terrors and mild, but devastating hallucinations."

Charlotte nodded. She carefully offered her hand to Flynn and helped him get off his knees. This was all ritual and tradition. Flynn was perfectly capable of standing on his own, but as a consort of human origin, all of his power would have come from Charlotte. What additional power he did have, he was granted by Nyx, who raised him to immortality and gave him an equal status as somnali. Charlotte took Flynn's hand in hers. She wanted Phobetor to know that her husband would stand by her side as her equal. The elder god took note of the action and growled.

"Day terrors in and of themselves aren't unusual," Charlotte observed. "As Flynn and I both know all too well, some humans have conditions that make us prone to waking dreams or visions."

Phobetor nodded. He was still angry about Flynn's mouthing off to him. When they interacted without Charlotte present, Flynn was always very respectful and deferential. Something about being with his mistress emboldened him. He really wanted to torment the boy further, but he needed Charlotte's help, and couldn't risk alienating her.

"I often see day terrors in little spikes here and there," Phobetor admitted. "It's the concentration in a single geographic area that I find disturbing. Even more disturbing is the purposefulness of the attacks. Most hallucinations don't result in someone driving in front of a train, for example. These are all connected to a suicidal action in the humans, and they are escalating."

Flynn got some sort of perverse pleasure from hanging off Charlotte's arm like so much supernatural eye candy, especially knowing that it was provoking Phobetor to do so. He knew by now that it angered Charlotte's uncle when he spoke. He was supposed to be making this conversation between them possible, not engaging in it.

And yet… he spoke.

"It sounds like something Mercy would do," he said casually. Phobetor gave him a dirty look for speaking out of turn.

"It does," Charlotte agreed. "But isn't she supposed to have been reincarnated as a human?"

"She was reincarnated," Phobetor confirmed. "The question is, how? Most earthly reincarnations are facilitated by the forgetting waters of the Lethe. Drowned in the river, she should have returned to Earth tabula rasa, no memory of the person she used to be, and certainly no power. If she returned to Earth with her powers, her memory… she must have been reincarnated some other way."

"Great," Charlotte said. "So, what do you expect me to do about it?"

"You're the Oracle," Phobetor said insistently. "Not the only Oracle ever, but the only living Oracle of Somnus. It's why your father chose your mother. It's why you can't stop writing and drawing that infernal comic series *Somnali*. Those are not just visions of what is now. They are also predictions of the future. I need you to give me a copy of everything you know."

"Let me get this straight," Charlotte said, "You came here to pick up some unreleased material from my comic book?"

"Anything having to do with these two," Phobetor said, holding up the drawing of the two black-eyed toddlers. "I think that one of them is Mercy. The other… maybe one of her sisters, or maybe just an unfortunate human conceived in the wrong place at the wrong time."

Charlie nodded. "Those twins are named Kit and Kat in the comic, but I'm sure that those aren't their names in real life. Probably something similar, though, that is usually the way it works. I'll get something together for you."

"No need to get anything together," he said, tapping his skull with his finger "Just download it all, right into here."

Charlotte nodded and put her hands on either side of Phobetor's head. He was bending down so she could reach him, and she was standing on her tiptoes because he was a foot and a half taller than she was. After a few moments, she let go.

"There you are," she said. "I hope it helps."

"Thank you," he said, offering her a gruesome smile. Even when he was happy, he was absolutely terrifying.

"I'll see you a bit later," he told Flynn with a wink. Then he was gone.

Espousal

The minute Phobetor left, Flynn wrapped his arms around Charlotte and whisked them away to their little home by the Lethe. There were windows in the cave now. Flynn had been concentrating, trying to learn how to master his powers and manipulate the dream world.

He landed feet first in the furs and let her go. Charlotte turned to face him and asked, "Did Phobetor hurt you?"

"Not exactly," Flynn told her. "He mostly just scared me. It's hard to explain. I was having a hallucination that this snake was getting ready to force its way out of my eye socket. It was terrifying, really. But when he stopped, it all sort of started to fade away, like when you wake up after you have a bad dream."

"Oh, so he gave you a nightmare," Charlotte said. "That makes sense. Does he usually do that kind of thing to you?"

"He only did it twice," Flynn said with a shrug. "He asked me first, though. He said he wanted me to let him know if he was doing a good job, you know as your proxy. Then he touched me, and I had the same nightmare as the last person he visited. It was really intense. The next time he asked me, I said no."

Flynn walked over to the fire and shoved aside the hanging cauldron. Off to one side was a smaller hanging pot for tea. He shoved it to the middle and filled it with water from a clay pitcher on the floor. He could have made tea instantly appear, the way Nyx did, but he practiced these more human rituals to gain better control over his environment. Having something to do freed him up from some of the anxiety Charlotte's interrogation caused.

"I see," Charlotte said. "So that's the first time he did it without your permission?"

"Yes. He always asks me first. Why? What are you thinking?" Flynn asked.

"I'm thinking that little display was for my benefit," she said. "Don't get me wrong… he enjoys frightening you, otherwise he wouldn't be looking for excuses to do it. He probably wasn't lying when he said he enjoys the taste of your fear. But he's trying to let me know that if I challenge him too much, he's going to take it out on you."

"Do you mean by giving me nightmares?" Flynn asked. "That doesn't sound all that threatening."

"He could cause you to enter a permanent state of dread and abject terror if he wanted to," Charlotte said. "He's the god of fear, not just the god of nightmares, really, not someone to fuck with. That was just a little warning."

Flynn frowned. "You're probably right. When I first met him, he nearly tore me apart trying to take from me what is yours. Nyx saved me from him. Even then, though, I was just collateral damage. It was clear he bore me no animosity. I was just in the way of something he wanted."

Charlotte shrugged. "To him, my relationship with you is no different from his relationship with the brood mare that bore him the first centaur. In his eyes, you are nothing but a prize possession of mine."

Flynn shook his head. "Great. Now I really feel loved. I think I need a hug or something."

She walked up beside him, tenderly slipped her arms around his waist, and said, "I'm sorry. I didn't mean to imply…"

"But that's just it," Flynn glowered. "A lot of people in your family view me that way, Charlotte. I'm just a sex toy and breeding device you happen to have ownership of. I don't have much of a separate existence, or much of a hope of ever gaining one. I'm totally dependent on you and sometimes I really resent that."

"Do you want to leave me?" Charlotte asked, moving her hand.

"No, I don't want to leave you," he whispered. "I want to have a job, or some kind of purpose other than just being your husband."

"You're also Faelyn's father," Charlotte reminded him.

"I'm trying to be," he said. "Do you think she even notices?"

"Well, she was singing songs I'm pretty sure you taught her," Charlotte said with a shrug.

Flynn's eyes lit up. "Really? She can hear me? I thought maybe Somnus was making that up."

"Yes, she can hear you," Charlotte assured him. "Maybe you can try singing that ABC song to her, or something you know, educational."

"Yeah, I could do that," he said with a sigh. "Can I offer you some tea?"

"Sure," Charlotte said. She walked over to the table, sat down, and waited for him to serve it to her. She wasn't sure what to do or say. Apparently, he was having some sort of existential crisis. She'd heard of people looking for a purpose in life, but someone trying to find purpose in death was a new one on her.

Flynn poured the tea into her little ceramic cup and took a seat across the table.

"Did you know that in six weeks I would have been thirty years old?" Flynn asked her, pouring his own cup of tea. "I guess you could say I am having a life crisis, only I'm dead, so it's more like a death crisis. Whatever. Shouldn't we be married by now?"

"We can get married tomorrow, if you want," Charlotte said with a shrug.

"I always thought I would be married in my thirties," he explained. "I thought I would have a B.A. by now, and a job like Danny's. Be married, have kids. Own a house."

"Well, we have a kid, and we own a fine bit of riverside property just off the Lethe," she said with a grin. "But if you feel restless and discontent, you can build a house-shaped home if you like, with a white picket fence?"

"How do you like the skylights I put in?" he asked, pointing up to the ceiling.

"I noticed them earlier," she said. "Nice. So, is all this about your birthday?"

"Can we get married before my birthday?" he asked. "I think that would be nice, kind of respectable, right?"

"You do realize you're immortal, don't you?" Charlotte giggled. "I mean, thirty is really young for an immortal."

"I should totally pimp out this pad," he deflected. "You're right about that."

"Right?" Charlotte agreed. "I mean, Faelyn should have her own room now, for when she visits you. I mean in a couple of years, she'll be awake here, right? She should have one."

"Then this is real," he said.

"Let's get married," Charlotte said. "It's not a job, but it's something. We believe in nepotism here. You'll be in the family business, dreams. I'm sure my grandfather can give you a job."

"So tomorrow?" he said.

"No," she said. "The last time we waited, you died. Let's not wait a moment. Let's do it now."

They were married that very night. Pasithea was delighted. Flynn was relieved. He not only got married that night, he got a job. Like most of the jobs he had in life, it was a temporary. Somnus called it a mission. Unlike his human work assignments, this undertaking was of critical importance.

He was tasked by Somnus to assist Phobetor in tracking down and capturing the fugitive somnali.

Evil Eye

Although he didn't know it, there was yet another kink in Phobetor's hunt for the elusive Kit and Kat, whose actual names were Candy and Cyn, although they were better known to Phobetor as Mercy and

Sympathy. Timothy and Alice Carter, for the first time since the twins were born, were getting some time off from work for a well-deserved vacation. Tim's parents, Thomas and Rebecca Carter, were taking them on a road trip in their Coachman motor home.

They were going to go down and visit Tim's big brother, Tom Jr., a career navy officer stationed at Naval Submarine Base Point Loma, just south of San Diego. It would be a thousand-plus mile trip down I-5, with plenty of layovers at rest stops. There would be a long stretch of travel down the Pacific Coast Highway once they got to California.

There would be lots of new, exciting places to stop at, and interesting people to meet and kill.

The twins were absolutely psyched.

Cyn was especially pleased, because for the first time in a long time, she'd learned an impressive new trick before her sister discovered it. In fact, she was teaching it to Candy now. It was sort of a psychic time-release capsule, a post-hypnotic suggestion based upon the victim's fears that would be unleashed at some point in the future, hours or maybe even days after the children had left.

Of course, it would have had to have been Cyn. Candy would have never considered an idea that caused the horrifying death scene to occur off-camera, as they say in the movies. She agreed, though. It would up the body count.

It would also help confuse the otherworldly authorities that were now on the trail, although the girls weren't yet aware that their activities were getting more and more attention in the Demos Oneiroi. As it happened, they didn't. Their evasion was purely accidental.

The Carter family needed to find a place to fill up the tank and get a bite to eat that had spots big enough to accommodate the RV. The first victim was found at a truck stop restaurant.

Cyn called the new technique "the evil eye." Although not as immediately intimidating as the black-eyed child gambit, it was more effective. If done right, it was just as creepy to the intended target.

No one could tell they were hexing their victim. To the casual observer, it just looked like two adorable little kids staring at a stranger.

However, if anyone looked at the wrong time, they would see two girls' heads turning simultaneously. The synchronized staring was jarring to most people. Their current victim, a burly trucker, was disturbed by it. He was minding his own business, eating his greasy spoon diner special of meatloaf and potatoes when the toddlers at the next booth turned to stare at him. A chill went down his spine when he saw their two heads swivel to the left at once. It looked as if they were carnival dolls being operated with old fashioned animatronics that consisted of a set of cogs controlled by a single pole.

This trucker was headed in the opposite direction, up I-5 to Seattle. It deflected attention away from the Carter's southbound route of travel. It couldn't have worked out better if it had been deliberately planned out by the two scheming toddlers. It wasn't though. It was mere coincidence.

He was passing SeaTac when first he began to feel a strange creeping sensation on his forearms. Thinking it was a psychosomatic reaction to his ever-growing exhaustion, he decided he'd take a break at the nearest rest stop. Sometimes, if he got tired away from a rest stop, he'd pull off for a little shut eye at a local gas station, what he called a micro-nap. He was behind schedule and really couldn't afford to do that now.

He was a few miles north at the Kent/Des Moines Road overpass when he finally looked down at the coffee cup in his hands and saw the plump black and red snakes crawling all over his arms. The burly man was screaming like a pre-pubescent girl, trying to shake them off his arms when he plummeted over the side of the freeway. His big rig slammed into the two vehicles in front of it before smashing into the guard rail. When it hit, the cab separated from the trailer, and the trailer rolled back into oncoming traffic.

Kent was to the west of the freeway, down in the valley, Des Moines to the east, near Puget Sound. A 2012 Chevrolet Sonic jetted over the edge like a circus clown shot out of a stunt cannon. It flew through the air with the greatest of ease until its trajectory was interrupted by the door of room 205 at the Motel 6. It slammed nose-first into the front door of that hotel room, where exploded on impact, instantly killing the driver and a hapless shoe salesman who was just about to open the door to go out for a smoke.

The other economy car, a 2006 Volkswagen Jetta flew over the side and landed in the parking lot of the bakery outlet store, where its front end folded like accordion. The passenger side airbag deployed, and combined with her seatbelt saved Mary Brokaw, the preschool teacher in the passenger seat from any injuries greater than a broken arm and a black eye. Due to a previous accident, the driver's side airbag failed to deploy properly. Her husband, Dean, a used car salesman, was the unfortunate driver of the car. He died of a heart injury after being impaled on what was left of the broken steering wheel.

After Dean breathed his dying breath, Mary saw the situation was hopeless and began unbuckling her seatbelt. The door was smashed in, and she couldn't get it to open. She was planning to attempt to squeeze out of the hole where the windshield used to be.

She had just finished getting the seatbelt loose when the truck went flying over the top of her vehicle. She threw her arms across her face in an instinctive move to cover her eyes in case the impact didn't immediately squash her. As it happened, she lucked out. The truck landed fifteen feet past her on the sidewalk. If she had gotten the seatbelt off a moment sooner, she might have been standing there when it hit.

Two local Great America RV workers on a smoke break were less fortunate. The cab of the truck smashed into them head on, killing both and the driver upon impact. The guardrail slowed the big truck down, so there was no impressive explosion as there had been with the Sonic, whose mangled remains now sat on an incinerated bed in the burning Motel 6. Instead, the trailer listed to one side like a boat taking on water, and finally, just flopped down to the ground.

It was close enough to a major airport for it to make it onto more than just the local news, and the twins were thrilled when they saw it on the television at the hotel room their parents and grandparents decided to rent. They were still in Albany, the town with the diner, about seventy miles south of Portland.

Their parents and grandparents weren't in any big hurry to get to San Diego.

Pillow Talk

Shelby bolted upright in bed.

When she woke up, Hannah was already awake, sitting up beside Shelby with her arms crossed over her chest, impatiently tapping her fingers. Shelby thought, "That's a gesture I will never make." Being a lot bustier than Hannah, she would have had to cross her arms over her belly, below her ample breasts, not over her chest. She liked reading an online comic strip about these kinds of issues by Paige Halsey Warren. It was called *Busty Girl Comics*.

She immediately knew why Hannah was making the gesture and that irritated face.

"You saw him too, didn't you?" Shelby asked.

"Fucking Flynn!" Hannah spat, "What the hell? Now Charlotte's married to her cat? What is he thinking?"

"Thinking? What does thinking have to do with love?" Shelby asked. "They were going to get married before, but he died. So, it's kind of like the movie Ghost, right? Really dreamy, except for instead of kissing Whoopi Goldberg, she'll be sleeping with a fleabag alley cat."

"I put Advantage on him," Hannah said.

Shelby laughed. "You put Advantage on Flynn? That's hilarious."

"Yea, him and that Nightmare Phobetor thing, holy fuck," she said. "I mean, even as a cat, Phobetor is fucking scary, very intimidating. But I still put Advantage on his neck."

"Yeah, well Kyle is allergic to them," Shelby said. "They have to stay out in the garage."

"Right," Hannah said. "And Faelyn can't sleep out there in the garage. It's way too drafty."

"Maybe they should get their own place," Shelby suggested. She slid back down under the sheets. Hannah was still sitting up, looking agitated, so she tossed her arm over her lap and put her head on her thigh. Hannah didn't have any clothes on, neither of them did.

"But then Charlotte will have to take care of Faelyn by herself," Hannah said.

"Faelyn is in preschool now," Shelby pointed out. "Charlotte's not in school anymore. She makes enough money working on *Somnali* to pay for her own place. It's not exactly like she's grieving anymore."

Hannah did not look convinced. She looked sullen and a little pouty.

"Look," Shelby said, "I know Charlotte is your best friend, but you're not married to her. You're married to me. Me, you, and Kyle are a family. Faelyn and Charlotte are friends of the family."

"That's harsh," Hannah said. She continued to ignore the proximity of Shelby's head and hands to her bare bottom. She was aware of the not-so-subtle hints that Shelby was eager to plant her face between her legs. Hannah was too moody to respond.

"It isn't," Shelby countered. "Would you be acting like this if she hooked up with someone new, someone human?"

"But he's not human anymore," Hannah said. "He can't even exist in human form on this plane. How is that supposed to work?"

"I think it's romantic," Shelby said.

Hannah did a double take. "You? Romantic? I had no idea."

Shelby laughed. "I think marriage is a silly convention, yet here we are, married. Why would I marry you, if I weren't so romantic that I believe our love is more important than arbitrary rules or politics? I think that if two people love each other, they should be able to be together. Fuck the rules."

"I'm not against them," Hannah said. "I'm just saying, let's be practical. Even before he died, they were both recent guests of the local psych ward. If you had been as unstable as I was, we never would have been allowed to adopt Kyle, and you know it. If Faelyn wasn't her biological child, Charlotte would have been challenged about her custody a long time ago. Hell, I think if she hadn't moved in with us, Maribelle might have fought her for custody."

"Um…" Shelby paused. "Um… didn't she murder Flynn?"

"Yeah, she got away with it, too," Hannah said. "Maribelle is bold. I've known her half my life. Take my word for it. You don't know her like I do. If she finds out Charlotte's talking to a dead man…"

"All of us are talking to a dead man," Shelby said with a shrug. "No one is going to be calling up Maribelle and telling her that."

"But what if Faelyn says something?" Hannah asked. "If they are on their own, she'll be forced to ask Maribelle for support. Being a single parent is difficult. What if Faelyn says something about Flynn?"

"What could she say? Her mom has a cat named Dada?" Shelby asked. "Charlotte is an artist. Dada was a surrealist painter. It's hardly suspicious. But tell you what… I'm not trying to kick them out. I am just saying that we should support them to be a family."

Hannah shook her head. "Talk about your non-traditional families. But okay, fine. I'll try to stay open minded."

"What if we get building permits and have the garage converted?" Shelby suggested. "Charlotte already works there, and the cat lives there. That way they can stay close. Will that make you feel better?"

"That sounds fine," Hannah agreed.

"So can we go to bed now?" Shelby asked.

"What do you mean, bed?" Hannah asked, raising her eyebrow. "You've been rubbing my thigh for half an hour, isn't that considered foreplay?"

"I thought you had a headache," Shelby said.

"I feel it clearing up as we speak," Hannah said. She slid back under the covers and kissed Shelby across the belly, where she knew she was ticklish.

"You stop that," Shelby said half-heartedly. These things had a rhythm, gentle and easy as if they had all of the time in the world. It didn't matter if Hannah tickled her or teased her, because they were more than just lovers. They were married. They would fall into one another's arms over and over again for the rest of their lives.

That's what it meant to Shelby, being married. It was just a promise to stay together forever. None of the rest of it mattered, no pomp, no ceremony, or government paperwork. She rolled over in bed and scooped her little woman up in her arms. Hannah always amazed her, this tiny, wiry little lady with her steely resolve and iron backbone.

Physically, Shelby was a much bigger person than Hannah. She was close to five-nine and around 165 pounds, while Hannah was barely five feet tall and ninety pounds soaking wet. There were a lot of situations where the size difference mattered, many of which both women thoroughly enjoyed. Hannah wasn't as submissive as someone like Flynn, but she definitely enjoyed it when Shelby lifted her up and threw her against the shower wall and had her way with her under the pulsating, streaming water.

Guilt

Shelby held Hannah with a different kind of urgency now. She rolled Hannah on top of her just to feel the weight of her, just to know she was there. Three years ago, in the wake of the tragedies that had marred Faelyn's conception, Shelby was consumed with one repeated, guilty thought.

"At least it's not my Hannah."

Her Hannah was with her now, straddling Shelby's chest, laughing, pressing her breasts against Shelby's face. It was her Hannah who was presenting her with a mouthful of petite breast. Shelby loved those little tits, so tiny that there was barely anything more to them than those fat little nipples. They were already hard, and as thick and long as the tip of her finger. Shelby put her arms around Hannah's back and pulled her closer, sucking and biting them until she could feel all of the taut little muscles stiffen in Hannah's wiry frame.

Shelby stopped just long enough to look up and say, "More than a mouthful is wasted."

She let her hand slide over the delicate curve of Hannah's rump.

She remembered a time she grabbed Hannah's ass in both hands and lifted her up onto her own shoulders, pressing her back against the wall before burying her face into Hannah's snatch. She remembered the way Hannah's fingers curled into the wall-mounted coat rack and held on to the hooks with her fingers. Hannah's legs were wrapped around her neck while she was bucking and riding Shelby's face.

She remembered and wished that tonight could be another passionate night like that one. It couldn't be. She was too sad. She tried traveling downward, from her chest to her tummy, but her heart wasn't in it right now. She could not stop weeping into Hannah's soft, sweet belly. She could not stop thinking of death.

She remembered the day Mike Shaw and Tess Allen died. She remembered Cory Landers and that poor girl, Linda Myers, the one he tortured to death. She remembered the series of deaths and funerals that culminated with Flynn Keahi.

She remembered holding Hannah's hand, trembling in lace black gloves. She recalled looking at her bowed head covered in a black pillbox hat with a puff of black lace. She remembered the mumblings and urban legends that followed *Somnalia* around that year… that the comic was cursed. The more people thought it was cursed, the more units sold. Human beings were morbid that way.

That year, that summer, that body count, and Shelby's selfish refrain, "at least it was not my Hannah." And when Flynn had finally died, she was relieved. Everyone knew his death would end it. He was the one that they wanted anyway. Shelby believed that. Mercy was no different than Cory Landers with his suicide by security guard. She had to keep killing until someone stopped her, and the only person who could stop her was Flynn… by dying.

They would circle them all, and kill them off one-by-one, until he died. And eventually they would come for her, and her Hannah. There was nothing she could do to stop them.

She felt guilty about it. She finally broke down and told Hannah.

"I was glad he died!" Shelby sobbed. "I knew when he died, they would stop coming for us. I was so afraid they'd come get you." Then she started blubbering all over Hannah's bellybutton ring.

Hannah was startled. This wasn't what she had in mind. She thought she was getting laid, but as it turned out, her wife was having a personal crisis of some kind. Seeing that Shelby could not continue touring her torso with that sweet little mouth, Hannah leaned over onto her side and looked at her wife. She kissed Shelby's cheek and brushed away her tears with her fingers.

"We all felt that way, Shel," Hannah said.

"But he was my friend," Shelby said, looking confused. "What is wrong with me?"

"I know, Shel," Hannah said gently. "Charlotte and I, and Flynn himself, we all knew that you were fond of Flynn. You always tried to make him feel included. You treated him like a kid brother, even though he was a year older than you. He loved you too, Shelby. Why do you think he came to visit you?"

"I thought he killed himself," Shelby said, shaking her head. "I thought he took his own life, and I was glad. I was glad. I thought that as long as he was alive, we were all in danger. And you're right, I cared about him, like family, but it still didn't seem to matter. I mean what are we? All humans, are we all this fucked up, this brutal?"

"I think that's why Maribelle killed him," Hannah said darkly. "To protect Charlotte, of course, but most of all she was trying to protect Faelyn. As long as Brash and his somnali had access to her, the kid was doomed, destined to become a meat puppet. You feel bad because you were happy he died? How do you think I feel? Sometimes I feel sorry for Maribelle. Sometimes, I think that in her position, I'd do the same thing."

"That's horrible!" Shelby said. Shelby was very conservative compared to Hannah. Both of them were into alternative rock and some lightweight kinky stuff, but Shelby was more culturally provincial. They met at a sci-fi and fantasy convention. Shelby was an almost Amazonian five foot nine black and Portuguese lipstick lesbian, fit, stacked, and hot as fuck in her Xena Warrior Princess costume. It was lust at first sight. But by day, she turned into a postal service worker. Shelby was a nice girl, a law-abiding citizen.

She didn't get high, or harbor dark thoughts about human sacrifice.

"Chill out," Hannah said casually. "It's not like I killed him. I wouldn't have, really. But think about it? Yes, I did. I thought about how all of our problems would be solved by him just dying. So stop beating yourself up. There is enough guilt to go around."

The Job

Flynn was basically apprenticed to Phobetor now. His assignment was to wander around Portland in animal form sniffing out clues to the whereabouts of the nefarious Bonnie and Clyde twin toddlers, Kit and Kat. In order to do this, he had to master shapeshifting. His current form was a non-descript stray terrier. Phobetor teased him and called him "Deputy Dog."

Without Charlotte to observe, the nightmare god refrained from being rough and handsy with him. As Flynn suspected, it was a dominance game, a territorial piss Phobetor took all over Charlotte's property. It wasn't personal. In that scenario, Flynn was a pawn, not a person.

The struggle for personhood seemed central to Flynn's brief existence. He'd always had a hard time existing as a being in and unto himself. He'd always seen himself as someone in relationship to others. From the moment his father's sperm had fertilized his mother's egg, Flynn had been the regrettable accident that had destroyed Samantha Keahi's life. He would spend his first nineteen years being a disappointment to the women in his life, first his mother, then Tamara. He was too emotional, too fragile, too crazy, and too weak.

He was a disappointment to himself. He compared himself negatively to other men, like his friend Danny. He was never as tough, never as slick, never as gainfully employed.

But he never disappointed a Metaxas woman. Not the one he married, not the one he spawned and not even the one who killed him. He didn't want to, but he knew he had to go see his mother-in-law. Even though she took his life, he knew that Maribelle loved him. It couldn't have been easy for her. She probably viewed it as a kindness. If she hadn't killed him, things would have degraded further and further until he was finally forced to kill himself.

Somnus had once told Flynn that Thanatos considered Flynn's a beautiful death. Executed by Maribelle Metaxas with some painless concoction that paralyzed him before causing him to fall asleep and gradually suffocate. He'd been terrified. He couldn't move, and eventually he couldn't speak, but he wasn't in pain, so they could say he didn't suffer. He had suffered. Watching Charlotte sitting there, witnessing his death was horrible. It was something people told themselves to feel better about it, a beautiful death.

Anyway, dying beautifully wasn't exactly a superpower.

Flynn wanted desperately to act, and not to be constantly acted upon. Being Phobetor's sidekick gave him a bit more freedom and independence. Besides, Flynn didn't want to think about how totally fucked in the head he was. He was thinking bad thoughts right now.

Phobetor wore the more gracious and conspicuous form of a purebred German shepherd. There were benefits to the canine form, one of which was a superior sense of smell. He could smell Flynn's body chemistry and it made him laugh.

"Stop worrying about your perversions, little one," he barked dismissively. "You're not human anymore, and no one cares. Focus. We need to find the two little bitches before their killing spree gets out of hand."

Flynn felt hot under his fur and began wagging his tail.

"You can be punished later," Phobetor said. "Did you like being punished in front of you wife? I bet you did, you bad little puppy." He growled, grabbed Flynn by the throat and tossed him over on his back. Flynn tucked his tail between his legs, started whining and pissed all over himself.

"Okay, what just happened?" Flynn asked, getting up from the puddle of his own urine.

"You're a dog," Phobetor said gruffly. "I'm a dog. I'm the Alpha dog. That was a little doggie domination. I mean we're animals. It's not even really sexual. It's just what we do to show who's in charge. I did the same thing in front of Charlotte. If it turns you on, you really shouldn't feel guilty about it. I'd be doing it anyway, whether you liked it or not, so if you enjoy it, that's just a bonus, really. Just accept it. You're submissive."

Flynn shook himself off and followed after Phobetor. Whatever just happened, he felt a lot more clearheaded now. "Okay, so what are we supposed to be doing here?"

"Sniffing them out," Phobetor said patiently, inhaling the aroma around the railroad tracks. There were smells of burned rubber from the tires of cars that stopped suddenly at the crossing. There was a vague undertone of urine, both human and animal.

Flynn sat beside him and took a deep whiff of downtown Portland. "Oh man," he said. "Something smells delicious."

"Those are rats," Phobetor said. "You're in a rat terrier body. They probably smell like filet mignon to you. Filter them out, if you can… but if they distract you too much, just go kill and eat one. We're here to memorize the human aromas, so we can determine which ones are showing up in more than one of these kill sites. If you smell anyone from the last spot, let me know."

"Oh, that makes sense," Flynn said. He went walking around and sniffing things. He ran off several blocks on his own, exploring things. He was so happy to be out in the sunshine that for a little while, he forgot what he was doing.

He fell into the now of dog-thought. He was naked, and unashamed. He didn't care that his white fur, with its black and brown spots was stained yellow with urine. He did not care that he smelled like pee. He felt completely happy and free now. He wondered why he didn't spend more time in the animal form, suddenly. It was very liberating.

Phobetor wasn't into micromanaging. Flynn's little dog form was inconspicuous and frankly, adorable. He could go places a German shepherd couldn't go, without attracting too much attention. Phobetor himself was currently traveling in the company of an elderly homeless gentleman named Wilson, the very same Wilson the Kit and Kat serial killers tried to wipe out recently. Both dogs were keeping Wilson company.

Some homeless people kept pets. Wilson wasn't such a man. Wilson was very mentally scattered. When he happened to enjoy the companionship of any living creature, be it a sparrow or a fellow human denizen of the streets. Their relationship was one of temporary traveling companionship. Wilson fed the two dogs the same way little old ladies on park benches fed pigeons. No one thought of the pigeons as pets. Wilson didn't think of the dogs that way, either.

No one messed with him as long as the big, fierce-looking Shepherd sat next to him. It was a win-win situation for the dog, as Phobetor collected tons of sensory information from the homeless man. He still wore the clothing he had on the day of the accident, for one thing. Wilson was enough in the dream world so that he knew the animals' names, although he didn't understand who they really were.

"This is Phobetor," Wilson slurred to a passerby. "But you can call him MoPho, because he's a bad ass motherfucker." Wilson cackled at his own joke. Some of the passersby threw coins into the dusty overturned fedora at his feet. That morning, a kindly old woman had given Wilson and his two friends a small bag of dog food, bottle of water, and double-sided food dish from the nearby Dollar Store. She even poured the water and food into the dish while a cheerful Flynn licked her hand.

"What a sweet little dog!" she said happily. She was tempted to take the little dog home with her, but they looked clean and well fed. Besides, the German shepherd growled when she tried to pick up the terrier.

"Ladies love Flynn," Phobetor laughed.

Flynn was down the street chasing after a delicious rat when he found the evidence. It was a big, juicy brown Norwegian rat. They were commonly known as sewer rats in the city, and easily could get to be as big as his canine head. This one, minus tail, was about as long as a fast-food hamburger and smelled twice as juicy.

He jumped after it into the dark of the rain gutter and found himself under the city sidewalks. His teeth tore into the scampering creature's haunches, and it let out a high-pitched squeal. It tasted delicious, like a really rare steak. He had expected it to taste like chicken, because he'd heard once, as a human, that's what rat tasted like. Maybe it did. He'd never eaten raw chicken. He'd had raw beef before, that sweet taste of salt and iron. He wondered if he been this totally yummy when Charlotte had eaten him? He didn't care if the rat hurt.

He bit its head off and gnawed on it like a rubber toy, growling his little dog growl. He didn't care if this was dominant behavior. He didn't care if he was a submissive dog. He didn't reason, he just reacted.

When he was done eating, he smelled it… the Thing, that Thing that he was there looking for.

It was a Thing that Kit and Kat's parents shoved out of the side of their automobile at the traffic light. Their mother slyly stuffed the Thing down the rain gutter so no one would see her littering. She did not want the Thing in the car. It was a putrid, pungent Thing.

Flynn didn't care because he was a dog. He snapped it up in his jaws and ran obediently back to the Alpha dog. He dropped it on the ground at Phobetor's feet.

"Oh, my garrsh," Wilson slurred. "That… that is a dirty diaper."

It was a dirty diaper. Mercy aka Candy was potty trained, but her twin sister Cyn had always been a little slower. She was still in diapers.

"That's a good boy," Phobetor said, sniffing the diaper Flynn laid at his feet. "We have to go now. Tell your nice human friend goodbye."

"Bye, Wilson," Flynn barked. He licked the old man's hand gently, and then held his body low, head bent, while Wilson patted him.

"I'll miss you guys," Wilson said. "Stay safe."

The dogs were gone before Wilson could finish his sentence.

Act III: Killers

She wasn't surprised to see him. She might have been if he had shown up last year. Last year, she wasn't sure if he still existed as the same person. He might have been reincarnated by now or spread out into the universe as stardust and the tiny particles that atoms were made of. She had no idea.

She carried the blood, but she was no oracle. Nonetheless, she was a member of the cult of Undoing. She also read Charlotte's *Somnali*. She followed all of the signs.

She was sitting at her kitchen table in the dream. Steam rose from a cup of coffee in her hand. She recognized the cup. She hadn't used it in years. It was buried in her backyard now; hidden on the offhand chance that it might contain any evidence.

So, when Flynn appeared in her dream, she merely asked, "What took you so long?"

"I've been a bit tied up," Flynn said sarcastically. "You know how it goes, the usual thing."

Maribelle frowned.

"I instructed her on how to make you her slave, even in the afterlife," she said hesitantly. "Perhaps I didn't do you any favors?"

"Let's not play, Maribelle," he said angrily, taking a seat across from her at the kitchen table. "This is the very place where you murdered me.

"Well, if you want to be technical," Maribelle said, "I just overdosed you on your own Seroquel at the table. Then, when you passed out at the campsite, I shot you up with heroin while you and Charlotte slept. I may have given you enough Seroquel to shut down your lungs, but I doubt it. I was afraid if I used too much, you'd taste it. I had to make sure you died with the overdose. Did it hurt?"

Flynn gave her a dirty look. "It was upsetting, Maribelle. What did you expect?"

"Well, I wasn't trying to hurt you," she shrugged. "I was just trying to kill you."

"That's cold," he said. "Why are you being such a bitch to me, Ms. Metaxas? I never did anything to you, never a damned thing to deserve to be slaughtered and trussed up like a turkey on Thanksgiving."

Maribelle laughed. "Well, damn. Okay. So, you're a bit bent out of shape about the whole sordid affair. Can I get you some coffee? Well, I guess that wouldn't help."

"Does it make you feel better about what you did to me?" he asked. "I mean being so rude and abrasive now. Even cruel, does it make you feel powerful? Do you feel in control now that you've taken my life?"

"What do you want me to do?" Maribelle asked. "Would you like me to apologize?"

"It might help," he said. He was starting to feel tired, sad.

"Then I'm sorry," she said. "I am. You were a sweet boy, very kind. After Faelyn was born, I felt reminded of you every time I saw that generous smile. I felt really bad because it is my fault that she would grow up without a father. But I did it for her."

"Really?" Flynn asked. "Is that how you justify it?"

"Someone had to make the sacrifice," she said.

Flynn blinked. "Is that what I am to you, Maribelle, the sacrifice? Not another human being, just a thing to be taken out and slaughtered in the forest. And I'm supposed to be okay with it because you chose to poison me, instead of crushing my skull with a stone? Why?"

"I'm sure Nyx did not intend to curse you," Maribelle said, "but she did. The somnali were a danger to all of us, my daughter and granddaughter especially. Charlotte knows I killed you, or at least she suspects it. So do Lorena, Jeanie, and Sunshine. None of them will speak to me. Charlotte called me the other day; I know because you asked her to. It was so tense, so artificial. I'll never have my daughter back. But it was worth it. The price I paid; it was worth it."

All of the color ran out of Flynn's face.

"I'd do it again," she said coldly.

Flynn wiped his eye with the back of his hand. He was going to cry.

"I have to go now, Ms. Metaxas," he said. He stood up and vanished.

Maribelle frowned. What had he come here for? Was he looking to her for love, for acceptance? She was a monster, a predator who took something she had no right to take from him. She didn't know or care if he would have any sort of self-aware afterlife when she killed him.

She just destroyed him and his little life like it was nothing. She treated him like he was nothing. He shouldn't want her acceptance now. He should hate her.

Goodness knew, sometimes she hated herself.

His blood was all over her hands. She was a murderer.

I-5 Corridor

Phobetor didn't know who the twins were, but he knew what they smelled like, and what they looked like. Charlotte kept painting pictures of them, two inconspicuous, plain faced little girls. Generally speaking, he didn't think it was possible for infant mammals to be ugly. They were all adorable in some way, especially to their own species. Even so, it was possible to tell when a child would leave the pupae stage and turn into a moth rather than a butterfly.

These girls had the kind of round, pie faces that looked precious on infants. In adults, they made for the impression of a slack-faced dullard. They both had brown hair, but neither had hair with any luster. One had ashy brown hair, the color of a dead tree branch. The other had hair the plain brown of a dead, lifeless mouse carcass. They were cute in an unremarkable way and would grow up to be the kind of women who blended into any crowd.

It was their non-descript appearance that made the baby spree-killers so hard to catch.

They looked like just about half the babies on the west coast, especially those from the landlocked areas. They had brown hair, brown eyes, and the wind burned skin of farmers. They might have been white, or Latino, it was hard to tell. They were very generic looking, with an almost chameleon like ability to blend.

The most distinctive thing about them was that they were twins.

"Only two percent of the population is twins," Flynn said confidently. "We can rule out the male-male and male-female twin sets. I realize that there is a possibility that they weren't born in or near Portland, but the chances are high that they were.

"I think we should check out all of the twin baby girls between one and three who were born in that area and see if they, you know, smell right?"

He was sitting in his office now. Phobetor had given him an office in his kingdom, so that now Flynn was officially a commuter within the underworld. The office was in Phobetor's castle, gloomier, grayer, and more gothic than the shiny black castle Charlotte now owned. Flynn's office was a room in a high turret overlooking the Lethe. It could be reached by climbing a long, spiral staircase, or flying in through the open window cut through the stone. He had a desk, a computer, an internet connection. It was the first office Flynn had ever had that didn't feel like a cubicle. There was a plaque on the door that read "Flynn Keahi, Executive Assistant to the God of Nightmares." Phobetor thought it was funny.

He also liked having Flynn call him Mr. Phobetor, or simply Boss.

"Good work, Mr. Keahi," Phobetor said. "Why, if you keep this up, we may have to give you a promotion. Perhaps I could ask father to arrange your marriage to a demigod. Oh, he already did that? Well, strike that one off the list."

"I wanted to show you something," Flynn said. He sat in one of those gray, swiveling office chairs, but he sat in it sideways so that his wings wouldn't get squished. He stood up and walked over to a big map of US Interstate Highway 5 that was pinned to the wall.

"Everywhere there is a red pushpin," Flynn said, "there has been a report, by you, of paranormal, fear-based activity. Everywhere there is a blue pushpin, there has been a police report of some sort of accident. The green pins are for police reports that included reported hallucinations, or incidents such as with Wilson, where the victim was hospitalized with hallucinations or other psychiatric symptoms."

"What is eye five?" Phobetor asked, scratching his head, or at least the top of his body. He was in his primordial form now and looked like a dead tree that had been struck by lightning.

"It's a highway, boss" Flynn said. "Interstate 5, humans travel on it with automobiles."

"I assume you meant to tell me that it is the name of a highway. As old as I am, I do know what highways are. They actually predate automobiles. Indeed, it is we gods who invented them. Have you not heard the saying, all roads lead to Greece?"

"I thought it was Rome?" Flynn corrected.

Phobetor glared at him. "Semantics," he said. He was tempted to cuff the lad. How dare this pup presume to correct him? Instead, he chose the path of civility.

"So, what are we looking at here?" he asked.

"These sticky notes with the arrows," Flynn explained. "They have times and dates on them. It would seem that the twins are escalating. And they are headed up or down the I-5 corridor, apparently. My guess is down because most of the deaths follow that trajectory. But... they are happening at once or very close together at times. If they are human, or at least in human bodies, I don't see how they can be in two places at once."

"That is interesting," Phobetor said. "So, I'm the boss, of course, but if you were to suggest a path, what next?"

"I think we need to search for them along I-5," Flynn said. "Not as dogs, it's too slow. As birds, we can fly over them and when we land, I suppose we could shift again. Well, you could. Perhaps you will show me how?"

"It is a sound plan," Phobetor admitted. "When do we leave?"

"I have to warn my wife first," Flynn said nervously. "She lives too close to the I-5 corridor. What if they're headed her way?"

"Fine," Phobetor said. "And will you tell her how you've been in your room, weeping because her mother was mean to you?"

"No!" Flynn said, horrified. "No, I won't, and you won't either! How did you know about that?"

"There is no privacy in the underworld," he said. "There is only the illusion. If no one happens to look your way, you might be alone. Or if they chose to look away, but it's hard not to stare when certain people are ravishing other people under trees on tiny islands."

Flynn blushed. "Oh my."

"Right," Phobetor said, shaking his head. "That's why my father and his wife are so nonchalant about going around nude all the time. But no one really cares, Flynn. But yes, I saw you crying."

"Why are you telling me this?" Flynn demanded.

"I think it is unhealthy for you to be holed up in that little cave," Phobetor said. "All you do is mope and brood over your own death. It's over. You aren't dead, you are Somnali. Your wife is the first female to inherit the role of an Oneiroi. Do you understand how important that is? You are Prince Regent of your own kingdom, Nyx elected you as her champion. Somnus arranged your marriage to his daughter. Yet all you seem to care about is the life you left behind. I'm no therapist, but I think it's time you moved on.

"I mean, seriously, fuck Maribelle Metaxas."

"Did you actually say 'fuck Maribelle Metaxas'?" Flynn asked.

"Yea," Phobetor said. "Fuck her. I know my brother did." He winked at Flynn, although in his current form, the gesture was rather terrifying.

Spree

Candy couldn't resist the temptation to run a little head trip on someone local with more immediate consequences. The unfortunate hotel guest, Merle Edwards, happened to be out getting a bucket of ice from the ice machine next to the hotel office when the Carters were on the way in. Timothy and Alice Carter each had a twin on one hip. Being separated by a good five feet as their parents meandered their way to the room did not make the twin's coordinated bobble-head swivel any less disturbing. If anything, it was creepier when Merle turned around and the two little girls were both tracking him simultaneously from different positions.

He jumped a little when he saw that.

His walk back to the hotel room was uneventful. He used the keycard to open the door, walked inside, and inhaled the musty aroma of roadside inn. He wasn't sure why, exactly, but so many of these cheap hotels had a slightly moldy odor. It was like they threw their bedding on slightly damp and let it air dry to save money. It wouldn't matter much longer, though. In a little while, he'd be shitfaced drunk and getting head from a girl he just met on Craigslist. Not necessarily in that order.

It wasn't one hundred percent about the blow job. When a married woman agrees to meet for some no-strings-attached fun in a hotel room, it may or may not include head. Merle just liked to believe that the head would be inevitable. There was nothing like some cheap champagne to bring on the urge to nibble the old nozzle.

Merle stuck both bottles of bubbly in the ice bucket before fishing a flask of cheap brandy out of his inside breast pocket. The bubbly stuff was for the little lady. He planned to get his drink on before she got here. He sucked it down fast, felt the hot liquid burning the inside of his lips and cheeks before it slid down his welcoming esophagus. As usual, it tasted better on the way down.

Then he decided to go into the bathroom and brush his teeth so he would smell nice and pretty when the woman got here.

That's when he looked in the mirror and screamed. Both of his eyes were darker than coal, no whites, nor irises. They were just deep hellish pits of despair, like demon eyes. Merle was deeply disturbed by the idea of possession. He backed away from the mirror quickly, and in his drunken state, slipped and fell backwards against the ledge of the bathtub. He tumbled in, fell hard, and instantly broke his neck.

He had left the door open, so Alyssa Daniels walked right on in after he failed to answer her knock. She screamed and, in her panic, all rational thoughts scattered. Then she called the cops. Realizing she was a married woman in the midst of a failed extramarital encounter, she got cold feet and decided to turn around and drive back home. Unfortunately, she had made the call on her cell phone, so the police later tracked her down. The death was ruled accidental, but the damage to her marriage was done.

Cyn was also getting greedy. She insisted they jinx the maid, who showed up around 10 am to clean the place just as they were getting ready to check out. The twins were sitting on the edge of the bed watching television when she came in. Their little heads rotated towards the door the minute Martha cracked it open. She was a bit taken aback by this strange behavior.

The girls continued to stare as she asked their parents if they wanted fresh towels or soap. Their grandparents, bless their hearts, were out sleeping in the RV in the parking lot. For some reason, they did not feel that comfortable around the girls – not that they would ever tell their darling son or his charming wife.

"Those little freaks give me the creeps," Becky Carter told her husband the minute they got back to the camper. "They always stare at things, at the same time, like they have a little hive mind. Have you noticed?"

"I have," Thomas said uneasily. "But Tim and Alice don't seem to notice it."

"I know," Becky said with a shudder. "It's like those kids have them brainwashed. Stepford Parents. Just don't let the little shits know we're on to them." Becky had quit smoking ten years earlier, but she grabbed one of Thomas' Newports and started huffing like she'd never stopped.

Meanwhile, Martha had finished her shift and headed back home to Salem. On her way up I-5, she spotted a dog running across the freeway, a dog that wasn't there. She swerved to avoid hitting the cute little cockapoo and caused a six-car pile-up. Two dead, four injured. Martha was among the dead.

So, the Carter twins were officially on a killing spree. Carnage spread up and down the I-5 corridor as they headed towards San Diego. And now they were pulling off to stretch their legs again. They'd only been on the road three hours. The older Carters were in no hurry, though. Life was one big sightseeing tour for them.

Next stop, Eugene.

Birthday

Flynn was surprised that Charlotte was waiting for him. He was busy lately, and between work and spending time with the baby, he didn't come to sleep with her every night. He was amazed by her choice of meeting place as well. They were in her old apartment, the one they'd shared when they were first dating. It was the place where he proposed to her, and where Faelyn was conceived.

He felt very vulnerable being there.

Charlotte approached him and took him by the hand. He followed as she led him to her bed. She sat down and beckoned for him to sit with her. Then she kissed him.

"Happy birthday, sweetie," she said, wrapping her arms around his waist.

Flynn was suddenly terrified. "I don't want to be here," he said.

"Then take us somewhere where you feel safe," she said tenderly. She stroked his cheek with her fingers. He didn't understand why she was coddling him.

He wrapped his arms around her and wished them away somewhere safe. He was surprised that when he opened them, they were in Brash's throne room in his fortress. In fact, they were sitting on his throne. More accurately, Charlotte was sitting on her father's throne. Flynn was sitting on her lap.

She was touching his back with her fingertips. He gave her a strange look.

"Charlotte, why are you being so gentle with me?" he asked.

"I know you went to visit my mom," she said. "I was worried about you." She was kissing the back of his neck. It tickled.

"I have to tell you something," he said. "You're scaring me. The last time you touched me the way you're touching me right now, I was dying. Please stop treating me like I'm this fragile little thing. I'm not. Something bad is coming, Charlie. I've got to be strong. I've got to protect you and the baby."

He shifted his weight in the big, stone chair so that he was on one side, facing her, and still partially leaning against her.

"I'm listening," Charlotte said. She'd moved on to absent-mindedly picking the lint out of his bellybutton, since he didn't seem in the mood for tenderness. Her being gentle reminded him of how she had acted when he was dying. It didn't help that he had just finished visiting her mom and was having flashbacks.

"Mercy and Sympathy both reincarnated with all of their memories," he said. "I know you know at least some of this, because Phobetor told you. What you don't know is that they're traveling down I-5 on some kind of interstate killing spree."

"They're what, two years old?" Charlotte said. "That's ambitious, going on your first killing spree in preschool. Are they in Headstart for serial killers? Is it a new program?"

"Mock me if you like," Flynn said, "but they will be after you and Faelyn, if they can get at you. Not to mention your mother. Especially your mother, I think, since she is the one who tried to eliminate them."

"My mom," Charlotte sighed. "Isn't she the reason you're all touchy right now? You visited her and now you're back to thinking about your death. She didn't just eliminate them, she eliminated *you*."

"That's true," Flynn said. "I had kind of a setback, and I feel a bit shaky since seeing her. It's not like we have therapists here. I'm sorry I'm so moody."

"I see why you feel safer here," Charlotte said. "It's a fortress. You are somnali now. It's the seat of power for all somnali. Especially for you, I would think, since you carry my power for me and I am the queen of all somnali or will be. Anyway, get off my leg. My ass is falling asleep." She gave him a little shove.

He flipped his legs over the side of the throne and climbed down. Charlotte moved back a little so he wouldn't hit her in the face with his wings. When he stood in front of him, she smacked him on the ass. He turned around and smiled.

Flynn stretched and shook his wings out.

"Phobetor said we should be living here," Flynn said. "Not in the little cave."

"He's right," Charlotte agreed, kicking her feet up in the air. She didn't rise from her throne. "I mean, technically, this is my kingdom now. As a human, I can't run it. But it is mine. When we were both human, you couldn't act as my proxy here. A human ghost, or a shade, is a very powerless creature. You're not a shade anymore, now you're somnali. You're also my husband now, as well as my consort. I could grant you the power to act on my behalf."

"Is that what you want?" Flynn asked her. "What about Phobetor? I thought he was your proxy."

"How is old uncle Phobetor treating you these days?" she asked curiously. She hadn't gotten up out of her throne. Flynn was standing there in his tight black jeans, barefoot and shirtless. She was also barefoot. She kept touching his thighs with her toes.

"Oh," Flynn said bashfully, "he um... We were dogs, you know. He grabbed me by the throat, flipped me on my back, and I was afraid and I started pissing all over myself. And then he said that he was the Alpha dog, and I should just submit to him. Then we'd both be happier. He said it wasn't about sex. And he said I should call him Boss."

Charlotte laughed. "Well, that's very honest of him."

"I mean I was a little terrier dog, and he was a German shepherd." Flynn said quickly. "There was nothing I could do; he was really big."

"You weren't supposed to do anything that you didn't actually do," Charlotte said. "He was just establishing the pecking order. If you were more aggressive, you'd be in a direct confrontation with Phobetor, one you'd probably lose in a very ugly way. It seems he decided it would be better to lead you than to tear you into tiny shreds. And he is the one who suggested that you move here?"

Flynn shifted his weight a little. "He said I was in an arranged marriage to a demigod, is that true?"

Charlotte laughed. "He's using some poetic license. I've been stripped of my powers, but they still exist, in a separate location. I guess you can say I'm a demigod, but temporarily deprived of my power. Was our marriage arranged? Yes, it was. Nyx elected you as her champion, Somnus elected me as his. Somnus later arranged our marriage. He hoped that if we fell in love, I would keep you from dying. That didn't work out. He had Cupid hit me with his arrow. Not you, though. You still had choice."

Flynn blinked. "You didn't have a choice about loving me?"

"Who, if infatuated, really does?" she said with a shrug. "You think with your heart, and your groin, not with your head. I wanted you like a junkie wants dope. To be honest, I still do. You always were the more level-headed one."

She slid off the throne and threw her arms around his waist. She kissed him in the middle of his chest, and said, "Are you sure I can't be gentle with you?"

"Well, of course you can," he said. He hugged her. "I'm sorry. I didn't mean to be a dick about it. Your mom was so fucking mean to me. She kept calling me the sacrifice."

"Yea, you're not a dick," Charlotte said. "She's dehumanizing you so she can live with what she's done. She wants to reinvent things in her own mind so it's like beheading a plump, juicy hen for dinner. Maybe like putting down an unwanted dog at the pound. It's her way of distancing herself from you."

"It's very hurtful," he said. "But you didn't have anything to do with it?"

"Of course not," Charlotte said impatiently. "I already told you that. Besides, I was under a love spell. I would have rather taken the poison and drank it myself to keep it from you, than to allow you to perish. Cupid doesn't fuck around."

At that moment, Flynn looked around him. The palace was huge, and intimidating. The ceilings rose to impossible heights, and light peered in from jagged holes in the craggy roof. The entire structure looked as if it had been carved from the inside of an active volcano. Tiny rivulets of hot red substance ran at irregular intervals just below the surface on which they stood. He marveled that it did not burn their bare feet.

He pulled Charlotte tight against him and tried to fly. When he rose off the ground, she started to slip out of his grasp. In mere seconds, he was hovering above her head, and she was standing on the ground, holding his foot."

"Wait up," she said. "You can't carry me like that. Come back down for a minute and I'll show you how." Flynn landed on the ground in front of him, and Charlotte threw her arms around his neck and tried to climb up his body, but she kept slipping.

"Okay you need to hold me up. Put your hands under my ass," she said. "I mean, I have to wrap my legs around you, I need you to hold me up, though."

He put his arms around her hips, propping her up on one forearm with his other arm wrapped around her back. She wrapped her legs around him, and he lifted her up. She was looking over his shoulder.

'Oh yeah," she said. "You did it right."

He was surprised to find his dick getting hard. Usually, Flynn couldn't get an erection unless Charlotte was inflicting some kind of pain on his willing and wanting flesh. Flying was exhilarating, liberating.

"We could probably make love up here," he said. Love making was generally a euphemism for some kind of gentle sex that Flynn never had. It involved stroking and petting, and wondering if he needed Cialis or Viagra because he could go for hours and hours giving and receiving tender caresses with no response from below the belt. He did enjoy it, though… all of the soft, affectionate little touches. They just failed to make him feel hot and bothered.

But he thought he might enjoy trying to make love up here.

"We can," Charlotte said, "once you master flying. If we tried it right now, you'd probably go tumbling below, dragging me down with you and we'd both hit the ground with our asses."

It sounded so dangerous. Perhaps the danger was what he found so stimulating.

"The palace was designed for flying creatures," "Charlotte said. "Turn to your left and you'll find a secret place, a series of niches and catacombs in the wall." Flynn did as instructed and found himself in a narrow passage, carved into the stone. He set Charlotte gently on her feet and landed beside her.

"This passage leads to my father's dungeons," she said. Her tone was cavalier. "My father had many consorts, otherworldly as well as humans over his long life. His appetites were voracious, and he often had dozens of consorts at once. Any depravity Phobetor accuses me of, I surely inherited. We could spend all year down there without using all of the restraints and implements of torture. I'm offering, since you don't want me to be tender with you on your birthday."

Flynn shrugged. "I keep trying to forget it's my birthday," he admitted. "I'm thirty. Wow."

"Or you're twenty-six for the fourth time," she said with a wink.

He swiftly unbuckled his pants and dropped them to the floor, along with his underpants.

"You don't have to be rough. You can pet me, Charlotte," he recommended. "You can touch me however you like. You can stroke my skin. I can present my belly to you, like I presented it to Phobetor."

Charlotte laughed when he shifted into the form of a little rat terrier. He rolled on his back and offered is belly to her. She rubbed it, and when he shifted back to his somnali form, he was prone on his back, naked, with her hand on his stomach.

She turned onto one side and snuggled up next to him, her head upon his chest, arm casually tossed over his belly. He caught her up in the crook of his arm, feeling strangely protective. She was warm, tender, and gentle. Her finger was tracing his clavicle. This was a lover's touch. He pulled her closer and returned her affection. He wanted her to know that he loved her, too. He would do anything to keep her and the baby safe.

"Do you have a choice in loving me now?" he asked quietly.

"Of course I do," she said, relaxing.

He could feel the weight of her body pressing into his. She wrapped one of her legs around him. This was how they had held and touched each other once when they slept together. They had shared the same bed, back when he was living. No wonder she took him to their old apartment for his birthday. She wanted to cuddle and touch and pretend that they were together the way they had been when he was alive.

It was just play-acting. They lived in two different realms now, and his wife slept alone. He could come to her as a dream, or as a senseless animal who slept beside her as a pet, not a husband. They were merely pretending to have a life that was over.

He was absolutely furious about dying. His tears came hot and angry. He tried to look away so she wouldn't see them, but of course it was too late. She saw everything.

"I was so lonely before I met you," he said finally. "The life we had together in that little apartment meant everything to me. It was the only time I was actually happy since childhood. It's hard to explain, really. One day, I was a normal, well, sort of a normal kid. The next day I was head case, a disappointment, someone primarily identified by my psychological condition, a non-person.

"Maybe I didn't have a choice in loving you, either. You loved me, and when your love came to me it was like water coming to the desert. Things could grow, and blossom, where there used to be no life. I never thought that I would be a husband or a father, but you gave that dream to me. I'll always be grateful for that.

"But when I died, I lost everything. I lost all my dreams and plans about having a job and a wife and a child and an ordinary life. I feel like it's my fault."

Charlotte rolled over on top of him and looked him in the eye. "I know. They were my dreams, too. This hasn't been easy for either of us, but perhaps you least of all. I know this place doesn't feel real to you, but it is real. The life we share here is real. One day in the future, when my journey on Earth is over, we'll live here together, forever. It's not your fault that you're here, Flynn. Never forget that."

He stopped crying and kissed the top of her head.

"I get to feeling very angry at myself," he admitted. "I feel like I have to punish someone for what happened, and you know, a lot of times that someone is me. Who else is there to blame? Nyx, because whether it was her intention or not, she cursed me? Your mother, because she thought she was liberating me from guilt, shame, and a possible act of suicide? Perhaps I could blame Mercy and Sympathy for being what they are, ruthless and practically a force of nature?

"It was a terrible time. People were getting hurt. Howard was wounded, terribly. Then Mike, and Tess, and all those other people I didn't even know died senselessly. I knew that other people were going to die. Your mom said it was a terrible burden for me, knowing my death could end it all.

"The way she tells it, she was doing me a favor. She was going to remove the burden of my guilt and take this terrible decision out of my hands. I was really depressed, you know? About Mike dying, about everything and I told her I thought I needed to go back in the hospital. But she had another plan, and I guess it all kind of made sense at the time. But when I think about it now, I feel sick."

"That's understandable," Charlotte said. "She took advantage of your emotional distress to get you to agree to something you wouldn't have ordinarily agreed to."

Flynn snapped his fingers. "Right, that's right. That's exactly what I've been feeling; that I couldn't figure out how to express."

If he still had a tail, it would have been wagging. There was a perfect blend of unselfconscious love and devotion he felt when he was a dog. It came back to him now. He still loved her as a husband loves his wife, but he also loved her like a dog loves its human, uncompromisingly. He needed her. He needed to protect her.

"And the fucked-up thing is I practically died for nothing," he said finally. "I mean sure, it slowed them down for a couple of years, but now Mercy and Sympathy are back, and they are worse than ever."

"So, what are you planning to do to stop them?" she asked. "I'm human and I'm not in the position to do all that much. Except as oracle, I suppose."

"We have been tracking them down, using human technology and animal senses," he said. "I'm pretty sure they're near Eureka now, but there's no telling when they'll travel on. We don't know yet how they are traveling, but by a private vehicle or a public bus would be my guess, based on their travel patterns. They definitely aren't flying. We will be, though. We will search for them as birds, that way we will be able to travel fast enough to catch up with them if they've already left."

"Big birds that can swoop down and pick up rampaging toddlers?" she asked.

He laughed. "I haven't thought it through that far but killing them is probably a bad idea. I mean, if they die, they'll just reincarnate again, won't they?"

She nodded. "I guess we have to figure out a way to make them into regular human children, or else put some restrictions on their future reincarnations. I have an idea about who might be able to help with that."

Sisterhood of the Undoing

Charlotte really didn't want to call her mother. She didn't even want to call the rest of her posse, or coven, or whatever she called the group of women who were adherents of the Undoing. One of those women killed her husband, and at least half of the others considered it.

Still, as Flynn pointed out, someone among the Sisterhood of Undoing very likely knew spells that could be used to stop Mercy and Sympathy. There could be rites to prevent them from reentering the world with their memories and powers intact. There might be a way to bind their powers, cause them to revert to the state of normal human children. Whatever the case may be, they were experts on the activities of the somnali in the physical world, and they needed to be contacted.

The current line-up for the Sisterhood of the Undoing would have been Lorena Young, Maribelle Metaxas, Nancy Allen, Jeannie Byrne, and Sunny Green. Gertrude Singer passed away shortly after Mercy and Sympathy's original killing spree, ostensibly of a heart attack during the evening news. She knew better than anyone the connection between the deaths of Tess Allen, Michael Shaw, Cory Landers, Linda Myers, and the others slain in Elroy Shaw's murderous rampage at the mall... She even guessed at the probable fate of the innocent Keahi kid, although she couldn't determine at whose hands.

She'd clutched at her chest and collapsed, dead, before she even hit the floor. Like Tess, Michael, Cory, Linda and even Elroy, Gertrude had been reincarnated. She was one of many toddlers born around the same time as Faelyn who were direct or indirect results of some action by Mercy, Sympathy, or Maribelle.

Gertie was reborn as a young man in Calcutta. Michael was a little girl in Belgium. Tess was in Guam, Cory was in Nepal, and Linda was in Thailand. They were all a safe distance from the U.S. west coast and any shenanigans the evil sisters might have in mind.

Nancy Allen had been recruited to replace Gertrude. There were always five Sisters of the Undoing. The Sisters of the Undoing were always women, women whose lives had been affected by the somnali.

The Sisterhood hadn't met since after the funerals. Everyone was bickering. Half the women suspected Maribelle of killing Flynn. The other half had suspected Lorena and Jeannie. They had been quite vocal about the benefits of allowing him to take his own life. These fights escalated, and with no immediate threat, the Sisterhood fell apart.

Now it was Charlotte who had the unpleasant task of bringing them back together. She chose to meet them on her own ground.

Charlotte, Shelby and Hannah had converted the garage into a one-bedroom apartment live/work space. They removed the garage door and replaced it with a sliding glass patio door that opened into the living room. The center was divided into a bathroom and a small kitchen. There was a bedroom in the back. A narrow staircase led up to her studio workspace in the a-frame roof. There were gorgeous picture windows installed to let plenty of light in. Although her kitchen was small, her living room had a patio in front of the sliding door on a small deck. There was plenty of room to host the five ladies socially.

One side of her living room contained a comfortable burgundy couch and two matching easy chairs. There was a mahogany coffee table in the center of the seating area. On the opposite wall there was a large screen television, and three paintings of Phobetor. One showed him as a man, another as a primordial, shadowy form that looked like it had escaped from a haunted forest, and the third, as a cat held by Flynn. It was the last painting she'd made of Flynn as a shade.

There was also a large painting of Flynn in his somnali form hanging over the sofa. He was wearing swim trunks of all things. He was standing in the throne room of Somnus, where the river Lethe ran down its center. His smile was bright and easy. He'd stood there three hours so she could sketch him.

It was an important image. It was Flynn on the day of their wedding. The swimming suits were an almost comical concession by Pasithea. She'd originally intended for the entire wedding party to be nude, but graciously modified her plans to accommodate Flynn's lingering modesty.

Charlotte had worn a fashionable black one piece with a low-cut, corseted front. Her hair had been an extravagance of tree branches, black crepe, and poppies. There had been poppies everywhere, emblems of Somnus and Pasithea, who had held the wedding in their home. In a nod to human custom, Phobetor had given away the bride in place of his absent brother, Brash.

In the portrait, Flynn wore her ring.

Everything was ready, and the women were beginning to arrive.

Lorena Young and Sunny Green were first. They weren't exactly the closest of friends, but they'd come to forge an alliance over the years. Sunny was the only person besides the guilty Maribelle herself who felt absolutely certain that Lorena had no role in Flynn's execution. This was partially because Nyx herself, in no uncertain terms, told her so. Of course, she was wearing Howard Lowe at the time, but Howard concurred.

"I was with them in the hospital," Howard/Nyx had insisted to Sunny on one of their few dates. "Believe me, that woman did not kill that child."

Lorena was far less snooty than Sunny had imagined. If she'd been in the hospital with Howard and Flynn, Sunny figured she had her fair share of challenges. They went to that grief group together – the one Maribelle and Nancy put together after the tragedies. Lorena had a car, so she'd sometimes give Sunny a lift to the grocery store and other errands around town, or just drop by to check on her.

When they came in, Lorena immediately ran up to Faelyn, who was sitting in her little pink Hello Kitty bean bag chair. She was hugging a Nightmare before Christmas Jack Skellington doll. It was very obvious that her mom was still the one picking out her toys.

Lorena sat on the floor with the girl. "Hi, honey, my name is Lorena." She held out her hand, and Faelyn grabbed two fingers and shook them. She said "Rena."

"That's good enough," Lorena said. "What's your name?"

"My name is Faelyn," the girl said, and then clapped her hands to show her enthusiasm for sentence-making. Faelyn was now two and a half years old.

Sunshine stared at the little girl. "My goodness, she looks just like him," she said.

"Not just like him," Lorena corrected. "She looks like her mother, too. She has eyes just like Charlotte, and the same itty-bitty nose, too."

Lorena was a grandmother now. Her eldest daughter had a three-month-old son. She was comfortable around children, and it wasn't long before she had Faelyn on her hip and was chattering away with her like a long-lost pal.

Sunny, who was not exactly comfortable being around small children, was taking in the artwork. She was especially intent on appreciating Phobetor's human form, which was long and lean with taut musculature. He had an athletic build, but not bulky like a football jock, more like a dancer or martial artist.

"Who is he?" Sunny asked, wide eyed.

"That's Phobetor, the god of nightmares," Lorena piped in from behind them.

Maribelle and Nancy showed up next.

"Come in, mother." Charlotte said with a sigh. "It's nice to see you, Nancy." This seemed like an opportune time to wander back to the kitchen, a small alcove adjacent to the bathroom that could be better described as a kitchenette.

Charlotte spent the next ten minutes heating up hard apple cider and cinnamon sticks so she could avoid being in the room with her mom.

Jeannie Byrne was last. The first thing she commented on, walking in the door, was the painting of Flynn.

"That's beautiful," she said. "He's somnali in that painting, isn't he?"

Charlotte nodded and handed out the hot alcoholic beverages. Clearly, they were going to be needed. It was obvious where this conversation was heading.

"Yes, he is," Charlotte said. "And thank you for the compliment on my work."

"Is it from your imagination?" she asked pointedly. "Or have you seen him and spoken to him? I thought the dead reincarnated. Why would he be somnali?"

"Charlotte performed a binding spell on him," Maribelle said critically. "It holds him to her, even in the afterlife, although I'm sure that would be as a shade, not somnali."

"Nyx granted him the form of somnali," Charlotte said casually. "He was, after all, her champion."

Maribelle blinked nervously and sat on the couch. When she saw Flynn in her dream, it had not occurred to her that he actually had any power. He could have caused her a lot of psychic pain, in the very least. Somnali were dream spirits, specifically, associated with dark dreams, nightmares, and the more terrifying forms of eroticism. That he had only spoken with her was an unexpected kindness. She was taken aback.

"So, you're sure he's somnali? Do you two speak often?" Lorena asked, suddenly developing an interest in the conversation. If Charlotte had spoken with Flynn, surely, she knew who had killed him.

"Either he's somnali," Charlotte said, "or he's just a particularly enjoyable reoccurring wet dream I've been having, and I've lost my mind. Whichever the case may be, I see him and speak to him every second or third night."

Maribelle slammed down the rest of her drink.

Nancy, not really hip to what was going on, said, "Charlotte! Watch your language! The baby is here."

"I don't think she knows what that word before dream means in that context," Jeannie said dryly. "Neither of the two words means anything s-e-x-u-a-l separately, and the first word at her age refers to the condition of a urine-soaked diaper."

"Speaking of diapers," Charlotte said calmly, "and babies and things being inappropriate around them, mother, can you take Faelyn in the other room and put her to bed? It's her bedtime, and it's been a long time since you two spent any time alone together. Mom, please make sure to turn the baby monitor on before you return."

Maribelle was relieved for the chance to escape the conversation and the unpleasant turn it had taken. She picked up her grandchild and went back to the bedroom. Faelyn's toddler bed still had a gate around it to keep her from falling out when she was asleep. Maribelle carefully tucked her in.

Meanwhile, back in the living room, the other women were sipping their ciders and interrogating Charlotte.

"Is he… okay?" Lorena asked. The question was sincere. Lorena always liked Flynn, even when she thought it might have been best for him to die.

"Yes and no," Charlotte said. "He's still traumatized by having died, and he can get a little moody. There isn't any therapy in the afterlife, so he's stuck with talking to my relatives. I guess it's a lot to take in. But all things considered, having been through so much, I would say he is doing remarkably well."

"Does he know who killed him?" Sunshine asked awkwardly.

"Of course he does," Charlotte said. "I know, too. But we are not here to discuss that or bring on round two of the old accusations. We're here because two of the somnali somehow evaded their just punishment and are here on Earth, killing people."

"Now how does that work, exactly?" Lorena asked. "I thought that if Flynn died, they all died."

"They did die," Charlotte said. "Then, they were all reincarnated as humans so they could learn some life lessons."

"Then they shouldn't have any powers," Jeannie said. "They shouldn't have any memory of who they are."

"No, they shouldn't," Charlotte confirmed. "We assume someone intervened on their behalf to allow them to reincarnate with their powers and memories, much as Nyx intervened on behalf of Flynn."

Just then, Maribelle came in. "I heard you on the baby monitor. It took me a while to get it working right. Well, you can stop accusing one another. I killed Flynn."

Nancy almost dropped her apple cider. "Why would you do that?"

"You know why," Maribelle said angrily. "You saw what happened to your niece, and that boy. They weren't the only ones. They wouldn't have been the last. The somnali had to be stopped. Someone had to offer the sacrifice."

Charlotte shook her head. "Mom, you really hurt his feelings when you call him 'the sacrifice.'"

Lorena and Jeannie looked at each other, and simultaneously shook their heads.

"Maribelle," Lorena said gently, "I hope you know that's not what Jeannie and I were suggesting. I don't think that any of us had this in mind."

"The baby would have never been safe if it didn't happen," Maribelle argued.

Charlotte threw her hands up in the air. "See, there you go again. 'It' had to happen, or 'the sacrifice.' You're going out of your way to distance yourself from the fact that that he was a human being. You committed murder."

Maribelle looked heartbroken. "I did it for you."

Charlotte shook her head. "We're not here for this. Mercy and Sympathy are traveling down I-5 somehow, leaving a trail of bodies in their wake. We need to know how to stop them."

"Maybe you can just have your mother go out and kill them," Sunshine said bitterly.

"Phobetor is hunting them down," Charlotte said, pointedly ignoring Sunny's jab at Maribelle. "He can appear on Earth in animal form. If that were the solution, he would just kill them. There must be any number of animals that might be found along I-5 that could kill a couple of toddlers. Mountain lions, wild bears, feral dogs. Then, they would reincarnate, possibly with their powers and memories still intact, and we'd be back to square one."

"I'm going to need more alcohol to have this conversation," Nancy said. "Poor Flynn, poor Charlotte, what you've been through. I'm so sorry." Nancy looked ready to cry. She threw her arms around Charlie.

"It's alright, Nancy," Charlie said, patting the woman on the back. "I still see him. We're going to be okay."

"It's not okay," Nancy said. "He should be here in this house, raising his daughter with you. Not living in the dream world. And he died in your arms. It's so sad."

"I was devastated," Charlotte admitted. "I didn't hear from him until about six months ago. It's like we've been in a relationship for four years but only actually been together for one of them."

"Let me help you bring in the rest of the snacks and drinks, sweetie," Nancy said kindly.

"I'll help, too, honey," Sunshine offered. She looked over her shoulder at Lorena. She and Jeannie needed to talk some sense into Maribelle.

Charlotte wandered off into the kitchen with Sunny and Nancy. The women helped her prepare snacks. They offered words of advice and sympathy about her situation with Flynn. They sent him their regards.

Jeannie and Lorena sat Maribelle down.

"I understand why you did what you did," Jeannie started. "You could be a little less callous about it, though. You killed someone."

"Don't I know it," Maribelle said unsympathetically.

"Are you crazy?" Lorena asked her. "Your daughter is crazy about that boy. Do you see her ring? Do you see his ring in that picture? That's her husband. Your daughter is married to a dead man. That's not good."

"Oh, I know just how that is," Maribelle said. "At least her husband used to be human. Her father certainly never was. At least he gave her a human child."

"Your child is human now," Jeannie said harshly. "Are *you* still human?"

"Am I?" Maribelle asked. "I poisoned my son-in-law and watched him die in front of my child. I convinced Charlotte to dump his dead body into the river on the offhand chance that they might be reunited in the afterworld. I didn't think she'd ever see him again. Ever since that day, I've been kind of dead inside. So tell me, am I human?"

"It was war," Lorena said. "He was a casualty of that war. I know you feel guilty, but you can't make yourself feel better by negating his existence."

Maribelle frowned. "I'll keep that in mind."

Charlotte, Sunny, and Nancy came back just then with a rescue round of refreshments. There were platters of cheese, crackers, and cold cuts, a fruit plate, and several bottles of wine. Maribelle decided to get her drink on. Her first generous glass of Syrah lasted about five seconds.

"Whatever we might feel about the things that have happened in the past, I think we need to move beyond all that," Jeannie said. "We need to see if there is anything in the Rites of Undoing that can help us with the situation at hand."

"All those rites you had me doing," Charlotte flashed on Maribelle accusingly, "what were they actually for?"

Maribelle slurred, already buzzed. "You're still with the guy. You have a beautiful child with him. What do you mean what were the rites for? They worked, didn't they?" At this point, Lorena and Sunny excused themselves to step outside for a smoke.

Shelby still smoked, but not inside, not with the kid. Kyle had his own room now, the one that used to be Charlotte and Faelyn's. The kids still shared a playground in the backyard, consisting of a sandbox and a swing set. She was out there smoking when Lorena and Sunny popped over and joined her. Shelby could see the Charlotte and Maribelle show through the sliding glass window. Drama. Boy was she glad that Charlie had her own place right now.

Poor Jeannie and Nancy, the non-smokers of the bunch, were stuck inside dealing with the fallout from Maribelle's icy confessions. Yes, she killed Flynn. Yes, she'd do it again. No, she didn't feel bad. Stop correcting her, he was the sacrifice.

Bad Dream

Somehow, they managed to get through the Sisterhood of the Undoing reunion, but both Charlotte and Maribelle drank excessively. Jeannie gave Nancy a ride home because Maribelle was too drunk to drive. For the first time in two years, the Metaxas women slept under the same roof. Maribelle passed out on Charlotte's couch.

She was visited by Flynn in her sleep again. He was not pleased.

He was very pasty and gray with a slack facial expression. His skin was flaccid and waxy, and the whites of his eyes had gone rheumy and yellow.

Maribelle blanched. This was a dead body, a walking corpse.

He stiffly pulled up a chair at the kitchen table and sat.

"You'll have to forgive my appearance," he said. "This is what I looked like immediately after Charlotte watched me die. I felt bad for her, you know. She was watching me die right in front of her. When I was too stunned or too numbed by the sheer volume of chemical substances you poisoned me with, I noticed how distraught she was. Other times, I wondered if she did this to me."

He reached beneath the table and pulled out a wooden cutting board and a large butcher knife from below. As Maribelle looked on in horror, he began cleaving his left fingers from the hand at the knuckle.

"This was my body," he said, although she had a hard time hearing him over the sound of steel striking against wood. "I shouldn't say it was mine, though. It belonged to others. It was a thing they could use to carry out their little plans. It was made to be destroyed and sacrificed. You want a piece of it, don't you?" He finally severed the smallest finger from his hand. He picked up and handed it to her.

"Here you are, Maribelle," he said casually. "Have a piece of this body. You're entitled, aren't you? That won't be enough, though. I'm sure you'll need more."

"Flynn," she gasped. "Stop it, that's just horrible. Why are you doing this?"

"Oh," he said. "It's the bone, isn't it? When Faelyn was conceived, Charlotte tried to devour my entire body, but she couldn't seem to deal with all of those aggravating bones. I think I have a solution."

He reached under the table and pulled out a meat grinder. It was the old-fashioned kind, the kind that used a handle to turn it instead of electricity. He stuck what was left of his hand inside and began to crank the grinding mechanism. Pulverized flesh and bone squeezed out of the little holes in the end, like so much hamburger or ground sausage.

"This will be easier to digest," he said gleefully. He pulled back the wrist-stump from his severed hand, and blood began to spurt around the room. Some of it splashed onto Maribelle's face. She threw her hands up to block it, but to no avail. She started to scream.

"Don't worry about it, Maribelle," he said coolly. "It was made to be sacrificed, wasn't it? It's one hundred percent Grade-A human meat. You want me to make you a burger?" Using the hand that was still whole, he balled some of the ground meat up in his fingers and began eating it.

Maribelle turned away from the spectacle.

It didn't do her any good. Seconds later, he was standing right beside her. He patted her on the shoulder with his bleeding stump. "As I rotted in the Napa River many creatures enjoyed my carcass. Flies and maggots, little fishes, rats, and even a feral dog ate me. Once I got caught for a little while at the mouth of Carquinez. Seafaring birds pecked at my desiccated flesh."

As he rattled off his narrative, his body began to rot before her. His eyes grew cloudy, flesh swollen and very pungent. Maggots and flies infested his carcass and flew in and out of his mouth as he spoke. Maribelle couldn't keep her eyes off it.

A seagull gouged out one of his eyes and sucked down little bits of it while he spoke. He continued orating over the little sucking noises. Maribelle started to dry heave.

"You only give lip service to environmentalism," Flynn chided. "I actually went green. I gave my corpse back to the environment. How many people can say that? Are you sure you aren't hungry?"

"Get out!" she screamed, waving him away.

She shoved him back, and her hand returned to her covered in rotted and corpulent flesh. It was runny, like an egg white, and the stench was unmistakable. Decaying human flesh had the same putrid stench as the dead rats that went undiscovered after she used poison for pest control. She could still remember weeks later, the stench of decomposition in the walls and coming from the couch. It smelled like a package of ground beef she once accidentally left with a bag of groceries in the car. She'd been in a hurry unloading the food, and forgotten it was there. It sat there the weekend, rotting in seventy-degree weather. When she opened the car Monday, the reek was ghastly. That car never smelled the same way again.

Flynn stank like that.

By the time he left, she was shaking uncontrollably.

Afterwards, Flynn returned to Phobetor. They were tying up loose ends before they went hunting the twins. Phobetor patted him on the back.

""Well done, boy! That's what nightmares are supposed to do," he explained. "They are supposed to help humans to process unfinished business, or to figure things out. Sometimes they contain life lessons or allegories. Other times they are warnings of what bad behavior can lead to. Mostly, they are just how the humans cope with and come to understand what they've been through."

"What could Maribelle possibly get from all that that?" Flynn asked.

"She has been minimizing your death, pretending it was inevitable," Phobetor said. "She can't really deal with you, or what she did to you. Sometimes she tells herself you asked for it. Other days, she thinks of it as you fulfilling your destiny. Most of the time, she tries to pretend none of it ever happened. The more she casts false filters over reality, the more icy and distant she becomes with her daughter and everyone else in her life. She can't function anymore.

"She needs to get her shit together. She has an important role to play in the Sisterhood. She can't do what she is meant to do while denying everything she knows of the supernatural."

"I feel sorry for her," Flynn admitted.

"Don't bother," Phobetor said, "She needs to pull her head out of her ass. Actions have consequences. The rites were completed, and she sacrificed the anointed human – no offense. Now she has to deal with the fallout. Whether she likes it or not, she has become the Priestess of the Undoing."

"So let me get this right," Flynn asked. "She killed me, and you gave her a fancy new job title for doing it? Wow. I feel special."

"Deal with it," Phobetor said.

The Flight

The North American subspecies of the golden eagle occupied the mountains and coastal areas of the West Coast of the continent from Alaska to Baja California. A very large, powerful raptor, it had a wingspan greater than the height of a grown man and could weigh as much as fifteen pounds. Its prey usually consisted of small, tasty mammals like rabbits and squirrels, but the birds of prey were known to work together to take down deer and other larger animals. Despite the name golden eagle, the creatures were primarily dark brown. They had a circle of golden feathers around their necks, like the ruff on an Edwardian collar. They were the fastest birds in North America.

Phobetor and Flynn weren't naturally eagles and had a bit more freedom in their range as long as they avoided the now of animal thought. Phobetor was Oneiroi, an ancient dream god. Further, he was one of the named and known, alongside Morpheus and Phantasos. He could travel endlessly in creature form without losing himself, but his young somnali companion could make no such claim.

Flynn was a bit smaller than Phobetor, and still had white markings on his tail and under his feathers than marked him as an adolescent.

He loved flying through the skies of North America in this form. It was so easy to stretch these wings and fly. Everything was built so well, so aerodynamically practical. He wished that flight in his somnali form could be this perfectly natural.

These birds were rarely seen in urban areas, but they would have to go to Eugene next. After several hours of searching up and down I-5, the cold trail went hot at a rest stop. Candy and Cyn had been at the Oak Grove rest stop, thirteen miles north of Eureka, within the past one to three hours.

Flynn and Phobetor shifted into their dog forms, sniffing and investigating the area. The act of shifting had a secondary benefit. It prolonged Flynn's conscious awareness of himself as somnali. It did so by disrupting the inevitable process of identifying with his current creature form. It did not take long for the dogs to determine that the twins spent an hour at the rest stop before heading south down I-5 approximately two hours earlier.

Before taking flight, they added new smells to their mental database. They now recognized the odor of the other twin, both of their parents and their grandparents by comparing them to odors from their previous locations.

The diaper at the rail crossing belonged to Cyn. Candy, who was already potty trained, left her scent in unexpected places. It seemed she was adopting a more hands-on approach for some of her violence.

The first animal was a pet. She was a two-month-old orange tabby kitten named Beanie, who was traveling with her human companions when she disappeared out of the backseat of her minivan. Beanie's humans just adopted her from the litter their grandparent's gray tabby Smoky had delivered a few weeks before. Beanie's new family had been visiting them on their farm upstate. The little female human named her Beanie because she thought she looked like a beanie baby toy. One of the older kids absentmindedly let the cat get out, and before the family could find her, Candy got her hands on her.

Flynn and the twins had the same birthday. Today, Candy and Cyn were two years old.

If it hadn't been their birthday, their parents and grandparents wouldn't have spent so much time at the Oak Grove Rest Stop. It was, though, so they did. They huddled around the picnic table eating cold cut deli sandwiches and potato chips. They drank fruit punch and lit the four candles that sat in groupings of two on either side of the strawberries and cream birthday cake with the giant pink icing bow in its corner.

They were so busy celebrating that they didn't even notice when the tiny kitten approached their picnic table mewling for scraps. They might have heard her hungry cries, but they were in the middle of singing the birthday song. The only one who did see it was Candy.

She dangled a piece of turkey from her sandwich in front of the kitten until it drew closer to her foot under the table. It was a tiny thing, not much bigger than a rat. She picked it up under the table. She hoisted it upon her knee, where she began to slowly strangle it to death.

She was afraid her parents might hear its mewing noise, so she shoved two of her tiny fingers down its throat. It bit her, so she increased the pressure on its tiny neck until it snapped. Satisfied, Candy smiled and let the corpse drop to the ground.

"Want some cake, cutie pie?" Timothy Carter asked his daughter.

"Yes daddy, cake! Candy wants cake!" she shrieked. She was so proud. She was using her words.

The messy strawberry filling hid the red marks on her fingers from the kitten's bites and scratches, and a few spots of red blood that might have belonged to either Candy or Beanie.

Autzen Stadium

More and more, Candy was starting to realize that she enjoyed killing. When she was trying to leave the Demos Oneiroi and enter the physical plane, it was easy to believe otherwise. She told herself that all of the human slaughter was a means to an end. It was necessary in order to enter the physical world. Now that she was here, on Earth, she could see that the killing was its own reward.

She loved it.

For the uninitiated and relatively innocent, murder darkened the spirit. It was what was eating at Maribelle Metaxas, the stain left on her very soul by Flynn's death at her hands. Her psyche was corrupted by the vile nature of the deed. This wasn't the case for the likes of Mercy, who was now Candy.

Every killing made the twin more powerful.

Killing was like sucking in all of the power that used to belong to whatever life form she destroyed. As time went on, Candy consumed more and more of the human essence of the victims. She became increasingly aware of how these actions physically and mentally strengthened her. These same could not be said for Cyn, who was being left behind developmentally. Cyn was also physically smaller than Candy. One day, Candy realized that she was growing so much faster than Cyn because she was cannibalizing her energy, the same way that both twins devoured the strength of others.

By the time they got to Austen, Candy was speaking in full sentences and totally potty trained. Cyn was still in diapers, and her spoken vocabulary consisted of only a dozen words. She wasn't just behind her twin Candy. She was now developmentally behind the curve for a twenty-four-month-old baby.

They would have been further away from Oak Grove, and the golden eagles on their tail, if they hadn't gotten caught in traffic.

The night after their birthday was game day at Autzen Stadium, home of the Fighting Ducks. The huge recreational vehicle got caught up in heavy traffic on Martin Luther King, Jr. Blvd. Street traffic was moving slightly faster than the parking lot of a Wal-Mart on Black Friday. Thomas was driving, and his wife, Rebecca was in the passenger seat. His son Timothy and his wife Alice were sitting in the back, around the half-circle kitchen table with their twin girls.

At first, it was impossible to determine the source of the traffic congestion, but as the vehicle got closer to the stadium it became apparent.

The clog of cars was crisscrossed by a horde of fans clad festively in green and yellow, the colors du jour. Crosswalks fell into disuse as throngs of eager fans jetted in and out of traffic.

Rosemary "Roz" Dyson wasn't wearing official team gear, but she wore a deep lemon sweater vest over her avocado mock turtleneck. Those were the colors the labels gave, but her twenty-year-old grandson Ken referred to them as pea soup and wino urine. Ken was already half a block ahead of her, having claimed that he needed to pee and could save their seats so he could escape.

Roz used to wear her hair in a strawberry blond poodle cut back when Ken was born, but she'd since fallen victim to female pattern baldness. She now wore a short, gray wig that looked like a dead guinea pig. Almost an affront to her designer outfit from circa 1991 Ross Dress for Less, an official Fighting Ducks baseball cap perched precariously upon her lady toupee.

"Why don't you try using the sidewalk?" Tom yelled out the driver's side window of his RV, furiously honking the horn.

"Fuck you!" Roz yelled back, presenting him with her grizzled and age spotted middle finger.

Becky shook her head. She picked up her mango cannabis milkshake and took a swig. There was not enough medicinal marijuana in the whole fucking state of Oregon to put up with this bullshit.

Roz was across the street and halfway through the thatch of dead lawn that bordered the sidewalk by the time the twins passed her in the rear of the camper. She probably should have quit while she was ahead, but she couldn't resist taking one last peek over her shoulder and flipping that final bird. As Ken would have told anyone who asked, his grandmother had to have the last word.

Unfortunately for her, so did Candy and Cyn. She couldn't see the twins as they spun their heads towards her in eerie unison like a pair of heat-seeking missiles. What she did see was a western rattlesnake in the low dry grass poised to strike at her ankle when she turned back around.

Roz screamed, and pin wheeled back into traffic. If traffic wasn't going about five miles an hour, she might have been hit. As it was, she twisted her ankle on the way down, and instead of landing on her big fat loud ass, her hip slammed down into the pavement. Seventy-two-year-old Roz Dyson fractured her pelvis and did not make it to the game that day.

Some young men on their way to the game ran over to assist the ornery woman, who could be seen waving them off and yelling at them. It would be some time before the ambulance got through, with all of the traffic, but she would live.

Candy looked out of the side window of the camper and laughed.

It was fun for a giggle, but soon she found herself dissatisfied with the lack of actual death and brutal carnage. She began idly wondering what it would feel like to kill her sister, Cyn. She daydreamed about causing grandpa to plow the RV into the crowd and kill a few more Ducks fans on the way out. What could he smash into that would be likely to make an explosion?

She was bored.

She hated this traffic.

Phobetor and Flynn came up behind the recreational vehicle just as it was passing a statue of some sort, composed of X's and O's, and marked with inspirational slogans. Phobetor made sure to take a nice, messy dump on it as he swooped down from the sky.

They couldn't get inside the camper, because all of the windows and doors were shut, so they alit on the roof.

"We've found them, now what?" Phobetor asked in a language no human could understand. "I can stick with the vehicle, trail them, but you can't stay in this form much longer."

Phobetor was the original shapeshifter, he could do this forever without forgetting himself, but Flynn was already starting to lose his somnali mind.

"I can go back to the office and look up the license number," Flynn suggested helpfully. "Find out who the owners are. See if they are related to any of the twins on the list. We could figure out who they are. That way they'll be easier to track if we lose them."

"I won't lose them," Phobetor said. "I'll do damage control here for a while and see if I can slow down their killing spree. Do me a favor, check on your wife and see if the Sisterhood has any information before you come back."

"Sure," Flynn said. He was anxious to see Charlotte anyway.

The Priestess

When she awoke on the sofa, Maribelle expected Charlotte to come in the living room and yell at her, something she was not looking forward to. She had a hangover, and her head was throbbing like a woodpecker had taken up residence on her temple. Instead, Charlotte walked into the room with a cup of coffee in her hand and a book under her arm.

She set them both down on the table in front of her mother.

"I imagine you have a headache," Charlotte said calmly. "I do, too. Let me get another cup of coffee and some aspirin. I'll be back."

When she came back into the room, there was a gray cat trailing at her feet. Maribelle knew that the color was actually called blue, possibly Russian Blue. The cat was a young British Domestic Shorthair, maybe a year and a half or two years old. Charlotte sat in one of the easy chairs that graced either side of the sofa, facing each other across the coffee table. The cat walked up to her feet and looked up at her expectantly until she picked it up and put it on her lap.

"I didn't know you had a cat," Maribelle said. "I thought Hannah's kid was allergic."

"He is," Charlotte said, petting the cat on her knee. "Different buildings, so it's no issue. Hannah and Shelby call the cat my familiar. You can call him Dada." The cat started kneading her leg and purring. She smiled.

"Oh, okay," Maribelle said awkwardly. She took her coffee cup in her hand and blew it, partially to cool it off, but mostly to buy herself time. She didn't know what to say.

"Have you read the book?" Charlotte asked.

"No, I haven't read it," Maribelle confessed. She picked up the tome, a leather-bound book which appeared to be a journal or diary of some sort. When she flipped it open to the first pages, she saw the words "Priestess of the Undoing" in familiar block print. She ran her finger over the text. It was her daughter's writing, the same lettering she used to title her comic books.

"What is this, Charlie?" she asked.

"Something I've been putting together for you for a while," Charlotte sighed. "You know what sucks? I'm the Oracle. Yes, I inherited some fucked up shit from dad, but that one is all you. Your bloodline is the blood of the Oracle of Somnus. That's why father chose you. You don't have the Sight, I do. But you do have a role to play. That's you. You're the Priestess of the Undoing."

"Why?" Maribelle asked. "Why I am the Priestess of the Undoing, and what does it mean?"

"You're the Priestess because you are the one who banished the somnali," Charlotte said simply, without accusation. "The whole purpose of the Rites of Undoing is to contain and control the somnali. The book I just gave you is an expansion of those rites. I know that some of the rituals have a darker purpose. You instructed me in the purification rituals and I performed them on Flynn with no idea that they were also cleansing him for sacrifice. I feel a little bit used when I think about it. Although I suppose that we wouldn't have had a child without them."

"I'm not going to sit here and listen to this," Maribelle said, setting the book down. "You act like I planned it all. I never planned to harm your husband, I just didn't feel, in the end, that I had any choice. I didn't set him up. Don't blame me for that."

"But you had to know that the rituals could be used that way," Charlotte accused. "Maybe you weren't consciously planning it, but it must have been there somewhere below the surface, sort of a back-up plan. Have the dreams started?" Charlotte asked her.

"What dreams?" Maribelle asked.

Charlotte rephrased the question. "Have you seen Flynn in your dreams?"

Maribelle slammed her coffee cup on the table. "You know what? What if I did? Dreams don't mean anything, they… I don't want to talk about it." He hands were shaking.

Charlotte shook her head. "Mom, you can't just pretend that my father and our entire history never happened to make yourself feel better. What about father? Do you miss him?"

"Things fell apart for us a long time ago," she said.

"But you loved him once," Charlotte said gently. "It couldn't have been easy to let him go forever."

"I loved him once," Maribelle said grimly, "but he could never love me. Understand me when I say it wasn't something he was capable of. The only creatures he felt any affection for were his offspring. Truly, he loved you. He loved Mercy and those other little monsters he spawned. For me, the only thing he felt was a sort of respect. I was the mother of his child, that's all."

"But you killed him," Charlotte said. "You killed them all."

Maribelle sighed. "I had to; don't you see? Your father was a monster. And now, so am I."

1988

Happiness Charlotte Metaxas was born in 1988. For obvious reasons, her father was unknown to everyone except for Maribelle. Brash insisted that his daughter's first name be some kind of human condition or emotion. He suggested human acceptable names like Joy, Chastity, or Prudence. Maribelle had no intention of giving her daughter a name like that, so she selected a middle name that she sincerely hoped the child would go by.

Maribelle Metaxas was twenty-six years old when Charlie was born. Her best friend, Jeannette Byrne, twenty-five, was married and pregnant at the same time. Maribelle and Jeannie had known one another since high school, back when people were still calling Maribelle "Mari." Back then, Jeannie Byrne was still Jeannie Morrison. Young Jeannie was gothic before Rose and Charlie were born. She was gothic before they were even called goths. She'd been a death rocker in high school.

Jeannie wanted to name her daughter Charlotte after her favorite Cure song, *Charlotte Sometimes*. Her husband Brian insisted that they name the child after his dearly departed grandmother Roshanara. Roshanara went by the Americanized name Roxanne, something Jeannie strongly objected to for her daughter. Jeannie thought of Roxanne as the hooker in the Police song of the same name. Maribelle suggested that Rose might be a compromise Brian would be open to. He accepted, and their daughter was Rose Byrne.

In turn, Jeannie suggested the name Charlotte to Maribelle. She knew Mari was a big fan of E.B. White's *Charlotte's Web*. Maribelle thought it was a wonderful name. That is how Charlotte came to be named after two songs and a book. In an act of secret defiance, she gave her daughter the first name Happiness after the Beatles' song *Happiness is a Warm Gun*. It tidily summed up her feelings about Brash on multiple levels.

Brash…

Maribelle sometimes blamed Jeannie for introducing her to those *Sandman* comics. Maribelle would have been just as happy if she'd just stuck with Richard and Wendy Pini's *ElfQuest*, with all of the romance and free love. Maybe life would have been better if she didn't develop a taste for bad boys. Bad boys like Brash.

He was the man of her dreams – and her nightmares.

As bad as he turned out to be, back then, she still loved him. She had no idea what he had done. She wouldn't find out for another ten years. When she did, she wouldn't be able to love him anymore.

She wouldn't find out about the terrible thing that Brash did to facilitate her pregnancy until the day of Charlotte's tenth birthday in 1998. But it was a month before Charlotte was born that Maribelle first had the inkling that something was terribly wrong.

It was the first time she'd laid eyes on the Rites of Undoing in the physical realm, but not the first time she'd seen it. She'd been having dreams about the book ever since the conception of Charlotte. She had been introduced to it through visitations by the author of the book himself, Phobetor.

Sandra Metaxas was the one who gave the book to Maribelle, her daughter, as a gift at her baby shower. It would be another two years before she introduced her daughter to the woman she'd gotten it from, Gertrude Singer. Sandra was already having an affair with Gertie by this time.

Sandra had been thirty-five when Maribelle was born. Her husband, Lionel Metaxas, had been fifty-seven. Lionel already had adult children in the old country and hadn't expected to become a father again so late in life. Sandra, previously divorced, had not expected to conceive at all. She had always assumed that her failure to get pregnant was a sign that there was something wrong with her. It never occurred to her that her first husband, Samuel Barry, was sterile. She'd met and married Samuel, only two years older than herself, when she was eighteen. She was thirty-four when she remarried a much older Lionel. That was two years after Sam left her and ran off with his nubile young receptionist, Margaret. Ironically, Margaret dumped Sam shortly after she learned of Maribelle's birth, angrily berating him for "shooting blanks."

By the time Charlotte was born, Sandra was sixty-one and eighty-three-year-old Lionel's Alzheimer's disease had taken a turn for the worse. She met Sandra in a support group for people who were caring for relatives with Alzheimer's. Gertie was close to Sandra's age and caring for her own mother, who also suffered from the disease. The two grew close. It wasn't until Lionel died two years later that the rumors started. Many suspected Gertie and Sandra were lovers. They moved in together after Lionel died and were inseparable for the rest of Sandra's life.

As for Lionel, although he was very affectionate with his granddaughter, he never could remember her name. He usually called her Maribelle, confusing her with his daughter.

Like Sandra, Maribelle had trouble conceiving. When she was a teenager, she had been in a bicycle vs. automobile accident, and the injuries to her abdominal cavity had been extensive. Although her ovaries and fallopian tubes were intact, the surgeon and her gynecologist believed that her uterus had been too damaged to carry a pregnancy to term. Her only hope was something she couldn't very well afford, surrogacy.

If she had waited ten or fifteen years, she would have been wealthy enough to afford a surrogate. Of course, then she would have had to worry about whether or not her aging ovaries would be able to produce viable eggs that could be used for a surrogate pregnancy.

She didn't wait, though. Against her better judgment, she trusted Brash, the "man of her dreams." Almost all of her interactions with Brash were in the Demos Oneiroi. When he promised to show up in the flesh and give her the child, she thought she could never have, she was intrigued, but she still didn't believe any of it was real. She thought she was daydreaming, or maybe losing her mind – until the day she met him face to face, in a new wave discotheque named Baby Doll.

As far as Sandra, Jeannie, and anyone else knew, Charlotte was the miraculous result of a one-night stand. A wanted pregnancy, desired by a mother who thought she would never have a child. No one chided Maribelle for her decision to keep the baby. Everyone understood. She was twenty-five when she got pregnant, old enough to start a family, surely. She already had a stable job at an ad agency, although nowhere near the success she would see later in life.

Her friend and family were mostly concerned about whether or not she would miscarry.

When Charlotte was born, everyone was overjoyed.

But by the time she was born, Maribelle wasn't the only one who knew that Brash wasn't human. Jeannie, Gertrude, Sandra, and another friend of the two older women from the Alzheimer's group, a young lady named Lorena Young, had all been visited by Phobetor and warned. The Sisterhood of the Undoing was formed.

Although they didn't know it, Phobetor's influence was always present amongst the Sisterhood of Undoing. His rivalry with Brash was more than a thousand years old. Phobetor himself had authored the Rites of Undoing. Their primary purpose was disempowering Brash and weakening his control over his bloodline. Phobetor disapproved of his brother. People needed their dreams to work things out, even their nightmares. Brash and his offspring diluted the purpose of dreams by polluting them with blood magic. They only used dreams as a platform to launch themselves into the physical world. They never truly appreciated the Demos Oneiroi for what it was meant to be.

Grants Pass

The journey from Eugene to Grant's Pass was largely uneventful for the human beings that the Carter family left in their wake. Phobetor had been interrupting all of Candy and Cyn's attempts to feed with his deft, and, to them, invisible hand. The toddlers were confounded as to why their usual tricks and attacks weren't working. In spite of their attempts to wreak havoc, the people with whom they came into contact remained mysteriously unharmed.

This was not the case for Cyn, who was growing weaker and weaker. Her twin, desperate for the nourishment Phobetor denied her, had redoubled her psychic siphoning of energies from her sibling. Cyn had been running a fever and throwing up for the past thirty miles, and Alice was insisting that the child be taken to the emergency room at once.

By the time Flynn came back from Charlotte's house, the twins were with their parents in a local community hospital emergency care waiting room, and Phobetor was trapped between a rock and a hard place.

They were loitering around the parking lot in the less conspicuous and far less glamorous avian form of common pigeon. They were still sitting on the roof of the RV, but it wasn't really necessary. They knew who the kids and their grandparents were now, and even where they were headed.

"I think maybe our interference has backfired." Phobetor complained. "If the stronger one kills the weaker one, she'll reincarnate somewhere else. We can't know for sure, but likely with her memories intact, and we'll be back to square one two years from now."

Flynn was always quick to tune into the bodily needs and rhythms of whatever form he shifted into. He was busy picking ticks and mites out of his feathers. He felt a bit conflicted about it. There was enough human type thinking to find the process disgusting. He was pecking at, picking at, and occasionally eating all or part of the parasites. He barely was able to resist an urge to start grooming Phobetor's feathers as well.

"So, what can we do?" Flynn asked, looking up from under his wing. "We can't very well just let them go around killing people."

"At the moment, I would say we have to." Phobetor countered. "They are in a hospital, it's not like we can just fly in there as pigeons or crawl in as rats. They keep a sanitary environment in there. If we did stop them, the death of the weaker twin might be too high a price to pay."

"You don't value human life all that highly," Flynn observed.

Phobetor considered ignoring the remark. Instead, he answered, "They will just reincarnate, they always do. What's the problem with that?"

"We lose our connections," Flynn argued. "We lose our identities."

"Speaking of connections," Phobetor said, changing the subject, "how is Charlotte?"

"She's fine," Flynn said. "Her mother is not. Maribelle seems almost as fucked up over killing me as I am over dying. I'm not sure what to do."

"I'll come over to talk to her with you," Phobetor suggested.

"Right now?" Flynn asked. "You mean leave the Chucky twins on the loose?"

"We need her help to stop them," Phobetor said. "We're kind of at an impasse until we figure out how to erase their memories. Besides, I have an alarm system. I'll know as soon as they start using their powers on another victim."

Reconciliation

It wasn't possible for two humans to share the same dream, but more than one dream creature could occupy the night visions of a single human with ease. When Flynn and Phobetor went to visit Maribelle in her dreams, she was doing something unexpected. She was on a settee in an unfamiliar living room, knitting little pink baby booties.

"How nice," Phobetor purred. "What memory is this? Are those for the granddaughter or the daughter? I can never tell age with you poor little temporary creatures."

Maribelle smiled and patted her obviously pregnant belly.

"Well, I've bought you a gift," he said, roughly shoving Flynn down on the floor at her feet. Flynn didn't know what Phobetor was thinking, and he was more than a little afraid. He decided it was in his best interest not to resist. "It goes with the book I gave you earlier. The Rites of Undoing, remember?"

Maribelle wrinkled her nose. "It's somnali. Is it one of Brash's little brats?"

"I'm sorry," Phobetor said. "It didn't look like that in 1988. Let me fix that." Phobetor ruffled his hair and Flynn recoiled in horror as his wings dropped off onto the floor. It was an instant measure. They simply fell, like dead things. He was watching them shrivel and dry up on the ground when he first noticed himself growing younger, and smaller.

As with assuming any other form, the emotions and mental capacity of his new form began to usurp his somnali mind. He remembered who he was, but with every passing moment, he felt and thought more like a three-and-a-half-year-old child. Flynn was standing in the middle of his black jeans, which had grown too large and fallen off. He was still wearing his boxer briefs, but they were so baggy and oversized they hung down to his knees as if he'd had an accident.

"I'm afraid," Flynn said timidly. He was shocked by the childish sound of his own voice. Maribelle set down her knitting, leaned down and picked him up.

"Well, aren't you adorable?" she cooed, sitting the child down on the couch beside her. "What's your name? Where did you come from?"

He graced her with a smile. As a man and as a child, Flynn had a very disarming smile. If he was smiling, it was one of the first things people noticed about him. There was no manipulation behind it. It was a totally natural smile. Still, it was the kind of smile that could, and often did, melt hearts.

"Awww," Maribelle said, smiling back at him. She lifted an afghan from the couch and tossed it across his little legs. "Are you cold?"

He looked at her funny when she did it. It reminded him of how she wrapped him in blankets at the campsite, when she was poisoning him as Charlotte slept. Everything he could remember about dying made a travesty of the word comfort. Maribelle and Charlotte had both been trying to keep him comfortable and free from pain as he slipped away. Comfort was so overrated.

"I'm not cold," he said, struggling with his rapidly diminishing vocabulary. "I am Flynn. I'm you son-in-law."

Maribelle laughed. "Don't you think you're a little young to get married? And to someone who isn't even born yet."

Just then, Phobetor interrupted their innocent conversation to hand Maribelle a knife. It had a fancy curved blade, in an s shape. The hilt was made of dark metal, shaped like the head of a snake. Rubies formed the serpent's eyes.

"What is this for?" Maribelle asked.

"It's so you can kill him," he said harshly. "Stop comforting the child and get it over with. Slit his throat."

"That's terrible," Maribelle said, throwing the knife down. "I'm not going to kill this little boy."

"You did kill me, lady" Flynn childishly attempted to explain. "To stop the somnom... nom... somnom..."

"Somnali," Phobetor said. "That is your little son-in-law. You did kill him, to stop Brash and his somnali offspring. He's your human sacrifice."

Maribelle blanched. "But he is just a little baby."

"He was 26 when he died," Phobetor shrugged. "That makes it better, right? Almost as old as Jimi Hendrix and Janis Joplin were when they died." He patted Flynn on the head and the little boy resumed his adult, human form.

"Not much," Maribelle said. "I'm twenty-six now, it's not very old." She looked at Flynn, who was nervously putting his pants back on.

"Calm down," she said, waving her arm dismissively. "You don't have anything down there I haven't seen before."

Flynn blushed. "Maribelle! You're my mother-in-law," he said, zipping his pants up. "It's really embarrassing."

Young Maribelle looked a lot like Charlotte. The differences were minor. Her eyes were wider and much darker than Charlotte's. Her hair was thicker and wavier, almost curly. She was bustier, and narrower in the hips. She wore dark eye shadow and mascara, but almost no other make-up. Unlike Charlotte's her complexion was perfectly clear. She was a bigger fan of the sunlight than her daughter, and her naturally olive skin was quite tan. That made the Persian heritage in her Greek bloodline more apparent. Her hairstyles and fashion choices were also calculated to play it up. Maribelle was a very beautiful woman, exotic, and very put together.

"I'm still not killing him," Maribelle said, refusing the knife Phobetor handed her. "I've read your book, Phobetor. I know what you're trying to do. I understand that you're trying to protect me and my child, but no. I can't do it."

Flynn looked at him, stunned. "This was your idea, the whole me dying thing?"

"Well, I didn't know why back then," Phobetor said with a shrug. "I did know it might come down to that, though. Be a good sport and bare your throat for Maribelle there. Make it easy. Just like last time. It's for the good of your wife and daughter, you know."

Maribelle raised her eyebrow. "I killed you? You let me kill you?"

"Kind of," he shrugged. "It wasn't exactly like that. You had to be there. I mean I kind of suspected you were poisoning me, it's not like I knew for sure." He felt a little ill, absorbing the knowledge that Phobetor and Maribelle had plotted against him. He always thought of her actions as a desperate, last-ditch measure. The idea that they might have been calculated sickened him.

"You need to grow up now, Maribelle," Phobetor said at last. "You were there. Deal with it." He patted Maribelle on the head and she grew older, until she was her current age of 52. She appraised Phobetor sharply.

"Phobetor. I recognize you now. It's been a while," she said suddenly. "Tell me, why are you punishing Flynn for what happened?"

"The real question is why you do?" Phobetor asked, "Why do you treat him like shit now? Would you be happier if he were angry with you? What did you want him to do, punch you in the face? Throw the coffee mug against the wall? Scream and wail that it was not his fault that Mike and the others died?"

"I guess," she admitted.

"Well, isn't he terrible?" Phobetor said sarcastically. "I don't think he's suffered enough, do you? Perhaps I should reach into his chest and snatch out his still-beating heart, and we can eat it while he watches."

"No, that's okay," Maribelle said. She trembled a little. She knew him to be capable of it.

"Did you think of Brash while you were killing him?" Phobetor asked. "And be honest, did you get satisfaction knowing that as Flynn lay dying, somewhere Brash was dying as well?"

"Of course I did," Maribelle said sourly. "And what of it? What if I did? He was evil, a monster. What he did so I would become pregnant. What he intended to do to my grandchild, he planned to possess her if he could. I hated him!"

"Right," Phobetor said. "I know. But do you hate Flynn?"

Maribelle looked at her feet. "No of course not, why would I? I just can't stand it, him coming around here smiling in my face after what I did to him. It makes me feel guilty. I feel like shit every time I see him. His wanting my approval only makes it worse."

"Don't be a bitch about it," Phobetor said. "He gave you his life – well, technically, he gave it to his daughter. Twice. But you took it. If he wants your approval, I think you should give it to him."

Flynn cocked his head sideways and grinned at Maribelle. "I do realize that it's neurotic for me to want you to like me. I have pretty serious self-esteem issues."

"You were a cute kid," she said quickly. "Faelyn looks so much like you did. She reminds me of you. I did some terrible things I have a hard time facing, and you remind me of that. But I don't hate you, Flynn. I love you."

She leaned over and gave him a big hug. Then, she started to cry. Maribelle was crying so hard it was difficult to understand what she was saying. She told him about how horrible it was watching him die. She told him how hard it was forcing Charlotte to watch his death and knowing that she was the reason she lost him. He shuddered when she said that she had considered leaving him to die alone, where Charlotte wouldn't have to know about it, but it seemed too cruel.

She confessed that when she helped Charlotte to dump his body in the river, she was less concerned with his afterlife and more concerned with evading police detection. She explained that she had a falling out with Charlotte because her daughter resented her insisting that Flynn's death must be a suicide. There was nothing in the coroner's report to refute it.

Flynn just held her and listened to whatever she said while she cried, but it was starting to wear him down. Phobetor came by and patted him on the back and freed him from experiencing these emotions as a human. He could feel the wings erupt from his back, and the weight lift from his shoulders.

It was better this way. He couldn't afford to sit there with his heart breaking while Maribelle confessed to him. They needed her whole. They needed her strong. He needed to be centered and emotionally detached enough to listen to her declaration of guilt, and he couldn't do it in human form.

He waited until she stopped her rambling, and then gave his mother-in-law a big bear hug.

"I forgive you, Maribelle," he said. "I know you were just trying to protect Charlotte and Faelyn and a lot of other people. I forgive you."

Maribelle wiped her face on the lovely, ruffled sleeve of her blouse. She liked wearing delicate, lacey blouses under her power suits. This one had beautifully fluted cuffs, now covered in snot and tears. Flynn couldn't help but laugh at that. His mother-in-law was such a dignified lady. If she wasn't in the middle of a serious bawl, she would have never done that. Flynn thought that everyone looked terrible when they cried – ugly, distressed. There was a part of human nature that made one want to comfort that red-faced, squalling infant. It was an instinct. It never went away. We still wanted to comfort the baby even after it grew up into a flushed, squalling middle aged woman.

Flynn produced a folded square of cloth from his jeans pocket and handed it to her. He was slightly impressed with himself, as he still hadn't mastered the control of objects in the dream world. It was a perfectly made handkerchief. Maribelle unceremoniously blew her nose in it with a loud honking sound.

Once again, he took note of his wings and resulting perpetually shirtless condition. His chest was damp with ocular secretions and mucous. The afghan kept sliding down and offered little protection. Maribelle, at least, had so many dealings with the Oneiroi and the somnali that she wasn't in the least concerned with her son-in-law's half nakedness.

"I'm so glad you forgive me," she said, finally sitting up. She straightened her jacket, attempting to make herself look respectable. Flynn smiled at her. She was so human.

"Do you forgive me?" Phobetor asked Maribelle.

"No, I don't" Maribelle told him. "How could you?"

Phobetor heard her words and seethed. He loved her. He had done all of these things for her, but she didn't seem to appreciate any of it. He was filled with a burning rage. He wanted to lash out at her, but he would never do anything to hurt Maribelle.

Fear

They returned to Phobetor's castle, not to the tiny office Flynn worked in, high in a turret, but to the ground floor, to the throne room. Like Somnus and Brash, Phobetor had his throne room built around the Lethe, the source of all of their powers.

Since Brash had died, Phobetor had built a door, a portal of sorts. It sat directly adjacent to the opening where the river entered the building and began its course through the middle of the floor. The door connected the throne rooms of Phobetor and Brash. He claimed it made it easier for him to manage both kingdoms. It was only necessary until Charlotte returned, he said. He asked Flynn to ask her for permission first. Charlotte was quick to grant it. She feared Phobetor, and with good reason.

Flynn was not so wise. He'd considered Phobetor a friend, and perhaps that was his mistake. He was sullen after the revelations of their recent meeting. He learned that Phobetor was behind what Maribelle did to him all along. Phobetor had lied to him, betrayed him. Flynn felt that he had to confront him for these transgressions. He didn't realize that Phobetor himself would never condone or tolerate Flynn's speaking to him as if he were somehow his equal.

"You lied to me," Flynn accused. "I trusted you, and you betrayed me. You let me go along believing it was all Maribelle's idea, you let me think you were my friend."

Phobetor raised an eyebrow.

"I hid the truth from you," the nightmare daemon said casually. "Whether or not you want to call that lying… well I suppose was a lie of omission, if you will. I care something for you now, but you were human then. Asking me to care about the fate of a human being is like asking McDonald's corporate headquarters to care about the slaughter of a specific cow."

He hoped the somnali-child would accept this answer and let it go.

Even in his somnali form, Charlotte's prince consort was simply riddled with human emotion. He related far too heavily to the human beings. He seemed not to understand yet that he was a dream daemon. All of the dream daemons were placed somewhere on the spectrum of dream pleasantries between Morpheus, the god of dreams, and Phobetor, the god of nightmares. Brash and his spawn occupied a niche immediately adjacent to Phobetor. These were the darker realms. Brash and his children dealt in horrifying wet dreams that left the dreamer equal parts terrified and titillated. How would Charlotte's sensitive little subject ever be able to accept that reality?

Boldly and without apprehension, this man-child dared to make accusations and question the judgment of his superiors. How dare he speak to his elders so freely? The youngster was barely thirty years old. Phobetor had blue jeans older than that. This boy was getting out of hand. Phobetor was already unhappy with the young man. Flynn's softhearted affection towards mortals was a large part of the reason Phobetor had agreed to prevent Mercy from feeding. Denied her usual prey, the former somnali in whatever mutated human form she currently possessed had turned on her sister. Now Mercy threatened to consume Sympathy and become more powerful than ever. Phobetor blamed Flynn.

He needed to be put in his place.

"Nyx warned me not to trust you," Flynn snarled. "How could you do it? How could you lie to me like that? I'm hurt."

Phobetor did a double-take. Was it raising its voice to him? The urge to damage Flynn was rising in him like bile in the throat of an angry human. Did it think that mentioning Nyx would keep it from suffering its well-earned punishments and humiliations? It was a very young somnali. Phobetor decided that perhaps another warning was warranted. With difficulty, he stayed his hand.

"Watch your tone with me, little man," Phobetor cautioned. "It is only your flimsy little human emotions that were wounded. You would do well to ignore them. You are no longer human. Nyx has elevated you. Forget the weakness of your humble mortal origins and move on. If you continue to accuse me, you may yet experience what it would truly be like to be injured at my hands. What's done is done," he concluded with a note of finality.

The situation with Mercy made Phobetor feel very angry and impotent. If he were either common or human, he might have felt guilty about taking his anger out on Flynn. He was neither. Phobetor was no mere dream daemon, not one of the nameless Oneiroi. He was one of the three, one of the named, one of the gods. Phobetor was proud of his absolute dominion over the kingdom of nightmares. He wasn't used to accepting responsibility for any miscalculations. He was used to making a scapegoat of some lesser being, such as the young somnali before him who acted as his advisor and employee. Who better?

Thoughts of what he could do to Flynn became increasingly enticing to Phobetor.

"You would do well to fear me," Phobetor threatened. "After his death, I came to lay claim to my brother's kingdom. I found it had been inherited by an infantile demigodling, stripped of her powers. I found it in the care of her defenseless, naive, and dead little human consort. I would have taken possession at once if Nyx did not interfere. You and your wife have powerful allies but make no mistake: I have powerful allies of my own.

"Nyx asked me to take you on as my charge in order to avert an all-out war amongst the gods. I only agreed because as regent I do have power over your kingdom. It is simply power I can wield without displacing you and your woman. One day, I will be asked to step aside. In the meantime, I intend to keep you both firmly under me until she is ready to rule. If you refuse to show me respect and deference, I can tell you now that your punishment will be brutal."

"You enjoy terrorizing me," Flynn charged. "You especially love to torment me in front of these women. You threatened me in front of Maribelle and did the same thing in front of Charlotte. Why?"

Phobetor shrugged. "I'm the god of fear. What do you want from me? Your apprehension, their panic and terror as they anticipate the horrible things I might do to you, are just too delicious. These emotions of yours and those the Metaxas women feel for you are so delectable, so delightful. They are too tempting. How could I resist? Would you like me to deny that I enjoy the sight of you trembling, on your knees? How can I? It is as the humans like to say, better than sex."

Phobetor gave him a rather salacious smile.

For the first time since the conversation began, Flynn was nervous. Up until now, his anger had blotted out all of his fear. He'd been mouthing off to Phobetor like a surly, rebellious teenager criticizing his parent. Now he was beginning to see his error. He was not Phobetor's child, he was his charge. Nyx had assigned Flynn to Phobetor as an apprentice, a trainee, and an underling.

Phobetor was regent over Charlotte's kingdom, managing most of its affairs. Although she was the heir apparent, Charlotte was human. Flynn had been deified by Nyx, and as somnali, he was now qualified to act as her regent. That made him potentially a threat to Phobetor. However, Charlotte and Flynn were both considered too young and inexperienced to manage affairs on their own. Flynn was like a somnali infant – he couldn't even conjure his own garments yet. Phobetor and Nyx had to offer him changes of attire like he was a kindergartener. He was still far from self-sufficient.

Phobetor had just enlightened Flynn to an additional unpleasant fact, one that he hadn't previously considered. If things went badly between Phobetor and the Metaxas women, Flynn's role as apprentice was subject to instant change. If Phobetor deemed it necessary, Flynn would become his prisoner of war. He was the puerile prince consort of a currently human somnali queen. As such, he was very useful as a bargaining chip.

Phobetor smiled with pleasure. "If your wife Charlotte Metaxas, queen of your realm, and Oracle of Somnus refuses to obey me, you will certainly come to harm," he announced. "If your mother-in-law, priestess of my temple, unknowing though she may be – head of the Phobetor's most sacred order, the Sisterhood of Undoing, rebels against me, I will break your tender bones. If you rise up against me, newborn somnali, I will enjoy inflicting the most brutal punishments upon your vulnerable person. The fact is that you already invite such chastisement. Stay your tongue."

Flynn should have known better, but he was still too angry keep his mouth shut.

"I can't believe you. You're just as bad as Mercy," he accused.

Phobetor laughed, and presented him with a cruel grin. "Oh no… I am much worse."

It was the last straw, a comparison between himself and the pathetic creature Mercy. That Flynn, this little somnali infant, should fear her, but not fear the great Phobetor was too great an insult to allow it to stand.

He assumed the nightmare shape of a broken shadow rife with elongated, sharpened appendages. He raised five long fingers, thin and sharp as awls. Flynn gasped as they pierced through the side of him. In a split second, Phobetor was behind him. The terror god had pinned him so that he couldn't escape. The talons laced through the young somnali's ribcage. Where they exited on the other side, they wound and curved around each other, knotted at the ends. He pulled his victim close to him and immobilized him against his chest. Flynn trembled.

Phobetor's laughter was like the jovial belly laugh of a sadistic school boy with a magnifying glass torturing ants on a hot summer's day. His delight was that of a cruel child plucking the wings off a fly. The overwhelming power and control he had over this pathetic, puny little creature gave him great joy. Soon, he forgot about the mounting troubles with Mercy, and the train wreck about to happen on planet Earth. Flynn's anger and brave posturing crumbled. Finally, Phobetor had his niece's consort impaled, terrified. The enchanting aroma of Flynn's dread made his mouth water. He couldn't wait to taste more.

Flynn recalled Charlotte's admonition to submit to Phobetor and avoid incurring his wrath. He also recalled Nyx's warning not to trust the nightmare daemon. He hadn't listened. Now he would pay the price for failing to heed good advice.

As his heart pounded against the inside of his ribcage, Phobetor touched and stroked the organ with his wicked fingers. Flynn had to hold very still in order to avoid the sharp protuberances that threatened to tear it asunder. Deep breathing pressed his lungs painfully against the barbed digits Phobetor had entwined around his ribs. The dream daemon's fingers and limbs were a thicket of tendrils, sharp and painful as thorny vines. Flynn made his breaths shallow, to avoid the discomfort.

The palpable dread was worse than the physical agony. Phobetor exuded a thick, dreary essence of unadulterated revulsion and dismay. He scratched and caressed the vulnerable flesh of his prey, threatening to slice and prod. Flynn could feel his skin crawl everywhere the ancient god lay a hand on him with those prickly digits. The young somnali was so very cold.

Phobetor wickedly whispered in his ear. "It is I who authored the Rites of Undoing. It is I who coveted Brash's kingdom for a thousand years. It was I who bargained with your youthful flesh in order to steal from him his kingdom. It was I who manipulated Maribelle, before Charlotte was even born. It is I who set the wheels into motion."

The terror god waved a hand in front of him, and the black cave wall's surface transformed into a crystal clear mirror. Behind him, Phobetor had transmuted into a creature with the face of a giant eel. A mouth full of razor-sharp teeth gnashed and snapped near his neck, threatening to bite. Multiple pointed and viscous fingers, like twisted coral, branched out at all angles. The ones piercing his chest began to wiggle, and Flynn started to cough up blood.

"I want you to watch," Phobetor said. "See yourself, caught like a butterfly on a pin. Watch. Observe everything I do to you. If you refuse, I'll excise your eyelids and force you to stare."

He wanted Flynn to look. He enjoyed the heightened panic that watching, and anticipating the devastating blows caused the boy. Phobetor took great pleasure in consuming the young somnali's raw, tender emotions. They were delectable.

He sank his teeth into Flynn's neck, and pulled back, tearing out a chunk of flesh. Blood poured down onto his chest. The terrified Flynn felt warm urine spread out across his crotch and upper thighs, making his black jeans grow heavy and stick to the skin.

"Whatever you do, don't scream," Phobetor warned. "If you scream, I will have to tear your throat out and render you voiceless. You may sob, whimper, or weep silently if you wish." These threats were designed to increase apprehension and anticipatory dread in the helpless subject.

Phobetor extended the arm which held him. The pressure and heat in Flynn's chest felt as though he had been forced to swallow burning hot coals. The angry god used the spikes buried within his chest cavity to elevate Flynn several inches off the ground. He rotated his imprisoned body until his reflection was sideways in the mirror. Powerless, the feeble somnali hung limply from the branchlike limb of mighty Phobetor,

With a free hand – and Phobetor had so many of them, so many hands, and so many arms all covered in sharp instruments designed to do his wicked bidding – he caressed Flynn's wings. The little somnali cringed in trepidation over what surely must come. He bit his lip until it bled to keep himself from screaming. The god of nightmares shattered his wing with a single blow, crushing its bones as easily as a child plucking the wings off a fly. What was left of the broken wing was dangling, half torn from his shoulder blade.

"Young immortals naively believe they are in no real danger," Phobetor lectured. He felt the need of an abusive parent to explain to his charge in some detail why this cruel castigation was required. "Ganymede innocently fulfilled his role as cupbearer and lover without knowing that Hera plotted his death. Prometheus knew better when he crossed Zeus, yet his immortal body healing only made him the apt victim of a gruesome torture that renewed every day with the regeneration of his damaged flesh. I could damage your body daily. I could watch it regenerate every night and return to abuse it again if I so desired."

As if to underscore this point, Phobetor reached out a single grizzled hand and plunged its needle-sharp fingers into Flynn's chest. He crushed the boy's heart in his hand, plucked it out. Flynn screamed in anguish until Phobetor fulfilled his promise and tore out his throat with his teeth in order to silence him. When Flynn could scream no more, he silently wept.

Phobetor casually destroyed his other wing before pulling back his fingers and dropping his broken body on the ground. When Flynn lay on the ground bleeding, Phobetor bore down on his legs with tremendous weight. He stomped down on the back of each of his calves until the bones were shattered.

"Now you will remember your lowly station," Phobetor said, patting the broken man on the head. "Stay on the ground, my little dog."

Flynn was forced to crawl. He had never experienced such intense and prolonged agony. The time when Charlotte had eaten him alive, she'd torn out his throat and he'd died almost instantly. He had been quickly released from his flesh and the pain associated with it. For the first time, he realized that she probably intentionally minimized his suffering. Now he was immortal and could not die. His torture could be potentially everlasting. Phobetor wanted to inflict as much anguish and torment as possible without causing him to lose consciousness.

"In a day's time, your injuries will heal," Phobetor said gently. "Until this day, I have been kind. I have been respectful of you and your ridiculous human customs. I have been willing to allow you and your wife to set up your little fiefdom and play house under the auspices of my protection. You should have been grateful. Instead, you have rewarded me with insolence.

"Your foolish mewling about the lives of irrelevant humans is to blame for Mercy's consumption of her sister and exponential increase in power. You and your wife are silly, emotional creatures, incompetent in your decision making, incapable of ruling. Tell your wife that if she does not give up her kingdom and swear her allegiance to me, your punishments will continue."

He kicked Flynn hard in the haunches. "You should nod to let me know if you have heard me, little dog."

Flynn nodded.

"Come," Phobetor said with an icy smile. "Follow me. We must show your wife what I have done." He slapped his leg and whistled the way a man does when calling a dog to heel.

Legs and wings broken, Flynn was forced to crawl. He followed behind on the floor, on his hands and knees. His shattered body was bleeding profoundly from gaping wounds in his throat, chest, wings, and calves. As he moved, he left a trail of blood and other fluids behind him on the ground like a snail's trail of mucous. Tears welled up in his eyes. He was afraid, in unbearable pain, and he felt very foolish. He had misjudged the situation, and Phobetor thrashed him for it. He had to be more careful moving forward. The nightmare daemon was not his friend, but an ally of convenience. The creature's best attempts at affection were the carrot and stick a farmer might offer the ass dragging his plow.

The fifty feet he had to crawl to reach the door to Charlotte's dream world seemed like a mile to Flynn. He had a lot to think about. He had been so naïve, believing that Phobetor aided him in his search for Mercy, in his management of Charlotte's kingdom, because it was the right thing to do. The nightmare god's goals were now revealed as strictly opportunistic. He cared nothing about right and wrong, all he cared about was power. Mercy was a threat to his power, so he wanted her eliminated.

Flynn was safe only as long as he was docile, and easy to control. He would be subject to further brutalization if he dared to step out of line. If Charlotte rebelled, Phobetor promised Flynn would experience retribution so consistent and violent that it would make Prometheus cringe.

Phobetor opened the door. He looked at Charlotte and said, "I had to punish the little dog. Teach him to heel, so I won't be provoked to further discipline. You will both kneel before me."

He kicked Flynn in the rear repeatedly until he finished crawling inside, and then slammed the door behind him.

Flynn found himself on the floor of the throne room in Brash's castle, in so much pain that he hoped he would pass out. Cruelly, he could not, no matter how much it hurt to stay awake.

Act IV: Bonded Pairs

Imelda

Charlotte picked up a fur rug and ran over to Flynn with it in her hands. She put it down on the floor beside him and rolled him onto it. He smiled when he recognized it. It was her skin, her leopard skin from her leopard body. He was bleeding all over it. The stains would never come out.

"It's going to hurt some but crawl up on here let me drag you across the floor," she told him. "I want some distance between us and Phobetor."

Flynn nodded and climbed upon on the skin and curled up into the fetal position. He was miserable. For the first time since Nyx created him as somnali, he understood immortality wasn't the same as invulnerability. He could still be placed in real danger. He had previously assumed that as an immortal he would be invulnerable. He did not expect to suffer the same indignities he had when Phobetor first encountered him as a mere mortal spirit. He assumed wounds would instantly heal. Therefore, he believed he would never be at risk of life or limb.

His injuries were not healing. They were extremely painful. The pain was not just physical. He had been betrayed by one of his trusted allies. It wasn't the first time. Maribelle had also betrayed him. Phobetor made him understand just how powerless he really was.

Charlotte opened a low-lying, hidden door so small it seemed to be designed for a household pet, perhaps a cat, or dog. It was rather small for anything as large as a human being. She dragged him inside the low ceilinged cavern and closed the little door behind her. The room was very small and positively claustrophobic. Neither of them would be able to stand, although it was possible to sit or crawl. When he looked up, there were stars on the ceiling. He smiled when he recognized them.

"That's the blanket Nyx gave you," Charlotte said, pointing up. Pointing down, she said "This other one, she gave to me as a child. The blanket of stars is a precious gift. It offers the wearer a little privacy. We don't really have much of it down here. I lined this room so we would be hidden from prying eyes and ears."

Being in the room was like being in a tent, or a very spacious sleeping bag. It was like they were sandwiched inside a pita pocket. It would have been cozy, but his ribs were broken and his knees were shattered. His busted wings made it painful to lie on his back, and one of his sides was torn open. He carefully propped himself up on one arm on the side that was uninjured. He raised his knees to his belly, trying to get in a comfortable position.

"I can ease your suffering, possibly even heal you completely, but it might be a little unpleasant," Charlotte said. "I haven't tried exercising my powers very often since I've been human, and I am only able to do so using you as a conduit. Would you like me to try?"

Flynn held his free hand out to her and nodded.

"Okay then," Charlotte said. "You might feel some pressure."

She ran her fingers over the hole in his chest and called the snake that lived under his skin to her. She touched the skin around the wound until the snake responded. It began to follow her hand. She stroked his skin over the serpent's head, and then she called it by name, "Imelda, emblem of my power, adhere to my will."

Flynn couldn't speak but he wondered at the name, Imelda. He had never considered that the creature sharing his skin might be feminine. It made perfect sense, though… she was Charlotte's, the personification of his wife's power, although she lived in his body.

Flynn felt the movement under his skin. It wasn't unpleasant, but it was very strange. Wherever it moved, the creature created friction and generated heat and pressure. He could feel it weaving through his battered flesh and shattered bone, swimming through his body. Everywhere it passed, he could feel the tingling and heat that accompanied regeneration. The snake was creating new flesh, growing new organs inside his body. He put his arms around Charlotte's shoulders and looked at her while she did her work.

He was reminded of the snake its original form, the circular Ouroboros tattoo. He thought of the snake on the rod of Asclepius, a healing deity. Snakes were often associated with medicine in Greek mythology and healing practice. Charlotte was using the creature to heal him. It strangely pleasurable, the tension he felt inside his body radiating outward.

It followed her hand wherever she brushed it across his skin. His neck injury was too severe for him to look down. He felt it, though. He could feel his flesh regenerating where she touched him. He found himself eagerly pressing his flesh into her tender caress. The snake Imelda did likewise, straining against his skin to find her fingers.

When she finished with his chest, she leaned in and kissed him. He felt the snake running up his throat, following the heat of her mouth. The slithering motion as the snake traversed through his esophagus caused him pain, but it also healed him. When it reached the surface, it bit the inside of his lip until he opened his mouth wide enough to allow it to escape. Charlotte kissed the snake. When she finished, it returned to where it lived inside him. Then she kissed and sucked at the skin on his throat until it was healed and he could speak again.

Flynn held Charlotte close to him and whispered in her ear. "Who is Imelda?"

"Imelda was the name of a snake I created in the Demos Oneiroi when I was a child," Charlotte said. "I wanted a pet, so I made her. This is her room, where she lived in the castle. She was the first real manifestation of my power. It took me a long time to recognize her when I saw you. She lives in your body now.

As somnali, you have your own power. As a pure human, I can't contain somnali power. My power occupies your flesh in the form of Imelda. Nyx split Brash's powers between the two of us. You and I are in essence, two parts of one whole. You see, somnali are not as powerful as Oneiroi, so it is necessary to keep my power dormant for the most part. It is waiting for me to take it from you. I just exercised my power through you, though. It's a little bit dangerous, because if I unleash too much of it, your somnali body won't be able to contain it. It would tear you apart."

She was running her fingers over his body, deciding what next to heal. His legs and his wings were still broken. She started to unbutton his jeans. She would need to remove them to heal his legs. The pants themselves were destroyed – shredded in some places, with bone showing through.

"Ow! Shit that hurts!" he yelped. He shifted his weight to make it easier for her to get them off. When they were off, he sat on his bottom with his knees bent. He kept his back hunched over so the wings wouldn't touch the ceiling. Any weight on them or pressure against them was painful.

In a moment, the pain seemed irrelevant. She was touching his leg, inviting Imelda to follow her hand down his thigh, to his knee. It didn't hurt him. It was tantalizing and delicious. Soon, it was traveling over his knee, into his shattered calf. Everywhere she touched, he was healed. Soon, she was working on his opposite thigh.

"Is it the same thing you did when we had sex under the tree?" he asked her.

"More or less," she said. "I should say, more, not less. I can't run my powers through my human body. When I'm somnali – after I die, you can return them to me safely. If you did it now, it would probably kill me. On that day, we might together, be able to stand up to Phobetor. But not today."

"But not yet," Flynn said. "So, you want me to continue to appease Phobetor until then?"

Finished with his legs, she moved around behind him and touched his wings. They felt different than the rest of his body. When she healed them, they itched.

"You must," she insisted. "He's not actually worse than Mercy, but he is more powerful. You shouldn't have said that to him. It's like you challenged him to prove that he's more dangerous than she is – than you are – than we are."

"That was brutal," Flynn said. "Thank you for healing me." He hugged her.

"Are you feeling alright?" Charlotte asked, touching his forehead. "You feel feverish."

"I think I'm okay," Flynn told her. "Everywhere you healed me, the skin is very sensitive. It's sore, like having sunburned skin or getting a rug burn."

"Whatever you did to anger him, don't do it again. Phobetor is one of only a hand full of Oneiroi who can exist in the physical realm in any form," Charlotte warned. "You really don't want to piss him off. That could lead to our daughter starring in 'A Dingo Ate My Baby.'"

"So, he could just show up as a wolf or coyote and eat the Carter twins if he wanted to?" Flynn asked.

"He could, but that would be ill advised," Charlotte said. "I think I told you, we feed off the emotions of others. Phobetor threatens you more often than he actually hurts you, because he doesn't feed off your pain, he feeds off your fear. He only throttled you because if he was never willing to cause harm, his threats would lose their teeth. He wants my kingdom for his own."

Coupling

After he was healed, Charlotte tried to explain to Flynn how their powers worked.

"You're my opposite part," she said. "I'm not just a human sexual sadist, the way you are aroused sexually, by pain… it feeds me, or at least it did when I was demisomnali. It will again when I am somnali. It's the opposite thing with you. The pleasure I feel when… well you know."

Flynn blushed. "I do know. It's why I begged you to under the tree." He was on his side, naked, with her spooned up against the front of his body. He wanted to beg her now to take him, to claim him, to hurt him with her teeth and her fingernails in all of the little ways that excited him so much.

"You require it now," she said. "Like food or water. Nyx made you somnali in that way. We are companion pieces, made to fit together. She took what was natural to you in your human form and amplified it so that we would always suit each other."

"Like the snake Ouroboros," Flynn said. "He could always be independent because he feasted on himself. Like an ecosystem of one. So, we are made interdependent, so that if necessary, we can feed each other?"

"Yes," Charlotte said, rolling over to face him. "We nourish one another, because we each have compatible needs." She started kissing and biting his chest, the kind of foreplay they both enjoyed. Coupling seemed natural, inevitable.

Champion of Thanatos

Phobetor had no way of knowing that the twins had Thanatos' seal of approval – or more accurately, Mercy did. She'd always been Thanatos' favorite. Ruthless, power hungry, insatiable Mercy was a force of nature. She was a non-stop destruction machine, like the Kraken. The god of death thought she was beautiful and wonderful and could not wait to see her unleashed on all of mankind. He was intoxicated by the idea of how powerful she would become, if she would only take the plunge and fully cannibalize her sister.

Thanatos was hoping that Mercy would give her sister a beautiful death, one for the legends. Those legendary deaths were few and far between. Most deaths were commonplace and of little note. Usually, the life of the dead overshadowed the details of their demise, but there were exceptions. There were legendary deaths, like Achilles. Everyone knew about his fatal flaw, his heel. One of the things he was most famous for was the circumstances of his death.

There were deaths on an epic scale, like Pompeii and the Titanic. These, and other large-scale deaths, were completely over the top in their sheer scale. The role of death, which Thanatos himself personified, was of greater importance in the storytelling than the individual dying. Thanatos had great hope that Mercy would bring such attention to death among the mortals. She'd done so well with the Elroy Shaw tragedy. Thanatos had more than a little salt in the game.

Mercy was his champion on Earth. She would have many names; Mercy the Ravenous, Mercy the Insatiable, Mercy the Bringer of Death. The Cult of Mercy would span the Earth in time, but not if these others interfered.

Of course, Phobetor didn't know that. If he did, he might have held his uncle Thanatos responsible, instead of throwing all the blame on Flynn's fragile shoulders. Blame never resolved anything, though.

Chimera

Phobetor needed answers. He sat on Maribelle's couch, seeking her counsel and guidance. She was not aware of Thanatos' role in it, but she had insight into why and how Mercy was able to consume Sympathy's essence. She even had a few ideas about where it might lead.

"So, tell me more about this vanishing twin syndrome," he said, leaning ever so slightly.

The current situation made Phobetor feel insecure. He didn't like the fact that Mercy, Sympathy, Charlotte, Flynn, and other lesser beings could pose any threat to his authority. Being in the company of a former lover was very soothing. He wondered if Maribelle still found him attractive. He stretched his arm out on the couch behind her and set it on her shoulder.

Maribelle giggled. It was conspicuous, and not very godlike. He was acting like an awkward teenager trying to cop a feel at a movie theater. She was not unmoved by his clumsy come-on. She felt a little flushed and tried her best not to look at him. She looked straight ahead as she launched into a technical discussion of how one twin might cannibalize another in utero.

"It is surprisingly common," Maribelle explained, shifting uncomfortably. "In fact, some scientists theorize as many as one in eight people started life as a twin. Usually, vanishing twin syndrome results in the complete absorption of one twin by the other. Of course, it usually happens in the womb, not just after the second birthday."

"Interesting," Phobetor purred.

He slid a little closer to her. Fetuses that absorbed their own twins were not the only thing he found interesting. He always found Maribelle fetching, partially due to the fact that she was his brother's consort. He coveted all things that belonged to Brash, including his woman. If he slept with her now, it wouldn't be the first time.

After learning of Brash's treachery, she'd sought comfort in Phobetor's arms many times. Of course, it was Phobetor himself who'd informed Maribelle of said treachery. It was he who had engineered the little break up. That was some fifteen years ago. Maribelle was fifty-two now and she was still a fine-looking woman.

Maribelle was flattered by his attempts at flirtation. Since murdering her son-in-law, eliminating her ex-husband, and alienating her daughter and all of her friends, she'd been lonely. She still dated, but she wasn't seeing anyone seriously. Most men were a bit put off by the bitterness and sarcasm she used to prevent herself from fully absorbing the extent of her fall from grace. She was a killer, repentant, but none-the-less, a cold-blooded murderer. That made her a little uptight on the social scene.

Phobetor was perfect and beautiful. He was always gorgeous. His tall and athletic build put even Brash to shame, and Brash had been very easy on the eyes. Brash was well-built and handsome, but Phobetor was absolutely intimidating. Of course, he didn't age, so he still looked as young and fresh as the day they met. It was tempting, but her previous dealings with the immortals left her a little wary.

Then there were her previous dealings with him, personally. It was just beginning to sink in, how wily his manipulation of her and the entire

Sisterhood of the Undoing had been. If Phobetor had influenced her to kill Flynn, it would have been for only one reason: to eliminate Brash. He insisted it was to free Maribelle from Brash's influence. She believed it was more than that alone if it was that at all. If he got rid of Brash, surely he wanted his kingdom. It was Charlotte's kingdom now. Would Phobetor try to take it from her?

Maribelle did not trust him. She would have to give him the brush off.

"I hate to tell you this," she chuckled, "but what you're doing there with your arm is a waste of time. I'm in menopause now. The way my hormones are fluctuating, if I even manage to have an orgasm, it usually gives me a migraine afterward."

"I can fix that," he offered sincerely.

Maribelle laughed nervously and began to fan herself. She could remember all of the creative ways he had for soothing her aches and pains with his fingers and tongue…and other body parts. She could only imagine what sort of plans he might have for remedying her headaches. He liked to be in control. When they had been together in the past, he prided himself in pleasuring her. Like Brash, he was very dominant. Unlike Brash, he demonstrated that mastery by handling her flesh the way a maestro works a fine instrument.

Brash and Phobetor both had other lovers, but when she was with Phobetor, he was thoroughly focused. He always made her feel like she was the only one. He would leave her in a state beyond the quivering delight of orgasm. Her skin would become so sensitive to the touch that pain began to blend with pleasure as he continued, pushing her beyond her boundaries. He drew every possible sensation from her until her fatigued flesh could endure no more. He was inexhaustible and insatiable. She tried desperately to shake off the memory of collapsing against his chest in a satiated little puddle of sexual satisfaction.

"Oh my," she deflected. "I think I'm having a hot flash."

Phobetor was not blind to her arousal, and he carefully brushed a hand against her thigh as he bent over her. He leaned across her lap to grab a box of tissue paper from the table on the other side of her body.

Handing it to her, he said, "You're wet. Here, maybe this will help." Then, without warning, he leaned in and stole a kiss. Maribelle couldn't prevent her body from responding to him, parting lips and arched back communicating an acceptance her words denied. It was all she could do to maintain her composure afterward, scooting away from him and straightening out her skirt.

The memory of having recently assaulted her son-in-law made his attempted dalliance with Maribelle all the more exciting for Phobetor due to the risk of her discovering his treachery. He'd flirted with Charlotte's naïve little consort several times before breaking him in two. He'd made Flynn trust him before devastating the boy. Thinking about it made him a little hard.

He had violated all of their weak, prissy little human boundaries. He broke all of the simpering lines of sentimental concern Flynn and Maribelle had tried to blackmail him into obeying. Did they think that he should have to act like a human to gain their friendship, their affection? No, he would not be bound by their rules. He would do as he saw fit.

But when Maribelle found out, she would not be pleased. Maribelle liked the bad boys, but only just so bad. She had her limits. She'd dumped Brash over the Sacrifice of the Innocents. Would she view this as harshly? Phobetor honestly didn't know. Humans were so complicated, with their morality and their delicious emotions.

He had to do it, to get the boy in line. Flynn was weak and would never be able to protect Maribelle's daughter or granddaughter. Phobetor wanted to rule Charlotte and Flynn for their own good. But Maribelle probably wouldn't understand. He wanted to bed her before she learned of the incident. Let her protest all she wanted. He was sure that she wanted him, just as she always had.

"Are you sure you don't want me to take care of your headache?" he asked. "I can also help you resolve this dampness that has suddenly come over you."

"I'll consider it. Perhaps some other time," she said prissily. She didn't trust him.

Phobetor smiled. The promise of future flirtations was interesting. She never could resist him in the past. He wasn't sure how long she could hold out now. But even if she did manage to resist him, he would enjoy the game. He remembered the delightful horror she experienced when he threatened to tear Flynn's heart out. That was followed closely by the delicious memory of Flynn staring at his own bleeding heart, less than an hour later. His smile took on a wicked edge of satisfaction. Even if she learned what he'd done and rejected him, he had to admit he would take some pleasure in her dread.

Maribelle did find him attractive. His long, tautly muscled body was very scantily clad. His clingy loincloth was a minimal concession to her human ideas of modesty and hid very little. He had chiseled features, high cheekbones, and the same long, feline eyes as Brash had had, the beautiful orange eyes of a lion, fringed in perfect, dark eyelashes.

Brash and Phobetor had eyes far more vibrant than the genetically watered-down brownish versions Charlotte and Faelyn inherited. They glittered like jewels. She remembered the way they looked in intimate moments, gazing hungrily over her flesh, watching her helpless, trembling. She had watched the way those eyes changed color when he came to orgasm. They went from tawny to crimson, red hot lava in an active volcano getting ready to explode. Sometimes they would explode in tandem, arms and legs entangled. When she lay in his arms afterwards, fragile and spent, he would gaze at her with a look so tender it might easily be mistaken for love. But she was not that foolish. She could not believe that a creature like Brash or Phobetor could ever truly love another. It must have been some trick of the light. She would never be fooled by those eyes again. Fortunately, she didn't have to look at his eyes or his mostly naked body on the couch beside her. She looked straight ahead and continued with the business at hand.

"Another type of absorption occurs in chimerism," she lectured. "The weaker twin is absorbed into and becomes a part of the stronger twin's body. Either of these outcomes is possible if Mercy consumes her twin. If the result were chimerism, it would be difficult to say whether or not Sympathy would remain as a conscious entity. She might just become a part of her greedier sister's genetic material, no more individually conscious than an earlobe.

"From what I can gather, not only from my research, but from having read Charlotte's notes or predictions, if this happens Sympathy will reincarnate as she was originally intended to. She'll be given a clean slate, like Brash and her sisters. Unfortunately, Mercy will become extremely powerful and dangerous."

Just then, the warning signal Phobetor set up to alert him to Mercy's activities went off. To Maribelle, it sounded like an alarm on a wristwatch.

"Speaking of the Mercy…" Phobetor said. "This alarm is set to go off if and when she kills a human. She's active again. I need to go look in on what's happening. We'll talk about this more later."

"Of course," Maribelle said. *Saved by the bell*, she thought to herself.

Hiding

Around the time Phobetor went back to Earth to see what Mercy was up to, Charlotte and Flynn were dozing off in their post-coital glow. After they woke up, the reality of spending the day in hiding in a very crammed space began to set in for Flynn.

"Why are we hiding in here?" Flynn asked.

"Phobetor can't know I have any power," Charlotte said. "He'll view me as a threat if he does. Nyx doesn't have time to babysit us. There is no chance we can stand up against Phobetor or any other Oneiroi right now. We are both too young, and besides, I'm human. Phobetor is all that is standing between us and his nine hundred and ninety seven remaining brothers. Have you noticed that your animal forms are very young?"

"Yes," Flynn said absently. "Why is that?"

"You are very young for a somnali," she said. "A thirty year old somnali is essentially an adolescent, but you're not a thirty year old somnali. As a human, you're thirty years old, but only six months old as a somnali. You're an infant. You won't have full adult control over yourself and your form until you're about two hundred years old. Be patient. You need to stay here twenty-four hours so he doesn't know you were healed. Otherwise, Phobetor will feel obligated to break your body repeatedly and very publicly so that I can't intervene."

Flynn yawned. He rolled over onto his belly so he could stretch his wings. He wasn't looking forward to being alone crammed up in this cubbyhole. Charlotte would wake up in the morning and have to leave. Humans slept about eight hours. He'd be here alone for an additional sixteen.

They were in tight quarters, so she nestled up against his side, under the crook of his arm. He was glad she was there. He adjusted his weight so that he was leaning on one hip, so she could slide in closer. When he turned his head to face her, she was looking at him, smiling.

"There is something about being human," he started, "you, being fully human. There is something about it that makes you want to be tender towards me, isn't there?"

"It's not just that," she said. "You died. I had to experience your death as a human woman. I had to mourn your loss. I'm always a little afraid of losing you now. Can you understand?"

"I understand very well," he told her. "It took me a long time to figure out how to get to you, how to see you. You could say in a way, I mourned too. I just wanted to let you know that I enjoy being with you. I'm glad we're still together, and I don't regret anything."

Charlotte nodded. She liked the way he was brushing against her bare skin with his wings. They were gently fluttering. She knew it was a subconscious gesture on his part, like a puppy wagging its tail. It was a thing that somnali did when they were happy. She reached over and patted him on the ass.

"I'm happy you're okay with the way things turned out," she said seriously. "You didn't have a lot of choices. I guess in many ways, your choices remain limited."

Flynn thought about it very carefully, and he said, "I like the way you always ask me, Charlotte. You never force me. You never break me. You never take anything from me, you just request it. You ask. And you let me give myself to you. I love being able to give myself to you repeatedly. I love you and I get to stay with you forever. Why wouldn't I be happy?"

"Stop it," she said. "You're making me all wet."

He pulled her a little closer to him. The idea that he had the power to sexually tempt her was very appealing to him in ways that he couldn't quite understand. He whispered in her ear, "When you healed me I could feel your power unleashed, coursing through my flesh. It thrills me, the thought of you using my body as a conduit. You should perfect your ability to wield your power through me. You should practice using me as your instrument. I'm more than willing."

"I must," she said. "You're my weapon. I'll need to wield you eventually. But it's dangerous. We need to be careful."

"You mean like Raziel in the video game *Soulcaliber*?" he asked.

Charlotte laughed. "Well, you did kind of look like him after Phobetor finished shredding your wings and tearing your throat out. But he skipped the whole ripping your jaw off thing. I wouldn't remind him. Do you think he's a fan?"

"No," Flynn said determinedly. "But will I be a weapon like that?"

"I won't be shoving you into a sword," Charlotte said lightly. "I'll be shoving you into me. That sounds like fun, right?"

He smiled and kissed her. "You know how much I love being in you."

They returned to a game of identifying constellations among the stars in the blanket of night that was installed on the ceiling. It was what they had been doing to past the time. After a long while, Charlotte turned to Flynn and took his hand.

"I don't know how to tell you this," she began, "but you should want more from your lover than just not to force you. That's very low on the hierarchy of considerate behavior towards your love. Of course I don't force you. I would never force you. What Mercy did to you was rape."

He frowned. "I know, but I don't want to talk about it. I don't want to talk about her. I told Phobetor he was worse than her just before he kicked my ass."

"He assaulted you," Charlotte said plainly. "He beat you so brutally that if you were human, you would have died. You're immortal, so he kept pounding you into the ground after he ripped out your heart and tore out your throat."

Flynn nodded "He did it because I compared him to Mercy. It made him furious."

"He hates her," Charlotte said simply. "He also thinks she's very much beneath him. He not only thinks she is weaker, he thinks she is amoral. Let me explain it in terms you can understand. Phobetor is ordered neutral. Mercy is chaotic evil. His purpose isn't evil; people need nightmares to work things out. However, he doesn't want the purpose of nightmares diluted. Brash, Mercy, and my other siblings corrupted the process. Phobetor wants to correct that and restore balance. Unfortunately, he's also a control freak. My dad died, and now Phobetor's on a big power trip. He wants to add my kingdom to his. The most expedient way to do it is to control you."

She crawled out from under Flynn's arm and stretched a little. It was too tiny in this fissure for two people to be comfortable without being almost on top of each other. Charlotte decided that was a good idea. She crawled upon his back and laid her head in the space between his wings. She wrapped her arms around his waist. She liked the way her bare skin felt against his.

Flynn murmured happily. "I like it when you're on top."

Charlotte laughed. She crossed her fingers together and made a pillow and set her head down on his back. She said, "That's a good thing. I love you. I want Phobetor to keep his fucking hands off you. I may be human, but I still have some power. Tell Phobetor I said that we're both willing to swear fealty to him, but he has to agree not to hurt you anymore."

"I don't want you to give away your kingdom for me," Flynn protested.

"I am still the heir apparent," Charlotte said. "It is still my choice. We aren't strong enough to fight him. Just do as I ask."

Flynn shook his head. "I won't do it. I'd rather be broken a thousand times than to give away your power. It's your inheritance, your birthright. Let him do his worst. I can take it."

Charlotte frowned. "I'll try to respect your opinion here and think about what you're saying, but I really don't like it. I love you and I don't like to see you getting hurt."

She could tell that Flynn was getting angry. His wings quivered with barely contained rage. The muscles in his back and shoulders grew taut and strained.

"I think you are folding your hand too easily," he grumbled. "Phobetor told me he knows we have powerful allies. Nyx has intervened on our behalf before. She might again. I think he is just hoping that you'll cave in if he hurts your precious little consort."

She kissed the little hairs on the back of his neck. "But you are precious. Like I said, I lost you once. I don't think I can bear it again."

"And he knows that," Flynn complained. "He can't kill me. He threatened to, but I don't think he has the power. Phobetor is bad ass, but he's not Zeus. He's never turned anyone into a constellation of stars. I bet Nyx could do that, but Phobetor? He's bluffing."

Charlotte started grooming his wings. Flynn only knew that was what she was doing because he remembered it from when he was a pigeon. He preened himself, picking away the dirt and parasites. He recalled being rebuffed by Phobetor for his attempt at social grooming. Preening, or feather grooming, was a way to not only keep the feathers clean but keep them aligned properly for flight. In humans, and other primates, grooming was a bonding activity. He realized that she was doing it to diffuse his anger. Her fingers in his wings and hair made him feel relaxed and a little drowsy.

"He's not just faking," Charlotte warned. "Look what he did to you."

"He beat the shit out of me," Flynn said. "But other than a bruised ego, I'm basically fine now. He deceived me. He got at me through my vanity. I should have known better."

"What do you mean?" Charlotte asked. She was still grooming him. Flynn was grateful. It wasn't easy for him to say what he had to say.

"I didn't want to accept my role in things," he sighed. "I'm your sidekick, Charlie. You're the hero here. If I hadn't felt, you know, that I had to prove how independent I was, he wouldn't have had the excuse to beat the crap out of me. He used my insecurities to manipulate me. He pretended to be nice until he got everything he wanted. I gave him the location of the twins. I helped him get access to your mother. Then when he didn't need me anymore, he just used me. He used me to influence you, don't you see?"

Charlotte shrugged. Flynn almost giggled because he could feel her body movement on his back. "So like the *Women in Refrigerators Syndrome*," she said. "Maybe, sort of, I would say, except you are actually more powerful than you were as a human. So maybe *Dead Men Defrosting*, but nonetheless you are being tortured to have an effect on me. Let's go old school and say, like a whipping boy."

Both of them were huge comic book fans. *Women in Refrigerators Syndrome* was the name of a comic book and television trope in which female associates of superheroes were violently killed or maimed in order to spur the male hero into action. *Dead Men Defrosting* was a secondary trope involving male sidekicks, who were killed likewise to affect the hero. The difference being that the guys usually come back just as strong, or stronger.

A whipping boy was not a fictional character. It was an actual role in human history. In 15th Century England, a whipping boy was an official scapegoat who would be punished for princely misbehavior. Princes were considered to be part of a divinely appointed bloodline. Common people such as tutors were responsible for the day to day training and upbringing of a young royal. They were not allowed to lay hands upon him, so a young playmate and companion was punished in his stead. The two were usually close friends. The guilty conscience of the prince at witnessing his friend's punishment for his own misdeeds was hoped to be a motivator.

"I think whipping boy sounds right," Flynn said. "Somnus and Nyx would intervene immediately if Phobetor laid a hand on you. He is punishing me to gain your compliance. Your mother's obedience as well, since she feels so guilty about killing me. He needs her help to defeat the twins. I suggest you don't let him blackmail you."

"Really? So let him just beat the shit out of you whenever he feels like it?" Charlotte asked.

"Yes," Flynn said. "That's exactly what I'm saying. He's just trying to manipulate you. Even Prometheus didn't have to suffer forever.

Eventually, Heracles rescued him. And Phobetor isn't Zeus. He isn't as powerful as Somnus or Nyx. He's just playing chicken with my body."

"You're a tough little shit," Charlotte said, smacking him on the butt. "But I don't think so. I can't let him use you as a punching bag. Besides, if he feels the need to "discipline" you again, his violence towards you will increase. I know my uncle. We'll figure something else out. In the meantime, can you at least promise not to provoke him?"

Flynn nodded. "Definitely, I've learned my lesson. I spoke too freely because I thought he was my friend. He's not my friend. I won't speak to him so casually again. In fact, I think I'll avoid him."

Mealtime

While all of this was occurring, five hours went by in Grants Pass, Oregon. Cynthia was currently receiving treatment for pneumonia at Three Rivers Community Hospital. Around the time Phobetor and Flynn left the roof of the camper to go visit Maribelle Metaxas, little Cyn was being seen by the triage nurse. She made the determination to have the child admitted immediately for treatment.

By the time twenty-six year old Maribelle Metaxas was picking up three and a half year old Flynn Keahi and setting him beside her on the couch, two year and two day old Cynthia was being treated with IV fluids and antibiotics. On the other side of the curtain, her twin sister Candice was being examined by an intern given the contagious nature of the condition.

By the time Phobetor crushed Flynn's heart and tore it from his chest, Cyn was receiving a chest X-Ray while Candy and her parents and grandparents were being issued a preventative course of oral antibiotics. This was also around the time that the twins were separated, to help protect Candy from the disease.

Thomas and Rebecca were also separated from Cyn. They were in their seventies, and pneumonia was a bigger risk for older people and infants, but that wasn't the only reason they left. Becky Carter had bone cancer and was on an oral chemotherapy drug. That was the reason for all of that medicinal marijuana she consumed. Pneumonia was very dangerous for people on any kind of chemo. The elder Carters were also glad to get a little space from at least one of their two creepy little grandchildren.

They took Candy to a nearby diner, and the distance did little Cynthia a world of good. Although she'd been admitted for bacterial pneumonia, the weaker twin was already starting to recover. Away from her food source, Candy was beginning to hunger.

She didn't need her sister to orchestrate her first tactile hallucination. She was seated at the counter with her grandparents, where she had an excellent view of the staff. Miguel, the fry cook with the vat of hot grease cooking a metal basket full of fries was annoyed by the invisible fly on his neck. He kept slapping at it.

Miguel was so busy smacking himself on the neck that he didn't notice Liam, the burly prep cook passing behind him. He accidentally smacked Liam in the face. Liam, a veteran of both the foster care and the prison system, did not think before punching Miguel in the back of his head. It was an instinctive, protective reaction. Miguel didn't intend to rotate on his heel and hit Liam square in the chest with a basket full of hot greasy fries, fresh out of the cooker.

Maybe if Candy wasn't there, feeding off of and feeding into their rage, the fight wouldn't have escalated. As it was, Liam struck Miguel with a left hook to the jaw. Shocked, Miguel dropped his basket full of hot fries on the floor. Melissa, a waitress who happened to be passing through the kitchen before this brawn broke out, slipped in the oily mess and was hit in the back of the head by Liam's oncoming fist. She fell square into Miguel's chest, knocking him into a vat of hot oil.

The scalding burn on his face didn't kill him, but at 6'3 Melissa was a very big girl. Unfortunately, when all five hundred and thirty-six pounds of her landed on Miguel, the edge of the vat impacted his neck with enough force to crush his larynx. Unable to move, Miguel began to suffocate in the oil.

Melissa wasn't a young gal, either. At fifty-eight years of age, twenty-one years at her present weight had taken its toll on her heart. Seeing his mouth move helplessly in the oil, she rolled Miguel over in the vat so he could breathe. Seeing his deep-fried eyeballs and bubbling, crisped skin freaked her out, sending her into cardiac arrest.

By the time Charlotte was working her healing mojo on Flynn, a riveted Phobetor was knee-deep into a conversation about the Carter twins with Maribelle. They had been chatting for about forty minutes when the alarm Phobetor set to alert him of any Candy and Cyn related paranormal activity went off.

Five hours had passed since Phobetor left the roof of the RV.

Timothy and Alice had just left the hospital and rented a hotel room in Grants Pass, Oregon, having been informed that Cynthia's stay would be at least a week long. They had decided it was best to allowed Tim's parents to continue their slow and meandering way down to San Diego in their recreational vehicle.

They were just checking in when their parents called on a cell phone from the diner. Around this time, the ambulance paramedics began to arrive for unfortunate Miguel and Melissa. Liam received a different sort of emergency vehicle with flashing blue lights piloted by a pair of police officers.

Miguel died before the ambulance arrived. Melissa passed away later, in the same hospital where Cyn was being treated. Most likely, her instinctual feeding on Candy's victim had something to do with Melissa's failure to recover. Liam was later convicted on manslaughter charges.

The Undoing

These were perilous times. Charlotte wanted to get as much information to Flynn as she could before she was awakened by her alarm clock. She stayed with him as long as she could.

"If somnali aren't as powerful as Oneiroi," Flynn asked, "why are Mercy and Sympathy even a problem?"

"They are twins," Charlotte said. "They can combine their powers, in much the same way as you and I will be able to do. They are also much older than you or I. Mercy is ruthless and she may consider taking Sympathy's life and her powers completely, making herself as powerful as any Oneiroi. If so, she would be a real contender for my father's post. She is a threat to me and you as well as to Phobetor."

Flynn shivered. "Would she really do that to her own sister?"

"Phobetor is afraid she will," Charlotte said. "That is why he was at home savaging your flesh, to take out his frustrations rather than interfering any further with the killing spree. He'd rather see fifty more humans die than unleash an Oneiroi-powered Mercy on the world."

"He did talk to his priestess," Flynn said. "I should say your mother. He's the one who wrote the Rites of Undoing. He's the one who convinced your mother to kill me. He wrote all of those purification rituals so that you… so that I…"

Charlotte nodded. "So, I had guessed. I am the Oracle of Somnus, after all. When I wrote the second book, I was given some indication of who the author of the original was."

"What about this one?" Flynn asked. "Where are you getting the information from?"

"I suspect Somnus," Charlotte said. "After all, I am his oracle. Only those directly in my bloodline, my forebears, can influence me. That would be Somnus, Pasithea, Nyx, Erebus, Chaos, and of course, Brash if he were still alive. My uncles and aunts and the like have no access. Phobetor must have used the hands of someone from his direct line to write the original."

"Interesting," Flynn said. "What do you think Phobetor is up to now?"

"Consulting with the Priestess of the Undoing," Charlotte said. "They've known one another for quite some time. I'm pretty sure they had an affair right after she broke up with my father."

"Really?" Flynn was incredulous. "How could she be with him? He's so cruel."

"I know it's hard to believe," Charlotte said, "but in some ways, many ways, he was better to her than my father was. My father was a liar. Phobetor never lied to her. Not once, about anything. Neither of them was faithful – like Zeus, they are both philanderers. But Phobetor never bullshitted her about it. He's the one who told her about the Slaughter of the Innocents."

"Slaughter of the Innocents?" Flynn asked.

"A blood sacrifice of unborn children and pregnant women he performed in order to make it possible for him to appear in a physical body and impregnate my mother," Charlotte said.

"That's… yikes!" Flynn said. "I think you told me but I tried to block out that memory."

"Phobetor told her. That's why she left my dad," Charlotte shrugged. "So she's crying on this guy's shoulder, and Phobetor is a dick, right? He wanted my father's kingdom and everything that came with it under his control. On the other hand, he resented the blood sacrifices and the encroachments into the physical world. He doted on mother like a prize pony. She represented everything he meant to take from Brash. If he was in charge, it would be better, much better for humanity. I don't think he's exactly evil, but even if he is, he's the lesser of two evils."

"You will tell your mom what he did to me, right?" Flynn said. "And that he's blackmailing you?"

"Definitely," Charlotte said. "My alarm is going to go off soon. Listen, I've been thinking – that spell I did, the one that lets you feel what I feel?"

Flynn carefully rolled over and caught Charlotte on his belly. He wanted to see her face before she left. As he twisted over, he caught her by putting both of his hands on her perky behind. She was laying on top of him now. Her body weight pressed her breasts softly against his chest. Her hair fell onto his face, tickling him.

"Yes, "Flynn said. "I was able to experience the same tactile sensations as you did. Once I tasted, too. You put your fingers in your mouth and I could taste what was on your skin." He didn't mention what he tasted on her fingers but he flushed a bit when he mentioned it. The stirring in his loins caused by the memory caused a physical reaction, one she could probably feel pressing against her upper thigh.

"Cool," she said casually, ignoring his erection. "I was thinking that since you are stuck down here for a while, I could try seeing if we can use that particular ability to communicate. I don't mean sexually, though. Regular things, it's just an experiment. If I can connect with you while I am on Earth, I might not have to remain completely powerless in the waking world."

"With the twins heading down I-5, I would be a lot more comfortable if you did have some power," Flynn said. "I can't exactly protect you as a cat, or a little rat dog. All of the animal forms I can make are very small."

"I noticed," Charlotte said. "You might want to ask why you're able to shift. You shouldn't be able to. A few Oneiroi can shift at will, but most lower-level beings such as human hybrids and somnali can't do it without blood sacrifices unless they are from Phobetor's bloodline. "

Flynn grumbled. "Seriously, fuck him right now. I just want to protect you and the baby from the twins. What the fuck am I going to do on Earth? Scratch them? Bite them? Give them fleas? Yea, maybe I could get myself infected with rabies and transmit it. I'm basically saying that I'm not very powerful. But if you can tap into whatever power I am storing for you, you should do it. I'll tell you know how it goes, later."

"Theoretically, you should be able to occupy the same body with me," she said. "Not exactly like possession, but sort of. It would be the same thing that Nyx did with Howard at my birthday party. You would be a passenger in my body. We could be powerful together. It will take a lot of practice, though. I just don't want to…"

Charlotte never finished the sentence. Somewhere in Suisun, her alarm clock went off and she was awakening into her world, out of his. Now that she wasn't watching, he hugged himself. The room reeked of the sex sweat and spilled blood in the soiled furs. The blood had smelled like raw hamburger at first. Now, it was starting to get a little gamey. Flynn decided to clean up a little before his wife came back home.

Matched Sets

On a microcellular level, Cyn and Candy exchanged genetic material when they bonded to one another psychically. This connection allowed them to act together in concert, attacking others. When the act was over, Cynthia generously returned Candy's essence to her, but Candy greedily retained all that she could of Cyn. That was why Cyn was growing so thin and weak. It was also why Candy looked more and more like her sister.

She wasn't just consuming her. She was becoming one with her.

Charlotte and Flynn were practicing a different kind of exchange. Charlotte was perfecting her ability to use their bond to transmit sensory information to Flynn from the human world. He was learning to feel with her skin. During their long night together, they both decided to see if that trick could be used for other purposes. If it could, then asleep or awake, they would be in constant communication with one another. Flynn had nothing to do all day except stay in his hiding place. They decided to use it as an opportunity to experiment. She was sending, and he was receiving. She held and touched people and objects. She picked up Faelyn and passed it on. She gave Hannah a hug and shared it with Flynn. She painted and cleaned her brushes. Flynn received and was delighted to find he understood what he was experiencing.

Like Cynthia and Candice, Somnus and Thanatos were twins. Somnus was beginning to suspect his twin brother's involvement in the unfolding drama. The failure of two somnali to reincarnate happened to involve Thanatos' two favorite grand-nieces. If that weren't evidence enough, there was little privacy in the Demos Oneiroi. Someone was always overhearing something. Nyx had overheard a certain conversation that occurred near the river Lethe just before Mercy and Sympathy went on their journey.

"Why did you do it?" Somnus asked his brother, sitting on a picnic blanket by the river Lethe. The blanket was red and white checked. A large wicker picnic basket full of snacks and sandwiches sat upon it, and there was a white oversized plate laden with fresh fruits. They didn't require food for sustenance, but they enjoyed it. Thanatos finished his grapes before answering.

"Of all of your grandchildren," he said, "Mercy was my favorite. She is brazen, wild, and free. She takes what she likes and does what she will the way that the beasts do. She doesn't hold back, that one."

"If this is about Mercy," Somnus asked, "why send Sympathy with her?"

"She might get lonely," Thanatos shrugged. "She might get hungry. Either way it goes, two are more powerful than one. I hear Phobetor is after her. Won't she need the extra power?"

Somnus gasped. "But that's her sister! How can you think of such an awful thing?"

He shrugged. "Her appetites have always been voracious. It will be interesting to see how things proceed, no matter which course she chooses. I see that Brash's other girl, the human one… she shares herself with her consort. It is odd."

"Nyx gave them the choice," Somnus said. "They are unhappy without each other."

"But you know that boy would let her consume every ounce of him if she didn't have the self-control to stop," Thanatos claimed. "Sympathy, I don't think she would stop Mercy, either. I think she loves her sister. She relies on her."

"Then what a cruel game you play," Somnus observed. "Mercy will never return Sympathy's affection or show concern, I know that girl. It is truly beyond her."

Thanatos didn't answer right away, because he was eating half a sandwich, roast beef on rye bread. He ate it slowly, and would not speak until it was done. Finally, he licked his fingers.

"Do you think," he supposed, "the sandwich would taste as well if the beef were still screaming? It is a cow, is it not?"

"What an absurd question," Somnus answered. He picked up the other half of the sandwich without thinking, and began to eat it. It was quite delicious.

"I think Mercy would prefer it if her meals screamed," Thanatos said with a laugh. "Whether it perishes before or during our consumption, we all eat life. In one way or another we gorge our bellies on other entities, plant or animal. So why do you think that makes Mercy particularly evil?"

Grandma

Rebecca looked on in horror at the two-body pile up in the kitchen. She watched in dismay as the ambulances arrived for Miguel and Melissa, and the police picked up Liam. She couldn't prove it, but suspected that her granddaughter, Candy, had something to do with it. She and her sister Cyn were always around when bad things happened. Becky no longer believed it could just be coincidence. There were too many incidents, always precipitated by the twins doling out the same creepy stare. With one of the sisters in the hospital now, sick as hell, Becky had hoped that the series of sinister events would come to an end. She thought it took both twins to make scary shit happen. She thought the separation would create at least a break in the paranormal activity. Well, no such fucking luck.

"We need to get out of here," she told her husband, Tom. "We seriously need to go,"

Tom was sitting at the counter with his mouth hanging open. Uneaten spaghetti pasta dangled from the end of a fork suspended before his shell-shocked visage. This absolutely could not be happening, he thought. It was like the grisliest episode ever of the Three Stooges had just unfolded before his eyes.

"Sure," he croaked. "Let me get the bill."

Due to recent events, his throat felt extremely dry. Acid was beginning to erupt from his stomach. It burned the inside of his esophagus. Gruesome diner tragedies had a very negative effect on his Gastro-esophageal reflux disease, or GERD. In the back of his mind was his doctor's admonitions against tomato-based sauces. Although he answered Becky in the affirmative, he was too stunned to leave his seat. He didn't even put his fork down.

"Not just this diner. I mean we should leave town," Becky hissed under her breath. She looked around to see if the child was paying attention. Fortunately for her, Candy was enraptured by the cavalcade of gurneys and emergency personnel currently exiting the kitchen.

"The other kid is in the hospital," she said quickly. "The child has pneumonia. Tim and Alice aren't going to be going anywhere anytime soon. We can leave, though. We have a valid reason to go. We are on our way to see Tommy Jr. They have a valid reason to stay and take care of their child. We need to get while the going is good, because something is very wrong in this town."

At that very instant, Candy swiveled her head to the left to look at her grandmother. Her neck moved so slowly, in undetectable increments, and with perfect precision. Her head seemed to glide through space. The innocent, childlike smile she wore a second earlier gave way to a wicked sneer. As Becky watched, her granddaughter's eyes appeared to rapidly fill with a thick, dark fluid until the whites and irises were swallowed up by the inky blackness.

Becky gulped, and quickly scooted her chair back several inches in shock. Just before her chair bumped into a man crossing behind her, she grabbed hold of herself and steadied her nerves. The child's game was one of hallucinations and deception. She only hoped that forewarned truly was forearmed.

"Tom," she said irritably, refusing to let her voice register any fear, "we need to go. Get the check. It's a madhouse in here."

The wait staff was calmly asking patrons to finish their meals so that they could close down. The sign on the door had already been rotated to the closed position. A gentle young waitress arrived and offered to help Tom by taking his bill and credit card over to the cash register.

Candy turned away from her grandmother again, facing the door so she could watch the exiting paramedics. From the corner of her eye,

Becky noted that the toddler wore a messy, goopy face covered with fresh strawberries and berry syrup. Chunks of fruit suspended in sugary, gelatinous liquid fell from the child's chin. The baby was gleefully gazing at the exiting gurney upon which Miguel's corpse was propped. Her once innocent grin became a ghastly gash of gore and horrid intention.

Becky probably only imagined it, the gradual change in appearance that turned sweet strawberry succor into a river of flesh-clotted blood. Maybe the baby was making her see things this way. It suddenly looked as though Candy had made a recent meal of human flesh.

By the time Tom came to his senses and wiped the grime off his granddaughter's face, his wife was a wreck. She was sitting in the corner, shaking uncontrollably, and looking away from the baby.

"I don't think we should leave," Tom said, zombie like, bending down to pick up the baby. "Tim is on shore leave for three whole months. We can wait here a week, for the little one to get better. We need to be here, for Tim and Alice and these precious girls."

Becky shook her head. There was definitely something wrong with him. His behavior hearkened back to the victims of certain sci-fi films that came out in the seventies when she was in her prime. The *Stepford Wives* and *Invasion of the Body Snatchers* were both about humans being replaced by inhuman doppelgangers. The first was about robots, the second aliens. Tom acted like either, or.

She was thoroughly spooked but decided that it was in her best interest to remain calm. She needed to pretend like he didn't notice that anything was wrong. Avoiding detection by the Bad Seed and her new Stepford Grandpa seemed key to her survival.

Human

Charlotte's weekday mornings all started the same way. She took a quick shower and grabbed a cup of coffee. She woke the baby and gave her a bath. She dressed herself then she dressed her child. They both walked across the yard to Hannah and Shelby's house and knocked on the sliding glass door. One of the ladies let them in, and they all had breakfast together.

Today, Shelby answered the door. She quickly picked up the baby and sat her on her hip. She always adored Faelyn. Like many an auntie, it was seeing her friend with a kid that ultimately made Shelby feel like she wanted one of her own.

"You need to talk to your husband," Shelby said sharply. "Both of the kids are in here singing Red Hot Chili Peppers songs, and I know I didn't teach them that. If I hear the phrase "ay o" one more time I swear… I thought he was supposed to teach her the alphabet?"

Charlotte laughed. She knew that on at least one occasion, Flynn had visited Shelby. Hannah and Daniel also reported seeing him once or twice.

"I'm trying to see if I can transmit sensory information to him. Specifically, tactile information. Do you want to see if you can send him a hug?"

"How do I do that?" she asked.

"Just hug me," Charlotte answered. "You should try it. Trust me, he really needs a hug."

"Sure, why not?" Shelby said. Without removing the baby from her hip, she gave Charlotte a big bear hug. Shelby was three inches taller, but she didn't have to bend over to hug Charlie. In his room, alone, Flynn received the affectionate gesture as intended.

The women went inside and sat down to breakfast.

More and more, Charlotte found herself keeping secrets from her friends. It was fine for them to know the basics, but too much information might get them in trouble. It was bad enough the way Flynn had to constantly suffer because of who she was.

If they hadn't known her, Mike and Tess, and Shelby's mad roommate Cory, probably would not have died. Elroy and Cory were both souls predisposed to murder, certainly. Without Mercy, though, they were like a bomb with no detonator. Mercy was the wick, the spark, the fire that started those explosions. She selected those victims from among her friends, on purposes.

When they were both alive, Charlotte and Flynn used to sit around in their crowded little apartment playing video games, reading comic books, and talking about movies. One of the things they liked to talk about was the roles women were relegated to in so many of these stories. They were helpless victims, to be rescued. Would Lois Lane even need Superman to rescue her if she wasn't always being put into danger because of knowing him?

She put Flynn in that kind of danger all the time just by being involved with him, just by being who she was. Now that she was human and he was somnali, she thought things would be different. In many ways, they weren't/ He might be physically more powerful than she was, but she was the heir apparent to Brash's kingdom. She thought about giving up that inheritance or accepting a reduced role in things. Even that idea – pledging her fealty to Phobetor in order to protect Flynn – seemed to make him feel emasculated.

When she was demisomnali, she really didn't give a shit. Everything seemed so simple. Her role was preordained, so was his. Now, things were different. Phobetor broke Flynn's body and turned him into a living *Woman in a Refrigerator* trope. In the comics, the hero was supposed to get angry – to get revenge. If she was somnali, or even demisomnali, she might have wanted that fight. Now, she was human. She was a mother. She had to worry about not only threats to her friends, but to her child. It was that maternal concern, for her child, her friends, and even her lover that made her think the best strategy was to back down.

She had a lot on her mind. It showed.

"What's wrong?" Hannah finally asked. "You've been staring out at nothing, chewing on your toast like a cow on its cud. Something is up."

Charlotte just sighed and set her toast down.

Shelby raised an eyebrow. "Ten bucks says it's about Flynn."

"Yea, I haven't seen the cat around lately," Hannah remarked. "What is going on with your boy?"

"One of my uncles," she said carefully, leaving out the name and other details, "he kind of mislead Flynn into thinking he was a friend. He let him think he had freedom and choices, and a job, and things I guess Flynn wanted as a human man. Kind of macho bullshit, I guess. I guess part of Flynn doesn't like always being up under a woman. Then this asshole took it all away. He pulled the rug out from under him in one swift and devastating blow. It was unbelievably cruel."

"And how is Flynn taking it?" Shelby asked.

"He's stuck back under me," Charlotte said. "I mean, I had to rescue him, and look at me. I'm human. It sounds like he felt conflicted about being rescued by a woman when I was still a demigod. Now he has to be rescued by a human woman."

"From what I remember, he likes being under you both literally and metaphorically," Shelby suggested. "Individuals in couples sometimes have conflicting emotions, and most newlyweds don't lose as much of their independence as he has. His ability to interact with his friends is very limited. It would be normal for him to try to make new friends, where he lives. It's hard for him to visit us."

"He's been through a lot of shit," Hannah said. "He's one of the most resilient people I know. I think maybe you should focus on his strengths, not his weaknesses. Most people couldn't recover from what he's been through. If he is having some adjustment issues, I wouldn't take it personally."

"Yeah, I think I'd been a drooling pile of mush if I had to die two or three times," Shelby said with a shrug. "He's a strong person. He just brushes himself off and keeps on stepping."

Charlotte didn't look convinced.

"Look," Hannah said, "if any woman we knew had been through half of what he's been through, we would definitely be telling her she was strong and a survivor. He would have to be traumatized. He's survived rape, assault, battery, attempted homicide. If that happened to a woman, would we be telling her to just crawl up under a big strong man? Maybe you should try not to let his gender cloud your judgment. A lot of what he is feeling has nothing to do with you. You shouldn't take it personally any more than a guy should take it personally if his old lady takes self defense classes after being assaulted."

Charlotte shrugged and sipped her cold coffee. "Okay, that's fair enough."

Hannah wasn't giving up. "You ever read this one strip in the Oatmeal comic, *How the Male Angler Fish Get Completely Screwed*?"

Shelby tossed her hand over her mouth. "Oh man… I've seen it! That's totally messed up."

Warily, Charlotte said, "No, I haven't. So…"

"So let me just tell you about the life cycle of a male angler fish," Hannah said. "I don't need the comic; you can read it later. The short story is that the males are essentially parasites, totally helpless and incapable of fending for themselves until they attach to a female. At first, he feeds off her. Then, she begins to absorb him until there is nothing left. Well, almost nothing left. All that is left is a pair of balls that now belong to the newly hermaphroditic female. You see, they are a chimera species. He just dies and becomes a part of her."

Charlotte remembered Flynn once telling her that he had a fantasy about her consuming him completely. Thinking about it made her feel sick to the stomach. She dropped a fork full of scrambled eggs back down on her plate.

"So, what is your point, Hannah?" she asked.

"So that is damn near what the normal course of an intimate relationship between a female somnali and a male human is like," Hannah said. "It's where Mercy was headed, wasn't it? She wanted to consume him until there was nothing left. Isn't that right?"

"Yea, basically," Charlotte said. "In another month or two, he would have died."

"But you were half human," Hannah said. "You wanted more than a meal and some sperm, right? Your love probably wasn't perfectly human. I am just saying that even then, you cared about him. You always wanted a more symbiotic. Something more equal, right? And you got that."

"Yea," Charlotte admitted. "That's true." She absentmindedly picked at the food on her plate. After a moment, she looked over at her daughter. Faelyn was happily eating lukewarm oatmeal and bananas. She didn't seem terribly concerned with the adult conversation. She didn't know they were discussing her conception.

Charlie thought about it, though. Many demisomnali were just as ruthless as their somnali counterparts. Many would have used him to perform the fertility rituals, and then continued to consume him until nothing was left. Like Mercy, she had had the power to drug him. She could have tampered with his hormones and her pheromones until he invited such a death. He would have begged her to devour him. On the night of Faelyn's conception, he nearly did.

Charlotte wasn't even trying to compel him to want such a thing. It was just the natural interaction of the chemicals in their bodies; he wanted it because it was part of what was required for them to procreate. It was instinctive, like the male angler fish with its sexual suicide. The worst part of it was that he would have died happy. Or maybe that wasn't the worst. She would have been equally satisfied by his sacrifice. In fact, her happiness wouldn't have worn off until several hours later. Then she would have been struck by a human emotion of loss. She would have been filled with regret and remorse. She would have missed him. Mercy had no such compunctions and would have just remembered the pleasure she would have derived from devouring him.

"Do you think you're going to hurt him somehow?" Shelby asked.

"No, I don't," Charlotte said. "I would never do anything I thought was bad for him."

"Well, do you think someone else is going to hurt him because of you?" she asked.

"Of course I do," Charlotte said. She had a hard time keeping her voice from breaking. "People are always hurting him because of me. My uncle just… I can't even say. He hurt him very badly, though. He did it just to get me to do something."

Hannah frowned. "I can see how that would be very upsetting for both of you. Well, for what it's worth, I don't think that has always been the case. Mercy hurt a lot of people. It was her nature. Like you said, she would have killed him. What your mother did was the desperate act of a desperate woman."

"I think your mom maybe hurt him to protect us," Shelby was ashamed to admit. "All of your friends were being killed off. Things were escalating. I'm just… I'm sorry for what she did, but it's not your fault."

Charlotte shook her head. It felt like her fault.

"Maybe you should let Hannah hug you guys," Shelby suggested. "Hannah, Charlotte's trying to see if she can get Flynn to feel what she feels. Isn't that trippy?"

"Well, I've done it before," Charlotte said.

Hannah gave her a weird look. "So, he feels with your skin?"

"Yea," Charlotte said. "I mean, I have to intend for that to happen. He said he could taste what I tasted, too. But I must focus, you know, on wanting him to."

Hannah shrugged. "You guys are a couple of freaks. You know that, right?" She walked up behind Charlotte and gave her a big hug anyway. "Is that okay?"

Charlotte turned around and hugged her back. "I think another one, just to be sure."

Faelyn and Kyle saw the hugs going around, and they both reached their little arms up towards their respective parents in anticipation. Charlotte leaned over and hugged Faelyn in her highchair. Shelby picked Kyle up out of his booster seat and carried him over.

"You better hug the kids two or three times," Shelby said. "Toddler hugs have amazing curative qualities. I'm sure that you and Flynn will both feel better in no time."

Grandpa

Tom and Becky had spent the night in their motorhome, parked on the side of the trucker motel Tim and Alice picked out the night before. Becky had been hard pressed to talk Tom out of spending the night in the hotel room with their son and daughter-in-law and their little spawn from hell. They were about twenty miles from Portland when she first noticed the hairy scary shit that seemed to follow in the wake of the twins.

At first, she thought that their parents didn't notice it because they were blinded by paternal and maternal love. Most parents thought their two-year-olds could do no wrong. Even if they did something bad, it was adorable.

But following the recent mental zombification of her husband, Becky was attributing it to another source. Apparently, the kids were able to somehow influence their loved ones. They influenced their victims as well, of course. It was just not in such a long-term fashion.

Tom was in the tiny RV kitchen now, preparing a peanut butter and jelly sandwich. It was an atypical breakfast for most, but not him. He'd been eating peanut butter and jelly with a glass of milk most mornings for many years. In a lot of ways, he was acting normally.

Only one thing was wrong.

Every time she bought up the idea that something was wrong with the kids, Tom acted like she was losing her mind. That would have been less strange if he hadn't been concurring with her opinion for most of the trip.

"Come in here, honey," he said sweetly. "I made you a sandwich. I've got a bottle of your favorite medicinal herbage, babe." He winked at her and patted the seat next to him. Becky was slightly apprehensive after last night's incidents, but she sat beside him. She smiled when he put his arm around her.

They had been married forty-two years. Ordinarily, she trusted her husband of four decades implicitly. Today, she was less certain. She was convinced that he was still under Candy's sway.

As she snuggled up against her husband, a loud "smack" against the door of the vehicle startled her. She had been kicking back on the seat, relaxed, until the noise made her bolt upright.

"What the hell? What is that?" she asked. Her inquiry was answered by a series of barks and scratching noises at the side door. It sounded like a dog was frantically trying to get inside. It sounded like it was trying to break the door down.

"Ignore it," her husband said calmly. "Just come back here and eat the breakfast I made you." Tom picked up a peanut butter and jelly sandwich and held it up in front of her face.

Becky sniffed the sandwich. She examined it closely for the first time. Then she gave Tom a peculiar look. "Peanut butter? Sweetie I can't eat that. You know it will wreak havoc on my dentures."

Suddenly, the arm Tom had gently dangled over her shoulder folded at the elbow. It began to tighten around her neck. "What in the fuck are you doing?" she yelled, smacking him in the face repeatedly with her closest hand. Her ring finger stuck him in the nose, and it began to bleed. That didn't slow him down any. Soon Becky was choking and unable to speak.

"If only you'd just eaten the damned poison," Tom complained. "Then the obstacle would be removed. Then her Lord Mercy would be satisfied. All who refuse to obey her lordship shall perish."

Tom wasn't a particularly big man, but Becky was a tiny woman. Her aging body had been weakened by her battle with cancer. Her body might be frail, but she was very strong willed. She was a fighter, with five years of chemo and radiation therapy under her belt. She wasn't going to give up the ghost that easily.

But Tom… he looked crazy as fuck. In fact, she didn't know who or what this was. The real Tom had left the building. Whoever or whatever currently occupied his body seemed as determined to kill her as she was to live.

In fact, Becky would have given up the ghost right then and there if the beast outside hadn't broken the door down. A huge German shepherd came barreling through the cramped camper kitchen and landed on the table in front of Tom. It was growling and frothing at the mouth. The dog snapped its jaw around Tom's forearm and sunk the teeth in deep until it bled. It began shaking it back and forth until he released her neck.

Moments later, Tom was sitting at the table, dazed and confused, nursing his arm. The dog turned around and fled.

"What just happened?" Tom asked Becky.

"That coffee I made this morning must have been really bad," Becky answered drolly. "You just tied to kill me. She scooted over a bit, away from her husband to be safe. However, she could see that Tom was quickly reverting back to normal.

"I don't give a fuck what you say," Becky said gruffly. "We need to get the hell out of here, like right now." She didn't say another word. She grabbed the cabin door's handle, and slammed it shut. Then she kept right on trekking until she got to the front seat. The determined little lady hoped behind the wheel, and belted herself in.

Before Tom, the kids, or anyone else could say fuck all, she had turned the key and stepped on the gas. Becky Carter was hauling ass towards the I-5 onramp as fast as she could without getting into an accident or causing the heavy vehicle to topple.

She was headed down to San Diego, to see her oldest son, Tom, Jr. He was a career navy man and spent months at a time out in a submarine. Between his limited shore leave and her grueling medical treatment schedules, they hadn't seen each other in years. She was determined to see him again while she still had breath in her body.

She turned over her shoulder and shouted back at a startled Tom, "And now just who in the fuck is Mercy?"

Misfire

Phobetor was starting to realize he'd seriously fucked up. The time he spent protecting innocent mortals from the twins was against his better judgment. He'd done it to lull Charlotte's naïve little consort into a false sense of security. He'd needed Flynn to trust him, to think he was a nice guy who cared about humans.

Phobetor actually did have a sense of justice and fair play when it came to the continued survival of the human race as a species. He cared about humans the way that some people cared about ecological balance and animal species. Mercy and Sympathy were like an invasive species, throwing off the natural balance. They could not be allowed to destroy the natural order of things.

But on an individual level, Phobetor did not give a flying fuck about human beings. Sure, there were special ones like Maribelle, ones he had a connection to. They were like pets. And Charlotte – Phobetor would never think of her as human. It was a temporary condition she'd been inflicted with, like a cold or the flu. Even if she was born with inferior human blood, she was still his niece.

The rest of mankind lived and died like any wild animal. Sometimes they grew out of control, and it was necessary to cull the herd. Even in times like this, they were hardly endangered. Why should he care if a Roz, a Miguel, or a Melissa died?

What he cared about was preventing Mercy from gaining any more power.

He had made a grievous error in judgment. By preventing Mercy from consuming lesser snacks with her sister, he had accelerated the parasitic relationship she enjoyed with Sympathy. Mercy had sucked her weaker sister almost dry, and now Mercy was way fucking out of control.

Her grandfather was just caught babbling insanely about the Cult of Mercy. She was apparently now strong enough to control a full-grown man. She also knew who she was, and wanted everyone else to know, too.

Phobetor had rescued Becky because he was well-aware of the power rankings when it came to blood sacrifice. Most people thought that the most potent offering was an innocent. Purity was a factor, but it wasn't the most crucial among them. Blood ties and blood lines were also relevant. For example, once Charlotte and Flynn had conceived, it became much more powerful for Maribelle to offer him because he was the father of her grandchild. It was at that moment Phobetor had decided that it had to be Maribelle, not any other member of the Sisterhood of Undoing. The only more powerful gesture would have been if he could have convinced Charlotte herself.

Becky was the biological grandmother of Candice, Mercy's current incarnation. Killing her was more powerful than murdering a stranger at a diner, and having her husband kill her would give Mercy even more to feed on.

Denied that treat, she would undoubtedly be feeding on her parents right now, if she didn't need them. She needed them to drive her back to the hospital, so she could finish consuming Sympathy.

Phobetor had to stop that from happening.

According to Maribelle, his Priestess of the Undoing, there was an upside and a downside to Mercy's complete consumption of Sympathy. The upside was that there was a very high probability that Sympathy would instantly return to the river Lethe and be reincarnated without her memories. Given her horrible behavior this go 'round, if the other religions were right, she might come back as a rat or a cockroach. Regardless, Sympathy would be a thousand years out of the running. She would no longer be a threat to Phobetor's power.

Unfortunately, Mercy would become an even bigger and more immediate threat. Consuming Sympathy would make Mercy as powerful as her father. If she became as powerful as Brash, she would be nearly as powerful as Phobetor.

If Brash had not been cursed by Zeus, he might have become as powerful as Phobetor. Unlike Brash and his line, Phobetor could enter the mortal world and procreate without blood sacrifice. He could shape-shift without blood sacrifice. He had only required one life, and that was the one Maribelle took in order to eliminate Brash and the somnali.

The third powerful element regarding a sacrifice was love. Maribelle loved Flynn as a son-in-law. She didn't love him like she loved her daughter, or granddaughter. She didn't even love him more than she hated Brash. But she loved him enough to add potency her decision to forfeit his life.

Mercy's love of Sympathy was even more potent. Although it was not as deep as human love, it was the deepest love Mercy ever knew. Mercy loved Sympathy more than any other being in existence. She was also her blood, her closest blood, her twin.

Blood sacrifices involving relations had been changing history since before Agamemnon sacrificed his daughter, Iphigenia, so that the Greek ships would be granted the proper weather conditions to sail forth and go to war against the city of Troy.

If Mercy were to become as powerful as Brash, she would be even more dangerous than she'd been before. The curse would still affect her, but she was ruthless. There would be no limit to the amount of blood sacrifice she'd be willing to make to increase her powers.

Seeing how fast her powers were increasing, Phobetor suddenly regretted his decision to challenge Charlotte. She was human, and fragile. Her weakness for her beloved consort made her easy to manipulate, and he was pretty sure she would cave in. But what if she acted unpredictably?

This would be a lousy time to have to fight a battle on two fronts.

Skin

It had been twenty-four hours, but Flynn was afraid to go outside. Phobetor probably had his hands full with Mercy and Sympathy. He might be busy talking to Maribelle. Still, there was no telling when he might show up. It reminded him, strangely, of being bullied on the school yard in junior high school.

Phobetor was a bully. He had chosen to bully Flynn. He wasn't beating him up for his lunch money. He was beating him down for higher stakes. He was after Charlotte's kingdom. Flynn couldn't stand being the reason his wife lost her inheritance. He had decided he would just take whatever it was Phobetor decided to dish out.

Still, he hoped he didn't run into him.

Flynn waited an extra hour just to be safe, and then went outside. He carried his bloodstained pants and fur with him. After a day in the cave, they stank like a sun-baked animal carcass. Brash's castle didn't have natural pools and exotic features like Charlotte's little cave. The bathing areas were modeled after the ancient Greek or Roman bathhouses.

There was a fireplace on the way to the pools. He threw his hopelessly ruined jeans in the fire and stood there for a while, watching them burn.

They were torn to shreds. They were covered in the blood, urine, and feces he excreted while Phobetor was dismembering him. They also reminded them of Phobetor – they had been a gift from him. He never wanted to see them again. He stood there a while and watched them burn.

Although Brash's lavish estate was carved into jet-black volcanic rock, stylistically it reflected his deep attachment to Roman architecture. It was also designed to accommodate his hedonistic lifestyle. The place was filled with rooms designed to host different types of feasts and orgies. It looked very empty now.

The vast open spaces gave Flynn the creeps. He liked tight spaces, and cozy environments. He often imagined this castle was haunted. Sometimes he felt lost here, like a little kid left behind in a vacant supermall. The oversized baths, bigger than Olympic swimming pools, were no different. Flynn picked one of the smaller ones. It was heated by natural hot springs. He carefully lowered his body into the steamy waters.

When he was covered up to his neck, he released the bloodstained leopard skin and let it float in the cleansing waters. He'd never bathed in somnali form before. He always shifted to human. Something about being somnali made him feel safer. Even when Phobetor was torturing him, the psychological makeup that accompanied his somnali form made it easier for him to fend off the emotions. The physical pain was bad enough without fully absorbing the guilt, betrayal, and feelings of foolishness regarding his deception.

He held his breath and dropped his body to the bottom of the pool. He was encapsulated in comforting liquid warmth. The feeling of water pressure against his wings was fresh and new. He swam under the water to the other side of the pool. When he popped out again, he was smiling. It was nice to play. Maybe he would come here with Charlotte sometime.

He still had the oatmeal soap from the little cave they used to live in. He fished it off the ledge of the pool and grabbed the stained leopard skin. Perched on a step under the water, he began scrubbing it, trying to get the blood out of the fur. Half an hour later, the fur was cleaner, but he still couldn't get all of the blood out.

He was still engaged in the now fruitless labor when a shadowy figure startled him. Flynn was terrified. He dropped his face down to his knees and clutched them with his arms. He was afraid to look up. When a hand touched his shoulder, he whispered, "Please, no…" under his breath.

"It's me, child," the dark figure said. Flynn looked up when he recognized the voice. It was Nyx.

"It's been a long time," he said, turning his body in the water so that he was facing her. He carefully placed the skin on the decorative tiles at the side of the pool. Then, he grasped the edge of the pool and set his chin on his fingers.

"It has," she said. "I've heard about your adventures. I am so sorry you got hurt. How are you?"

"I'm okay," he mumbled. He really did not want to talk about it.

"That skin," she said, pointing at the leopard skin rug. "You are trying to preserve it?"

"Yes," he said. "It used to be Charlotte's. Now it's mine, I guess I find it comforting."

Nyx smiled. "Yes, I know where it came from. It has a lot of history. Perhaps you'd like to try it on, to wear it. It wouldn't be the first time you have shared her skin."

Flynn shivered. Her words evoked intimacies that he liked to believe were private. As Charlotte had informed him, very little was concealed here. Someone or the other always seemed to know.

"Do you mean, shift into that form?" he asked. Flynn's shifting abilities were very limited. The only form he had ever learned without Phobetor's assistance was his own human one, and Charlotte had helped him to master that. Phobetor taught him three additional other forms. The only way he could enter the physical realm in animal form was with Phobetor's assistance. Now that they were on the outs, he couldn't be a cat in Charlotte's apartment anymore. It was just another loss he tried not to think about.

"Yes," she said. "You only know a few forms. Perhaps you would benefit by another."

"I would," he said. Every form had a different set of emotions attached to it. He wondered what it would feel like in that skin.

"Show me all of the forms you are capable of," she asked. "I want to see what you've learned."

Flynn shyly stepped out of the bath. Nudity still made him feel self-conscious, after all this time in the Demos Oneiroi. He resolved this dilemma by quickly transforming into a golden eagle there on the clay tiles. He was still wet. He shook the water out of his feathers.

"Delightful," Nyx said. "Can you show me the others?"

Flynn shifted into the shape of a blue gray British shorthair cat. Nyx nodded. She knew that shape. He shifted into the little brown, black, and white rat terrier. Nyx smiled. He shifted into his younger human self, him as a toddler. Nyx leaned over and playful tousled his hair.

Finally, he shifted to his human form. He was seated, naked and damp, cross-legged on the ground. Before he could shift back to somnali, Nyx said, "Wait."

She walked behind him, picked up the leopard pelt, and placed it over his back. It was still soggy and felt cold against his bare skin. He began to shiver. She ran her hand over the animal skin, and the instant she touched it, it fused into his skin. He fell forward onto his hands and knees and began to shift. The transition was swift and painless. Soon he was sitting on the floor in leopard form, licking his damp fur clean.

The rough, bristly tongue made short work of the somnali blood trapped in the fur. Flynn was not yet consumed by the animal mind, but the thought of tasting his own blood did not bother him. Occupying a form that once belonged to his wife was a bit more jarring. He stopped cleaning his coat and looked around, confused. Something felt strange and different. He sniffed himself and inspected his figure. Soon, he figured it out. Unlike his other forms, this one was female.

Nyx laughed at his bafflement. She patted his back and said, "There's a pretty girl. We can change that if you like." She ran her hand over the spotted fur, and Flynn began to shift slightly. The body was now male. It wasn't a major change. It was just a bit more complicated than when he shifted his housecat form, Dada, from an unaltered male to a neuter. He felt confident that he could easily switch between the male and female variant of his leopard form. That was a new trick.

It was easy to learn from her.

"Nyx," Flynn quietly asked, "how am I able to shift? Charlotte says that's something that only higher order beings should be able to do, like Oneiroi. Phobetor is a god, I'm not… I mean, somnali are lower order, like nymphs and other lesser spirits. She said the only lower level beings that can shift are related to Phobetor. I'm not, am I?"

"In a manner of speaking," Nyx said. "Not in the usual way, though. Do you remember when you were still a wandering human spirit? Remember when Phobetor stuck his arm in your chest, trying to get that one, Imelda, who lives within you?"

Flynn nodded.

"Well, let's just say she bit him and he left a little something behind," Nyx explained casually. "He left a bit of his blood inside of you, his genetic material. I used that when I created you as a somnali. You are a hybrid of a sort, on the cellular level. Phobetor wasn't told about donation to your creation, but certainly he would suspect it." She laughed.

"You are a wily one," Flynn said admiringly. His animal forms could never speak to other species in the physical world. It was interesting to speak to her from his leopard form now.

She smiled. "I am. Wisdom is occasionally accompanied by humor. Some would call it wit. Most would never suspect it of me. I am very fond of you, child."

She patted Flynn on his furry spotted back.

"I have a gift for you," she said, holding out a tiny black pouch. He couldn't pick it up very easily without opposable thumbs. He gracefully transmuted into his default somnali body. It was not his original form, but now, it was his natural one. When he shook the pouch, it furled outward into a long stretch of cloth. It was a long dark cloak, made of night sky. This design was thick and starless, like the horizon during darkest hours of early morning.

He shifted back to his human form because it was too hard to wear it with wings on. Pulling it on, he noticed it had sleeves. It covered his entire body from his head to his feet. When he finished putting it on it began to change shape until it fit his body like a second skin. Although he could see perfectly, when he bent over to look at his reflection, all he saw was a shadow.

"In case you should need to hide from anyone," Nyx said with a wink. "You will be very difficult to find in this. It works in much the same way as the blanket."

He realized she was talking about Phobetor. If she didn't want to name names, he wouldn't either. For the third time that he knew of, she intervened on his behalf. He wondered if there weren't other instances he didn't know about. He was an ordinary person. He had no idea why she took such an interest. He was at a loss for words, so he simply said, "Thank you."

"You might wish to be able to travel back and forth in your animal forms without the aid of Phobetor. He has betrayed you. I am able to discern how much this wounds your human heart. Brace yourself. Perilous times are coming. Mercy is rising in her powers. You must be strong in the way you always have been, resilient, and determined. You must be strong enough to protect your family."

Flynn nodded. "I don't know how to get to Earth without Phobetor. I know that Mercy and Sympathy are coming. I fear for my family. I would be indebted to you should you offer me a way to protect them."

She laughed. "Why, you are already indebted to me. But you owe me nothing except that you should protect your wife and your child. Charlotte needs you. I'll make a portal for you, in your little room – hidden from prying eyes. You can use it to enter and leave the world of men at your whim, but you will always arrive in the same spot. You will always arrive in the home of your wife and daughter."

"Thank you again," he said. "I was wondering if I can ever appear on Earth as myself."

"You are forbidden," she said tersely. "The walking dead terrify mortals and give them strange ideas. You are very fortunate that you can appear as an animal without making a sacrifice. Brash's somnali were not able to walk the Earth in any form without blood sacrifice because of the curse. But Brash did not father you. I gave you the form of somnali. You are no more cursed than any other member of my clan. Be grateful for what you do have."

"I'm sorry," he said. "I didn't mean to appear greedy or ungrateful."

"You aren't greedy," she said. "You have a generous spirit. Perhaps too many have taken advantage of that. I wish I could promise you an end to such malfeasance, but I fear I cannot. Your trials are far from over. Even now, Phobetor fumbles upon the surface of the Earth. His vanity has him attempting to stop Mercy the Insatiable on his own. He may yet regret his treatment of you."

Flynn had remained in his human form for too long. The impact of Phobetor's betrayals began to weigh on him heavily. It was not just the brutal assault, which was the most recent and overt transgression against him. There was also the plotting, the bending of Maribelle to his will. That Phobetor could conceive of using Maribelle's hand to take his life proved to Flynn that the man who pretended to be his friend had never been anything but contemptuous.

"Phobetor's attack seemed to have as much to do with undermining Charlotte's authority as it did with disciplining me. Why is Phobetor so determined to control her?"

"Who knows?" she answered. "Sibling rivalry, I suppose. He was always jealous of Brash. Now with Brash gone, Somnus dotes upon his grandchildren, you, and Charlotte. Charlotte is his oracle. She is the grandchild of his beloved Pasithea. How Pasithea adores the two of you and your precious little romance. How difficult it must be for a son to hold the attention of his father when he is one of a thousand? How frustrating it must be for Phobetor when his rival is dead, yet continues to thwart him at every turn? But I must go. I need to speak with my sons."

And with that, she vanished and Flynn was once again on his own in that big, lonely palace. He did not want to be alone. He went to find the portal and return to Earth and the arms of his loving wife.

Insatiable

Alice and Tim were staying in a flea-bitten dive motel in Grants Pass, Oregon. Flea bitten was a nicer euphemism for the true nature of the infestation. The motel was plagued by bedbugs. The tiny, vampiric creatures had begun drinking from the annoyed couple hours ago, right after checkout, back when Tim's parents were still babysitting little Candy at a local diner – before the grandparents ran screaming for the hills. The marks from a quarter of a day's worth of feasting were apparent on their bodies. Alice was wearing a knee-length cotton nightgown. When she lay down, red welts began to cover her forearms and calves. Turning the lights on made the disgusting little creatures skitter across the thin cotton sheet that covered the stained mattress. The mattress was covered in small spots of blood, from where patrons had squashed the creatures in the middle of their meal. When caught in the act of eating, the bugs were no longer black. Filled with blood, their formerly flat bodies became bulbous and red.

They weren't the only hungry creatures to enter the room that night.

If she had possessed the power, the feast would have come to an end the moment Candy got home. Try as she might, she could not use her mind to control more than one of the filthy little vermin at a time. She soon grew tired of expending her energies on the horrid little monsters.

She needed to feed.

Alice Carter was the most accessible target. She was serious about modern parenting and her Earth mother image. Extended breastfeeding was a part of that identity. She didn't believe in weaning her children off the breast until they voluntarily relinquished it. The twins asked for the breast less and less these days. In fact, Alice was a little surprised because it had been weeks. She was beginning to think they'd moved on. She wasn't totally shocked, though. They were in a strange place, and it was normal for Candy to want comfort. The separation from her sister must be tearing her apart.

As the insatiable toddler nursed, she also fed on Alice's life force and emotional energies.

Even when she was still known as Mercy, Candy had always been greedy. She wanted it all. Everything that was available to her, and everything that was available to others. Her acquisitiveness when it came to the property of others was one part envy and three parts entitlement. It was less that she coveted what others had, and more that she felt it was owed to her.

She felt innately superior to others. Her narcissism extended to her feelings regarding her family. Her somnali sisters were naturally superior to other beings unrelated to her. Even her demisomnali kin were better than other demisomnali. As an extension of her wondrousness, these fleshly beings she had been born to in this incarnation must also be superior.

It would be a shame to consume her parents. But she was so hungry. She had her needs.

As the toddler continued to feed, Alice took on an increasingly gaunt, pale appearance. She looked anemic and a bit nauseated. It had always been hard for her to say no to her baby. Candy was always the ravenous one. Even as newborns, she fed stronger and longer than her sister. She was soon bigger and fatter than her sister. Often, Alice's nipples became cracked, or even bled due to Candy's vigorous feeding. The more they hurt, the more difficult it seemed to be to get the greedy child to take a break from her relentless eating. If the baby wasn't already fat, Alice would have felt guilt ever pushing her away. It seemed impossible for one so young, but sometimes she wondered if the infant might be a big sadistic.

Tonight, a dozen tiny insects joined Candy in feeding on and pestering her poor, beleaguered mother. Alice was looking sicker. She was beginning to develop bags under her eyes. The baby was tempted to let her go now.

She was afraid she might go too far. She didn't want to kill her parents. There were many reasons for trying to preserve them. For one thing, she preferred their company over that of anyone else except for her twin sister. Besides that, she needed them. They would have to transport her down I-5, after those wayward grandparents of hers. They would need to make a brief detour, of course.

Maybe not so brief, she wasn't sure how long it would take. All she knew what that she needed vengeance. The woman who did this to her had to pay. Someone had to pay for killing her father and all of her siblings. Someone had to pay for forcing her to reincarnate into this puny, yet useful form.

That someone was Maribelle Metaxas. She and her Sisterhood of Undoing would pay for what they'd done to her! Mercy would see them all destroyed!

Unfortunately, her human body was only two years old. It could not drive.

That was why she had to be careful not to eat all of her mother.

Reluctantly, Candy let go of her earthly mother, and set aside her true identity, as the somnali Mercy. She let the human body that was now her own take over her needs with its own. It wasn't a lot different than when Flynn slipped into the animal thought of his hosts. She was far better at resisting her human flesh with its pathological neediness. This time, she let it take over because its affection for Alice would stop her from consuming the young mother entirely.

Alice was too drained to move from the spot where she lay with her daughter on the bed. She simply fell asleep there, with her legs dangling off the side of the bed. There were no blankets to warm her. Candy curled up into the space of her mother's armpit. She put her tiny head on her mother's chest. She was lit up and filled with energy. It would be hard for her to fall asleep.

Instead of counting sheep, Candy decided to focus her mind on the bugs. One by one, she convinced the bugs to turn and feed on their own kind. Like insectoid zombies, the controlled bed bugs drank from their friends until they were dried up and dead. They drank until they themselves burst from gluttonous over engorgement. The baby laughed and smiled while they died.

Tim lay in the second queen bed, being feasted upon by insect life. In the morning, he awakened with a series of itchy red dots on the exposed parts of his flesh. Alice, on the other hand, sustained not another bite. Mysteriously, all of the bugs found on her mattress in the morning were already dead.

Anger

A German shepherd spent half of the night sitting in a dark corner behind the industrial-sized dumpsters about twenty feet away from the Carter's infested hotel room. Once it became apparent that Mercy wouldn't be killing her mother tonight, Phobetor abandoned his post and returned to the Demos Oneiroi.

There was nothing to be done if he couldn't figure out a way to separate Mercy from her ever-increasing power. He needed more information. He was going to have to visit his Priestess of the Undoing. Phobetor was a bit reluctant to see Maribelle at this point. She would have undoubtedly heard about his savaging Flynn not long ago. Flynn himself was hiding. The somnali was too inexperienced to know how to do this on his own, so he would have had to have had some help. Perhaps Charlotte assisted him, or perhaps Nyx or Somnus. Either way, he was out of the reach of Phobetor.

Maribelle was not.

Phobetor did not know what to expect when he entered her chambers. Perhaps she would be weeping, begging him not to act so rashly in the future. Perhaps she would have no reaction to the news. After all, she was the one who had killed the boy. He wasn't sure.

What he didn't expect was her unadulterated fury.

He appeared in the modern kitchen of her Berkeley Hills home. He was fully clothed today. He wore a black turtleneck, black jeans, and an ankle length black leather duster.

"I refuse to allow you to come in, you bastard! Fuck off, seriously. Get the fuck out!" she yelled, plucking a cup off the table and flinging it at his head. Phobetor was too busy ducking to take notice of the fact that it was the same cup she offered Flynn poisoned coffee in.

Phobetor was used to experiencing a vast array of emotions coming from Maribelle. Even anger, for she felt a great deal of it towards Brash when she learned of the Slaughter of the Innocents. For whatever reason, his transgressions seemed to have finally reached a tipping point. Maribelle was as furious with him as she had been with her husband. That same husband was dead, with Phobetor's assistance of course.

He wasn't sure how he should feel about all this, but he was amused.

"Why are you so angry?" he said, standing in the doorway. He was honestly mystified. Human emotions fascinated and tantalized him, but he had very little insight into how they actually worked. He declined to march further inward, since it would probably provoke her further.

"You!" she said, her face turning red. "You! Fucking you! You authored the Rituals of Undoing. I didn't even know it, but fucking fuck, fuck it all, I'm your priestess. How? How in the hell? You manipulated me, used my feelings of protectiveness towards Charlotte and Faelyn and my secret hatred of Brash to manipulate me."

Phobetor nodded. "You did hate him, after you found out about the Slaughter of the Innocents."

"I hate you!" she screamed. "You tricked me into killing Flynn. You tricked me into coming out from under the protection of Brash, by getting rid of him. Now you're trying to steal my daughter's inheritance. I heard what you did to Flynn. You're a monster!"

"I am?" he asked calmly. "Do you really want your daughter to take Brash's place? She has long life ahead of her as the only living Oracle of Somnus. When that dies, do you really want her to become the new goddess of freaky sex nightmares?"

Maribelle quietly flipped him the bird. Phobetor was rather relieved that she didn't yell or throw anything at him.

"Let us not continue to be at odds with one another," he said evenly. "Even now, Mercy is beating down a pathway to your door. Don't you think she knows it was you who betrayed her? You and all of the Sisterhood of the Undoing are in danger until she is dealt with."

"Betrayed her?" Maribelle said. "Are you fucking kidding me?"

Phobetor decided that her use of profanity was not a good sign. Earlier, her entire vocabulary had reverted to a string of "fucks". He couldn't afford this. He needed to get the information.

"Perhaps I chose my words poorly," he said carefully. "Of course, you owed her nothing. Yet, you are her sister's mother and perhaps, she did not expect you to end her immortality."

"She can continue to reincarnate with all of her powers and memories," Maribelle pointed out. "Doesn't that make her essentially immortal?"

"I suppose it does," he admitted. "And we must end her reign of terror. She is, as she always has been, completely out of control."

She spat on the floor in his general direction. "You are one to talk about being out of control."

"I am perfectly in control," he argued, finally daring to step back into the room. "It is the rest of you who have lost all your senses. Charlotte and Flynn are infants. They cannot be allowed to run an Oneiroi kingdom. It is unconscionable!"

"Take it up with your grandmother," Maribelle sarcastically suggested. There was no way in hell Phobetor was going to bring this up to Nyx. "But keep your hands off my children."

He raised an eyebrow. "Children? But you only have one child." By now he had managed to get past the food preparation areas and was standing behind the counter that divided the kitchen from the dining room. Maribelle sat at a small table in the kitchen proper, the one used for cozy breakfasts and coffees. The one she poisoned Flynn at.

"He is my son-in-law," Maribelle argued. "First word is son."

"Forgive me for saying so," Phobetor began, leaning casually against the counter so that his feet were now facing her. "It was for Charlotte's protection that you killed Flynn. Your stepchildren, Mercy and her kind, as well as this son-in-law, you killed. This suggests, to me, that you have a unique relationship with you only child. Your relationship with the boy is a lesser one."

Maribelle sighed. Tears began to well up in her eyes.

"Right, I feel terrible about it," she sobbed. "I was so busy protecting my family, I treated him like nothing. But don't you see? He's my son-in-law. I was supposed to treat him like my son."

He slowly took a seat across from her. He handed her a paper towel he had pulled from the roll when he passed it on the way to the table.

"I have some emotions, too," he confessed. "They don't always work the same way as yours do. Human emotions are complicated, nuanced. Somnali have simpler emotions and we have far fewer. One emotion we do experience is anger. I was very angry when I punished… I mean, when I hurt the boy."

"Why were you angry?" she asked. She had nervously gotten up from the table and walked over to the coffee machine. It was something she did on automatic. It gave her something to do with her hands. It allowed her to distract her mind. She poured two cups of coffee and bought them to the table. She'd known Phobetor for a long time. She knew how he took his coffee, with that horrible Hazelnut creamer. She didn't keep it in her house in the real world, but this was a dream. It was there when she opened the fridge.

Phobetor remembered the human ritual of politeness that said he should wait for her to return and sit before he spoke. Soon, she returned and handed him his coffee.

"Thank you, Mari," he said, taking the coffee. "I was angry because he impressed upon me a necessity to protect the humans from Mercy and Sympathy. I did as he saw fit, and so Mercy, in her desperation, turned to feed on her sister. Now she grows more powerful than ever. She plots to make blood sacrifices of her parents and grandparents. If she does so, and fully consumes her sister, she will very likely become very powerful. If only I hadn't prevented her from eating those humans. Humans are expendable. What was I thinking?"

"So, you regret your choice," Maribelle observed. "Rather than admitting you made a mistake, you choose to blame your closest advisor. Should I be worried? You come to me for advice now. If it goes badly, will you throttle me as well?"

"Well of course not," he protested. "I know it is hard for you to believe, but we do have emotions. Maybe not like yours, but we have them. Look at Somnus and his great love for Pasithea. Is it so hard for you to believe that I could love you, just a little bit?"

Maribelle shook her head. "Why would I suppose that? I would have to be a fool."

Phobetor regretted the fact that his actions caused Maribelle to mistrust him, but there was no sense in dwelling on that which could not be undone.

"Think what you will of me," he said. "But know this: Mercy is coming. Charlotte is protected by Somnus as his Oracle. But Brash is gone now. You have only me. You are my priestess, and I will protect you. You should not be thinking only of yourself. Who do you think will protect your grandchild? Her father is unable to wield Charlotte's powers. He is so inexperienced he only knows how to use the most basic of his own. You need someone stronger to protect Faelyn."

Maribelle leaned back and folded her hands into one another.

"I'm listening," Maribelle said. "Tell me what you have to offer. Then I will tell you my conditions."

Phobetor rose from the table. "Conditions? Insolent woman. Very well, then, die if you wish."

Maribelle shrugged. After a moment, she smiled at him and waved. "Don't let the door hit you in the ass on your way out, Phobie."

He bristled. It was obvious to him that she was still pissed off. She hadn't called him any pet name in fifteen years. She was being sarcastic, which was typical for her when angry. He turned around and vanished.

The moment Phobetor left, Maribelle's other guests were revealed by Nyx. The goddess of Night had concealed herself, her son Somnus, and her daughter Pasithea for the duration of the conversation.

"Do you see?" Maribelle asked. She was trembling with a rare combination of fear and fury. She was extremely angry with Phobetor. Pasithea was perhaps equally ticked off with Maribelle. Before Phobetor's arrival, Pasithea had been threatening to squish her like a bug.

The common wisdom was that all of Somnus' thousand sons had been the result of parthenogenesis and had no mothers. The truth was that one of the lesser known Oneiroi had been his child with Pasithea. That was Brash. Although her son was out of control, Pasithea loved Brash. She wasn't very happy with Maribelle or Phobetor right now.

"All I see is that having destroyed my son, Phobetor now wishes to steal his legacy, Charlotte's inheritance," Pasithea said huffily. Her arms were crossed over her chest, and she looked both sullen and dangerous.

"I tried to discipline Brash and his heirs," Nyx said noncommittally. "They were difficult."

"Charlotte and Faelyn are his sole heirs, and how dare Phobetor threaten them!" she shouted.

"Well, that's not true," Somnus said with a shrug. "Because my twin brother Thanatos intervened on their behalf, Mercy and Sympathy also survived with their memories intact beyond the sacrifice."

"Surely you jest," Maribelle said, nervously sipping at her coffee. "If it wasn't for their behavior, Brash would still be sitting on his throne. They are the ones who forced my hand. I would have never made the choices I did otherwise."

Pasithea narrowed her eyes. "I know who and what they are. They use my powers to provoke hallucinations in humans even now. One of Phobetor's better known flaws is hubris. It is why he cannot admit that it is he who miscalculated regarding Mercy. This pride is also what leads him to attribute all of Mercy and Sympathy's powers to something akin to nightmares. The influence he has over the sleeping was inherited by him from his father, Somnus. Clearly, Mercy and Sympathy affect the waking. Hallucinations are my domain."

"So they are," Somnus conceded, gently patting his wife on the shoulder. "They also use hypnosis, though. They seem to have retained all of the powers of their bloodline except for the ability to affect the sleeping."

"Thank God they can't show up here," Maribelle said.

"Which of the gods do you give thanks to?" Somnus inquired.

"Never mind that," Maribelle said with a sigh. She didn't feel like getting into a conversation about Christianity with him. Sometimes she wondered if she'd removed Flynn from the natural course of his afterlife by encouraging Charlotte to put that little spell on him. It was one of the many burdens of guilt she carried.

"What about Flynn?" Maribelle asked. "I don't want to see him throttled senseless on a whim. Can't you protect him?"

Nyx waved her arm. "Do not trouble yourself. It was I who deified the young somnali. I created him in his deified form as a fitting companion to your daughter. Would you like to see him made unfit with your coddling? Did Zeus interfere every time Heracles skinned a knee?"

Somnus laughed. "I think not."

"But Charlotte and Flynn aren't strong enough to protect themselves," Maribelle protested.

"Individually, neither is strong enough." Pasithea declared. "They are not meant to fight as two, they are meant to fight as one. They are paired. If they cannot learn how to work together, then I fear it is hopeless for them."

"Not hopeless," Nyx countered. "They can always accept Phobetor's offer and learn to live on their knees."

"And Mercy and Sympathy?" Maribelle asked.

Pasithea looked first to Somnus, and then to Nyx. They nodded their agreement, and she spoke.

"They are my granddaughters," Pasithea said. "I would not have them harmed, not even by each other. Your daughter assumes the Rites she has transcribed for the Sisterhood are from Somnus himself. She is nearly correct. They are by my hand. They would leave Mercy and Sympathy with their identities intact but stripped of their powers. They would be much as Charlotte is now. Is that acceptable?"

"It is to me," Maribelle said. "Whether Phobetor will agree to it, I do not know."

"You have your ways," Pasithea hissed. "You have been able to convince him to do many things before. You have been his partner in many things. You were co-conspirators in execution of Flynn. The usurping of my son Brash, whose throne your daughter now sits on. Because of you my son Brash is all but dead. Human, lowered to your pathetic condition. He does not even know his own name. I would at least have my granddaughters know their own names. If he does not agree, then convince him. Perhaps you can bed him again. That worked the last time."

Maribelle got up and went into the kitchen cabinet, the one she kept her booze in. She pulled out a large, skull-shaped bottle of overpriced vodka and poured herself a screwdriver. She was going to need it if she had to sit here and be essentially called a whore by Brash's mother.

Nyx gave Pasithea a cautioning look. "You can hardly blame the human for what happened," she said. "Phobetor has wanted all that belonged to Brash since before she existed. He had always been envious of Brash's relationship with their father. This is all Phobetor's doing. She was merely his instrument."

She looked at Somnus next. "It is you who should ask Phobetor. He seeks your approval."

Passenger

Flynn stepped through the portal Nyx had established for him and entered the human world. Charlotte was in the bathroom, brushing her teeth when he arrived. He recognized its high, industrial ceilings and its black on purple color scheme. The *Nightmare Before Christmas* towels, soap dish and toothbrush carousel were holdovers from their old apartment in Berkeley.

It was weird, though… how could he see things so high up if he was a cat?

Something weird was sticking out of his mouth, and it tasted overwhelmingly of peppermint. The pungent aroma and intense flavor were unforgettable. He hadn't needed to brush his teeth in three and a half years, but he knew it was toothpaste. He tried to spit it out, but nothing happened. It was as if he was paralyzed.

But he wasn't paralyzed. It was worse. His hand began to move without his consent. He was brushing his teeth, even though he didn't want to. Something, or someone, was controlling him. He was terrified.

Hello, Flynn, Charlotte said. *Try looking in the mirror.*

Her voice echoed in his head. It came from nowhere and everywhere at once. He did as she suggested and turned to face the mirror in the medicine cabinet. He was shocked by what saw there. Charlotte's face was staring back at him. A toothbrush was sticking out of the corner of her mouth. He was starting to panic.

It's okay, sweetie, she said. *Welcome aboard."

The figure in the mirror wrapped its arms around itself in a self-comforting gesture. A chill went down his spine. Charlotte was trying to give him a hug. He was inside of her.

I was trying to be a cat he thought defensively. *How did this happen?*

He was very uncomfortable with this. She kept touching him, trying to soothe him. She was rubbing his arm, stroking his hair. The problem is, it wasn't his arm, it was her arm, and her hair.

I was trying to communicate with you at the same time, I guess. she said. *I know its nerve wracking, but can you try to calm down?*

Why can't I move? he asked.

Oh, you want me to let you be behind the wheel? she asked. *Why didn't you say so? No problem.*

He felt a little more comfortable now that he was able to move his, or rather her body. It still gave him the creeps, looking at her face in the mirror through her eyes. At her request, he finished brushing her teeth. Meanwhile, she was explaining to him that she believed that if he could ride along inside her body, she might be able to access her somnali powers. Not just the demisomnali powers she used to have, but powers that were Brash's. She said she would have to be careful not to do it for too long. She said it might injure one or both of them.

The more she talked, the more nervous he became.

This is really freaking me out, Charlie he thought. He was so stressed out by it that he bounced right out of her skin and appeared on the sink in front of her as a cat.

Charlotte finished brushing her teeth and spat the toothpaste out. Dada hissed and skittered away from the sink. She shook her head. She had been hoping that Flynn would be able to hold on to his somnali state of mind a bit longer. Still, she knew he would remember his feline experiences later, when he got home. She decided to just keep talking to him.

She dried her hands and picked up the warm little gray fur ball.

"Are you my little scaredy cat?" she asked, rolling him over on his back in the crook of her arm. She rubbed his belly playfully until he began to purr.

"That's my good boy," she said. "That's my pretty boy." She carried him into the bedroom, where Faelyn was still asleep in her toddler bed. Charlotte hoped that having a simple, more immediate goal would help Flynn to focus.

"Let's try it again," she told her feline companion. "If we both want the same thing, we should both be able to operate this body at the same time. So, pick up the baby with me, okay? If you get scared, you can always jump out and become a cat again."

It hadn't been that long. Flynn was still present enough in Dada's mind to understand everything she said. Doing his best to focus, he pressed his small, fuzzy body against her. He thought about falling into her skin, becoming one with her. Try as he might, nothing happened.

"Huh," she said. "Maybe you're nervous." Charlotte put the cat on her shoulder and began petting his soft fur. After a little while, that loud little pepper grinder churning sound started up in his belly. It only took seconds after that for the cat to collapse into her shoulder and disintegrate into her skin.

I'm going to try to relax Flynn said, not realizing that he had already entered her body. Charlotte held her hands up in front of her eyes to show him. Flynn saw where he was and found it easier to adjust to than the first time. Together they walked over to the baby's bed, bent over, and picked up Faelyn.

That was easy, he said.

It can be that easy, she said. *But we have to both be on the same page.*

He wasn't sure what to do next, so Flynn just went along with things for a while. Charlie was picking up the baby and changing her diaper. It smelled awful, like the inside of a dumpster. He remembered what the inside of a dumpster smelled like from when he was homeless. He used to dumpster dive looking for food. Sometimes, if it was cold enough, he might sleep in one. He wasn't homeless now. He was living inside his wife… inside his wife's castle. His mind was beginning to wander, just coasting here inside Charlotte's body.

They carried the baby into the bathroom and ran a very shallow bath. They bathed Faelyn in warm soapy water. She hit the water over and over again with her little hand, making ripples. The water bounced up and down. She had a little rubber vampire ducky with fangs and a bowtie. The splashing made the ducky bounce up and down.

Flynn felt lightheaded, dizzy, and a bit emotional.

You do this every day, without me he said. *I should have been here.*

Moments later, he was blubbering like a baby. *I wanted to be here every day for her. I didn't want her to grow up without a father like I did. I let her down. I let us all down!*

Oh hell no, Charlotte thought. *Get out of me now, Flynn. You're getting moody because I'm on my period.*

What? he asked. *You're on what!?*

I'm menstruating, you're in my body, and now you're hormonal as fuck. Charlotte said. *Welcome to the estrogen experience. Now get out!*

Flynn bounced out of her body and returned to the form of the cat. Dada rubbed against her ankle as Charlie took Faelyn out of the tub and dried her off.

"I'm so sorry about that," Charlotte told the cat. "You know how you start feeling and thinking like that cat when you are in that form? Well, when you're inside of me, it's not entirely the same. You still think more or less, like yourself. You think like yourself if you were suddenly dumped into the body of a twenty-six-year-old chick on the rag. I mean, I'm used to my hormones. You're totally not."

Charlie sighed. This was not going to be easy.

The only way she could defend herself on the earthly plane would be by tapping into his powers, or rather, her powers which were stored inside of him. The same applied in reverse. The easiest way for her to empower him to stand up to Phobetor would be to lend him her abilities. She would have to practice merging with him in the Demos Oneiroi.

The urge to merge… thinking about it made her want to giggle.

"We can practice merging with each other some more a bit later," she told Dada. "Let me give you some breakfast. You can chill out in the kitchen while I finish getting the baby dressed." Both the man and the cat versions of Flynn were very relieved.

Charlotte wrapped Faelyn in a little child's terrycloth robe, sat her on her hip, and walked to the kitchen. When she got there, she sat the girl on a chair and fished a can of cat food out of the cabinet. When she pulled out the can opener and opened it, Dada began to purr. She deftly dumped it into the cat dish and freshened up the water.

She left the cat in the kitchen eating while she got Faelyn dressed.

Fifteen minutes later, she walked back into the kitchen holding her toddler by the hand. "I want to have breakfast with Shelby and Hannah," she told the cat. "Their son, Kyle, is allergic to cats. Maybe you should try being inside me and see how it feels."

As soon as the words left her mouth, she recognized the accidental double entendre. "I like it when you're inside me," she teased. "You like being inside me, don't you?"

The cat turned around and leaped into the air. He launched himself at her, and she stood still, waiting and unafraid. Seconds later he disappeared into her chest.

"Well done," she said aloud. They were together again, trying to function inside of the same flesh. They bent down and picked up their daughter, and the strange little family walked next door to spend time with their friends.

They walked up to the door, knocked on the window, and waited. This time, Hannah answered.

"I've got some Flynn in me right now," Charlotte said.

Hannah raised an eyebrow. "Already? That was fast." She leaned over and gave them and the baby a hug. "Well, come on in. All of you, I suppose."

Before Charlotte could say anything to Shelby, Hannah announced, "Charlotte's got Flynn with her today."

Shelby looked up from behind the kitchen shelf, where she was toasting English muffins for the family. "Hi Charlotte! Hey Flynn, long time no see! Okay, technically, I still don't see you, but you see me, right? So heeeeey. Hi Faelyn, how's my cutie pie?"

Hannah elbowed Charlotte. "Are you going to let him speak?"

Charlotte nodded. "Fine. But let me warn you right now, I'm on my period. Which means he's on my period, can you deal with that?"

"Aw, don't hassle him," Shelby said. "We miss him. Let him come out and play."

Charlotte nodded and handed Faelyn to Hannah.

Flynn gained control of the body and immediately burst into tears. "I missed you guys too. I missed you so much. It's really boring in the Demos Oneiroi, and I don't have any friends."

Shelby walked into the room with a tray full of muffins and patted him on the back on the way to the dining table.

"Come sit down and talk to me, dude!" she said cheerfully. "It's been a long time."

"This is so embarrassing," he said. "I mean I feel really emotional. I don't know what to say. This is weird." He went to the table and sat down, though. Shelby shoved a cup of coffee and a breakfast platter in front of him.

"Charlotte said you guys have Wonder Twin powers," Shelby said. "What's that like?"

They both laughed. "We can barely control them."

"Maybe you can use them on that," Hannah said, pointing at a big black furry shape in the window. It was Phobetor's cat form, Nightmare.

"Oh, hell no," Charlotte said. Flynn relaxed and let her take over. She raised her arm and pointed the palm of her hand at Phobetor. No one could see what came out of her hand, at least no one human. Flynn and Phobetor both saw it, though. The beam of light struck Phobetor in the chest and knocked him back into the Demos Oneiroi.

She was still standing there, in shock, when she felt a tiny hand on her calf. Flynn felt it, too. They both looked down at once and saw Faelyn hugging Charlotte's leg. They bent down and picked her up in their arms.

"I would never let thing hurt you," they told their daughter.

For Flynn, it was the perfect moment. He was holding his daughter in the physical world, in the world that had always been real for him. They were both holding her, and she was safe. They could protect her. He had what he always wanted, a family. Granted, it was a strange one. But it was his. He was not going to let anyone take it from him.

A warm glow of affection settled over the three of them, and for a little while, nothing else mattered except for their love. Flynn didn't care about the gender of the body he occupied. He no longer cared that his own body was a pile of bones buried under six feet of soil in Colma. He stopped noticing that he had breasts, and menstrual cramps. He only knew that he was there, with his wife, and his daughter. None of the crazy shit that had happened had managed to tear them away from him.

He felt a little teary eyed. But this was no time to get emotional. They needed to deal with Phobetor and whatever threat he might represent.

"We've got to find out why he was here," Charlotte and Flynn said at once. Acting in concert was strange. It was like performing a duet. Someone was always a bit in the lead. Right now, it was Charlotte. Flynn was singing harmony and backing up her act.

"I think we should go see my mom," Charlotte added. "It's Saturday. She'll be off work. She's probably clear on what Phobetor is up to."

"She'll be glad to see that little one," Hannah said, pointing at Faelyn, who was still on her mother's hip. Hannah and Shelby were both glad that Charlotte and Flynn were on speaking terms with Maribelle. What she did was terrible, but she was not a monster. She had just been misguided and manipulated by Phobetor.

"Don't be a stranger." Shelby told Flynn. She slapped Charlotte on the back bro-style, like she was acknowledging that there was a dude in there somewhere. Charlotte and Flynn immediately caught her up in a hug, with little Faelyn in the middle.

Flynn felt like there just weren't enough hugs in the world. Life in the dream realm with his formal and distant guardians, Nyx, Somnus and Pasithea, was terribly lonely for Flynn. Nyx took a hands-off approach and rarely visited him. When Charlotte wasn't with him, Phobetor had generally been his only companion. This was a fact that made his betrayal even harder to bear.

"I guess I'll see both of you later," Hannah told Charlotte's body and its various occupants. She stood in the doorway with Shelby and Kyle, waving goodbye to what appeared to be a little girl and her mother. If any neighbors had been looking, they might have been surprised when a little rat terrier appeared at the woman's heels. The cheerful little dog was off leash but remained faithfully at her side.

Charlotte was driving again these days. She opened the back door to her twenty-year-old cobalt blue Toyota Corolla and strapped Faelyn into the baby seat. She climbed to the front and put on her seatbelt. When she was seated Flynn wound up his tiny dog body and leapt into her lap.

She laughed as he began licking her face. "I love you too, but I've got to drive. Sit over there, in the passenger seat." He whined a little, but obediently moved over to the passenger side. Charlotte rolled down his window very slightly, and he pressed his muzzle out of the crack. He had a goofy doggy grin on his face and his tongue was lolling out of the side of his mouth. He was a happy boy.

When they were gone, Hannah shook her head and said, "Hah! It was nice to see him, but that was fucked up on so many levels."

"They are very determined to be together," Shelby said. "I think it's touching and romantic."

Hannah smiled and gave Shelby a big hug. "Yea, I could see that. I guess it is. I'm just glad we don't have to go through so much weird shit to be together." She reflected upon how truly blessed they were. Life was so short, and sometimes so incredibly unfair. It was desperately unfair -what had happened to Mike. They would never see him again.

Maybe Charlotte and Flynn never got their storybook happy ending, but they were still together, working shit out. They were the least traditional couple Hannah knew. That was saying a lot, since Hannah knew a lot of unusual people.

"Sharing a body is a level of closeness I'm not sure I could endure," Hannah joked.

Shelby laughed. She was holding Kyle's hand, with her other arm wrapped around Hannah's neck. "I heard that! I mean, I thought we were close. Remember when we told people to call us Hanby?"

"Yea, I do," Hannah said, holding her lover even closer. Loved ones were precious. They could be taken away without notice, sometimes forever. "That was a fun night. We had some good times back in the day, before everything got scary."

"I think they need a celebrity couple name," Shelby said. "Charlyn? Fylette? Charlene?"

"That's messed up," Hannah said. She laughed nervously. Shelby was in good spirits, but Hannah was overcome with apprehension. An ancient god was visiting their home. The god of nightmares just showed up out of nowhere, whenever he pleased. Charlotte and Flynn had recently had a falling out with Mr. Tall, Dark, and Terrifying. Mercy and Sympathy were barreling down I-5 with a death-ray lock on Charlotte's mother and the rest of the Soccer Mom Coven. Shit was about to get hairy.

Shelby must have known that she was nervous. She turned to Hannah and said, "I just want to let you know that I wouldn't let anything bad happen to you or Kyle, either."

"I know that," Hannah said with a gulp. "I do. Just don't die or anything, okay? I don't think I could stand it."

"I won't," Shelby said. "I promise."

Act V: Factions

The Sisterhood

Things were still awkward between been Maribelle and the Sisterhood. Knowing who killed Flynn eliminated some of the tension. They met at her home in the Berkeley Hills for the first time in three and a half years.

Lorena Young, Nancy Allen, Jeannie Byrne, and Sunny Green had not entirely recovered from their earlier falling out. But politics make for strange bedfellows. There was nothing as blatantly political as being on the verge of war.

The messy past and impending doom were no reasons to ignore social niceties. The five middle aged women were gathered around a gorgeous fireplace in the living room. They were sipping Napa wines and eating from vegetable platters and little trays with multicultural finger foods. Chinese egg rolls, and Filipino spring rolls called lumpia served with various sweet and sour, sweet plum, or soy-based sauces.

There was a giant bowl of fancy blue corn chips sitting next to bowls full of sweet corn salsa, mango salsa, and guacamole. Greek salad, olives, pita chips and hummus, and rice stuffed olive leaves called dolmathakia covered the coffee table. There were little signs denoting which foods were vegan, and gluten free. It was so very Berkeley.

Lorena Green was sipping a glass of chardonnay and eating a sweet Turkish desert called baklava. It consisted of layers of flaky pastry laden with honey and pistachio nuts. She wore strappy high heels and a turquoise sundress that ended mid-thigh. She'd lost forty pounds and was determined to show off her shapely legs. No longer concerned about being accused of murder, she felt comfortable sitting next to Maribelle. Lorena was ready to have a frank discussion.

"I know you had your reasons, Maribelle," Lorena said boldly. "I'm not excusing what you did to Flynn by any means, but I know you had your reasons."

"At least his daughter isn't cursed," Jeannie Byrne piped in from the other side of Lorena. Like Lorena, she was relieved that Maribelle's confession had taken her off the hot seat. Jeannie had a fashion sensibility Charlotte used to call "gothic secretary."

Another affectionate if slightly derisive nickname Charlotte and Hannah had for Mrs. Byrne when they were in high school with her daughter, Rose, was "Gothy Spice." Back then, she wore platform heels like the Spice Girls. Today, she was in slightly more conservative chunky square heeled Mary Janes. She was wearing one of her usual knee-length black dresses. They were invariably convertible from office to nightwear, and always from some store like Ross, J.C. Penney, or T.J. Maxx. Her jet-black dyed hair was piled into two Princess Leia buns, held in place with red lacquered chopsticks. She wore adorable cat knee-high stockings. They were shaped like cats and had tails on the back of their knees.

"Right," Maribelle said dryly. "I'm sure that's a big comfort to Flynn in the afterlife."

She was in a fashionable ankle-length purple sheath, with her wavy brown hair piled on her head in an old Roman style. However, confessing to everyone and their dog had left her emotionally exhausted and looking haggard. Her usually fashionable smoky eye shadow, eye liner and mascara clung in the microscopic wrinkles in her under-eye bags. She really wasn't sleeping well. She felt a stress headache coming on.

Exhausted though she was, Maribelle stood up and clicked her fork against the side of her wine glass. "Excuse me, ladies… may I have your attention?"

The other four women gathered around as Maribelle stood in front of the fireplace to address them.

"I have a lot to tell you ladies," she began. "I have tried to be generous with the wine and comfort foods, because a lot of it is very unpleasant. The Rites of Undoing, the very basis for this Sisterhood, I have learned, were originally authored by Phobetor. They were designed for the express purpose of ending Brash's reign in the realm of dreams, as well as eliminating his non-human bloodline."

Lorena raised an eyebrow. "Phobetor? The god of nightmares? Isn't that Brash's brother?"

"Yes," Maribelle said. "Apparently, everything we did to try to limit Brash's influence here on Earth and protect the world from his offspring was a part of a larger plan. Phobetor believed that if he could reduce Brash and all of his children to mere mortals, he could take his brother's place. His intention was to rule two kingdoms from one throne."

"Did he succeed?" Sunshine asked, sipping at her organic orange juice and local sparkling wine mimosa.

"Not entirely," Maribelle said. "Somnus intervened on Charlotte's behalf, and preserved her powers and estate, if you will, in trust for her until the day she dies. She's been promised deification in the afterlife, to rule as Brash's heir."

"Wow," Jeannie said. "So, in the meantime, there's kind of a vacuum of power? You have an heir apparently who is, I guess you might say in immortal terms, too young to take the throne. I could see how this could cause trouble."

"It has," Maribelle continued. "Thanatos intervened on behalf of two of Brash's other offspring, Mercy and Sympathy. Meanwhile, Phobetor is demanding that he be allowed to run the kingdom until Charlotte is ready, as her proxy. Only lately, he says she'll never be strong enough and demands she just hand it over. So it's like a War of the Roses, but with dream deities."

"And what does any of this have to do with us?" Nancy demanded, eating her fat free kettle corn.

"Well, all of the rituals we performed were to get rid of Brash and his offspring," Maribelle said. "To make Charlotte fully human, and force everyone else to reincarnate. The problem is that Mercy and Sympathy still have some of their powers. They still know who they are. They still know who we are. And more to the point, they want revenge. Phobetor said they've gotten down to Redding now, making a bee line for the Bay

Area. They want to see us dead."

"Well that most definitely *is* unsettling news," Lorena admitted, slugging the rest of her chardonnay down in a single gulp. Sunny Green burst into a nervous, tittering laughter. Those who knew her well began to worry about her sanity.

"Isn't Phobetor the guy who manipulated you into killing your son-in-law?" Nancy asked. "Isn't he the one who has been influencing all of us, through the Rites of Undoing? And to what end? Is it really to protect humanity from creatures like Mercy? Or is it just a part of his personal grasping for power and glory?"

Maribelle was going to say something when Jeannie Byrne began a contrived, noisy effort to clear her throat. Maribelle assumed it was an effort to get her attention, perhaps the attention of the group. She decided to give her the floor.

"Besides Maribelle," Jeannie said, "I'm the only one here who actually has met Phobetor. Now I don't have a thing for winged beings, so I can't say that I knew him as intimately as Maribelle did."

Maribelle huffed. "That was uncalled for!"

Jeannie sneered. "Do you deny that you had an affair with your brother-in-law?"

Sunny Green's eyes widened with envious disbelief. "Did you really?"

Sunny was more than a little fascinated with Phobetor. She'd been lusting over Charlotte's painting of him that afternoon the Sisterhood met in Suisun. When she went home that night, she immediately ordered a copy of that issue of Somnalia. She also purchased the Phobetor t-shirt. Then she googled up and read every single reference to Phobetor on the internet. She ordered several relevant books of mythology.

You could say she was a raging fan girl.

Lorena knew all about that. She just looked at Sunny and winked. "Yes, I'm sure that Sunny here absolutely has to know all of the gory details about that affair."

Maribelle blushed.

"He said he was trying to save her from Brash," Jeannie said with childish glee. "He claimed that Brash was a terrible person, a supernatural serial killer. I asked Maribelle then, 'how can you trust this guy? He's the friggin' god of fear, the god of nightmares!' But she just took Phobetor's word for it, that Brash had slaughtered seventeen innocent people."

Maribelle snarled at Jeannie. She'd forgotten how much Gothy Spice used to buy into Brash's whole übergoth "I am the brother of Morpheus" bullshit story back in the day.

"You jealous little bitch," she said. "Take my word for it, the Slaughter of Innocents was real. Brash admitted it all with no hesitation when I confronted him about it. He said, and I quote, 'Well technically, it was only five people. I killed five people and aborted twelve fetuses.' All very casually, like he couldn't understand why I was so upset."

"The Slaughter of Innocents?" Sunny asked. She grabbed the first tome of the Rites of Undoing off the shelf over the fireplace. "Wait, that's in the book. Let me see… I almost remember."

"Don't bother looking it up," Lorena said. "I remember it. It's the sacrifice of twelve unborn children required for anyone in Brash's cursed line to conceive a demisomnali. The slaughter of the mothers is not required, but it often happens as a consequence of some of the methods employed."

"That's absolutely the most horrifying thing I've ever heard!" Nancy said. She was very upset and feeling lightheaded. She had to take a seat on the couch before she spilled her merlot.

"I felt the same way when I found out," Maribelle assured her. "That's why I left Brash."

Nancy shook her head. "This is worse than the Jerry Springer show. It's like a reality television program with demons, Real Housewives of the Demos Oneiroi." She tittered nervously at her own joke. An equally stunned Sunny took a seat beside her.

"So how and when did you find out?" Lorena asked. By now, Lorena and Maribelle were the only ones left who were exuding a semblance of calm. Sunny and Nancy were totally freaked out, sitting on the couch inhaling glasses of wine. Jeannie was in the middle of dumping her twenty-seven years' worth of resentment over the Oneiroi on Maribelle's head.

"Phobetor told her!" Jeannie accused, seeming more like one of the over-the-top hysterical reality show vixens Nancy had alluded to by the minute. "And after he told her, he offered her a shoulder to cry on. What a nice guy, right?"

Maribelle lowered her eyes. She was about to shoot back a salty remark pertaining to Jeannie's inadequate love-life when the doorbell rang.

"I better go get that," she said. Crossing the threshold, she breathed a sigh of relief. She wasn't expecting company. She wasn't sure who it was. She'd been ordering a lot of books lately, perhaps it was a package delivery. Whoever it was, they'd provided a welcome reprieve from the awkward conversation.

She took a deep breath and then opened the door.

Twins

Pasithea had accompanied her husband on a visit with his brother in order to plead with Thanatos to intervene on the behalf of Sympathy. All three were sitting outdoors, in front of Thanatos' castle. The couple sat together on a curbed bench. Pasithea looked unusually vulnerable today, leaning against her beloved as if she lacked the strength to sit up on her own.

"Please, I beg of you, spare my granddaughter, Sympathy," she cried to Thanatos. "Unbind her from Mercy, for only you have the power to do so,"

He shrugged. "Twins may be many things. They may be at one another's throats, as Romulus was with his twin brother Remus. Romulus took his place in history as the founder of Rome. In this very city, which he created, to which he gave his very name, did he spill his brother's blood? Perhaps the blood of Remus was a sacrificial sacrament spilled into the soil of the newly established Rome? Perhaps it was required, before his brother could be allowed to take his true place in history.

"Twins may be many things, but as my brother and I both know, one thing we can never be is unbound. Be glad that they are not identical, for they might have been bound even closer. The future remains to be seen, but perhaps Sympathy may yet live. I think it more likely that Sympathy's blood will be the sacrifice required for the establishment of the Cult of Mercy. Let us see."

All three gathered closer to the object at the center of the circle of benches on which they sat. The river Lethe made a perfectly good scrying glass, but Thanatos had chosen to use the bottom of a well. The well was deep, and its waters were dark and murky. Leaning over, Thanatos dropped a coin inside. The shadowy waters cleared, and the scene being played out between Candy, Cyn and their mortal parents played itself out on that screen.

Pasithea gasped in horror when she saw what unfolded before her.

Sympathy

All of her very long life, Sympathy, lately known as Cyn, had trusted her sister. Only now was it occurring to her that this was a mistake. Mercy was tearing Sympathy apart.

She was beginning to see the light now. Now knowing how things were, she saw her sister didn't care. Mercy would take all and everything without a thought. It was her way. She was like a ravenous shark. She just consumed everything in her wake and kept swimming.

Sympathy was not, and she was starving.

Alice Carter and little Sympathy "Cyn" Carter were sitting in the bathroom of a crappy roadside motel in Redding, California. Now that they were driving around in a rental car, rest stops were no longer as practical as they had been with the RV.

Mercy "Candy" Carter was out with her daddy picking up some breakfast. They'd get food to go for Alice and Cyn. Both of them were looking way too haggard to be taken out in public.

By the time Sympathy had been released from the hospital in Grants Pass two days ago, she had put on a little bit of weight. There were no signs of pneumonia. Her mother, however, looked a bit under the weather. When they first came in, a nurse had expressed some concern and suggested that Alice be admitted. Afraid of arousing suspicion, Tom ordered her to go sit in the car. He was completely under the sway of Candy by now.

For some reason, Candy's mind manipulations worked better on men than on women. Like his father before him, Tim was firmly wrapped around Candy's little finger. This was probably a holdover from when she had been a somnali named Mercy. Sympathy and other somnali had their own personal skill sets. Mercy more than any other somnali, had the seductive qualities of a succubus or a siren.

Since Tim looked perfectly healthy, and was the easiest of the three to control, he was selected for the away mission. That left Cyn and Alice alone.

Alice was sitting on the toilet in the bathroom. She'd just finished vomiting, and now she was trying to pee. She'd barely had enough energy to flush the toilet before crawling up off her knees to sit on it. The mother of two was increasingly emaciated. Her skin had a grayish sheen to it. The bags under her eyes were so deep and dark that they looked like they might have been caused by a physical injury, like a black eye. Her eyes themselves were jaundiced. Two days ago, her hair had been brown. Now it was thinning and patchy and mostly gray. It stuck to her forehead in damp clumps because she could not stop sweating. She had hot flashes because she had just started menopause.

Alice was only twenty-eight years old.

If Alice looked like she was on death's door, Cyn looked like death warmed over. She was sitting on the edge of the sink, with the mirror behind her. She had been looking into it recently, realizing just how badly things were going for her. Her tiny, fragile arms had gone beyond emaciation. They were skeletally thin. All of the bones in her forearms were visible. Her ribcage protruded out of her caved-in chest, which sat above a distended belly. Her lifeless, bony legs dangled from the counter, useless. She could no longer walk. She couldn't speak, either.

What truly frightened her was that her senses were starting to fade. She couldn't feel, smell, or hear as well as she used to. Her sight was beginning to dim.

There was only one thing she could do, though. She could communicate with her mother telepathically. Telepathy between mothers and daughters was not as strong as it was between twins, but it was present. It was scientific – neurons were transferred from the brains of unborn children into their mother's brains and vice versa through the placenta during pregnancy. This process was called microchimerism.

But Cyn was weak, and so was her internal voice.

We have to go, mommy she whispered into her mother's head. *She's killing us*

She'd been trying to talk to Alice for the past fifteen minutes, since Candy left. She had been trying desperately to call out to the only person she still had access to and failing. Perhaps, now that she wasn't throwing up, it would be easier for her to hear. At least they had eye contact now.

Alice looked back at her, dull and listless.

Sympathy decided to give it one more try. *Mommy, please! We have to go!*

When Alice finally parted her dry, cracked lips, and spoke, it was a croak barely above a whisper.

"I know, honey," she said. "I know."

Alice understood at last that she wasn't going to be able to pee. Her bladder hurt because she had an infection. It was one of the many health problems she'd mysteriously developed over the past forty-eight hours. Her health was deteriorating quickly, and she knew that she was dying. So was her daughter.

With great effort, Alice lifted her weight up onto her swollen, arthritic knees. She slid back into her now oversized blue jeans. The pain in her fingers was so bad that she began to cry when she pulled up the zipper.

When her pants were on, she leaned over and picked up her poor, withered daughter. Cyn was wearing nothing but a soiled diaper. Alice was too sick to clothe her properly. She bundled her up in a clean, white towel to keep her warm. Tim and Candy would be home soon. She had to hurry.

Her legs were killing her, but she knew she had to hurry.

Alice was too tired to close the hotel room door behind her. It took all of her effort to get to the side of the road, and to stumble across the highway without being hit by a car.

Tim was alarmed when they returned home and saw the open door. He immediately approached the hotel night clerk and asked where his wife had gone. The young man at the desk, and several hotel guests reported that a woman had left the hotel, holding what appeared to be a baby.

Everyone saw her walk to the edge of the road. When she got there, she stuck her thumb out and hitched a ride south, towards Sacramento. After a few minutes, an eight-wheeler stopped and picked her and the baby up. That was maybe fifteen minutes before Tim came back. Now a half an hour had gone by.

Candy and Tim checked out of the hotel room. He packed their bags into the rental car and headed down the road, due south. They hoped to catch up with them.

The thing was that Alice wasn't on her way down I-5. She had wandered into a vacant lot across the street. A stack of four-by-four boards next to a smaller stack of two by fours indicated that construction would begin soon. There was also a portable toilet there. It was unlocked, and thankfully, unused. Alice crawled inside with the baby and pulled close the latch. She was too weak to go any further. They were still inside of the toilet when Candy and Tim got back to the hotel.

Cyn used the last of her energy to glamour the hotel residents into thinking that they'd actually climbed into a passing truck. It was the last conscious action she was able to take. She used the last of her mental energy to try to protect her mother and herself and aid their escape under the cover of darkness. Then she fell unconscious. The toddler was in a comatose state by the time Alice locked them into the stall.

Her losing consciousness might have been fortuitous. If she had been conscious, Candy might have been able to detect her. Her unconscious mind put out fewer noticeable brainwaves. Alice was not as strongly connected to the twins as they were to each other.

Even with all that, they might have been found if they didn't have a protector.

An unusually large German shepherd was lying on the ground, immediately outside of the portable toilet. Phobetor stood guard, waiting until he was sure that Candy and Tim were long gone. It was quite easy for him to cast a protective shield over his sleeping niece and her semi-conscious mother. He couldn't afford to continually guard them, but at least he could give them a head start.

He didn't hold much hope for Cyn. She didn't look well enough to make it through the night.

Pasithea's Tears

Pasithea stood at the edge of the well, watching. Her thin and milky fingers were clasped so tightly that what little color they had to begin with drained from the pallid. The stone at the edge of the well began to crumple a bit, and a soft spray of dust drifted into the well below her. Her tears fell hot, hard and inconsolable. They splashed at the bottom of the well, causing the scrying waters to ripple and distort. Even the warm touch of Somnus, who stood beside her, arm around her waist, was not enough to comfort her.

"Is there nothing you can do?" she cried. "My grandchild lies dying and I have no one to defend her except for the foul beast of nightmares, Phobetor. It is he who caused this abominable predicament. He and yourself, Thanatos, and yet you refuse to offer her aid?"

Thanatos shrugged. "I do not think only Phobetor defends her. Even now, her earthly mother holds her against her withered breast. See how she attempts to nourish her child with her last breath? Does it not evoke pity in even the likes of you? You and Somnus, with your everlasting and untouchably perfect love, do you not see how much deeper the love of humans is?

"Alice tries to feed her daughter, but her body is a desert laid to waste by famine. Her breast is a reservoir emptied by drought. While she tries in vain to feed her child, that same child uses the last of her precious magic to cloak and protect them from Mercy. Watch as the fragile mother and daughter desperately cling to one another in need. Theirs is a tableau of pathos and tragedy. Alice and Cynthia Carter are on their way to experiencing a beautiful death."

Somnus grew angry and impatient with Thanatos and his insipid death poetry. He left his wife's side and flew upon his brother at once, cuffing him in the side of the head. Thanatos did not strike him back, but instead, stood there laughing.

"You are so gentle, brother," Thanatos said. "Your hands are as tender and downy as the cumulus clouds your granddaughter Charlotte draws to indicate dreams in her comic book. Your slap is as gentle as a milk maid's. Perhaps you have grown soft, with all of your many years tenderly romancing Pasithea. Perhaps you always were soft, dreams being the weak, transient state mortals gather their rest in before I offer them permanent release from the dull, dreadful lives they lead."

Somnus placed his hands at his sides, and stood unmoving, glaring at his brother. His red-yellow eyes grew fiery and determined. Perhaps he could not best Thanatos, but neither could he be moved.

"You have always been morbid," Somnus sneered. "You have always tried to cast everything in your dark and tragic light. You might have named the twins Castor and Pollux. You might have told the story of how the demigod Pollux offered a portion of his own immortality to Castor so they could be together. You might have even mentioned our own sometimes tumultuous, but generally copacetic relationship as twins.

"Instead, you choose the example most conducive to your own proselytizing. Your story of Remus and Romulus is designed only to manipulate."

Thanatos turned his body to face Somnus, staring at him with a gaze as hard and incorruptible as that of a blank eyed marble statue. Both twins stood and stared as if they had been overcome by the notion that a strong posture and hardened grimace were enough to win a war or a battle of wills.

"The Cult of Mercy shall be marvelous indeed," Thanatos proclaimed.

"Her followers shall be many. I have seen the jihad she will lead. Mercy is destined to become the harbinger of death, greater than any Reverend Jim Jones or Pol Pot. The Eyes of Mercy are the eyes that will launch a dozen death cults, a hundred. Who are you to stop her from beginning her order on Earth?"

"You are obsessed with death," Somnus spat.

"As are you with your gentle sleep and tender resolutions," Thanatos countered. "You corrupted Flynn's beautiful death sacrifice and turned his tragic love story into an insipid bit of eternal god and goddess fuckery such as you enjoy with your nauseatingly well-loved Pasithea."

"Enough, boys!" shouted a familiar, angry voice, impatient and dripping with authority. Nyx stood beside a grieving Pasithea, lovingly holding her hand.

"How dare you speak so crudely of your sister-in-law so as she stands here before you?" Nyx chastised Thanatos. "How dare you accuse your brother for the choice I made, to deify Flynn, my champion? If you choose Mercy as your champion, your bringer of death, then with what authority do you to impugn the choices of others?"

Thanatos scowled but said nothing. Nyx was more powerful than any of them. She rarely interfered. But if she so chose, she might cuff him so hard that he would find himself ejected from the Demos Oneiroi. Once, he angered her, and found himself cast on a heated rock afloat in a sea of boiling lava at the heart of Tartarus.

His senses had been so scrambled that it had taken him twenty years to find his way back home.

"Very well, mother," he said coolly.

"If you would prefer that Sympathy be freed from Mercy," Nyx told Pasithea, "then you have it in your power to give her over to her mortal mother and let her retain her mortal form. Free her from yourself, and she will also be freed from your ravenous Mercy."

"But what will become of her if I do?" Pasithea sobbed.

"If she dies, her reincarnation cycles will be connected with her earthly mother, Alice, instead of Mercy," Thanatos said, as diplomatically as he was capable of given his underlying resentment. "She won't remember who she was, but she will be met by Alice in some form or another for the rest of her cycle.

"If she lives, she will remember who she is as long as she is Cynthia Carter. Of course, she may grow older and decide it was a dream or a delusion. So many humans exposed to the supernatural as children eventually do. She will recognize you if you visit her in her dreams. But she won't have any power. She'll be mortal. So, it would be with you much as it is with Flynn and his child."

"Does Flynn know that when Faelyn eventually dies, she will be reincarnated like any other mortal?" Somnus asked solemnly.

"No, he does not," Nyx answered hastily. "Why should he? It would only trouble him. They may have fifty years, or even a hundred. Whenever she does die, he can mourn her as humans mourn their dead. Why should he mourn her now when her life is just beginning?"

"But their lives are so short," Somnus complained.

"He's only thirty years old," Nyx reminded Somnus. "Her life will seem very long to him."

"But Sympathy's life won't seem long to me," Pasithea mourned. "Only eighty years. It's so unfair."

"Not eighty minutes if you do not intervene on her behalf," Nyx warned.

Pasithea accepted her offer. She let her immortal child go, and Thanatos severed the ties between the mortal Cynthia Sympathy Carter and the increasingly powerful monster she had been born with. Alice and Cynthia were withered, and dry. Pasithea moistened them with her tears. It wasn't much, but it would give them a little extra time… several hours or maybe a day. Nonetheless, if someone didn't find them, and soon, both would die.

Nyx was about to leave when Pasithea stopped her.

"Did Somnus speak truly when he said that Phobetor loved that woman, Maribelle Metaxas?" she asked.

"Only in the selfish, acquisitive way he loves anything or anyone," Nyx shrugged. "Phobetor loves Maribelle the way a mortal man may love his fancy new sports car. He loves her the way a betting man loves a prizewinning horse. He does not listen to her. He does not consider the consequences of his actions as they would be viewed through mortal eyes."

"But he would be hurt if he lost her," Pasithea suggested.

A dark look came over Nyx's single, white eye. She narrowed it until it looked like the barest slit of a fingernail moon. At first, Pasithea was sure she was angry. Then Nyx took both of her hands.

"Sweet Pasithea," Nyx said thoughtfully, "stay your hand. Vengeance does not suit you. Wicked though my grandson Phobetor has been, your granddaughters Mercy and Sympathy have been far more malevolent. Their behavior, and that of your son, made it clear why his name was Brash. He was brash and reckless as well. He would have bought the fury of Zeus down upon all of our heads. Mercy and Sympathy forced Maribelle's hand with their outrageous attacks on Charlotte's inner circle. They sent warning flares as they circled their prey. They were rash, and foolish.

"Even now, I exercise great patience and forgiveness in allowing your Sympathy her redemption. I show restraint in my dealings with Mercy as well. It is only her distance from me, her placement on Earth that protects us from Zeus' wrath. Make no mistake, though, she invites it – if only on herself.

"If Phobetor did not guard Sympathy, Mercy would have killed her this night. I ask that you reconsider your urge to punish him, and leave his priestess be."

Nyx turned again and left.

When she was gone, Pasithea said. "I am surprised that Phobetor would assist my granddaughter Sympathy. However, that doesn't begin to erase the crimes he has committed against Brash, my son. It doesn't make up for his banishment of my grandchildren from this realm."

Cats and Dogs

Maribelle was surprised when she opened the door and saw her daughter and granddaughter standing there. Charlotte was wearing an outfit so similar to Jeannie Byrne's that it made Maribelle laugh inside when she saw it. Charlie looked way better in it. Jeannie was going to just die of envy.

Faelyn was going through a stage where she preferred to walk everywhere. She was beginning to refuse to be picked up. She was holding her mother's hand with her own tiny fingers. Mother and daughter wore matching purple fingernail polish, and Faelyn's jet-black hair was in the two-pigtail configuration. She wore little purple bow barrettes. She had black shorts, a purple Dora the Explorer t-shirt and black tennis shoes with little white lace-cuffed socks.

"You guys look adorable," Maribelle said. She was pleasantly surprised when her daughter leaned over to give her a hug. That was something that hadn't happened in a very long time. It seemed that all was forgiven. Maybe Flynn spoke to her.

"You look great, too, mom," Charlotte said. "Wow, all three of us have purple on. We should take a picture."

Maribelle was about to turn around and go back to the living room was when she noticed for the first time the little dog they had with them. It was cowering in fear, doing its best to hide behind one of Charlotte's shoes. It was terrified of Maribelle. She turned and looked at it.

"That's him, isn't it?" Maribelle asked pointedly. She dropped down on one knee and offered the frightened little rat terrier her hand to sniff. The tiny dog was still trembling, but he sniffed her hand. After a little while, he licked her fingers.

Charlotte nodded. "Yes, he is Flynn." She stood and watched, not interfering with the interaction between her mother and the dog.

She couldn't blame the little dog for shaking. However, Flynn the man felt, it was being filtered through the sense of the little rat dog. She petted him gently until he calmed down. He was a tiny dog, no more than ten pounds. Once he seemed comfortable with her, she picked him up and set him on her forearm.

"Maybe I can get him a little chicken out of the kitchen when we settle in," Maribelle said calmly. The dog seemed happy and settled and was panting with a big doggy grin on his little doggy face. She didn't want to alarm him.

"I'm sure he'd like that," Charlotte said. She was relieved that her mother was okay with Flynn being here. In the past, Maribelle's feelings of guilt had been taken out on him. Scapegoating was such an ugly, yet predictable part of human nature. Given Phobetor's behavior, apparently it wasn't unique to humans.

"The last time I saw him, he was a cat." Maribelle noted. "That's two shapes he's shifted into that I am aware of. Don't you wonder why he has these powers? Did you know that all human shapeshifters are related to Phobetor?"

Flynn was having his ears scratched and didn't seem to take notice of the fact that he was being talked about in the third person. Later, when he went home and returned to his natural form, he would remember the conversation and understand it. At the moment, though, they might as well be speaking a foreign language.

"He's not a *human* shapeshifter," Charlotte corrected. "He is no longer human. He's taken the form of a somnali. I should say, the form was granted to him. The gods were always showing up as swans, horses, showers of gold, what have you. Somnali are the grandchildren of Somnus: why shouldn't they be able to shift?"

"Because a blood sacrifice has been required for the cursed somnali," Maribelle said with a shrug. "Of course he isn't from Brash's bloodline. Perhaps he isn't cursed."

They walked straight into the kitchen. Maribelle set Flynn down on the tiled floor and opened the refrigerator. She pulled out a baked boneless breast of chicken and tossed it on a chopping board. She diced it in half, and then cubed one quarter of it. She tossed the cubes on a tea plate and put it down on the floor for the little dog.

Charlotte shook her head. "How many great-great-great grandchildren does Phobetor have anyway? He was very prolific, wasn't he? I don't really care if Flynn's human bloodline was infiltrated by one of the thousand or hundred-thousand hybrid species spawned by Phobetor. Why should I?"

"I didn't think you would, but Phobetor might care," Maribelle said mysteriously. "Speaking of Phobetor, his order is in the house right now, the Sisterhood of the Undoing. Why don't you and Faelyn go say hi to the girls? I'll be out in a bit."

Charlotte nodded. She walked into the living room, where she was immediately greeted by the Sisterhood of Undoing.

"Hi Aunt Jeannie, you look great!" Charlotte said enthusiastically, immediately running up and giving the older woman a hug. Charlie had known Jeannie all her life. She grew up with her daughter, Rosie.

"Oh, you both look so cute!" Sunshine squealed with delight. "You should take a picture together. You match!"

Charlie's shoes were Demonia brand platform Mary Janes, a less matronly version of the shoes Jeannie wore. She had the exact same fucking knee-high cat socks on as the older woman did but paired with a much shorter skirt. Jeannie's skirt came to the knee, while Charlotte's covered less than half of her thigh. It was a black pleated mini skirt with a built-in tulle and lace underskirt. She wore a matching black and purple tube top.

She had cut her long hair short during the hair-grabbing stage of Faelyn's infancy. This happened when Faelyn was about ten months old and extremely into grabbing things like glasses and hair. Charlie's hair had grown considerably over the past year and a half, but it was still only chin-length. Today she had it on top of her head in a pair of messy pigtails that stuck straight up, like the puppet from Fraggle Rock. Each pigtail had a cute little black and purple striped bow on it, with a skull glued to the center.

As Maribelle anticipated, Jeannie was envious and not taking compliments very well.

"Where is your mother?" Jeannie demanded. "We need to get this business sorted out about Phobetor."

"I think we should be more concerned about Mercy and Sympathy," Lorena gently suggested. "Redding is a three-hour drive from here. They could easily arrive tonight."

Nancy scooted over a bit and offered Charlotte a seat. Charlotte accepted it graciously and sat Faelyn in her lap. It wasn't long before the toddler had crawled over to Nancy. Not much longer still before she hopped down to the floor. She was circulating the room, exerting her fresh toddler autonomy. She was being the natural little social butterfly she was.

Just then, Maribelle came in the room, with Flynn at her heels.

Flynn was so excited to be in this room, surrounded by giants. His mistress Charlotte was seated between two of them. He ran up to her and pawed at her ankle, begging to be picked up. She reached her great hands down and plucked him up. He curled his body up into a little ball in her lap.

He recognized the other two women on the couch, Sunny and Nancy.

The one called Nancy offered him her hand to sniff. He sniffed it several times, and decided she was safe and could be trusted. He lifted his head up to Charlotte's knee and let the Nancy woman pat it. After a little time, his mistress plucked him out of her comfortable lap and set him on the floor.

"It is okay, sweetie," she said gently. "You're safe here."

Flynn ran off to play with the baby, who was already on the carpet whizzing around in manic circles. He ran up to her and wagged his tail. She grinned wildly and chased after him. Soon, they were playing tag in the living room, among the feet of the giant women.

"Mom," Charlotte said. "I've got a lot to tell you. Maybe I should get a drink."

For Flynn, the house was large and filled with strange aromas associated with many kinds of food and several human women. Some of the humans were not as familiar to Flynn as others. He knew and loved Faelyn. When the tiny human came to play with him, he wagged his tail. She was excited and smacked him roughly on the back with her little hands, which were as large as his tiny paws. She decided to ride him like a horsey.

When she climbed up on his back and sat on his back, he wasn't big enough to carry her. His tiny body was squished to the floor. Instinctively, he shifted into a form large enough to support her. The baby giggled rowdily and held on with her arms around his neck.

"Whoa! Holy shit!" Nancy shouted when she noticed the big leopard in the middle of the living room floor. "I like cats but damn… that's a big one."

"That should come in handy," Lorena said drolly.

"Let's just hope he's impervious to mind control and hallucinations," Maribelle said with a sigh.

"If they'll be here tonight, I guess there is no sense in going home," Charlotte acknowledged.

Captured

She was crawling across the parking lot on her broken knees. Pain radiated outward from her fractured tibia where it protruded from her torn-open calf. She could feel the pressure against her exposed bone as it rubbed against the pavement. The movement caused it to shift under her skin. If she had a choice, she would have stopped right then and there and passed out on the ground.

But she didn't have any better options. That evil little bitch was right behind her. When she first showed up, she was riding on her daddy's shoulders like he was a fucking prize pony. Now, Candy and Tim were both on the ground and running like a father and daughter maniac tag team.

"Shit!" Becky Carter yelled as the toddler grabbed her by the hair. Only, Candy didn't look like a toddler anymore. She certainly had grown; she looked like she was old enough to start kindergarten. The child sat on Becky's broken legs, pinning them to the ground.

"Hi. Good to see you, Grandma," the menacing child said in perfectly pronounced English well beyond her two years. Flashing her pearly whites at Becky, she added, "By the way… I meant to tell you. Please don't call me Candy. I hate that name. My name is Mercy."

Mercy aka Candice Carter originally intended to high tail it straight to the Bay Area. Sometimes things don't go according to plan. By a coincidence, that was either happy or unhappy depending on the point of view, she spotted her grandparent's RV at the Elkhorn rest stop, located at the Sacramento Airport. Phobetor wasn't there to interfere this time. He was still guarding Alice and Cyn and couldn't be in two places at once.

Tom Carter, Sr. was already dead.

Becky knew that it was a bad idea, performing routine maintenance at a rest stop. They still had the Wicked Witch from the Womb on their asses. Unfortunately, Tom didn't have the same sense of immediate and impending danger as she did. Tom was emptying out the camper's shitter when Candy pulled in. She strolled right on up to him on Tim's shoulder, did her little hypnotic eye zombify thing, and it was on.

The enraptured Tom yelled, "I offer this sacrifice to the Cult of Mercy! I offer my life!"

Becky looked on in horror as her husband picked up the hose that was sucking waste from the RV and shoved it down his throat. Never mind that it was caked in shit and lined with piss. That was not the worst of it. The device was like a vacuum cleaner. It began to suction out his insides. He was well on his way to dying of an inverted digestive tract when Candy stopped him.

"No," the child said forcefully. "It's not enough. I need more lives. More."

That was when Becky turned and ran.

Tom knocked her down on his way to the front door of the camper. He sprinted, moving like an Olympic track star in his prime. She fell down in front of the mobile home. She was not able to get up before he started the vehicle. Her knees and calves were busted open when he took off. He drove over her legs as he hauled ass towards a row of parked campers. The fact that she was not his target was the only reason she survived the initial impact.

She looked up just in time to watch him plow into the side of the nearest vehicle, knocking them over like a row of dominoes. The camper at the end was in the middle of loading its propane tanks. Hank Martin, the fellow doing the loading, had an ill-advised habit of chain smoking while doing everything. His daughter, Amy, repeatedly warned him about the dangers of smoking while handling hazardous liquids like gasoline and propane. That never stopped him from lighting up at a gas pump. His wife, Deborah, used to say, "Hank never met a potential smoking area he didn't like." She said that before she ran off with their plumber, Bill, leaving Hank with two teenage children, sixteen-year-old Amy and seventeen year old Sam.

Sam Martin was a huge fan death metal, scream and fireworks. The Martins were on their way back home to Redding after a trip to Tijuana. Little Sammy managed to sneak back through the border with all kinds of contraband. There was a bullwhip, a set of handcuffs, and a big black domesticated raven onboard. The guy who sold him the later claimed it was a mynah bird. Sam couldn't get it to talk, but it was fucking hardcore. He loved it.

All of those things would have been confiscated at the Mexican border if the Martins had been pulled over. Fortunately for Sam, they weren't. The shaggy haired, H.I.M. t-shirt wearing, black lipstick sporting Sammy Martin might have raised an eyebrow or two, but Hank and Amy were both very clean-cut all-American tourists.

Also among the contraband were several M-80s, cherry bombs, and other types of explosive fireworks legal in Mexico but banned in California. When Tom Carter plowed into the motor home, he knocked Hank Marin and his lit cigarette into the propane tank. The RV, the tank, the fireworks, and Hank himself all exploded into a ball of magnificent fire.

The flames from that vehicle spread to the next, and soon, the rest stop and refueling station looked like something out of a disaster movie.

Satisfied, Mercy ordered Tim to drag his mother into the back of the rental car and take off before the emergency vehicles arrived. They didn't have time to kill Rebecca right now, but that was alright. Mercy might need a snack later.

Rescue

Two hours had passed since Candy and Tim fled. There was no guarantee that they wouldn't turn around and head right back up, but they had checked out of the motel before leaving. At approximately 9:14 pm, the German shepherd that was Phobetor began barking and howling to draw attention to the construction site.

He ran back and forth between the portable toilet and the chain link fence, barking at the top of his lungs, until he attracted the attention of a passing pedestrian. The Good Samaritan was a young black man on a skateboard, nineteen or twenty years old. He was wearing board shorts and a Dre Dog t-shirt. Although a human probably couldn't smell it, to Phobetor he reeked of ganja. It was lightly bathed in the aromas of the Febreeze, lavender gum and Visine used to mask the recent marijuana use.

His name was Kenyatta Frazier.

The stoned young man followed the yowling dog to the portable potty. He was about to turn around again and leave when he heard a weak sound from inside. Kenyatta did a double take and noticed the "occupied" sign was visible on the locking mechanism. A woman's voice was mumbling "help me." She was tapping on the inside of the door.

Kenyatta pulled out his cell phone and dialed 911. He thought about taking off before the police and emergency services came but changed his mind. He took the small baggie of weed out of his shorts pocket and dumped the contents into his mouth. After swallowing it, he picked up an empty Snapple bottle from off the ground, twisted the lid of, and shoved the baggie inside. He picked it up and flung it away from him as hard as he could. He didn't have any warrants or record, and the baggie, even if was linked to him, was only paraphernalia.

Then he did what he had wanted to do just about all of his life. He decided to try to be a hero.

When he picked up a two by four and forced it under bottom corner of door of the portable toilet, he was working on more than just adrenaline. He was working on the knowledge that he'd gained sitting in four years of high school science classes no one thought he was paying attention to. He was working with leverage. That's what he used when he kicked the board until the door propped open.

He was working with frustration. He could hear all of the little nitpicking voices in the back of his head. He heard his foster father telling him he was lazy and would never amount to shit. He heard his ex-girlfriend, Sheila, telling him he didn't have a real job and wasn't a real man.

The door popped open and what he saw horrified him. He didn't know how long the emaciated woman and child had been trapped inside, but they both seemed to be starving to death. There wasn't any smell except for the chemicals, so clearly the toilet had never been used. Something, though, must have attracted the vermin. The floor inside was littered with dead insects and rodents. He saw roaches, flies, field mice and one big ass rat.

Cyn had invited them all in and sucked up their essences, before Pasithea made her fully human and took away her powers. It wasn't much, but she was trying to avoid taking anything but milk away from poor, beleaguered Alice. The woman was desperately trying to breast feed her, but she was so dehydrated her attempts were mostly unsuccessful.

Kenyatta told the skeletal woman in the pajama pants and terrycloth robe, "Help is coming." Looking at her and her baby made him want to cry. He wondered what their story was, were they homeless? The lady almost looked too old to have a baby, about fifty, but he knew older ladies could have babies. After twenty years of trying, his then-forty-eight-year-old foster mother had finally conceived two years ago.

Some of the neighbors gossiped and said that she used the money she got from the state taking care of kids like Kenyatta to pay for it. Kenyatta told them to fuck off. He had just turned eighteen then, and he knew that a lot of foster parents just kicked their kids out on the streets. Lacy Benson let him stay there and pay rent with the money he got from his little side business slinging weed. All she said was that he had to go to college. Kenyatta didn't mind, he liked school.

That's why he understood leverage.

This baby didn't look good at all. He had a six-month-old baby of his own now. Between his own child and his foster sister, he knew something about infants and toddlers. This kid was so malnourished it was hard to tell how old she was, but she had all of her front teeth. That meant she was old enough for solid food. Her mom was trying to breast feed her, but her milk had dried up.

Kenyatta smoked a lot of weed and he always had the munchies. He pulled his snack stash out of his pocket and rifled through it, trying to find something that was alright for a kid. He found some raisins and decided they were healthy. He fed them to her. Watching that frail little thing inhale them so fast that they could not have been fully chewed, he felt himself starting to choke up again.

Fuck! How could anyone do this to a baby?

By the time the paramedics arrived, the dog was gone. Kenyatta told the paramedics and the police about that dog. The dog was some kind of hero.

But by the time the news crews showed up, there was only one hero left to report on, and that was Kenyatta Frazier.

Weakness

Mercy was pissed off. The whole time she'd been double teaming people with Sympathy in their mortal shells of Candy and Cyn she'd believed that each twin possessed identical powers. Now that she was on her own, she was seeing it simply was not so.

Sympathy had been able to influence and control women in a way that Mercy simply could not. That was probably how she was able to convince Alice to take off with her. She didn't know where they went, but it sure in the hell was not to Sacramento.

Mercy's control over Tim was absolute, but her attempts to control his mother failed completely. She could make Becky hallucinate, but she knew the visions weren't real anymore, so she ignored them. Mind control had no effect on Becky at all, and she was pissed off, screaming and trying to escape. Or at least, she *had* been, before Mercy had Tim pull over at the side of a deserted side road off I-80 and strangle his mother somewhere between Dixon and Vacaville.

The old broad had some spunk. Even Mercy had to admit that. She wouldn't stop flipping Mercy the bird, even as she was being strangled to death. She was still giving them the middle finger when Tim tossed her lifeless corpse under a bush.

Mercy suspected that if or when Sympathy died, she would inherit her sister's ability to control women. For now, though, she was without it.

She wasn't sure where her sister Charlotte lived these days but her mother in Berkeley or her two friends in Suisun probably did. She was going to use mind control to force them to tell her, but she didn't seem to have that anymore where women were concerned.

So, she came up with an alternate plan: torture.

Tim wasn't going to be able to control two or three women, so they were going to need to pick up a few extra bodies. She wasn't sure where she was going to get them until that motorcycle cop pulled her dad over for speeding. Fortunately, it was a male motorcycle cop.

Under her influence, he was quite handy with the information. There was a county jail in Fairfield. In about an hour, the prisoners who were to be released that day would be streaming out of the aforementioned prison. With any luck, some of them would be big, strong fellows with an affinity for violence.

Fairfield was right next door to Suisun.

Protection

None of the Sisterhood was willing to remain sitting ducks in Maribelle's home. Mercy might want to kill them, might even be able to figure out where they lived. One thing was for damned sure, though: Mercy and Charlotte's entire family knew where Maribelle lived. They were leaving, and advising Maribelle and Charlotte to get the hell out while the getting was good.

Charlie was trying to negotiate the details of how she would manage to leave the building with Flynn's stubborn adherence to his current form. There was a leopard in the living room, curled protectively around his cub. She was using English to attempt to calmly explain to him that a leopard walking around Berkeley would be likely to draw negative attention. The police might show up and shoot him. Animal control might pick him up.

None of that worked. Finally, she settled on the floor beside him and patted him on the haunches. She realized that this was him, her sweet, sensitive husband doing his best to be a father to their child. He refused to return to the Demos Oneiroi and stayed by Faelyn's side. He was determined to keep her safe. Charlotte understood. She put her arms around him.

Then, because she knew him well, she whispered something dirty in his ear. Flynn hastily shifted forms, back into the little rat terrier. He rolled over on his back with his little paws in the air and his tongue lolling out of the corner of his mouth. Charlotte put her hand on his chest and rubbed his body hard enough to make it rock back and forth on the carpet. He smiled, barked twice, and rolled over. Shortly after, Charlotte was at the door with her toddler holding her hand, and a yappy little dog at her heel.

"What on Earth did you tell him?" Maribelle asked her.

"I said that I noticed that when he's a dog, he has ten nipples, and when I put my hand on his chest just right, it covers like eight of them. Then I asked him if that was why he liked having his belly rubbed, and did he want me to rub it right now?"

Maribelle shook her head. "What a dog. I guess it's a good thing he's not fixed."

The four of them hopped into Charlotte's car because it was the one with the car seat. They drove down to the hotel Maribelle had booked out on the water. Running away from imminent danger was no reason not to have the luxuries her economic status could afford them, Maribelle believed. The rest of her world might have fallen apart after Flynn's death, but her career path was on an upswing. She had nothing other than work to occupy her time.

Charlotte explained to a bitchy desk clerk that Flynn was a service animal. She shoved the paperwork in his face, and hoped he didn't notice it was for a cat named Dada. The ruse worked, and the two women checked into a hotel room with two queen beds and a mini kitchen. After they got settled in, Charlotte asked her mother a question.

"Mom," she started, "before we came down to see you, Phobetor appeared in the window at our house up in Suisun. Flynn and I zapped him with our wonder twin power. I was just thinking, though… if he wanted to hurt me, or Faelyn, wouldn't he have chosen a larger form? Like that leopard shape Flynn has, or hey, even a big dog."

"I don't think he was there to hurt you," Maribelle said. "He was probably there to protect you and the baby. He knew Mercy and Sympathy were on their way down here. He told me that he didn't think Flynn was capable of doing it. He says that's why he beat Flynn up. He said it was for his own good, and that he wants you to give up the kingdom for your own good. In his own arrogant, sadistic way he believes he's protecting you. He's a tyrant. He wants you all under him. He doesn't want you dead."

Charlotte blinked. "Wait a minute. He thought Mercy and Sympathy were on their way to my house? You mean my place with Hannah and Shelby up in Suisun?"

"If he was there, apparently so," Maribelle said.

"Fuck!" Charlotte yelled. "I've got to warn Hannah!"

She picked up her cell phone.

The phone rang through several times. Then the answering machine picked up. Charlie hung up and dialed Shelby. There was still no answer. She was getting very worried by then. Upset.

Suisun

The guy stank. He was a big, burly fucker with copious amounts of armpit and back hair. Both of these types of hair, when not kept clean, held in the rancid stench of his body odor. He smelled like the rancid slime at the bottom of the dumpster at the fast-food restaurant Hannah used to work at as a teenager.

She would have laughed, but he was holding a soldering iron four inches from her eye.

"I already told you," Hannah lied, "Charlotte went out to the grocery store. The one in the mall you passed when you got off the freeway. She took the baby with her. If you leave now, you can probably catch her."

He pulled his arm back and punched the soldering iron forward.

Hannah screamed until she felt like her lungs would give out. The pain was worse than she had imagined. She was so stunned, that it took her a moment to realize that she hadn't been blinded. The man shoved the hot metal at the end of the soldering tool into the flesh just above her eyebrow.

She could smell the hot, burning flesh. She expected the aroma to be nauseating, but the fact of it was worse. It smelled like a frying pan full of hot bacon. Her parents were Orthodox, so she never ate pork growing up. Old habits were hard to break, and even though Hannah did not adhere to a kosher diet, she didn't eat pork. Shelby and the rest of the household did. Hannah was pretty sure she would never be able to stand the smell of cooking swine again.

Her stomach flipped and she vomited. She would have doubled over, but she was tied to the chair she sat in. She was forced to spew all over her nice new Tank Girl t-shirt. A stray bit of non-terrified thought flitted through her mind, wondering if the shirt could be salvaged.

Then she returned to her screaming.

"Stop playing games, bitch," the big man growled, slapping her across the face with his free hand. "The next time, you get it in the eye. Get it? I'm not fucking playing."

Shelby was sitting in a chair across from her, also bound, but unharmed. The idea of watching her wife blinded while she watched was apparently too much for her.

"She's at her mother's!" Shelby screamed. "I swear she is. Don't hurt Hannah anymore. Don't hurt her! I'll tell you anything!"

Mercy was standing behind the men, ordering them around like a sawed-off Godfather. She had a sharp kitchen knife in one of her child's hands. She looked like a kid, though a very evil one. Shelby mentally calculated what the offspring of Damien from the Omen and a Chucky doll would look like and that's what she came up with.

"She's telling the truth," Mercy said. She nodded and gestured towards Shelby. "I won't hurt Hannah, I promise. Tell us everything. How much do they know?"

All the while Shelby was uttering a silent prayer thanking God that Kyle was visiting her parents. Thanking all benevolent power in the Universe for the fact that their son would not witness this, or God forbid, be hurt by this. She also prayed that God would forgive her for what she was about to do.

She was going to tell Mercy everything. She was going to tell her about the Rites that would render her powerless and without identity. She was going to tell her where all of the drawings Charlotte kept in her studio were, especially the prophetic ones. She was going to tell her everything.

But then she looked up and saw a big brown bear standing behind Hannah. He was staring right at the hairy, stinky man who put the hole in Hannah's forehead. Before anyone could speak, the bear sliced its arm through the air and neatly detached the man's head from his body. It rolled backwards and fell to the floor at Mercy's feet.

The little girl glared at the animal. "Phobetor!" she screamed.

The bear ignored her and began systematically dismembering the other members of her entourage. Perhaps Phobetor couldn't kill her, but he thought she might find it difficult to fight back without her minions.

Mercy lifted the knife over her head and ran towards him He thought she was going to stab him in the legs, but at the last minute, she spun around and started to stab Shelby in the kneecaps. The injured woman cried out in pain. The room was beginning to stink of freshly spilled blood. It reminded her of the way the bottom of a pack of hamburger smelled once the meat was out.

Phobetor didn't have time to worry about the human and her suffering. His mission was to reduce Mercy's army until she turned tail and ran. He would not interfere with the stabbing.

Mercy proceeded to stab Shelby in the knees and calves fifteen times. She would have continued, if a leopard didn't show up from seemingly nowhere. The animal growled and bared its teeth. It ran into Mercy and knocked her across the room.

The startled child saw that she was outnumbered, and ran out to the car where her father, Tim, was waiting for her. She was suddenly happy she'd had the foresight to ask him to provide a getaway in case things went wrong.

Now that Mercy was gone and her posse dead on the floor, the bear turned and growled at the leopard. It raised its paw high in the air, ready to fight.

The leopard lowered its body to the floor and put its head on Shelby's feet. It sat there, motionless, waiting. The bear seemed confused by this. It sniffed the air and was about to approach the big cat when the wails of police sirens split the air.

Charlotte had called the police. Both of the animals vanished before the cops arrived.

Ritual

Maribelle was on the phone with the other members of the Sisterhood. If things weren't so dire, Charlotte would have laughed. Her mother was such the businesswoman. She had her coven on a five-way conference call.

"We need to start the ritual, now!" she insisted. "There is little time."

Charlotte sat on the bed, guarding her sleeping toddler. With Flynn gone, she was powerless. She knew it was a risk, but it was one she had to take. She owed Hannah and Shelby everything.

"Light your candles, now," Maribelle instructed. The one she lit was purple and matched her dress. Charlotte neither knew, nor cared what it represented. She did not understand the words her mother was mumbling in Latin, even though she was the one who had written them down. She was a mere vessel, a conduit for whoever wrote the message. She wasn't sure who, but it had to be one of her forebears. That ruled out Phobetor and Thanatos. It should be safe.

Maribelle was murmuring the last phrase of the spell when a milky-white figure appeared behind her, as pale and stealthy as a ghost. Charlotte gasped and scooted backward on her bed. It was Pasithea. She stood there naked, directly behind Maribelle.

"Did you know that the higher-level gods can appear on Earth in humanoid forms?" Pasithea asked, slitting Maribelle's throat. Charlotte wouldn't have recognized it, but Maribelle did. With her dying breath, she saw it. It was the self-same serpent handled, winding bladed knife Flynn offered Maribelle in a dream when he offered her his neck. Too late, she realized its significance.

The life of the person who made the sacrifice was being taken. Pasithea was undoing some portion of what Maribelle had done when she killed Flynn. There was no telling what the consequences would be.

"Did you know that I was your father's mother?" Pasithea asked sweetly, winking at Charlotte. "This is the whore who betrayed him with Phobetor. This is the whore who killed my Brash."

Charlotte instinctively picked up Faelyn and pulled her against her. She watched in horror as Pasithea let go of her mother's body, and it slumped down to the floor. Charlotte did the only thing a human woman could do in that situation. She screamed her head off.

"Help! Someone help! Oh my god, help!" she screamed. "Help!" She didn't know how soon help would come, but it was a hotel room in the middle of a city. Sooner or later, someone would come.

"Oh, never worry," Pasithea said in that same insipid, creepily cheerful voice. "I would never kill anyone in my bloodline. You and your husband have a beautiful love story. I'm a big fan. I certainly would not harm you or your precious child. But your mother, I'm sure her death will bring great sorrow to Phobetor."

"Not as much sorrow as it brings to me," Charlotte said sadly.

"I'm so sorry, but I have done what must be done," Pasithea explained. "Now I love you, but Mercy is very good with the hallucinations. I am so proud of her. I really have to go now. The rest of the Sisterhood needs to die, so the Cult of Mercy can rise."

"No! Oh please, no!" Charlotte cried. But it was too late. Pasithea was off to kill Nancy, Lorena, Jeannie, and Sunshine.

Charlotte sat there stunned. She was still in shock and could not process these events. She was about to call the police when she heard a keycard in the door. The hotel manager let himself in. She assumed he had heard the screams. Charlotte's relief that help had arrived was short-lived. Tim and Mercy were standing behind him.

Death and Sleep

Somnus and Thanatos were playing chess by the river Lethe. Neither had the inclination to rise or look into the well. Fortunately, the river itself made a perfectly good scrying glass. They were watching the events unfold below on Earth.

"I think my story is much better," Thanatos told Somnus. "Don't you agree that much death, and on such an epic scale is superior to your dull little love story with Charlotte and Flynn?"

"No, I don't," Somnus said. "And I wish you had not involved my darling Pasithea in all of this. Mother will not be pleased. Surely, a production on this scale can and will attract the attention of Zeus, and none of it good."

"Nonsense," Thanatos disagreed, moving his pawn on the chessboard. "The humans will blame it on this Tim Carter. Look at how he has conveniently arrived at Charlotte's doorstep, where he can accept blame for Maribelle's untimely death. Soon, the police will arrive to arrest him."

"My queen is about to take your pawn," Somnus warned.

"Yes, indeed," Thanatos said with a laugh. "And look in the river! Your queen is about to take Phobetor's pawn!"

In the river Lethe, both of the men could see Pasithea standing behind Lorena Young. Lorena was in her kitchen, cooking dinner for her family when she performed the ritual. She had a heart attack. Pasithea ran her hand over Lorena's back gently before reaching into her chest cavity to grasp it with her cold, clammy hand. She clutched it, and Lorena collapsed.

The scene disappeared and was replaced with a new one. Sunshine Green was sleeping outside in her cardboard box these days. She hadn't told any of the Sisterhood that she'd lost her place in the boarding care home. She was sitting next to the makeshift structure she lived in when she performed the ritual. Several bottles of alcohol were emptied and strewn in the corner beside her. Pasithea shoved her spectral hand into Sunshine's liver, and she began to spit up blood. Her liver was failing.

Next, she appeared in Jeannie Byrne's bathroom. She had been hiding there, performing the ritual while her husband watched television. A full bathtub would hide any suspicions her husband might have if he should happen to wander up there and demand admission. She would say she was just about to get in. She was standing in front of the bathtub in her fine silk robe when Pasithea arrived. She ran her hand over Jeannie's feet, and they gave out from under her. She slipped and fell into the tub, striking her head. She died instantly, although the corner had to perform an autopsy to rule out drowning since she was found with her head under the water.

Poor, sweet Nancy was the last. She was sitting in her living room when she performed the ritual. She had cooked an entire chicken for dinner and was sharing pieces of it with her cats. When Pasithea ran her hand over her throat, Nancy Allen choked to death on a chicken bone. She fell over on the couch, suffocating. Her favorite cat, Percy, sat on her chest licking her for hours, hoping to wake her up again. Bad little Mittens and Moppet devoured the rest of the whole chicken that was left sitting on the table. With Tess and Maribelle dead, Nancy had no human friends. She left her house to the cats in her will.

Thanatos turned to Somnus and smiled. "And you see? So, it is done. Phobetor's order has been destroyed. He has been weakened. A new order will arise. The Cult of Mercy. The final Rite of Undoing is complete."

Somnus sighed. "I can't believe Pasithea would consent to such a thing."

"You believers in true love," Thanatos said without malice. "You are always so blinded by it, so deceived by it. My ending is much better."

"I think there is still love," Somnus argued. "Look at where Pasithea is going. Look at what Flynn is doing. Even Phobetor can feel love."

Cry for Mercy

When the ritual was completed, a change came over Mercy. The little girl was transformed into a woman, one Flynn would have quickly recognized. She was tall, and freckled, buxom, and possessed the brightest red hair. She was the Mercy of dreams. She was Mercy, the demisomnali.

"I feel like such a princess!" she cried out with uncharacteristic joy. "You can keep the kingdom in Demos Oneiroi. I have what I have always wanted, power here on Earth. I am a djinn, released from a bottle. As a show of my gratitude, I might let you live. However, blood-related blood sacrifices are powerful."

"I am no longer your blood," Charlotte said dully. "Neither is Faelyn."

"I know," Mercy said. "But for old time's sake…" As she slid closer to Charlotte and Faelyn, a black glaze covered Mercy's eyes. It extended out from the dilated pupils like a black cloud, covering the red-brown irises and the whites alike until her eyes were solid black. She grinned wickedly. When she raised her hand, it still held the same bloody kitchen knife she'd stabbed Shelby in the knees with. She approached the bed.

She was no more than six feet into the doorway when two big cats appeared between her and the bed. Flynn and Phobetor arrived simultaneously, a leopard and a black panther respectively. Neither of them looked pleased. Flynn began pacing the length of carpet in front of the bed his wife and child sat on, establishing a protective perimeter.

Phobetor was bolder. He walked right up to her and growled.

"Let's talk about this, guys!" Mercy said. "We have a lot of history, don't we?"

Staring down into Phobetor's golden eyes, she smiled brightly, the corners of her eyes crinkling with saccharine sweetness. She hoped to penetrate, to establish mind control. Unfortunately, it wasn't working. Having spent a great deal of time observing Mercy's earlier interactions with the Carter family, Phobetor had noted the fact that female family members had seemed able to resist Mercy's control. He had appeared as female panther and was immune to her mind tricks.

Mercy backed away from the door a little. Then she giggled.

"Oh wow," she said. "My giggling sounds very strange. Perhaps I swallowed too much Sympathy. At any rate, Phobetor, shouldn't you get going? After that scene up in Suisun isn't animal control after you, or something?"

She ordered Tim Carter and the hotel manager to stand in front of her and protect her from the wild animals. The manager, Loren Delaney, was a firm believer in the right to bear arms. He had a permit to carry a concealed weapon. Some of the hotels he managed were in rougher neighborhoods, and he happened to have his gun on him. He pulled out his little 9mm Beretta and pointed it at Phobetor's head.

Phobetor reared up and raised a paw to disarm the man. Mr. Delaney began slowly backing away, towards the door. He intended to keep his gun out of the animal's reach. The panther charged at him. A lesser gunman would have lost an arm, but Delaney shot the animal in the forehead, square between the eyes. The force of the impact sent the big cat flying several feet backward before it finally collapsed on the floor. The animal's body quickly disintegrated, as the nightmare god returned to the Demos Oneiroi to regroup.

Mercy knew that the gunshot would not stop Phobetor. It would only slow him down for bit. She needed to finish this before he returned.

Flynn was much younger and far less experienced. Mercy could tell that although he wore a female skin, his essence and his instincts reminded masculine. She turned her black eyes on him with glee.

"I bet you're hungry," Mercy cooed. "I've been thinking about it, and Charlotte is a bigger threat to me dead than alive. But that baby… she's related to me. So, what do you say, Flynn old buddy? Why don't you do me a favor and jump on the bed and eat your daughter. You don't have to hurt your wife – not unless she gets in the way, of course."

Flynn felt a sharp, burning sensation at the base of his spine. His head hurt like hell and was filled with a buzzing sound. It was as if his skull was filled with a hive of angry bees. He smacked his head with his paw to try to get them out – to try to get her, Mercy, out… but it did no good.

Against his will, he found himself turning to face them. He was horrified when he found his body lumbering forward on sharpened claws of death against his will. He was mere inches away from his helpless family when he decided to do it.

Charlotte gasped when she saw what he was about to do. "Flynn… no!"

He decided to surrender, and to give himself over completely. The giant cat leapt right into Charlotte and disappeared into her chest. She could feel every part of him knitting together with every part of her on the microcellular level. The flesh on her arm danced and tingled. Risen and writhing, the image of the snake Imelda appeared on her skin. She felt it trace the curve of her neck and extend down her side.

Flynn was letting go of his form, his essence and all of the power he held. He was melting into her, becoming nothing but fuel. She could feel all of his power coursing through her body, but there was no resistance. He did not try to control her body. In fact, she couldn't feel his consciousness at all. She had his power, but he was gone.

"Look what you made him do, you bitch!" Charlotte screamed, lifting her palm and sending out a bolt of lightning that caused Mercy to fly back against the wall, hair singed.

"Wait, Charlotte!" Mercy screamed. "Stop, you don't want to do this!"

"Yes, I do!" Charlie shouted, angry and determined. "I want you dead! You need to die!"

"It's still not too late to save him," Mercy said calmly, sliding her burnt and blackened body down from the wall. As she placed her feet on the ground, solidly, slightly apart, she raised a hand. Charlotte lifted an arm across her face automatically, in defense.

Mercy wasn't after her, though. She extended her arm and began to use her powers to suck life force from an increasingly gray and haggard looking Tim Carter.

"You know, on second thought," Mercy quickly told Charlotte, "I have other family members. They've reincarnated somewhere. I can go on a world slaughter tour, gaining power. We can divide things up. I'll start my order on Earth, you keep dad's kingdom. I'll even leave old Tim Carter here. He's a blood relative of this body. That's a blood sacrifice, right? I can let the kid go."

"You're bargaining," Charlotte said. "That must mean you're losing."

"Fine," Mercy spat. "Fine, but if you want your precious Flynn back, you will need to kick him out of your body before it's too late. You're absorbing him, the way I absorbed most of Sympathy. Is killing me worth it? Is it worth your life?"

Charlotte lowered her shoulders, defeated. It wasn't worth it to her. She used all of her focus to shove Flynn out of her body. Slowly, she felt the snake tattoo that was etched into her skin begin to rise. The places where it moved, upward and outward, were hot and itchy. When it was done, it wrapped itself around her shoulders like a stole made not of fur but living reptilian flesh. It was Flynn in the form of Imelda.

Now that she'd freed him into this form to rescue him, Charlotte was once again powerless. She knew that Mercy could easily betray her now. She expected to die, but right at that moment, Phobetor reappeared. He sat at her feet, eying Mercy hungrily.

"Okay so let me paint my little tableau here," Mercy said quickly. "Loren, hold your gun up to Tim's head. You just caught him in Maribelle Metaxas' hotel room. You just caught a serial killer. He murdered one of your guests. Congratulations! You're a hero."

Loren Delaney nodded and smiled. He turned his gun on the man beside him, Tim Carter.

"Hey, Tim, I mean dad, do me a favor," Mercy said. "Send that text message you wrote earlier—that confessional suicide note? When the police arrive, refuse to surrender and make sure they kill you. Suicide by cop, it's a perfectly good way to make a sacrifice, don't you think?"

"All for the glory of the Cult of Mercy," Tim said, pulling his cell phone out of his pocket. He quickly sent the message and dialed 911.

When he looked up from his phone, Mercy was gone. So were the two animals, the woman, and her child. The only people in the room were Tim, Loren, and the dead body of Maribelle Metaxas.

Transport

Phobetor transformed into his Oneiroi form while Tim and Loren weren't looking. He sighed. He hated being seen on Earth this way. He quickly cast a cloak of invisibility over himself and the little Keahi family.

Then he walked over to Maribelle and took her pulse. She was already gone.

"Goodbye, my angel," he told the dead woman. He bent down and kissed her on the cheek. "May your next life be joyous and uncomplicated, and free of the pain and suffering this one caused you."

His love for her wasn't a great love, but it was a love. A petty and selfish love perhaps, but the only kind of love he could ever be capable of. That made it matter to him. He would miss her, but nothing could be done. He could only honor her wishes and protect her progeny as she had asked him to do.

He looked at Charlotte and Faelyn and Flynn. "Come. Let me take you away from here."

Flynn shifted into a small dog and leapt into Charlotte's arms. Phobetor put his arms around all three of them and transported them to Maribelle's house.

Tim Carter stayed. The cops already received his text confessing to the killing spree. The police would later assume that Maribelle rented the room for a clandestine affair, although not necessarily with Tim.

Loss

Shelby and Hannah loved Charlotte, but living with her was too dangerous. In fact, knowing her might be a risk that was great for any mere mortal to bear. However, that much was a risk the ladies were willing to take, at least for now. Living with her was not. Charlie moved out a month after the attack.

Hannah recovered with nothing but a scar over her eyebrow, but Shelby was off work on disability. She was in a wheelchair right now. She had been a mail carrier. She'd be moved to a desk job when she returned, possibly working in a post office as a clerk, or in administration somewhere. She'd gone through surgery and was in physical therapy now. Doctors had hope that she would walk again, but she would probably need some sort of assistive device like braces for her knees, maybe crutches. It was bad.

Hannah was very angry about it. "You could have been killed!" she shouted, storming around the kitchen the morning they decided that Charlotte should move. "What if Kyle was here? What about him?"

"I wasn't killed," Shelby said. "Flynn saved me. Remember?"

"That's great," Hannah sighed. "But I'm not taking any chances with my family. She needs to go. And I need a break. I'm not saying we'll never see her again; we work together, for fuck's sake. I would be fired if I lost Charlotte as a client now. *Somnalia* is our top seller."

The police blamed everything on Tim Carter and what they claimed was a cultish devotion to *Somnalia*. They said he constantly referred to Mercy, the character from the comic. As the news reports of the stalking maniac circulated, Charlotte's comic book became increasingly infamous – and popular. More and more copies sold. Charlotte was rich now, and Hannah was ten percent of rich, which was pretty damned well-heeled.

Maribelle had left Charlie the house in Berkeley. She moved in there with Faelyn and their pet cat Dada. In one form or another, Charlotte and Flynn spent time together on a daily basis now. Still, most nights, Charlie fell asleep crying in her mother's bed. With Brash gone, there was zero chance of Maribelle appearing in the Demos Oneiroi. Perhaps, if Phobetor had taken her as his consort, it would have been different. He could have bound her to himself, like Charlotte did with Flynn. But he hadn't, and she'd been reincarnated.

Phobetor sat alone in his castle, brooding and mourning his losses. How could he claim to be a better ruler than Charlotte or Flynn when his pride had caused him to lose his war with Mercy? He'd badly underestimated Pasithea. He discounted her rage. He hadn't imagined that such a sweet and seemingly passive woman might carry a spirit of vengeance. He brought all of this down on their heads the day he convinced Maribelle to eliminate Brash by offering a blood sacrifice – Flynn.

Pasithea would never tolerate allowing anyone outside of Brash's bloodline to sit on his throne, ever. That left only three possibilities: Mercy, Sympathy, or Happiness. Sympathy was ineligible. She was a mortal stuck in a thousand-year reincarnation cycle. Even if she wasn't, she was in no condition to run anything. The undersized, developmentally delayed human she was now, Cynthia Carter, had years of specialized care ahead of her. No one was sure if she would ever be able to live independently. Fortunately, Alice Carter was devoted and determined to see things through. No one blamed her for what happened with Tim. Clearly, she and her child were victims. The other twin was presumed dead.

The other twin, Mercy, had no interest in Brash's kingdom. She was living her dreams, establishing her own kingdom on Earth.

There were urban legends now, coming in from so many places around the world about a red-haired girl with glowing red eyes, who called herself Mercy. Wherever she walked, a plague of death was left in her wake. Reports were coming in on the news about death cults. Mass suicide and mass murder were increasing.

Somewhere, in another kingdom in the Demos Oneiroi, Thanatos laughed.

The Cult of Mercy was on the rise.

He lost his Order, his Priestess, and any claim he thought he might have on Charlotte's kingdom. Although it took him a long time to figure out, he'd also lost his best friend. He actually missed Flynn, but he didn't know if the young somnali would ever forgive him.

Grief

Charlotte was the inheritor of a palatial estate, and all of the powers associated with it. Neither she nor Flynn felt inclined to immediately return to it. He liked to be alone with her in those tight little spaces where she first introduced him to the mysteries and pleasures of her world.

She took him to the cave he'd lived in when he first awoke into his afterlife. She held him naked in the furs, bare skin against skin. He wanted to surprise her, so he showed her something new. He presented himself to her in a human hybrid form. His skin was covered in short, soft, leopard-spotted fur. She rolled him over onto his back and ran her hand over his chest and his belly. He could feel her tracing the curve of his belly. She ran her finger over the bare flesh where his fur parted slightly to reveal a nipple. Then another … she was counting them. There were eight of them.

Flynn inhaled sharply as she grabbed one of them between her thumb and forefinger and twisted it hard.

"I thought I was going to lose you," she said softly. "I could feel you in me, melting inside of me." She released his tender flesh briefly, teasingly only to pinch and pull at it moments later. He'd transgressed, and she intended to punish him for it.

"But I didn't…" he began. He didn't finish the sentence. She silenced him, first with a gesture, finger to lip. Next with her mouth pressed against his, kissing him roughly so he could not speak.

When she finally came up for air she said, "Don't ever take a risk like that again! I've already lost you once. I couldn't bear to lose you again. I've lost so much now. I have so little. But I have you. Please don't take you away from me."

He put his arms around her and whispered the expected reassurances. He made promises he had no way of knowing that he could keep, the way lovers always do. He promised he would never leave again, that he would always be hers. He spoke until his words were exhausted, and the only thing left to do was hold her. She pressed her face into the crook of his neck and let her tears fall. She cried so hard that the sobs rocked both their bodies. He held her close, remembering the time Maribelle had cried on his shoulder.

Charlotte spilled the essence of her pain out onto his shoulder. She coated his skin in her mucous, sweat, and tears. She cried until his fur was soaking wet and stuck to her cheeks and chin where she nuzzled against it. She wept until she felt that she had no fluids left in her body that she could pour out onto the canvas of his flesh.

When he saw that she was all cried out, Flynn touched her. His hands settled against the small of her back and caressed her shoulders with the soothing touch of a somnali. Her body relaxed a little. He touched her the way she used to touch him when he was fragile and human. He held her and understood that human or not, he could feel with this same great intensity. He could share in the experiences that made a person human. Love and grief were great equalizers. Charlotte was a queen now, but rulers and ragtag, rambling, broken men all owned their own legacies of love and loss.

Charlotte understood what Flynn was doing. She looked at him and smiled. "Thank you."

"I grieved when I died," he told her. "I didn't only cry because we were separated. I cried for all of the people I would never see. People like Mike, who died. People like my mom, and Danny. People always say they are in a better place, words of comfort. But the trouble is that you can't be in the place they are. You can't see them or touch them. They are just ripped from your life all at once."

"I grieved when you died," Charlotte said. "And now, I've lost my mother. Sometimes all I do is long for simpler times. I remember the days when I was spared the harrowing specter of grief. It's like a stalker. It just won't leave you alone. It shows uninvited like a freak storm. It batters you with its hard winds and cold torrents. It leaves you soaking and cold in its wake, and it feels nothing. And that's just not fair, is it? And death… and loss, how are mortals supposed to cope with it? Maybe if I wasn't born mortal, I wouldn't know what grief and loss are. They are a kind of madness.

"Thanatos can be so cruel. My kind can be. How will we ever be able to be that callous? How can we rule a kingdom at the heart this misery?"

Flynn mulled it over for a bit. He watched Charlotte using his fur to dry her tears, and he almost laughed. He used to rub his face in the leopard skin just like that. It was dead and inanimate and couldn't respond. He could respond and did, kissing her cheeks and brushing her tears away with his furry fingers.

Finally, he said, "Phobetor says that nightmares are supposed to help human beings, not hurt them. They are supposed to help them process and overcome their fears, grief, and loss as well. We don't have to be heartless and cruel; don't you see? We can help people."

"Perhaps," Charlotte said. "You don't know my family members as well as I do. They are prone to interfering, and they always have ulterior motives."

"But we can try?" Flynn asked hopefully.

"We can try," Charlotte agreed.

They stayed for a while and had their fill of each other. When they were done, they returned to the Palace, where Charlotte at last took her place on the throne.

Love

With Mercy dedicated to her mission on Earth, Sympathy incapacitated, and Phobetor essentially banned from the running, Charlotte ruled her kingdom unopposed. After the slaughter of the Sisterhood of Undoing, Charlotte was restored to her demisomnali status. It was the only reason she could survive Flynn's entering her body. As a demisomnali, she could now enter and navigate the dream world at will. Her status was one Mercy shared with her. Both could walk the Earth and enter dreams now, but Mercy hated the Demos Oneiroi and wanted no head-on confrontation with Nyx.

Charlotte's became known as the Kingdom of Happiness, as tradition dictated the territory carry her somnali name. She located and recruited her father's old household staff to work in the Kingdom of Happiness. The estate was no longer dreary and empty. It was filled with her father's former lovers, and servants, and a group of acrobats he'd employed for his entertainment. As a demisomnali, she could invade the dreams of others, but she decided not to. Flynn was sensitive about that kind of thing, and a bit jealous. Besides, her delegation skills were impeccable. She was, after all, Maribelle Metaxas's daughter.

One night, Phobetor showed up on Charlotte and Flynn's doorstep, looking morose.

Flynn was sitting on her throne. Charlotte was sitting on Flynn's lap. It was a pose they frequently adopted. His arms were around her waist, and her legs were draped over the side of the armrest. She was relaxed and sure she wouldn't fall. He had her. He always had her. He always held her safe. Always.

Faelyn sat in a little throne beside them. It was the same one Charlotte used to sit in at that age. Faelyn was still too young to stay awake in the Demos Oneiroi, but her parents liked to keep her nearby. They wanted to watch over her.

"You make a good chair," Charlotte said. She winked at him. "This throne is made of volcanic rock. It's really rough and uncomfortable. But you are so soft and squishy. I should chain you to my throne so I'll always have something cozy and warm to sit on."

Flynn poked his belly self-consciously. "You think I'm soft and squishy? Do you think I should work out more?" he asked.

"No," she told him. "I like you just the way you are. In fact, I love you. Very much."

"I know that," he said. He leaned forward and kissed her neck. "I love you, too."

Life and the afterlife were both fraught with uncertainty. They had lost so much, and there was still more they could lose. But they had each other. They had their daughter. They could comfort one other and shield each other from danger. They were a family.

"Come in," Charlotte told Phobetor, who stood in the doorway between their kingdoms. "You're welcome to visit, but you don't get to flirt with and hurt my Flynn, do we understand one another?"

Phobetor nodded. He looked sad. "Maribelle… you look just like her," he told Charlotte.

Charlotte bit her lip. "I miss her too, Phobetor. I'm pretty sure I'm always going to miss her. Sometimes I pick up the phone, to call her. I think I gotta let her know about this idiot who just cut me off in traffic, you know? But I can't, not ever again."

She wiped a tear from the corner of her eye. She'd been very close with her mother before the first sacrifice. They were just getting close again before the second. It was hard. She was tempted to tell Phobetor what she told Pasithea. She was tempted to say that this loss was more painful for her than it could possibly be for him. But then she realized that all love was love. All grief was grief. It should not be rated, measured and compared. It just should be accepted for what it was.

"I know you loved her," she told Phobetor kindly. "My father neglected her, but you made her feel alive. I'm glad you loved my mother like you did, and I'm sorry things turned out so badly."

"It's my fault," Phobetor said. It wasn't a question. "I deeply regret my choices. I am not easily able to admit such things, but I was a fool. Nyx tried to warn me. She tried to warn me that a show of strength is not true power. She told me that quiet, passive people are not necessarily weak. But I would not listen. How appropriate is it, then, that whimsical and delicate Pasithea destroyed all of my plans?"

"None of us will ever be as wise as Nyx," Flynn said simply. He didn't rise, but he held his wife tightly against his chest, and looked over her shoulder at Phobetor. Flynn knew that conversations about Maribelle were difficult for Charlie. The tears would come, although he didn't think she would ever let Phobetor see them.

"Pasithea has her regrets, too," Charlotte added. "To this day, she stands watch over Sympathy and Faelyn, to protect them from Mercy the Insatiable. She loves them, you know. She can't bear the thought that Mercy will come for them and take them from her. They're human. They'll reincarnate, like Mike and Tess. Like Nancy and Sunshine and Lorena and Jeannie. Like dad and like mom. You know better than any of us how short their precious lives will be."

"I watch over Faelyn sometimes," Phobetor admitted. "You and she are all I have left of Maribelle now. I would hope that she has children of her own someday to carry on Maribelle's earthly line. It is the only immortality most humans know. I wouldn't have thought that it mattered, but somehow it does."

"I'm sure Somnus feels the same," Charlotte said gently. "She is the last in the line of his oracles, and even if she doesn't have the gift, some child of hers may."

"I can't even think about it," Flynn said. "Faelyn is three now, and every time I see her here, in the Demos Oneiroi, I wonder when she will be able to speak with me. But I am afraid to have the time go past. I am afraid of the day I will never see her again."

He leaned over in the throne where he sat squished behind his wife and reached out to touch Faelyn's little, sleeping face. She was sleeping curled up around a giant stuffed Sanrio doll. He recognized it as Bad Badtz-Maru.

"I have had and lost many mortal children," Phobetor said. "I know what you mean. One day they must leave you, and you never see them again. But don't think on it too much. If you do, you will waste the precious time you do have. Grieving is something that should be reserved for those who are gone."

Phobetor looked away for a while. He was glad that Flynn was speaking to him again. Sometimes when he thought about them not speaking, he wondered if that was how Maribelle felt. Isolated, and cut off from others because of the things she had done. Because of the things he asked her to do.

"I have thought on it," Phobetor said to Flynn. "When we met, I mentioned that humans keep felines as pets. But they also keep canines. I always wondered why it is that the humans call these creatures man's best friend. But now I think I know why. They are fiercely loyal creatures. They would lay their lives down for their masters. I think anyone would be lucky to have such a pet."

Flynn laughed. "Are you trying to say I'm your dog? Tight! Does this mean I can have my old job back?"

Charlotte chuckled. It was cathartic to express amusement after being confronted with so much crushing, unbearable grief. "He's not your dog, he's my dog. But I'll let you come by and take him for a walk some time. As long as you promise there won't be any more animal cruelty."

Flynn gave her a dirty look. "Hey!" He pinched her on the butt. "I can speak for myself."

Charlotte giggled and shifted over. Their playfully affectionate behavior made Phobetor uncomfortable. They were starting to remind him of Somnus and Pasithea, and he couldn't stand it. He never liked his father's wife before. In light of recent events, he had come to loathe her and anything that reminded him of her. He didn't want to take that hatred out on the innocent young couple. He'd taken too much out on them already, and without just cause.

Someone had to stop Mercy, and he couldn't get these children involved again.

"I should go now," Phobetor said.

He disappeared before they could protest or say goodbye.

The End

Glossary of Terms for Somnalia

PEOPLE

Nyx */niks/: Goddess of the Night, mother of Somnus and Thanatos*

Thanatos */than-uh-tos, -tohs/: God of Death, twin brother of Somnus.*

Somnus */som-nuh s/: God of Sleep, twin brother of Thanatos. Also known as Hypnos.*

Morpheus */mawr-fee-uh s, -fyoos/: One of the Oneiroi, God of Dreams, and brother of Brash.*

Phobetor */foe-bah-tohr/: One of the Oneiroi, God of Nightmares, and brother of Brash.*

Phantasos */fan-tuh-sos/: One of the Oneiroi, God of Surreal Dreams, and brother of Brash.*

Pasithea */puh-sith-ee-uh/: Wife/consort of Somnus, mother of Brash.*

Brash */brash/: One of the Oneiroi, son of Somnus and Pasithea, God of Erotic Nightmares, cursed by Zeus.*

Maribelle Metaxas */mə'tæksəs/: Human mother of Happiness, Consort of Brash, and Priestess of the Undoing.*

Happiness */'ha-pē-nəs/: The somnali name of demisomnali Charlotte Metaxas.*

Flynn Keahi */kay-ah-hee/: Human consort of Happiness.*

Mercy */ mur-see/: Somnali daughter of Brash.*

Sympathy */sim-puh-thee/*: *Somnali daughter of Brash.*

Zeus */zoos/*: *King of the Gods.*

Eros */eer-os, er-os/*: *God of Love. Also known as Cupid.*

GROUPS

Oneiroi */own-nuh-roy/*: *Sons of Somnus, personified aspects of sleep.*

Somnali */somn älē/*: *Grandchildren of Somnus.*

Cursed Somnali */kur-sid, kurst/ /somn älē/*: *Children of Brash.*

Sisterhood of Undoing */sis-ter-hoo d/ /uhv, ov/ /uhn-doo-ing/*: *Coven of "soccer mom" mages in opposition to Brash.*

PLACES

Demos Oneiroi */dahy-mos/ /own-nuh-roy/: Domain of sleep gods.*

Lethe */lee-thee/: River that runs through Deimos Oneiroi.*

RITES

Rites of Binding: *Bind a human consort to a sleep god or demigod.*

Sacrifice of the Innocents: *Blood sacrifice to allow cursed Brash or somnali to procreate.*

Feast of Tears: *A lesser blood ritual to allow a cursed demisomnali to procreate.*

Rites of Undoing: *Rituals to reduce somnali influence over bound consorts and their offspring.*

About the Author

Sumiko Saulson is an award-winning author of Afrosurrealist and multicultural sci-fi and horror whose latest novel Happiness and Other Diseases is available on Mocha Memoirs Press.

Winner of the HWA Scholarship from Hell (2016) BCC Voice "Reframing the Other" contest (2017), Mixy Award (2017), Afrosurrealist Writer Award (2018), HWA Diversity Grant (2020), Ladies of Horror Fiction Grant (2021).

Sumiko has an AA in English from Berkeley City College, writes a column called "Writing While Black" for a national Black Newspaper, the San Francisco BayView is the host of the SOMA Leather and LGBT Cultural District's "Erotic Storytelling Hour," and teaches courses at the Speculative Fiction Academy.

More From Sumiko Saulson
&
Mocha Memoirs Press

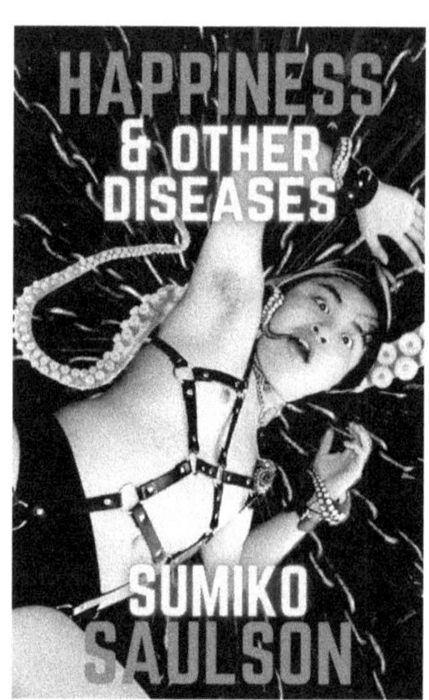

Flynn Keahi has had a rough year. His nightmares are starting to manifest in reality, but no one believes him. Terrifying creatures are trying to cross out of dreams into the physical realm. Only Flynn can stop them – but doing so might cost him his life.

Complicating matters further, one of these creatures cannot help wanting him -- in every forbidden way.

Will she be able to save him from his fate?

Can she even protect him from herself?

Imagine horror where black characters aren't all tropes and the first to die; imagine a world written by black sisters where black women and femmes are in the starring roles. From flesh-eating plants to flesh-eating bees; zombies to vampires to vampire-eating vampire hunters; ghosts, revenants, witches and werewolves, this book has it all. Cursed drums, cursed dolls, cursed palms, ancient spirits and goddesses create a nuanced world of Afrocentric and multicultural horror. Seventeen terrifying tales by seventeen of the scary sisters profiled in the reference guide "100 Black Women in Horror."

Includes the stories Appreciation by Mina Polina, Death Lines by Nuzo Onoh, Sweet Justice by Kenesha Williams, Bryannah and the Magic Negro by Crystal Connor, The Lost Ones by Valjeanne Jeffers, Tango of a TellTale Heart by Sumiko Saulson, Blood Magnolia by Nicole Givens Kurtz, Labor Pains by Kenya Moss-Dyme, Return to Me by Lori Titus, Here, Kitty! by LH Moore, Left Hand Torment by R. J. Joseph, Dark Moon's Curse by Delizhia Jenkins, Killer Queen by Cinsearae S, Sisters by Kai Leakes, Black and Deadly by Dicey Grenor, Trisha and Peter by Kamika Aziza, Alternative™ by Tabitha Thompson, and The Prizewinner by Alledria Hurt.

Blackened Roots is a unique collection and will be a must-have for zombie lovers. Blackened Roots takes the zombie mythos back to its roots. Drawing from a variety of cultural backgrounds, Blackened Roots imagines a world of horror and wonder where Black protagonists take center stage – as zombies, as hunters, as heroes. From a haunting recipe to sibling rivalry, a singing zombie cowboy, a slave ship, and disobedient gods stories, Blackened Roots is a groundbreaking Afrocentric zombie anthology celebrating the rich cultural heritage of the African Diaspora

About Mocha Memoirs Press

Established in July 2010, Mocha Memoirs Press's mission is to amplify marginalized voices in speculative fiction genres (science fiction, fantasy, horror). We publish bold, fearless fiction that pushes boundaries and smashes gatekeepers.

We invite you to review our catalog to review the diversity in our stories. You can access the catalog at https://www.mochamemoirspress.com. Join our newsletter here.

You can also find us online:
YouTube- https://www.youtube.com/@MochaMemoirsPress
Instagram - @mochamemoirspress
TikTok-@mochamemoirspress
BlueSky-@mochamemoirspress.com
Twitter (X)- @mochamemoirspress
Facebook facebook.com/MochaMemoirsPress